SAD GIRLS

LANG LEAV

Andrews McMeel
PUBLISHING®

In memory of
Nicole Lewanski

*May your love of books
live on in others.*

PART ONE

The Girl Who Cried Wolf

But you can't make people listen. They have to come round in their own time, wondering what happened and why the world blew up around them.

—Ray Bradbury, *Fahrenheit 451*

Death, like fiction, is brutal in its symmetry. Take this story and strip it down—all the way back—until you are left with two points. Two dots on a vast, blank canvas, separated by a sea of white. Here, we have come to the first point, where the bath is drawn and the hand is reaching for the razor blade. I will meet you at the next, by the axle of a screaming wheel, the revolution of a clock, the closing of an orbit.

One

I WAS THREE weeks shy of turning eighteen when I was struck with the cruel affliction of anxiety. It came in the form of a panic attack, seemingly from nowhere—a bolt from the blue. Like a thunderclap in my chest, an icy river down the length of my spine. Terror and confusion clawed at the edges of my brain as I clutched fistfuls of the sweat-soaked bedsheets I had slept fitfully in, just moments before. As my mind struggled to comprehend this new and frightful development, there was a dim thought that echoed through the midst of my blind panic. It told me, with a chilling certainty, that nothing would ever be the same again.

I have no doubt that the sudden onset of my anxiety had everything to do with *the lie*. To this day, I do not know why that terrible untruth spilled from my lips. But as soon as it did, the lie formed a life of its own. It became an evil presence, a curse. I told this wicked lie one ill-fated night to my two best friends, Lucy and Candela, who were sworn to secrecy on the lives of their loved ones. Lucy offered up her mother, and Candela, her sister Eve.

Perhaps I had wanted to create some kind of commotion, something to break the monotony. Like the boy who cried wolf, tricking the nearby villagers for his own amusement. Whatever the reason, the lie caused a chain of events that I did not foresee. The culmination of which still haunts me to this very day. For I have no doubt that my life and the lives of my two best friends would have been different if that night had never happened. If the lie that left my lips had only slipped away without the opportunity to persist, like a brewing storm, pushed out to sea, to dissipate over the restless waves. Like the night I absentmindedly boarded the wrong bus, carrying bits of change in my pocket and a phone with a dead battery, only to realize I was being driven farther and farther into a bad part of town. And my dilemma was whether I should trust the bus driver to take me back to the depot where I could call my parents to collect me or whether I should alight at the next stop and try to find my way back to familiar territory.

I chose the latter, and it just so happened that my father, on his way home from a late meeting, had turned the corner just as I was getting off the bus. If I had stayed on the bus, perhaps the man who reeked of gin, who had looked at me sideways once too often, had become aware of my predicament. How many stories do we hear about young girls who find themselves in the wrong part of town and are never found again? I could have become another statistic, but, instead, I was safe, riding shotgun with my dad, stopping by our local supermarket to pick up groceries on our way home.

The situation I was in led me to think of all the possible outcomes where I could have been abducted, raped, or murdered. At times, the scenarios I pictured were so graphic they left me wondering whether, perhaps, there is another version of me somewhere that has lived it. Maybe we slip in and out of alternate worlds through our minds and our imaginations, picking up scar tissue from other dimensions.

My recollection of the night I told that lie is just as vivid as if it were yesterday. I remember how the words tumbled from my mouth, my mind unsure of how the story was being formed, like a spider that spins its first web without any comprehension of where the ability was acquired.

I can recall the looks on the faces of my two best friends, their eyes wide with horror and disgust. "I saw them through the window," I had said earnestly, "when I was collecting for the Red Cross." I was known to be an honest person, and unless it was completely outrageous, my word was as good as any. The window I was referring to belonged to a house I walked by every day on my way to school, and it was easy to furnish it with my half-truths and utter fabrications. Shortly after the establishment of the lie, a fight broke out between me and Candela, who cried tears of disbelief and wanted to confront the protagonist of my carefully crafted narrative. Realizing this would implicate me, I did my best to dissuade her from doing so—a decision I now deeply regret.

Indeed, if the lie had been kept contained among the three of us, it would have ended there. If it were to come up in conversation years later, I would have admitted it was purely fictional and that I had no idea what drove me to create such a story. However, without our knowledge, Eve, Candela's kid sister, had her ear pressed against the other side of the door, and she later relayed our conversation to Candela's mother. It was the opening the lie had been waiting for. Through this channel, it slipped beyond my reach and spread through our small town of Three Oaks like wildfire.

All at once, everyone knew the sordid details of the lie I had fabricated; it was blindly accepted as truth. It was apparent that

Candela's mother had not given away any specifics of how she came by the rumor, as no one seemed to know its true origin. In the dying embers and blackened twigs of a ravaged forest, who could distinguish where the first spark was lit? Only the arsonist knows the exact location where that match was struck.

Days later, the victim of my deceit—seventeen-year-old Ana—was found in her family's white porcelain bathtub, with blood gushing and bubbling from her two delicate wrists. It was on the same night that I suffered my first panic attack.

Two

ANA WAS THE original sad girl. She held the unofficial title long before her death. We all became sad girls after that. At her funeral, everyone wore black because it was customary and because it was the color that best defined Ana.

We learned in art class that, technically, black is not a color but, rather, the absence of it. Black is a shade—one that holds its presence in every gradation of gray, departing only with its transition into white. I have always thought of white as a clean slate, an unwritten page. A snow-covered field or a wedding dress. White is starting over, an absolution from your sins. That day, I was the furthest away from white that I could possibly be.

Ana's funeral service was held at Holy Trinity, our local church. I sat in the back pew with my mother, who was staring straight ahead, her mouth set in a hard, firm line. The Peter Pan collar of my dress felt constrictive around my neck, and when I pulled at it with my forefinger, she shot me a look of annoyance. "Stop fidgeting, Audrey," she muttered under her breath. I let my hand fall into my lap.

Earlier that morning, I had stood in front of the large mirror above my dresser. As I stared at my reflection, I felt the oddest sensation that it was someone else staring back. The girl in the mirror had the same auburn hair that hung straight and low past her shoulders. Her eyes, gazing fixedly into mine, were an identical shade of forget-me-not blue. Like me, she was cursed with a smattering of freckles across her nose, courtesy of the hot Australian sun. But she was someone I didn't recognize, like an imposter who had stepped into my body and was acting of her own accord.

The black dress my mother had purchased specifically for this occasion was made from a rough woolen fabric that rubbed unpleasantly against my skin. It felt almost like a punishment, like so many of the decisions my mother made on my behalf.

I spotted Lucy sitting a few pews up between her doting parents, her forefinger twisting absentmindedly through her honey-blonde hair. For as long as I had known her, Lucy had a habit of playing with her hair. She did it unconsciously whenever she was thinking hard about something. Autumn was Lucy's favorite season, and I couldn't think of a more befitting way to describe her. She had eyes that were the color of burnt amber and a dewy peaches and cream complexion. She radiated a soft, mellow warmth reminiscent of fall—an old soul in a young girl's body. Two weeks before, she'd had her braces removed, and her smile was like a burst of sunlight piercing through a raincloud.

On Lucy's right sat Candela, who was with her mother and her sister, Eve. Where Lucy was soft, like a watercolor, Candela was bold and headstrong. She carried herself like a storm or a melodrama. She could walk into a room and instantly change the atmosphere. Her beautiful olive skin (an ode to her Indian heritage) and sultry bee-stung lips were the envy of every girl at school. She had emerald-green eyes that could turn from warm to icy within the space of a millisecond.

When Ana's father stood up to speak at the podium, I watched as Lucy glanced over at Candela and the two exchanged a knowing look. Then Candela turned her head around and caught my eye, sending a wry smile in my direction. She began to mouth something to me when her mother tugged sharply at the sleeve of her dress and she abruptly swung her head back around, her raven-black hair sweeping across her slender neck.

After Ana's eulogy was read, we were each given a white rose (passed down the wooden pews in cane wicker baskets), and the minister instructed us to place them inside the open casket. I was last in line, so by the time I saw her, Ana's frail body was already covered in flowers. She was even more beautiful in death than when she was alive—if that were possible. She looked like an angel in her white satin dress; her pink glossy lips were set in an expression of peaceful serenity. The locks of tawny-gold hair that framed her perfect heart-shaped face were immaculately brushed and shone like a halo. "I'm sorry," I whispered, placing my rose somewhere among the other apologies.

AT THE POST-FUNERAL reception, the mood was just as somber. There were no philosophical musings or fond recollections. Ana had left the world too early. As I passed the buffet, the sight and smell of food made my stomach turn. But not so much as the murmurings that caught my ear. ". . . mother didn't turn up to her own daughter's funeral . . ."

". . . brought in for questioning but no charges laid . . ."

". . . can't be true."

". . . why else would she kill herself?"

"So tragic. Poor girl."

". . . disgusting . . ."

It was my moment, then, to clear it all up. To stand on one of the many folding chairs scattered across the room and tell everyone the truth. To say out loud what my mind was screaming in my guilt-ridden silence. That it was my fault Ana was dead.

I was sitting by the window, on a smoky gray chaise lounge, when Candela came to join me.

"Hey, Audrey," she said.

"Hey," I replied.

"Where's Duck?" she asked.

"He's sick with the flu."

My boyfriend, Brian Duckman (whom we all called Duck), was the proverbial boy next door. He lived only a few houses away from me, and we could wave at each other if we stood out on the respective decks of our suburban bungalows. We had been friends for as far back as I could remember. One summer, I went away with his family to their lake house up north. At the tail end of our trip, Duck and I were hanging out with some kids down by the lake. We were taking turns running down the length of the jetty and hurling ourselves in the water. When it was my turn, I tripped just as I was about to launch myself into the air, hitting my head on the edge of the decking and tumbling into the lake. Everything went black. When I came to, I was sputtering water freshly pumped from my chest. Murmurs from the crowd around me washed over my ears like a radio signal; the sun blazing overhead seeped into my shut eyelids. Duck had found me at the bottom of the lake. He had to dive twice before he was able to locate my limp body and carry me back to the surface. That night, with my near-death experience on my mind, I snuck into his room, slipped into his bed, and our friendship turned into something more. It was my first time and his as well. For a while, we kept it to ourselves, but eventually it became apparent that we were more than friends. Our mothers had always been close, and it was no secret that they had long since held the romantic notion of Duck and I living happily ever after.

Across the room, Lucy was standing next to her boyfriend, Freddy, and they were in mid-conversation with a boy I didn't recognize. Lucy had begun dating Freddy only a year ago, but they reminded everyone of an old married couple.

"Who's that guy Lucy and Freddy are talking to?" I asked Candela.

"That's Rad—Ana's boyfriend," Candela said, and I felt a lurch in my stomach. "He was at St. John's with Freddy when they graduated last year."

"Oh," I said. "I didn't know Ana had a boyfriend."

"Yeah, they've been together for ages. Kind of like you and Duck."

All of a sudden, a memory I had forgotten came back to me, sharp and piercing. It must have been about a year ago. I was standing in line behind Ana at the library. I don't remember what we were talking about, but when she went to remove her borrowing card, I caught sight of a photo behind the plastic film of her wallet. "Who's that?" I had asked casually. "Just my boyfriend, Rad," she had shrugged, removing the photograph and handing it to me. "Isn't he dreamy?" My eyes had fallen on the monochromatic portrait of a boy standing against a seaside setting, with dark windswept hair and brows softly knitted as though the camera had caught him by surprise. I realized with a sinking feeling that it was the same boy who was now speaking to Lucy and Freddy across the room.

As though sensing he was being watched, Rad looked over, and for one brief moment, our eyes locked. He attempted a half smile—it looked more like a grimace—before turning his attention back to Lucy, who reached out and put her hand on his arm. A few moments later, Freddy and Lucy made their way over to us as Rad strode out of the room.

"How is he?" asked Candela.

"Not good," said Freddy, with a shake of his head. It was weird seeing Freddy in a suit. He was always in some quirky getup—checked shirts and contrasting ties, Vans with bold floral patterns. He wore black Buddy Holly glasses that teetered at the edge of his nose, and he was always pushing them up again.

"Poor thing," said Lucy, shaking her head. "He must be going through hell."

The air seemed to grow thicker all of a sudden, and I stood up quickly. Candela's eyes darted upward.

"Are you okay, Audrey?"

"Yeah," I mumbled, "I just need some air."

I STUMBLED OUT onto the back porch a little unsteadily and clung to the wrought iron balustrade, my breathing quick and ragged.

"Are you all right?" came a voice from behind me. I looked back, startled. Rad was sitting on a swinging chair that creaked softly as it swung gently back and forth. He dug his shoes into the ground and walked toward me, a look of concern crossing his face.

"I'm fine," I said.

Ana is dead because of me. The words flashed unbidden through my mind, and my body gave an involuntary shudder. Rad stood there for a minute or so, his gaze fixed steadily on me. It was the first time we had ever stood face-to-face, and I noticed that the color of his eyes didn't quite match. One was a stormy gray, the other a summer blue.

"Do you want a glass of water?" he asked.

"No, thanks," I said. I bit down hard on the inside of my cheek, and the sharp pain gave my mind a much-needed diversion. We stood like that for a while, until my breathing began to steady. Rad looked relieved.

"Did you go to school with Ana?" he asked.

I nodded.

"Were you close to her?"

"No," I said. "Not really."

He turned away from me, looking skyward and sighing deeply.

"Can I ask you something?" he asked.

"Sure," I replied.

"Do you believe in heaven?"

I looked at him, a little taken aback.

"I don't know," I said truthfully, with a small shake of my head. "I believe there is something, though."

"How do you know for sure?" he asked.

"It's a feeling, I suppose."

"A feeling?"

"Yeah, kind of like . . ." I paused, searching for the right word. "Like intuition," I said finally.

He nodded. "I suppose that makes sense."

He was quiet for a few moments, and then he turned to look at me, his eyes level with mine.

"What about hell?"

I felt my heart seize in my chest. For one irrational moment, I thought, *He knows about the lie.* But then I realized it was just my own paranoia.

"Yes," I said, thinking back to my panic attack the other night. "I believe there's a hell."

There was a loud crash that came from inside the house, and we turned our heads in unison.

"What was that?" asked Rad.

"I don't know. We should go back inside."

THE LIVING ROOM was a mess. The table was overturned, and there were plates of food scattered across the floor. Ana's dad was standing amidst the chaos, one hand cradled protectively over his left cheek, a trickle of blood running from the side of his mouth. Everyone watched in stunned silence as Ana's uncle stood with his fist partly raised, his face twisted with rage.

"You sick fuck!" he snarled. "She was a child, for Chrissake!" He was about to throw another punch when Ana's mother pulled him back.

"Stop it!" she screamed, stepping between them.

"Why didn't you stop him, Mia?" he said spinning around to face her. "You must have known what was going on."

She shook her head helplessly. "I didn't know," she whispered.

Ana's dad turned to face her, his eyes filled with despair. "Mia," he said helplessly. "You know I never touched our daughter—"

She shook her head in disgust. "Don't you dare talk to me," she hissed, before turning on her heel and striding away.

There was a tense silence in the room, broken only when someone began to pick up the shattered plates. Quiet murmurs floated from all directions as Ana's mother was led up the stairs by a pair of somber-faced relatives. With his head bowed and averted from everyone's gaze, Ana's dad turned and left the room.

I glanced at Rad and knew that the look of horror on his face mirrored my own—although for different reasons.

"Let's get out of here," he muttered under his breath.

OUTSIDE, THE SKY was a dark, moody blue. There was a strip of orange along the horizon, one rolling spark of flame the impending night would soon extinguish.

"Want to go for a drive?" asked Rad.

"Okay."

We walked to his car, a white sedan, which was parked across the street. I got into the passenger seat. There was a small tear in the upholstery, and I ran my fingers over it, thinking about the countless number of times Ana must have sat there. A flash of guilt opened me up like a fresh, gaping wound.

Rad got into the driver's seat beside me and shut the door behind him. The silence between us was comfortable despite the strange turn of events that led us there. As we pulled away from the curb, I turned my head back for one last look at Ana's house and could just barely make out her dad sitting bent over on the porch step, the light from the end of his cigarette glowing pitifully against the graying sky.

"ARE YOU HUNGRY?" asked Rad. We had been driving aimlessly for the last ten minutes through the suburban streets. We barely said a word the whole time, but it was a companionable silence.

"A little," I admitted. I couldn't remember the last time I ate.

"There's a burger place nearby called Alfie's Kitchen. Have you heard of it?"

I shook my head. "No."

"It's a hole in the wall. They only serve one type of burger, but it's pretty damn good. And their strawberry milkshake is the best thing in the world. What do you think?"

"Sounds good," I said.

ALFIE'S KITCHEN WAS a small beachfront kiosk that sat atop a grassy hill. Like Rad had mentioned, the place looked unassuming, but the crowd of people waiting to be served suggested there was something special about the place. A canvas awning the color of sandstone extended from the brick front, casting a block of shadow over the sprawling lawn where a number of plastic tables and seats were scattered across the patchy grass. A girl in a crisp white uniform and bouncy ponytail stood behind the counter, taking orders while two chefs behind her worked away in the busy kitchen. The air was filled with the rich smell of fried onions and the sound of sizzling patties. As we progressed farther in the queue, I noticed several photographs of celebrities taped to the sides of the walls, burgers clutched triumphantly in their hands and grins plastered across their faces.

By the time we got our meals, the tables were all taken, so we made our way over to an empty park bench a short walk away. The bench sat near the edge of a rocky cliff and overlooked the ocean. The sky was growing dimmer by the minute, and aside from the crowd in the distance, we were now alone. Toward the horizon, a man was preparing to launch a large multicolored kite into the sky. "I come here pretty often," said Rad, sitting down on the park bench.

"Yeah?" I said, sitting beside him.

"The light is beautiful this time of day, especially during the summer. The sunsets go on forever."

"It's nice here," I agreed, pulling my burger from its brown paper wrapper.

I didn't realize just how hungry I was until I took the first bite.

"Strange day, huh?" he said, taking a sip of his milkshake.

"Yeah," I agreed. I felt queasy all of a sudden and put my burger down on the bench. My fingers gripped the wooden slats.

"Are you okay?" Rad asked. He put his burger down too and turned to face me.

"I'm okay," I said, taking a deep breath to steady myself. "It just occurred to me that I've never known anyone who's died before except my granddad, but I was just a kid at the time."

"Me too," said Rad quietly. For a moment, he had a faraway look in his eyes, and then he shuddered as though shaking off a memory. "Hey." He turned to me. "Can we make a deal?"

"What kind of deal?"

"Let's not talk about Ana tonight. The last few days have been a nightmare, and I just want to feel normal again. Even if it's only for a few hours." His eyes looked into mine. "Is that okay?" He extended his hand to me.

"Yeah," I said, secretly relieved. I took his hand, and we shook on it. I noticed the strange coloring of his eyes again. I wanted to ask him about them but wasn't sure how to bring it up without sounding rude.

"Why are you looking at me like that?" he asked. "Do I have sauce on my lips or something?" He fumbled with his napkin.

I shook my head quickly, feeling the heat rise to my face. "No," I said, looking away. Then I turned my head back to face him. "It's just, well, your eyes. They're amazing, incredible. Like, they're really, really cool." My words came out all fragmented, and I wondered whether he thought I was a complete idiot.

"Oh, you mean the heterochromia," said Rad.

"Is that the scientific term?" I asked.

"Yeah," he smiled. "I hated the fact that my eyes were different when I was growing up."

"Are you kidding? I would love to have your eyes."

"Well, we can swap if you want; I'm not that attached to them."

"You don't want my eyes. They're kind of goofy. My mum says they're too big for my face."

"I think your eyes are really pretty," he said and then looked immediately embarrassed. "Sorry, I didn't mean it like that."

"Of course not."

There was an awkward silence.

"You know there's this series where the main character has different-colored eyes," I said.

"Yeah?"

"Uh-huh. His name is Spike Spiegel."

"From *Cowboy Bebop*?"

I nodded. "Have you seen it?"

"Yeah, but it was a long time ago. It must have been when I was going through my anime phase."

"I'm probably still in that phase."

"You are? What's your favorite?"

"Uh, Macross . . ."

"Which series of Macross?"

"*Super Dimension Fortress.*"

"That's definitely the best one," said Rad. He shook his head and smiled. "Talk about a trip down memory lane."

"I can't believe you've actually seen Macross. I don't know anyone else who has."

"Me neither, come to think of it," said Rad.

"I tried to get my boyfriend to watch it with me once, but he wasn't keen."

"Your boyfriend?"

"Yeah, Duck."

"You have a boyfriend named Duck?"

"Well, that's what we all call him. His actual name is Brian Duckman."

"Oh, that makes sense." He picked up his burger again. "So

how long have you been together?"

"Since we were kids, basically. But we have literally nothing in common."

"No?"

I shook my head. "We disagree on just about everything. I can never play my music out loud around him. And he's not really into books. But I suppose they say opposites attract."

"He doesn't read books?" said Rad.

"No. Well, actually, there's a book he's reading at the moment. I think it's called *Yes—Now What's the Next Question?*"

"Isn't that a self-help book?"

"Yeah, something like that."

"I suppose you prefer fiction?"

I nodded. "Definitely."

"What's your favorite book?"

I thought for a moment. "*The Land of Laughs,* I think."

"That's a good one."

"Do you remember the scene where Thomas is traveling through mountain towns while working on his father's biography?"

Rad nodded.

"I think that's always been my dream."

"To write your dad's biography?" There was a hint of a smile on his face.

I laughed. "Not exactly. But I would love to write something, maybe a book. I want to travel to a small town someday—one with fir trees and snowcapped mountains. Then I would spend an entire winter writing to my heart's content."

"I like the sound of that," he said.

We were quiet for a few minutes.

"Actually," he looked embarrassed, "I've been working on a book."

"You're writing a novel?"

"Yeah, I mean, it's early days."

"What's it about?"

He frowned. "I'm not sure exactly. It's a little hazy at the moment. I'm still waiting for the idea to come together."

"I know what that's like."

"So I guess you're working on something too?"

"Not really," I said, looking away. "Only stuff for the school magazine."

"Well, that still counts," he said. "What have you been writing?"

"Mainly short stories. A few articles here and there."

"Short stories are so underrated."

"I know."

"Have you read 'All Summer in a Day'?"

"By Ray Bradbury?"

He nodded.

"I love that story," I said.

"My teacher read it to our class in the third grade, and it's always stuck with me. I remember feeling bad for the girl."

"Yeah, me too."

I thought of Margot, the sad, pale girl in the story who was shut up in a closet and robbed of her time in the sun. A cold shiver ran through my body.

"'Mars Is Heaven!' is great too," Rad said after a few moments.

"I love that one as well."

By now the stars were coming out one by one like pinpricks through a veil. I let the cool, crisp air into my lungs and tried not to think about small, confined spaces.

"There was a book I read when I was a kid," said Rad. "I can't recall the title or the author. But it was about parallel worlds. Sometimes I feel like I'm in an alternate universe. Like I switched places with another version of me, and I'm stuck here, in this world. I don't know if that makes sense."

"It does," I said. "I feel like that sometimes too."

"You do?"

I nodded. "Absolutely."

"I suppose it's like being a character in a book. The author has this idea of where the story line is going, and she sets up her characters accordingly. But it changes as she goes, right? All of a sudden, it's the second draft, and you're stuck with a different name and a whole other backstory. Then she writes you into an alternate ending. You know, sometimes I get this tiny glimpse of what things were, before the new reality takes over."

"Exactly," I said. "I know what you mean by a glimpse. It's more of a feeling." I frowned. "Well, I don't know what it is exactly, but it's something intangible. Which is why it's so difficult to explain. There is a sense of something else—a different reality altogether—but then you're snatched up by the present one, and you're stuck here. I suppose the most obvious comparison is that moment when you wake up from a dream, and there are those first few seconds of adjustment. Only, I think I have felt that while I was wide awake."

"You've just described it perfectly," said Rad. "But the idea is crazy, right? I'm sitting here on this park bench talking to you, and it feels solid and real. But maybe in the original version of this story, we were never here."

"Which means the park bench never existed in the first place."

"Scary thought, huh?"

"Yeah," I said. "But I like your theory—about us being characters in a book."

"Do you think it's possible?"

"I do," I said.

"Then who do you think created us?"

"I don't know. Maybe it's like one of those mirrored rooms where you see a thousand versions of yourself. Someone created us, someone else created *them*, and it goes that way in an infinite loop."

"Well, if that's the case, my creator must be a masochist."

I could tell he was only half joking.

MY MOTHER WAS up when I got home later that night. She was standing in the hallway, her face a storm cloud of anger. "It's two in the morning, Audrey," she said. "Where the *hell* have you been?" I opened my mouth to speak, but she held up her hand to stop me. "You know what? I don't want to hear it. I know it's going to be lies anyway." She glared at me, wrapping her sleeping gown tighter around herself. Her voice dropped, but it still retained every bit of its venom. "Everyone at the reception saw you leave with that boy," she hissed. "Do you have any idea how that looks?"

"We were just talking, Mum," I said, looking down at my feet.

"Talking?" she said, raising her voice again. "Until two in the morning? What's wrong with you, Audrey?" She crossed her arms and sighed loudly. "Ana—*your friend*—is barely cold in her grave, and you're trying to get your hands down her boyfriend's pants."

I looked up at her, furious. "How dare you!" I screamed. "You don't know what you're talking about!"

"Yes, I do," she said coldly. "I saw the way you were looking at him. How do you think Duck would feel about that?"

"Duck wouldn't care, Mum." The words didn't come out as confidently as I had intended. Until now, I hadn't even thought about Duck.

"He wouldn't?" she said. "Are you out of your mind, Audrey? I hope you haven't forgotten that if it wasn't for Duck, you wouldn't even be here right now."

Tears sprang to my eyes, but I didn't want to give her the satisfaction of seeing me cry. I pushed past her roughly and was halfway up the stairs when I heard her call after me. "I don't want you seeing him again. Do you hear me, Audrey? It's finished."

"Shut up!" I screamed. "You can't tell me what to do!"

I slammed the door shut, anger rising inside me. I took a few deep breaths, willing myself not to cry. It had been such a strange night, and I wanted to collect myself and make sense of what I was feeling. Deep down I knew my mother was right, and I felt a bubble of self-hatred rise to the surface. It was clear to me now that I shouldn't have left Ana's house with Rad. But it happened so quickly that neither of us had time to think about the consequences. And now it was too late to turn back.

Three

CANDELA CAUGHT UP with me just as I was walking through the school gate.

"Hey, Audrey," she said, a little out of breath. "What happened last night?"

"What do you mean?" I asked.

"Well, you left Ana's house with Rad. Everyone was talking about it."

"How crass."

"People can be assholes," she agreed. "So, what happened, anyway? You didn't answer any of my texts last night."

"Sorry," I said, "I got home really late."

"Really?" She raised an eyebrow.

The school bell sounded.

"Hey, let's skip class today," said Candela.

"I can't. I've been falling behind."

"Audrey." She grabbed my arm. "You look like you need a break. And besides, one day won't kill you—will it?"

A FEW HOURS later, we were sitting on the sandy shore of our favorite beach, watching the surfers glide across the waves. It was unusually warm for August, and we were enjoying the rare bits of sunshine that broke intermittently through the gray clouds. Candela passed me a joint, and I took it from her gratefully.

"Thanks," I said. "I really needed this."

"Me too," she said. "What a god-awful week it's been."

I held the end of the joint to my lips, drawing the smoke into my lungs.

"Go easy, Audrey. You know that stuff can make you weird." I nodded, handing it back to her. She took a couple of quick puffs and then stubbed the joint out on the sand. I watched as she placed the rest of it carefully into a pillbox.

"I know I shouldn't have left with Rad last night."

"I thought you didn't know each other. I mean, one minute you were asking who he was, and then the next thing we knew, Lucy said the two of you left together. So what happened?"

"Well, I was feeling anxious," I looked at her. "You know . . ."

Candela nodded. Her mother suffered from panic attacks, and she knew I had started having them.

I took a deep breath. "So I went outside for some air, and Rad was there, on the back porch. We talked for a little bit, and then the fight broke out and we left."

"God, the fight," Candela's face was suddenly animated. "Did you see what happened?"

"I missed most of it."

"It was nasty. Ana's uncle turned up a bit drunk. He walked right up to Ana's dad and hit him. Really hard too!"

"Yeah," I said softly.

"Not that the bastard didn't deserve it," she added.

I remained quiet.

"You know, I can't believe the police haven't arrested him yet. I mean, you're the one who saw them through the window with their clothes off and going at it, so maybe you should speak to the cops."

My heart leapt to my throat, and it was on the tip of my tongue to tell Candela the truth—that I had made it all up and Ana's dad was innocent. I opened my mouth, but the words wouldn't form. I felt panic grip me like a vice.

"Audrey, are you okay? Oh shit, I shouldn't have said anything." Candela put her arm around me, stroking my back as I struggled to get my breathing under control. "God, I'm such an idiot," she said, shaking her head. "I'm so sorry, babe."

"It's okay," I said, between quick, ragged breaths.

She kept her hand on my back, rubbing in a slow circular motion. It took awhile before I began to feel okay again.

"I saw Ana the day before it happened, you know," Candela said. "Just when the rumor was turning into a shit storm. I know I promised you I wouldn't say anything to her, but I had this really strong feeling that I should. Now I wish I had." She bit her lip and began drawing arbitrary shapes in the sand with her fingertips. "I mean, she was my friend, and I let her down. I don't know if I can ever get past that, you know?"

"I'm so sorry, Candela." I could feel my throat tightening up again. "This is all my fault."

"No, it's not. Don't ever say that. You had no idea that Eve was listening at the door."

"I should never have said anything," I said, my voice dropping to a whisper.

"Hey." She let out a sigh. "Come on . . . let's just—fuck it. Let's not talk about Ana anymore. Okay? Tell me about Rad. How was he last night?"

"He was okay," I said. "I think he just needed someone to talk to. Maybe someone who didn't know Ana."

"I get that. Really I do. Did he say anything about Ana?"

"No," I said, with a shake of my head. "He didn't want to talk about her."

Candela nodded. "To be honest, I don't blame him. It messes me up, thinking about it. I'd rather think about anything else."

"Same. But I know it must be a million times worse for you, because you were always close to her."

"Yeah," said Candela. A shadow seemed to pass over her face. "We had some great times."

We were quiet, lost in our own thoughts.

"Are you going to see Rad again?"

"I don't know. Mum went completely feral when I got home last night."

"You should have seen her at the reception when Lucy told her you left with Rad." A tiny laugh escaped from her lips. "She was livid." Candela and my mother were mortal enemies.

I smirked. "Anyway, she has forbidden me from seeing him."

"She forbids you from seeing me," Candela pointed out. "Yet here we are."

"It's kind of messy. I mean, I'm not sure Duck would be keen on the idea."

Candela rolled her eyes. "Duck is way too possessive. You know I adore him, but the guy needs to lighten up."

"He can be a little moody sometimes, but he's a really good guy. Besides, I'm probably the last thing Rad needs right now."

"Or," said Candela, giving me a long, meaningful look, "you could be exactly what he needs."

I ARRIVED HOME late that afternoon to the smell of chicken soup wafting through the house. My mother came out of the kitchen, undoing her apron and sliding it over her head.

"Oh good, you're home. I was going to take some chicken soup over to Duck, but you can if you want to."

"Okay," I said.

I followed her into the kitchen, putting my school bag down on a chair. She ruffled through the cupboards and found an old thermos. After rinsing it in the sink, she carefully spooned in the soup with a ladle and screwed it shut tight. She wiped at the sides with a cloth and then handed it to me. "Here," she said. I tucked the thermos under my arm and set out on the short walk to Duck's house.

DUCK'S MOTHER, ZOE, answered the door on the third knock. "Audrey!" she said, smiling brightly. "Come in." She opened the door wider and I followed her inside.

Each time I walked through Duck's front door, I was greeted with a picture of the two of us that Zoe had hung in the entrance of the hallway. We were thirteen, and our mothers had entered us into a local ballroom dancing competition. In the photo, Duck was in a hideous powder-blue suit, and I was wearing a strange sequined dress my mother had sewn for me. It always made me cringe.

"How is Duck feeling?" I asked.

Zoe rolled her eyes. "You know what he's like."

"Man flu?" It was a private joke between us.

"Exactly," she laughed. "He's a bit grumpy, but maybe you can cheer him up."

"I'll try," I said, with a weak smile.

DUCK WAS SITTING up in his bed playing Grand Theft Auto.

"Hey," he said, eyes glued to the screen.

"Hi." I sat down on the edge of his bed and put the thermos on the ground. "I brought Mum's chicken soup."

"Oh great," he said, his tone sarcastic. "I've been craving chicken-flavored water all day."

"You get so grouchy when you're sick," I said, ruffling his hair.

"So what's the story about you leaving with Ana's boyfriend after the reception?"

"God, word travels fast around here," I mumbled, looking away.

He paused his game and put down his controller.

"So what's the story?"

I shrugged. "I don't know. We were just talking. No big deal."

"No big deal? You took off with some guy you'd never even met before, and it's no big deal?"

"His girlfriend just died; I think he just wanted someone to talk to, okay?" I could feel Duck's eyes boring into me, and I turned to meet his gaze. I could tell by his expression he had been brooding about it all day. He looked a little off-color, and there was a patch of rough stubble on his chin. Despite that, he was still as handsome as ever. His hair was dark brown and scruffy, and his eyes were a dreamy blue.

"What did you talk about?" Duck asked. He had always been jealous of me around other boys.

"Stuff, I guess. I don't know. Things that friends usually talk about."

"So you're *friends* now?" he said, his tone irate.

I glared at him. "I'm allowed to have friends, Duck."

"Sure, next time I'm at a party, I'll just leave with some random girl and make *her* my new friend."

"It wasn't a party," I said, my voice rising. "It was a *funeral.*"

"What's the difference?" he challenged.

"It's just different."

"How?"

"Oh, forget it. You wouldn't understand."

"And I suppose he does?"

I stood up. "What's the matter with you?" I said angrily. "We just hung out; it's not a big deal. His girlfriend just died, and I think that would be the only thing on his mind."

"Right," said Duck, with a shrug of his shoulders. He looked away. "Whatever."

"Look, you're just sick and feeling like shit. I get it. But you don't have to be jealous of Rad."

"So, he has a name."

"Can you stop?"

"Stop what?" He looked defiant.

"Stop being a jerk about this whole thing. I did nothing wrong, and you know it."

He looked at me for a few moments, a blank expression on his face. Then, he sighed and said in a resigned voice, "Sorry."

"It's fine," I said tightly.

"It's just that I've been stuck in my room all day, and I hear all this stuff about my girlfriend going off with some guy. How do you expect me to feel?"

"It's not like I planned it, you know. It just happened that way." I threw my hands in the air and sat back down on the edge of Duck's bed.

He picked up the PlayStation controller and began playing his game again. "So how is he doing, anyway?"

"He's okay, I suppose. I'm sure he and Ana were really close. I mean, I can't imagine how I would feel if I were in his shoes."

"Me neither," said Duck quietly. He glanced up at me. "You know, I still can't get my head around what happened to Ana. She was there last week. She lent me a pen in English class. How can someone go from lending a pen to being dead?" I felt the room spin a little, and I clutched the sky-blue comforter on Duck's bed. "Do you ever think about not existing?" he continued, missing my sudden bout of anxiety. "I mean, doesn't the concept terrify you?"

"Of course it does."

"I remember when I was twelve. My dad was talking about someone's kid at work who choked on a piece of apple and died. I think it traumatized me. I mean, I kept obsessing about death after that. To the point where I was sick about it. Like, imagine that. Not being anything."

"It's a scary thought," I agreed.

"It's like *The NeverEnding Story*. You know, how the Nothing starts to take over."

I nodded, thinking back to the day at the lake, my unconscious body settling down among the moss-covered rocks, an audience of tiny fish darting anxiously to and fro. How long would it have taken for my life to ebb away? What if Duck didn't find me on the second dive down? What if it had been the third, the fourth? Would it have been too late? If Duck hadn't saved me that day, would Ana still be here?

I looked at Duck, his eyes fixed to the screen. Sirens and radio static boomed from the television set. A car chase was under way. I tried to imagine how I would feel if the shoe was on the other foot and Duck had left Ana's funeral with another girl. I felt nothing—not even a pang of jealousy. Was it because he never gave me reason to doubt his feelings for me? Why was he always doubting mine?

"So," he said, casting a sidelong glance at me, "are you going to keep hanging out with this new friend of yours?"

I stood up, my fists clenched tightly at my sides. "Look, stop trying to pick a fight with me, okay? I've been having a rough time lately; you know that."

"Audrey, you were never that close to Ana," he pointed out. "I mean, Candela seems to be handling this better than you, and they were really close."

"Hey," I said defensively. "Some kid you didn't even know died from choking on a piece of fruit, and it messed you up, so maybe this is the same thing for me."

He was quiet for a few moments.

"I guess," he said finally.

"Anyway, I should head back before it gets dark."

"Okay."

"Are you going to school tomorrow?" Duck and I were both in our final term at Barrett, one of the few co-ed private schools in North Sydney. It was a short bus ride from Three Oaks and where most families in our town sent their kids.

"I think I'll be fine by tomorrow," he said. "I'll pick you up in the morning."

"Okay, I'll see you tomorrow."

LATER THAT NIGHT, I was lying in bed when I overheard a conversation between my parents.

"I think it's time we send her to see someone."

"Do you really think that's necessary?"

"Well, she's barely eating and those mood swings . . ."

"I don't know what has gotten into her . . ."

"For Chrissake, Edwina, her friend just slit her wrists."

"They weren't exactly close."

"They've known each other since they were kids. Ana's been around here plenty."

The conversation continued, but it began to rain and their words were lost to the soft drumming sound on the roof. I sighed and reached over to turn on my reading lamp. I propped myself up with some pillows and took the half-read copy of *My Sweet Audrina* from the nightstand.

A few hours later, I was on the final chapter when my phone beeped with a text message. It was Rad.

Are you up?

I texted back. Yeah

Can't sleep?

No

Me too. Want to go for a drive?

I checked the time. It was almost two in the morning.

Now?

Yeah.

I thought about it. My parents would murder me if they knew, but it wasn't the first time I had snuck out in the middle of the night. "Screw it," I muttered under my breath. I felt a small, unexpected thrill at the thought of seeing him again.

Okay, I texted back.

See you outside your house in 10.

RAD WAS PARKED outside when I closed the front door as quietly as I could and made my way quickly to his car.

"Hey," he said, as I slid into the passenger seat.

"Hey."

He pulled away from the curb and turned into the next street.

"Where are we going?"

"Actually, there is something I need to do, and I was hoping you could help me."

"What is it?"

"Ana had this gold necklace she was really attached to. It was a gift from her parents . . ."

Rad shifted gears and pulled over onto the side of the road. He dug into his jean pocket and drew out a gold chain with a heart-shaped locket attached. I recognized it at once. I was sitting at my desk in class one day, with the teacher droning on about algebra, when a glimmer of light caught my eye. Outside, a ray of sunlight had pierced through the clouds, briefly illuminating a gold necklace around Ana's neck like a wink. With lazy curiosity, I had noticed a dent at the center of the heart-shaped locket.

"I always wondered why that dent was there," I said.

"Her puppy, Starflash, chewed on it," said Rad. "I think she liked it more because of that. She used to say that the most beautiful things are damaged in some way." His expression saddened. "Anyway, I found it tonight. She had stuck it in a copy of *Brighton Rock,* as a bookmark I suppose, and then she forgot about it. We looked for it everywhere, and I kept telling her not to worry, that it would turn up eventually. Tonight, I was putting away some of her stuff in a box, and the locket fell out of the book. I know she would want to have it, so I thought I should return it to her."

It took me a few moments to comprehend what he meant by returning the locket to Ana. "You mean now?"

Rad nodded.

"You want to go into the cemetery at this hour?"

"You don't have to come if you don't want to," he said. "I can take you back home."

"Why don't you just wait until the morning? Cemeteries are so scary at night."

"I don't want to leave the necklace on her tombstone, in case someone takes it," said Rad. "I was thinking of burying it next to her, and that's not something I want to be doing in broad daylight."

"I suppose you have a point," I sighed.

"So do you want to come?"

I thought about it for a few moments. "Okay," I said finally.

He looked relieved. "Thanks, Audrey. To be honest, I didn't like the idea of going there alone."

I BEGAN TO regret my decision when Rad turned into the entrance of Woodlands Cemetery, where Ana was buried. As we drove past the weeping willows and tombstones jutting up from the ground like crooked teeth, a feeling of trepidation washed over me. When he came to a stop, I began to feel tiny pins pricking the back of my neck. This was always a bad sign. "Are you okay, Audrey?" said Rad, releasing the catch of his seat belt. "What's wrong?"

"I'm fine," I said, but my voice came out strangled and my entire body was trembling.

"You don't look fine," Rad frowned. "Do you want to leave?"

I shook my head and frantically felt for the door handle. "I just—need some air," I gasped. I stumbled out of the car onto the grass, desperately trying to suck air into my lungs.

"Audrey!" Rad had materialized at my side. "It's okay; calm down." I felt his hand on my shoulder. I brushed it away.

"Don't tell me to calm down!" I snapped, feeling disorientated.

"I'm sorry," he said, taking a step back.

My hands had turned numb, and I shook them furiously as I paced up and down the grassy field. I must have looked like I was having a mental breakdown, but I didn't care. All I could focus on was the horrible *thing* that had taken possession of my body. I was desperate to get back in control again.

"What can I do?" I heard Rad say, through the fog clouding my brain.

"I'll be okay," I panted. "Just—just give me a minute. Please."

A few moments later, I was starting to feel a little better. I glanced at Rad, standing there with a look of worry etched across his face.

"Are you all right?"

I nodded. "I'm sorry."

"Don't be."

"Sometimes it feels like—like there's a boa constrictor around my body and it's squeezing every last atom from my lungs. I don't know how else to explain it." I drew in a deep breath and let it out slowly.

"You don't have to explain," he said, and somehow I sensed that I didn't.

"Thanks." I gave him a tight smile.

"Hey, why don't you just wait in the car while I go and do this?"

"No." I shook my head. "I'll come with you."

ANA'S TOMBSTONE WAS barely visible beneath all the cards, decaying bouquets, and other tokens of grief.

A full moon hung in the sky like a Chinese lantern, and though I was grateful for the light, my mind kept playing random scenes from horror movies in a sinister montage.

Rad had brought a small trowel like the ones my mother used when she was gardening. He got onto his knees at the foot of Ana's grave, and with the sharp point of the metal, he carefully cut out a small patch of grass. He put the grass to one side and began digging at the fresh soil. I sat down next to him cross-legged and watched. My mind shot to my panic attack earlier. I thought he wouldn't want anything to do with me, that he would think I was a freak. But he didn't seem to mind or make an issue of it, and I liked him more because of that.

"You know, I used to hear stories about kids who hung out at cemeteries in the middle of the night. I never thought in a million years that I'd be one of them," I said.

Rad shook his head. "Me too."

After a few minutes he stopped and stood up, fishing the necklace from his pocket. He looked at it with a mixture of curiosity and sadness. "You know, I've never opened it," he said. "I don't know what she put in there."

"I'm sure it's a picture of you." I stood up and looked at the gold locket cupped in the palm of his hand.

He nodded. "I think I should just bury it and walk away." But there was a hesitancy to his voice.

"Maybe Ana would have wanted you to look inside."

Rad seemed to be thinking it over, and then he pried at the edge of the locket with his fingers. It clicked open with little resistance.

"It's not a picture of me," he said. I leaned in closer to examine the photograph stuck in the heart-shaped frame.

"It's Candela," I said, looking at him with surprise.

"Yeah," he said. I couldn't read the expression on his face.

Without a word, he snapped the locket back into its original position. Then he dropped to his knees again and placed it slowly into the freshly dug pit.

We were silent as he scooped the dirt onto the locket, filling in the void. Then he took the patch of grass and put it carefully back into position, patting it down gently. It looked like we were never here—as though the locket and its mysterious significance had been swallowed up by the earth. Rad glanced at his watch. "It'll be daylight in a few hours. Let's get out of here. I know a great place where we can watch the sun come up."

Four

It was a dreary, downcast day. I was riding to the bus stop in Mum's car, booked in for my first appointment with a psychologist just before noon.

Mum had been grilling me about Rad since breakfast and hadn't let up. "I'm only trying to stop you from making a huge mistake, Audrey," she said as she pulled up at the bus stop. "You'll thank me one day." She adjusted the rearview mirror to catch her reflection before smearing bright red lipstick across her lips.

"Mum, I'm not seeing Rad anymore," I lied. "Can you please just drop it?"

After we left the cemetery that night, Rad took me to an old lighthouse at Widow's Cove. It stood at the end of a battered wharf and wasn't much taller than a lamppost. We climbed up a rickety ladder and onto a balcony edged with thin metal railing. It was still dark, and the moon—large and glowing—threw a pale shimmer of light across the water. That night, we talked the way old friends do, with candor and ease. We were still deep in conversation when the sun announced its arrival with an astonishing flourish of orange and pink.

"Well, the damage has already been done." My mother's voice, always on the verge of hysteria, drove a wedge into my thoughts. "I was in the grocery store the other day, and I heard the Baker sisters gossiping about it in the next aisle."

"That's because they're assholes, Mum. I can't live my whole life worrying about every damn thing people are saying about me."

"No, you can't. But in the future, you can try to be a little more considerate. Imagine how Duck feels, you taking off with some guy."

"We just talked; that's all. And Duck knows that. Rad needed a friend that night, and I was there for him. You're just trying to turn it into something that it's not. Maybe you're projecting your own guilt onto me," I said, my words coming out in a rush before I could lose my nerve.

Her eyes narrowed. "What are you talking about?"

"You know exactly what I'm talking about. What you did to Dad."

Her face turned an ugly shade of red. "How dare you," she hissed. "That happened years ago. Your dad has gotten past it. You're the only one who won't let it go."

"Well, what choice did he have?" I spat at her. "At least we kept your dirty little secret to ourselves." As soon as the words were out of my mouth, I knew I had gone too far.

"Get out!" she screamed. "You ungrateful brat. Get out *now.*"

I got out of the car as quickly as I could, slamming the door behind me.

As THE BUS pulled away from the stop, I sat in my seat pinching hard at the skin between my knuckles. I took a deep gulp of air through my mouth and exhaled slowly. Feeling self-conscious,

I looked up to see whether anyone noticed how jittery I was. But the bus was crowded, and all the riders looked like they were in their own worlds.

My mother had a way of making everything seem ten times worse than it actually was. She watched me like a hawk, scrutinizing every move I made, looking for an opportunity to call me out. When I was thirteen, she came to pick me up at a birthday party. She caught sight of a cake stain on my new dress and yelled at me in front of all my friends. Though it was years ago, the humiliation I felt that day remains fresh in my mind.

As the bus continued, starting and stopping in the heavy morning traffic, I reached into the pocket of my jeans and fished out the crumpled piece of bright yellow paper my dad had given me the night before.

Ida Summers & Associates
24 Sentinel Street, Cremorne

Ida Summers was a name already familiar to me. I heard it dropped every so often in the school playground, like a status symbol. She had a reputation for treating damaged adolescent girls.

It was strange. The words "panic attack" were thrown around so often that I used to think nothing of it, applying the expression to the most trivial things. But now whenever I heard it, my stomach turned itself into knots. I used to be bulletproof, and I didn't even know it.

Describing a panic attack to someone who has never experienced one is impossible. However, to one who has, no explanation is needed. You just have to say the word "anxiety," and their eyes would light up with a knowing look. A mixture of "Welcome to the club" and "I know it sucks, but at least you're not alone."

The other night I was watching a movie when, midway through, it went out of sync. As the actors spoke, their words no longer matched up with the movement of their lips. I picked up the remote and tried the pause button. When that didn't work, I tried to restart the movie, hoping it would fix the problem. In the end I gave up and just stopped watching it altogether. That was when the realization hit me; that out-of-sync feeling is exactly what anxiety is. Only, imagine it is not on a movie screen but in your brain. The worst thing is you have no control over it. There is no fix. You have to wait until things begin to feel normal again, but when you're in that state of mind, you can't tell if it ever will. And that's what makes it so terrifying.

I ARRIVED AT the clinic twenty minutes before my appointment. I was still in a bad frame of mind from the argument with Mum earlier. I tried my best not to think about it.

The building was a two-story brick terrace house next to a row of boutiques, a mini shopping mart, and a secondhand book store. I pushed through the wrought iron gate and made my way up the concrete footpath to the bright red door. To my right was an intercom next to a rectangular plaque that read *Ida Summers*, along with two other names I didn't recognize. I pushed the red button labeled *Call*.

I heard a burst of static, and a female voice, almost childlike, came on.

"Hello?"

"Hi, it's Audrey for my eleven-o'clock appointment with Ida," I said into the speaker.

"Wonderful, come in."

There was a buzzing sound followed by a click as I pushed the door open. I walked into a small reception room and was greeted by a petite lady dressed in a gray pantsuit.

"Hello," she said smiling at me from behind her desk. "Is this your first time with Ida?"

"Yes, it is."

She stood up and began riffling through a filing cabinet before pulling out a piece of paper.

"Can you please fill this out?"

"Sure," I replied, taking the form from her tiny hands.

"AUDREY?" I HEARD as I was flicking through a magazine. When I looked up, I saw a lady in her early thirties standing by the doorframe. Her inky black hair was cut into a sharp bob, and a pair of tortoiseshell glasses framed her china-doll features.

"Yes."

"I'm Ida," she said with a smile. "Come with me."

I followed her up a narrow flight of steps and through a wood paneled door. Ida's office was small and stark, the furniture sparse. It was almost monochromatic, with eggshell walls and abstract art; geometric patterns flourished and faltered within frames of brushed aluminum. A neat row of certificates were displayed on an otherwise bare wall proclaiming to Ida's numerous areas of expertise. A tall, narrow window positioned behind a solid oak desk cast little light into the dimly lit room. "Over here, darling," she said, waving at a brown leather lounge chair in the center of the room. "You can sit here. Put that shawl over you if you get a bit chilly; I like to have the window open. You can smoke in here if you want."

"It's okay; I don't smoke," I said, settling myself into the lounge.

"Wonderful to hear, love; I wouldn't recommend it," she said with a quick, throaty laugh. "Though you don't mind if I do?"

"No, I don't mind," I replied. She drew a cigarette from a silver case and lit it with a fluorescent pink Zippo. She took a long drag and sighed with pleasure, blowing the smoke out the window. Then sitting at her desk, she regarded me carefully.

"You're a pretty one," she said. "How old are you—sixteen? Seventeen?"

I pulled the dark blue shawl across my body. "Turning eighteen. It's my birthday in a few days."

"Well, happy birthday in advance!" she said brightly. "Are you comfortable, dear?"

"Yes, thanks."

"Any plans for your big day?"

"No, not yet."

"Anything you're hoping for?"

Rad's face filled my mind in the same way a camera lens brings a blurry image sharply into focus. I felt a tug of longing in my chest—one quickly replaced with a wave of guilt.

"No, not really," I lied.

She gave me a thoughtful look.

"So," she said with a smile, "tell me what brings you here."

I shrugged. "My parents, I suppose. They think I have issues."

"And how do you feel about that?" she asked.

"I don't know. Mum drives me crazy."

"She does?"

"Yeah, she's always on my case. We had a huge argument just this morning."

"Oh?" said Ida, taking another drag of her cigarette. "What was it about?"

"It's a long story," I mumbled, looking away.

"Well, we have almost an hour to kill."

I smiled in spite of myself.

"She cheated on my dad a few years back. I don't like

thinking about that period in our family's history."

"And that's the reason why you were arguing? About something that happened years ago?"

"No, not really. Once in a while I bring it up."

"As a weapon against her?"

"Only when I want to go nuclear. I know it's wrong."

"So what was the argument really about?"

I shook my head. "Something stupid, I don't know."

"About a boy?" she guessed.

I was about to deny it, but I could see from her expression that I had given myself away.

"It's so cliché, isn't it?"

"There's a reason why things in this world turn into clichés. It's because they're common," she said with a smile. "So does this boy have a name?"

"His name is Rad. It's a messy situation."

"Why?"

"I met him at a funeral—he's Ana's boyfriend." After a short pause I added, "She's a girl I went to school with. It was her funeral."

"Oh," said Ida. "What happened to Ana?"

"She took her own life." I bit down on my lip and looked away.

"I see," she said, with a heavy sigh. "What a terrible tragedy." She stubbed out her cigarette on a red heart-shaped ashtray, her eyes meeting mine. "So, you're feeling guilty about your attraction to Ana's boyfriend?"

"Yeah," I said, twisting the tassel ends of the blue shawl around my forefinger. "Plus, to complicate matters, I have a boyfriend too. His name is Duck."

"How long have you known him?"

"Since forever."

"And how do you feel about him?"

"Well, he's like family to me. He lives just down the street, and our mothers are best friends. Duck's been there for every birthday, every Christmas, practically every milestone in my life. I suppose it was a natural thing, for us to wind up together."

"How long have you been an item?"

"Since we were fourteen. He saved my life."

Her eyes widened. "He did?"

I nodded. "I had an accident, down by the lake. I almost drowned, but he saved me. After that, I suppose I felt like . . ." I paused.

"Like you were in some way indebted to him?"

My mind shot back to that night I snuck into Duck's bedroom. Up until then, there was a firm line drawn, at least for me. Until he pulled me from the bottom of that lake, from certain death, I thought of him as a friend and nothing more. Although I never said it out loud, I did wonder from time to time whether we would have been a couple if I had never gone to the lake that day.

"When someone saves your life, I suppose you do feel a sense of obligation." I frowned. "Not that I don't love Duck; I just feel like we don't have anything in common."

She nodded. "And do you know how he feels about you?"

"Duck has this fixed idea in his mind about the two of us. He's studying law next year like he always planned, and once he gets his degree, he wants to settle down."

"What do you think about his plan?"

"I think it's something I always went along with because it was so far off in the future that it didn't feel real to me. Now that it's getting closer, I feel panicky about it. I don't want that life. Maybe I did once, but since I met Rad, it feels like there's a whole other dimension." I paused and chewed on the tip of my thumb. "It's almost like there was only an up and down before him, but now I have discovered you can also go sideways too. Does that make any sense?"

Ida nodded. "Actually, it makes perfect sense." She reached across her desk and grabbed a notepad and pen. "It's clear you're going through a tough time," she continued. "Are you in your final year at school?"

"Yeah."

"So you have your upcoming exams to deal with too." She gave me a sympathetic look. "No wonder you're finding it difficult to cope."

"I am. Everything seems to be happening all at once."

"You poor thing," said Ida as she scribbled something on her notepad. "Were you close to Ana?"

"No, but my best friend, Candela, was really close to her."

"And how is she doing?"

"I'm not sure," I frowned. "She seems to be okay, which is weird. I thought she would be a lot worse."

"Everyone grieves in their own way."

"I suppose."

"And your problems began only recently?" Ida asked. "After Ana's death? How did you feel, when you heard the news?"

"Shocked at first. Numb, if anything." I felt a chill go down my spine, and I pulled the blue shawl tighter around my body. "But later that night—well, it was weird. I had this sensation I've never experienced before. It was like . . . my mind was being pulled from my body. That's the only way I can explain it. I thought I was going crazy. I've been looking up the symptoms online, and I think it was a panic attack."

Ida nodded. "I would say that's what it was. Have you had another one since?"

"Yes, and I feel like I'm always on the verge of one. Do you think it will keep happening?"

"It's likely." The look she gave me was almost apologetic, and my heart sank.

"The worst thing is the constant anxiety."

"I know, darling," she said. "The worrying is a vicious cycle. Most people tend to think themselves into full-blown panic attacks. But I have something that might help you."

She reached into her drawer and pulled out a small glass jar containing a cluster of rubber bands. She unscrewed the cap, fished one out, and came around to where I was sitting, handing the piece of brown elastic to me. I gave her a bemused look as I took it from her outstretched hand.

"Slip that onto your wrist," she said.

I did what she asked.

"Good girl." Without warning, she pinched the elastic with her thumb and forefinger, pulled it right back, and then let it go.

"Ouch!" I cried, as the sharp sting of rubber bit into my skin. I pulled my hand away from her. "What the hell?"

"Sorry, honey. You see, when you find yourself getting into a cycle of worry, that sharp *ping* snaps you out of your own head. It's a way to ground you and bring you back to reality."

"Oh," I said softly. I began to see the logic behind the idea and was filled with a spark of hope. *Maybe this will work.*

"When you start to feel anxious, pull the rubber band back and snap it against your skin. That should ease the anxiety."

"Okay, I'll give it a go."

"Good." She glanced at the clock on the wall. "Looks like time is up, sweetie."

"Already?" I said, surprised.

She nodded as I stood up. "Is there anything else you want to ask me?"

I shook my head. "I can't think of anything."

"Remember, Audrey," said Ida, her eyes looking straight into mine, "you can say whatever you want here. Nothing leaves this room, okay?"

I wanted to tell her about the lie right then and there, but I just couldn't bring myself to do it.

"Okay," I said, looking down at my feet.

"I'll see you again next week, honey. Same time? Gloria will send a text the day before to remind you."

Five

I WASN'T IN a celebratory mood when my birthday came round the following week. It fell on a school day, and my friends organized a short message that was broadcasted over the loud-speaker at school. That night, my parents presented me with a simple chocolate mud cake, and when I blew out the candles, I thought of Ana.

Later, Lucy and Candela came by and we drove out to Blues Point Park, a local hangout, with a bottle of Sailor Jerry vodka and a six-pack of Red Bull. "Swig and sip session," Candela declared.

Lucy was the designated driver as usual. She was the respon-sible one among the three of us, and she also owned a car. It was a bottle-green Mini nicknamed Octopus One. Lucy had a habit of naming inanimate objects. After we left Octopus One parked on a quiet side street, we walked through a dense area of shrubbery and found our regular spot, under a large elm tree. Lucy spread out her old fraying tartan rug, and we sat down, breathing in the cool night air. Candela uncapped the vodka and took a long swig. She passed it to Lucy, who shook her head. "I hate vodka," she said. "Besides, how do you think you're getting home tonight?" She took out a Red Bull and flicked back the tab as Candela passed the vodka to me. I took a couple of gulps and waited for the liquid to warm me. The city lights of Sydney sparkled in the distance. We sat in silence for a time, lost in our own thoughts. Pretty soon the vodka was working its magic, and I began to feel buoyant and light, like nothing was really as bad as I thought.

I began telling Lucy and Candela about my meeting with Ida. "I heard she's the best," said Lucy, yawning and stretching herself out on the rug with my lap as her pillow.

"She gave me this rubber band." I held my left wrist up, pulling the sleeve of my sweater back. "I'm supposed to snap it when I get anxious."

"Seriously? No meds?" asked Candela. She gave me a disappointed look.

"Nope. Just this shitty rubber band." For some reason, we all found this wildly funny and broke into hysterics. Then we took turns trying on the rubber band and flicking it against each other's skin.

"Ow! That *really* hurts!" cried Lucy.

"Only because you're sober," I teased.

Still wincing, Lucy handed the rubber band to me, and I slipped it back onto my wrist.

"I'm still not talking to my mother," Candela said suddenly. We knew at once what she was referring to, and the mood turned sober. "I can't believe she couldn't keep her goddamn mouth shut about Ana."

"Yeah," I said quietly, and suddenly everything was bad again.

"Well, I've had enough. That was the last straw. I'm moving out next week."

"You are?" Lucy sat up.

"Yeah. Honestly, I'm so over her shit. No wonder my dad walked out on her." She reached into the side pocket of her backpack and pulled out a fresh pack of Marlboro Lights and a tin of Jelly Bellys. "I'm going to rent a place in Alexandria."

"Alexandria," said Lucy. "Isn't it a bit dicey down there?"

"It's fine," said Candela with a shrug. "I met my flatmates yesterday. They seem nice." She passed the Jelly Bellys to me. I shook out a handful and passed the tin on to Lucy.

"What are your roommates like?" I asked.

"Well," said Candela, "there are two of them." She pulled out a cigarette and lit it. "There's Ramona, who is *so* punk. She works in a record shop and has a stack of piercings and tattoos." Candela took a quick drag before shoving the pack of cigarettes back into her bag. Turning her head, she blew the smoke away from us. "And the other one is Ally. She's kind of bookish and is studying business at Sydney U." Candela must have caught the look I exchanged with Lucy because she quickly said, "As far as I can tell, the two do *not* get along. I peeked inside their fridge and half the stuff in there is labeled 'Ally.' How anal can you be?"

"Anal Ally," I said, and we all burst into laughter.

"Are you going to have a housewarming party?" asked Lucy.

"Yes and you're both coming to celebrate my emancipation."

"Sure," I said, "count us in."

Lucy's ringtone—which was set to the shower scene from *Psycho*—rang loudly from her purse.

"Jesus Christ, Lucy!" Candela jumped. "You've got to change your stupid ringtone."

Lucy stuck her tongue out at Candela and fished the phone from her purse. "Babe?" She said, holding it up to her ear. There was a pause. "You're breaking up; I can't hear you . . . Yeah, we're at Blues Point. What? You're almost here? Oh good. Okay. He is? Yeah." She laughed. "Okay, see you soon."

"Freddy's on his way here," Lucy said, tucking the phone back into her purse. "Also, Rad is coming too."

"Rad?" I said, surprised.

"That's okay, isn't it?"

"I suppose," I said, picking at a piece of cotton thread that had come loose from the picnic rug.

"Is Duck coming tonight?" Candela asked.

"No, his friend is sick, so Duck had to cover for him. But he's taking me out somewhere tomorrow to make up for it." Duck worked as a delivery driver at Kappys, the local pizzeria.

"That shitty flu is still going around," said Candela. "I should drag my lazy ass to the doctor and get my shots."

"Does Duck know you went to the cemetery with Rad the other night?" asked Lucy.

"You went to the cemetery with Rad?" Candela asked. "When did this happen?"

"A few nights ago." Lucy was the only person I had told about that night, although I left out the part where Rad and I found Candela's picture in Ana's locket.

"Why didn't you tell me you met up with him again?" said Candela. She looked hurt.

"I don't know." I wasn't sure why I didn't tell Candela about that night. I told her everything. Even more than Lucy. When I was a little girl, my dad and I had a code. The rule was if I said the words "yellow submarine," he wasn't allowed to get mad at me, no matter what I said next. It was like a safe zone, where I was free to confess anything without consequence. With Candela, that code was something unspoken between us. I could tell her any-thing, and I knew she would never judge me. But I couldn't tell her about that night because her photo had been in Ana's locket, which meant there was something she was keeping from me.

"So what happened?" Candela asked.

"They went to visit Ana in the dead of night to return her necklace," said Lucy.

"The gold one with the heart-shaped locket?" said Candela. She had an odd look on her face.

I nodded. "Rad said she was really attached to it."

"She was," said Candela quietly. "I'm glad she got it back."

"I still can't believe you went into the cemetery at night," Lucy shuddered.

"It was really creepy. Your eyes keep playing tricks on you."

"I can imagine," said Lucy.

My eyes were riveted to Candela's face. She looked like she was lost in her own world. I knew my friend better than anyone. I could tell she knew her picture was in Ana's locket. Lucy followed my gaze.

"Are you okay, sweetie?" she asked Candela.

Candela's head snapped up. "Of course I am. Why wouldn't I be?"

"Just asking, jeez," said Lucy, taken aback.

Candela quickly gathered herself. "Sorry, Lucy," she said with a small shake of her head. She leaned in and gave her an apologetic peck on the cheek. Then she turned her attention to me. "So what else did you guys get up to?"

"We went to the lighthouse at Widow's Cove and just talked for the rest of the night."

"What did you talk about?" Candela probed.

I shrugged. "Don't know—stuff."

I couldn't tell either Lucy or Candela that our conversation had centered around the locket. Rad said he suspected Ana had been involved with someone else before her death. Candela and Ana were always good friends, but they had grown especially close in the last year. Had their friendship blossomed into something more?

"So I'm guessing Duck doesn't know anything about that night?" said Lucy.

I shook my head. "No, and it stays between the three of us. Okay?"

They nodded in agreement.

"Before we forget!" said Candela reaching into her backpack again. "We got you something."

"You did?"

"Yes!" Lucy's face was suddenly animated. "I almost forgot."

After rummaging round in her bag, Candela pulled out a package wrapped in red cellophane and finished with a black ribbon bow.

"Thanks, guys!" I said, taking the present from her outstretched hands.

"It's something Lucy and I came across at that store in Crows Nest—you know, the one that sells vintage stuff. As soon as we spotted it, we thought of you. It has your name on it—literally."

I tore open the package to find a stunning cream-colored jacket made of the softest suede. It was lined in blood-red satin with a tag stitched into the neckline, bearing my name.

"See? It's an Audrey jacket," said Lucy. "Must be some old, obscure label."

"The label pretty much sealed the deal," said Candela. "I mean, how perfect is that?"

"It's gorgeous!" I pulled off my sweater and put the jacket on.

"It fits like a glove," said Lucy happily. "It was made for you."

"I love it! I'm going to wear it all the time!"

In the distance, we heard voices, and then two figures emerged from behind the shrubbery.

"Freddy!" Lucy got up and raced over to him. She threw her arms around him, and he picked her up, swinging her through the air.

The trio walked toward us as Candela and I stood up.

"Happy birthday, Audrey," said Freddy, putting his arm around my shoulders. "Rad decided to tag along; I hope you don't mind."

I shook my head. "Not at all."

Rad smiled at me. "Happy birthday, Audrey."

"Thanks."

We proceeded to arrange ourselves awkwardly on the picnic rug like a game of Twister. I wound up sitting between Rad and Lucy.

"Sheesh, I can't believe it's already your birthday. That means our exams are just around the corner," said Lucy.

"Don't remind me," I groaned. The thought of all the years of my education culminating in one crucial point was nothing short of terrifying.

"Hey, Rad, aren't you studying journalism at Charles Sturt?"

He nodded. "Yeah, but I've decided to take the rest of this year off. I don't go back until next February."

Lucy turned to me. "Isn't that the course you were looking at, Audrey? Wouldn't it be funny if you both wound up at the same campus?"

"It's in my top three, but it depends on how I score on my exams," I said. "Plus, I'm still thinking about whether or not to take a gap year. We've always talked about the three of us traveling through Europe. Remember the pact we made about sunbathing topless in Ibiza?"

"Well, I'm definitely tagging along for that," said Freddy as Lucy gave him a sharp jab in the ribs.

"That was before we had any concept of money," said Candela with a sigh. "I sure don't have the funds to travel anytime soon."

"I probably would have taken a gap year if I could do things over," said Rad. "I mean, I like the course I'm doing so far, but I don't know if I want to be a journalist."

"That's the crazy thing. How can they just expect us to know what we want to do with the rest of our lives when we're fresh out of school? I mean, it's not like flicking a switch," I said.

"Well, I'm sure enjoying my gap year so far," said Freddy, a Cheshire cat grin on his face. "Other than the fact my parents are going a bit nuts and I still have no idea what I'm going to do next year."

"How about clown college?" Lucy suggested.

Candela snorted.

Freddy grinned at Lucy. "Only if you want to be my assistant, babe."

"You're thinking about magicians; clowns don't have assistants."

"That's not true. What about Sideshow Bob?"

"Hey! I'm no sidekick!" Lucy protested. "I want us to be a power couple like Bill and Melinda. You know, that 'us against the world' mentality."

Lucy and Freddy continued their back and forth exchange for the next few minutes as we looked on with a mixture of amusement and envy. When they got started like this, it was as though there was no one else in the world.

"Hey, it looks like someone's coming over," Candela said suddenly. We turned our heads in unison to see a light shining through the shrubbery. A few moments later, a figure appeared, holding a pizza bag in one hand and a flashlight in the other.

"It's Duck," I said, getting up and walking over to meet him. "Hey, I thought you had to work tonight."

He grinned. "I managed to sneak away for a bit. Couldn't miss seeing my girl on her special night." He switched off his flashlight and latched it to his belt before taking my hand in his. We began strolling back to the group when he stopped abruptly. "Who's that guy sitting near Lucy?"

"That's Rad," I said, biting down on my lip. This wasn't going to go down well.

"Rad? What the fuck is he doing here?"

"I didn't know he was going to be here," I said truthfully. "Freddy brought him."

He gave me a dubious look. "Well, it's your party. You can invite anyone you want."

"I didn't invite him. He came with Freddy!"

"Sure, Audrey," he said, looking unconvinced.

"Look, everyone's staring at us, Duck. It's my birthday—can't we just drop it?"

"Fine," he said, resignation in his voice.

Freddy stood up to greet Duck when we reached the group. They locked their palms together the way boys do, playfully combative.

Freddy asked, "Have you met my friend Rad?"

Rad stood up and stuck out his hand. "Hey, man," he said.

"Hey," said Duck, shaking Rad's hand with reluctance.

"Did you bring pizza?" asked Lucy. "I'm starving!" She was perpetually hungry.

"It's Audrey's birthday cake, actually," said Duck, smiling shyly. With a practiced motion, he withdrew the pizza box from the red bag and passed it to me. I opened it to find a pepperoni pizza crudely fashioned into the shape of a heart. "Extra cheese, just how you like it."

"I love it!" I exclaimed.

"Aw, that's cute," said Lucy, peering over my shoulder.

Duck fished around in his pockets and came up with a handful of candles. I carefully laid the opened pizza box on the picnic rug as he stuck the candles arbitrarily into the fleshy dough.

"Anyone got a light?" asked Duck. Candela passed one to him, and he lit up my makeshift birthday cake.

"Happy birthday to you," started Lucy, and everyone else chimed in, singing off-key with their own different renditions about monkeys and zoos.

"Hip, hip, hooray!" they chorused as I blew out the candles.

"Did you make a wish?" asked Lucy.

Without meaning to, my eyes shot involuntarily to Rad—it was like a knee-jerk reaction. I looked away quickly, hoping no one had noticed.

"Yeah," I said to Lucy, "but the wish only comes true if you keep it a secret."

"Okay, everyone, dig in!" said Duck.

We all took turns grabbing a slice of pizza.

"Mmmm," Lucy moaned as she took her first bite. "You make the best pizzas, Duck."

"Thanks, Lucy."

We ate the rest largely in silence.

"I have an idea. Let's play truth or dare," said Candela.

"Yes!" said Lucy.

I groaned. "Really, Candela?"

Duck glanced at his watch. "Good thing I have to get back to work."

"Already?" I said.

"Uh-huh. Everyone's sick with the flu, so we're really understaffed tonight."

"Oh. I'll walk you to the car."

"No, you stay here. I'll see you tomorrow night. Okay?"

"Okay."

"See you," he said and gave a mock salute to the group as

we all called out goodbyes. He picked up the red bag, tucked it under his arm, and strolled away into the night.

Candela turned to Freddy, her eyes glinting with mischief. "Truth or dare?"

"Dare."

"Okay, run up to Duck and give him a goodbye kiss. Quick, before he disappears."

We laughed as Freddy sprung to his feet.

"On the lips!" Lucy called out as Freddy raced over to Duck.

We watched as Freddy ambushed Duck in the distance and pounced on him.

"What the—" we heard Duck cry, as Freddy planted a firm kiss on his lips, while we fell over ourselves laughing. Duck turned and shook his head at us, as Freddy gave him another peck on the cheek before walking back looking victorious.

"Well done, babe!" said Lucy.

"He's a great kisser, Audrey. You're a lucky girl."

I laughed. "Did you get any tongue action?"

"A little," he joked.

Freddy sat back down crossed-legged on the rug and turned to face Candela. "Your turn, missy. Truth or dare?"

"Uh, truth."

"Who was the first person you had sex with?"

"Novak Blackwood."

"Seriously? I thought it was Drew," I said.

"That didn't count as sex."

"Ah, what exactly constitutes sex for you, Candela?" asked Lucy.

She grinned. "You know, the definition they give you at the White House."

"Okay, let's rephrase that, then: who was the first person you fooled around with?" asked Freddy.

Candela thought for a few minutes. "Lisa Sadler."

Freddy's mouth fell open.

"Seriously?" asked Lucy.

Candela nodded. "Uh-huh. Fourteen, sleepover, found her dad's stash of weed. I think we made it to third base."

"Nice," said Freddy with approval.

"It was a fun night," said Candela with a shrug. She took a gulp of vodka and wiped her mouth with the back of her hand. "Okay, Audrey, your turn. Truth or dare?"

"Truth."

"What did you wish for earlier, when you were blowing out your birthday candles?"

"World peace," I said, batting my eyelashes at her.

"That's my girl," said Lucy.

"She *did not* wish for world peace," said Candela.

"Okay—Rad's turn," I said quickly, eager to move on from the subject. "Truth or dare?"

"Truth."

"Who was your first celebrity crush?"

"Pamela Anderson," he shrugged and grinned.

I rolled my eyes. "Typical."

"I had a poster of her above my bed."

"In her *Baywatch* gear?"

"No, it was a PETA ad, I think."

Freddy cupped his hands around his mouth like a megaphone. "Nerd!"

Rad turned to Lucy. "Truth or dare?"

"Dare."

"Okay, you have to call the first person on your contact list and tell them you love them."

"Sure, that's easy enough," she said, reaching into her purse for her phone.

"But," continued Rad, "it can't be a family member or friend."

Lucy froze. "Oh shit. No. No way!"

"Yes way!" Candela said, her face lit up with glee.

"Yeah, Lucy, rules are rules," I agreed.

She shook her head. "Nah-uh."

Freddy began to make clucking noises at her, moving his elbows in and out in a flapping motion. She glared at him.

"Lucy, Lucy," Freddy began to chant, and we all joined in. "Lucy, Lucy, Lucy."

With a look of dread on her face, Lucy scrolled through her contact list. "Fuck!"

"Who is it?" I asked.

"Dr. Mahajan, our family GP." She looked at Rad and shook her head. "Jeez, no way. I can't do it."

"You can't back out now, Lucy," I said.

"Come on, babe," said Freddy. "I had to make out with Duck."

"I am happy to make out with one of you instead."

"Sorry, you're not going to get off that easy," Candela said.

"Oh shit." She held her hand up to her forehead. "Shit, shit, shit." She took a deep breath and dialed his number while we all cheered her on.

"Shhhhh," she waved her hand at us.

"Put it on speaker," I whispered.

We all held our breaths as the dial tone echoed through the air.

There was an answer on the fifth ring.

"Hello?"

"Hello, Dr. Mahajan, it's Lucy—Lucy Locket. Um, Brenda's kid."

"Oh, hello, Lucy. Everything okay?"

"Uh, yeah, there's something I have to tell you."

"Go on."

"Um—I love you," Lucy blurted.

"I beg your pardon?"

"I love you, Dr. Mahajan."

A short pause.

"Are you feeling okay, Lucy?"

"Yes, I'm fine."

Her lips quivered at the corners as she tried to contain her laughter.

"Well, thank you, Lucy. I am very flattered, but I have been happily married for the last thirty years."

"Oh," said Lucy. "Well, if it doesn't work out with Mrs. Mahajan . . ."

"I'll be sure to keep you in mind."

"Okay, thanks, Dr. Mahajan."

"Good night, Lucy."

"Oh my God!" she cried when she hung up the phone. She clapped her hand over her mouth. "I can't believe I just did that!"

We all burst into laughter.

Freddy gave her a congratulatory pat on the back. "Well done, kiddo."

"Ha," said Candela. "I love how cool he was about it. Like, 'Hello, I love you, Dr. Mahajan.' 'Okay, Lucy, thanks but no.'"

We all broke into laughter again.

"I was a victim of the same dare once," said Rad.

"Whom did you have to call?" I asked.

"Cameron, my mechanic."

"How did he take it?"

"He was pretty cool about it. And he gave me a discount the next time I brought my car in."

"You stud," said Freddy.

"Oh God," said Lucy, burying her face in her hands. "That reminds me—I have to go in for my flu shot next week. No way I'm doing that now."

"Hey, it looks like we're out of booze," said Candela, draining the last of the vodka.

"Lucky for you we picked up a six-pack of Coronas on our way here," said Freddy.

"It's chilling in the trunk of my car," said Rad. "I'll go and grab it."

"I'll come with you," I said, getting up.

We began the short walk to his car. Tonight the moon was barely visible, and I tripped on a loose rock as Rad's arm shot out to steady me. Without a word, I laced my arm through his and we continued walking.

"Hey, Audrey," he said, when we were out of earshot. "There's something I need to talk to you about."

"Yeah?"

"These past few weeks . . . well, you've been really great . . ."

There was something in his tone that made my stomach drop. Even though I knew that Rad and I couldn't keep going down this path forever, I didn't want it to end just yet.

"Okay," I said and waited for him to continue.

"It's hard to believe it's only been a few weeks since I've met you. I mean, I can talk to you about stuff that I've never been able to tell anyone else."

"Me too," I said.

"But we're friends—we know that. That's where it starts and ends with us. It's just—" he frowned. "Everybody is turning it into something else, something it's not. Your boyfriend looked at me with daggers all night, and to be honest, I don't blame him. I wouldn't want some guy hanging around my girlfriend, either. And you know, with Ana—"

"Rad, you don't have to explain. I know what people are saying about us, and I know what we have to do."

He nodded. "It sucks, though, doesn't it? I really like talking to you."

I felt tears prick the back of my eyes. "So do I."

Soon, we were at his car, and he reached into his pocket for the keys.

"Hey," I said, turning to face him. "Do you think there's an alternate universe where we didn't have to worry about all this stuff? Where we could keep hanging out and no one would care?"

"Yeah," said Rad with a smile. "We're just characters in a book, remember? There are millions of books out there. We could be living all sorts of different lives."

"Which book would you put us in?"

He thought about it for a moment. "*The Princess Bride*."

I laughed.

He opened the trunk and rummaged around in the dark. He stopped when he heard the rustle of paper. "Oh, I almost forgot! I got you a present."

"You did?"

"Yeah," he said, handing me a brown paper bag. "I saw it in a shop window and thought of you."

I put my hand in the bag and drew out a hard round object.

"It's a snow globe!" I peered at the miniature scenery of a tiny town set against the backdrop of snowcapped mountains. "Oh, it's so pretty." I tipped it upside down then back up again. We watched as the bits of tiny white confetti swirled around the globe.

"I remember what you said that day we met, about snow-capped mountains."

"Oh." I was suddenly overcome with emotion. It felt like the person standing in front of me knew me better than anyone else. On impulse, I took a step toward him, and we put our arms around each other. It felt like the most natural thing in the world.

"Thank you," I said, putting my head on his shoulder. He was wearing a blue-and-white checked shirt that felt both soft and rough against my cheek. My face was inches away from his neck, and I caught the scent of soap and something else that was warm and comforting, like freshly laundered sheets.

"You're welcome. I'm glad you like it."

"I do."

"I hope you'll find your way there someday, to that little mountain town, and write your book."

"I hope you'll write yours too."

I pulled away from him reluctantly. "We should get back or they'll send a search party."

"Okay."

"So this is it then, I guess."

"It feels kind of like a breakup, doesn't it?"

"Yeah, in a weird way it does." I couldn't imagine how I would stop myself from calling him, and I sensed he felt the same way. It was a new thing for me, feeling this attached to another person, especially since we'd known each other for such a short time.

"Do you think we'll stick to the plan?" I asked.

"The one where we stop talking?"

"Uh-huh."

He seemed to think it over. "Have you got your phone on you?"

I reached into the pocket of my new Audrey jacket and pulled it out. At the same time, he fished his phone out from the back pocket of his jeans.

"Let's delete each other from our phones."

"Now?" I felt a wave of sadness wash over me.

"Yes, on the count of three." He gave me a sheepish grin. "Otherwise we'd never stick to it. I know I won't."

"Okay."

"Ready?"

I nodded.

He began to count. "One . . . two . . . three."

I pressed the delete button on his contact page and looked to see that he had done the same.

"You know, I'm really glad I met you, Audrey," he said, putting his phone away.

Tears began to well up in my eyes. I looked away, hoping he wouldn't notice.

"I just wish I had met you sooner," he continued.

"I know."

"Maybe one day we'll end up at the same campus, like what Lucy said. Things might be different then."

His words gave me a sense of optimism. It sounded like a dream, studying at the same campus as Rad, seeing him every day. And it wasn't unrealistic. If I did well in my exams, I could be there next year.

"I like the thought of that," I said.

Six

I brought a bottle of Pinot and a small yellow cactus plant to Candela's housewarming party. I had stuck googly eyes on the cactus and made him a tiny paper top hat.

"He's sensational!" Candela declared holding him out for everyone to see. "I'm going to name him Reginald." She set Reginald down on a nearby coffee table and introduced me to the guests. There were a handful of people I knew, and I guessed the rest were friends of the punk flatmate on the account of all the piercings and tattoos. "Ramona!" Candela called out to a girl who was coming down the hallway. She grabbed my arm. "Come and meet my friend Audrey."

Ramona wasn't her real name. It was Sheila. She had always hated the name, so on her eighteenth birthday she walked straight into the registry and changed it to Ramona. "Look at me," she said, her large, expressive eyes boring into me. "Do I fucking look like a Sheila?"

"Not at all." I meant it—she looked every inch a Ramona.

"What was your name again?"

"Audrey."

"Audrey—?" She tilted her head to one side and studied me carefully.

"Field."

"Oh, nice," she said approvingly. "Audrey Field sounds like a writer's name. Like Charles Bukowski or Virginia Woolf. It's almost like they were preordained. Do you write?"

"Not really."

"Yes, she does!" Candela countered. "She rarely shows her work to anyone, though."

"Well, you'll be a writer; mark my words. You have the name for it," she said with an assertive nod. "Although I knew a guy named Brady Leclair. Sounds hot, right?" she asked, looking at us for confirmation. Candela and I both smiled agreeably. "Well, sorry to disappoint ladies, but—" she stuck her fingers in her mouth and made a gagging noise. "Absolute troll and personality to match. Great name, though. I'd fuck that name."

"RAMONA'S A RIOT," Candela said, "but Ally is a real bore." We were sitting outside, on the patio steps, while Candela had a smoke. "I don't think I've seen her at all tonight."

I tipped my head up toward the inky black sky. It was a beautiful, clear night, and I could see the cluster of stars that spelled out Sagittarius, my mind projecting the outline of a centaur, arrow poised and ready to launch. I thought about Rad and wondered whether he was thinking of me.

"No one ever sees her," Candela said. "She's always in her room, with her head in a book. It's a Saturday night, for Chrissake." She shook her head. "Anyway, looks like Lucy is still a sick puppy."

"I spoke to her earlier. She sounded awful. I can't believe that flu is still going around. Duck couldn't get the night off because there are too many people off sick."

"Oh God, I hope I haven't caught it. I missed my flu shot this winter," Candela moaned. "I literally cannot afford to get sick anymore." She stuffed her cigarette butt into an empty can of Asahi and fished around in her jacket pocket for another one. "I went for a job interview the other day. Beauty assistant."

"Beauty assistant?" I looked at her amused. "You?"

"Yeah," she said with a shrug. "The pay wasn't too bad." She held the cigarette between her lips and lit it before taking a drag. Tilting her head up, she blew out the smoke, a little at a time. "The lady who interviewed me was so fucking weird, though. I mean, she made me peel a hard-boiled egg."

"What?" I said.

"Yeah, for real. She went off in the back room and returned with this sad-looking egg and told me to peel it."

"And did you?" I asked.

"Yeah," she laughed, "but I butchered it. The whole thing was a mess. Then she pressed her hand to her forehead like this—seriously, Audrey," she continued when she saw my incredulous look. "She basically said in this whiny bitch voice, 'Our clients have *very* delicate skin, and what you just did to that egg'—then she closed her eyes and shook her head like she was so disappointed."

"She had such high hopes for you, Candela," I said, laughing.

The door opened suddenly, and Ramona burst out from behind it. "What are you cocksuckers doing out here?" she shrieked. She was off-balance and clearly wasted. "Dex is getting ready to paint up my tits; you're missing out on all the fun." She pouted.

"He's a body painter," Candela explained, seeing the look of confusion cross my face.

"A bloody good one too," Ramona drawled. "But first I'm going to give him a lap dance." She began swaying her hips suggestively, looking dangerously unstable. "Not that it's gonna do anything for him. He's gay as fuck." She hooted with laughter just as someone called out to her from inside the house. "I'm coming," she called. "Hold off on the orgy 'til I get inside." She shot us a lascivious wink, then blew a kiss in our direction. "Don't be too long, bitches." With that, she turned, slamming the door shut. I looked at Candela and raised an eyebrow.

"Mum can't stand her," she said. "Thinks she's a bad influence."

"I wonder why she would think that," I said under my breath.

Candela grinned. "Don't be a smart-ass, Audrey. Ramona can be a little wild, but she's really nice once you get to know her."

"How is your mum coping with you moving out?" I asked.

"She's pretty pissed about the whole thing," said Candela. "Especially with exams coming up. Anyway," she stretched her legs out and sighed, "I'm thinking of quitting school."

"You're what?" I said, alarmed.

"I've given it a lot of thought."

"But Candela, school's over in a few months. You might as well stick it out."

"Yeah," she said, with another shrug. "But it's getting to be a pain, you know? I have to get up at seven every morning now, to make the bus. And I've taken on all those extra shifts at Lambell too, now that I'm paying rent." Lambell was an upmarket steakhouse where Candela waitressed.

"Why don't you just move back home for a while? You've made your point."

"No way," said Candela. "I'd rather die than give my mother the satisfaction of seeing me come back."

"Seriously, your mum isn't that bad. I have to live with mine, and she's a million times worse."

Candela knew what my mother was like, so she didn't have a good enough comeback.

"Why are you doing this, Candela? I thought you wanted to go to college and do an arts degree or something."

She was quiet for a few moments, and then her face began to crumple.

"Candela," I said, putting my arm around her. "What's wrong?"

"I just can't do it anymore," she said, tears rolling down her cheeks.

"Do what?" I said, feeling my stomach clench. I've known Candela my entire life, and I had seen her cry only a handful of times.

"I can't walk through those school halls or run the track or sneak a cigarette behind the bike sheds without seeing Ana's face. I can't keep pretending that everything is normal, not while I'm still there." She was sobbing now, and I tried my best to comfort her, the way she always did for me. "I'm trying to be strong about it, Audrey—I really am," she gulped. "But I let Ana down. She was like a sister to me. I just—I can't be there anymore." She shook her head, wiping her tears with the back of her hand.

"Candela," I said, as a fresh new wave of guilt washed over me. "I don't want you messing up your future because of what happened to Ana. It's not fair."

She sighed deeply and was quiet for a while. "I don't care about my fucking future."

"Don't say that."

She shrugged. "Anyway, I don't want to talk about it anymore."

"Maybe you should see someone about Ana."

"I don't want to. Besides, I can't afford a shrink, and there's no way I'm asking Mum."

"Do you have to quit right now? Why don't you think it over for a couple of weeks?"

"Stop fretting about me, Audrey. I'll be fine, honestly. I know what I'm doing."

"I don't know if you do," I said, still unconvinced.

"Anyway, let's face it," she said with a smirk. "I'm not as brainy as you and Lucy. I was never going to ace my exams."

"You don't know that."

She gave me her best "don't-bullshit-me-Audrey" look. I opened my mouth to protest but closed it again. I knew my friend. I could talk until I was blue in the face, and it wouldn't make an iota of difference. It was clear that Candela had made up her mind.

"So how is the boy?" asked Ida, an unlit cigarette dangling between her brightly painted nails.

We were in the middle of our third session together. It was a particularly warm day, and the fan was whirring noisily above us. The lazy drone of a plane flying overhead made me feel suddenly sleepy.

"We're not in touch anymore."

"Oh? What happened?"

"It was a mutual thing," I shrugged. "I suppose it was getting kind of messy. We thought it was best we keep our distance for now."

"That's very mature of you both."

"It is?"

She nodded.

I leaned back into my chair and stared up at the ceiling, mesmerized by the hypnotic spin of the blades.

"How do you feel about your decision to end the friendship with Rad?"

I thought about it for a minute.

"Lonely," I said finally. "It's a lot harder than I thought it would be. I mean, it's not like anything romantic happened between us. But I miss talking to him. Every time I come across something I think he'd like, I just wish I could call him up or send him a text. Like the other day, I saw this movie, *Coherence*. It was about parallel universes, and I just know he'd love it. That's the thing; he's the only person I know who would appreciate it the same way I do. And I wish I could watch it with him and talk to him about it. Why is that so important to me? I don't get it. I didn't even think about all this before I knew him."

"It's human nature, I suppose. To have another person validate your own unique view of the world."

"I can't even talk about it, which makes me think about it more."

Ida nodded. "Things tend to grow bigger in your mind if you let them sit there. It's always better to get it off your chest. That's why I'm here."

We were quiet for a few minutes.

"My friend Candela just quit school."

"Really? In her final term?"

"Yeah. It almost feels like she's on this self-destructive path. I think Ana's death has been really difficult on her."

I told Ida about the time Rad and I went to the cemetery and found Candela's picture in Ana's locket.

"I don't know exactly what their relationship was, but it obviously went deeper than I thought. Whenever I try to talk to Candela about it, she clams up. And then just like that, she switches to her old happy-go-lucky self, and I think I'm just imagining it all. It makes me uneasy. I'm worried sick about her, but I feel so helpless."

"I know the feeling, sweetheart. But it's up to Candela to sort her own life out. All you can do is be a friend to her. Keep a line of communication open."

"I know," I said quietly. "It feels almost like she's a different person now. She moved away from home a few weeks ago, and she's hanging out with a weird crowd. I met them at her housewarming, and I didn't feel comfortable around them." I shrugged. "But maybe it's just me."

"It's good to trust your instincts; they're usually right." Ida reached for a lighter and finally sparked up her cigarette. She took a long drag and looked at me. "How about your mother?"

"She's driving me insane. I've stopped seeing Rad, but she's still not happy. I don't know what the hell she wants from me."

"I see," she said and let me continue.

"She's just so—I don't know . . . *miserable.* I can't seem to do anything right. There's always a problem. It's like walking on eggshells. When it's just Dad and me, things are easy. I just want her to not be so crazy all the time."

"Have you spoken to her about how you feel?"

"I've tried, but there's no point. It's like a monologue with her. Lucy talks to her mother all the time. It's a two-way street with them. They're, like, best of friends. I don't know why mine has to be so difficult."

"Relationships are complex things. On the surface it should be simple. But it's like an onion. So many layers there. The mother-daughter relationship seems to be a particularly tough one. But they tend to work themselves out as you get older."

"I don't know," I said, unconvinced. "It seems to get progressively worse every year."

She gave me a sympathetic look. "Is the rubber band still working?"

"Yeah. It's pretty much a requirement for me now. I carry spares with me too."

"That's good to hear, honey. I think you're coping remarkably well, considering what you're up against. It would be a tough time for anyone, even under ordinary circumstances."

"I suppose," I glanced at the clock and was surprised to see my hour was up.

"It goes by quickly, doesn't it?" She stubbed out her cigarette. "Well, you take care, honey."

I picked myself up from the chair. "I will."

"Just take it one step at a time, okay? Don't beat yourself up so much."

I nodded.

"Good girl. I'll see you next week."

Seven

THE BELL SOUNDED, signaling the end of sixth period. I breathed a sigh of relief and began packing up my desk. Duck, who was sitting next to me, stood up and slung his bag over his shoulders.

"Audrey," my English teacher, Mr. Sadowski, called to me across the chatter in the classroom.

I looked up. "Yeah?"

"Can you come here a minute?"

"Sure," I said, shoving the rest of my books into my bag.

"I'll meet you at the front gate?" said Duck.

"Actually, I have to stay back today to do some work on the school mag. But I'll drop by your place afterward."

"Okay, want me to pick you up?"

I shook my head. "No, I'll take the bus."

I swung my school bag onto my shoulder and, doing my best to avoid my jostling classmates, made my way to the front where Mr. Sadowski was waiting.

"What's up, Mr. Sadowski?"

"I've finished reading some of the recent pieces you've written for the school magazine. Great work, really great. You've always been a strong writer, but it's gone up a notch in the past couple of months. Well done."

I smiled, pleased with the compliment.

"But I thought I should just check in with you, make sure everything is okay."

"Of course it is. Why would you think otherwise?"

"You've been a little quiet in class lately, and your writing, well . . ." He gave me a look I couldn't quite interpret. "It's taken something of a dark turn."

"Oh."

"Is there a reason for this?"

I shook my head and smiled. "No, not really."

"No?" He looked unconvinced.

"Why do you ask?"

He sighed. "Since Ana's death, the running theme in your work seems to focus mainly on suicide, and I've been a little worried."

"It's okay. I'm seeing someone about it. Ida has been great. I'm sure you've heard of her."

"I have, and from what I know, you're in good hands."

"So was that all?"

He nodded. "Yes, that was all."

"Okay. Thanks, Mr. Sadowski. See you tomorrow."

I MADE MY way over to the school library to meet up with Anton, who insisted we call him Angie. He was editor of the school magazine and the most popular kid in school, well liked by the teachers, the kids, the ladies at the school cafeteria, and even the grumpy caretaker whom everyone steered clear of.

"Hey, Angie," I said when I walked into our headquarters—a small study room tucked away in the back corner of the library. "Sorry I'm late."

"Hey, Audrey," he said, his eyes pinned to the screen of his laptop.

I dropped my school bag down and pulled out a chair.

"What are you working on today?" I asked.

His fingers paused over the keys, and his eyes flickered up to meet mine.

"I'm working on a tribute to Ana."

I drew in a deep breath. "Yeah?"

Angie rubbed at his chin. His fingernails were painted with bright pink polish and finished with a smattering of rainbow glitter. Today he had rolled up the sleeves of his white polo shirt to show off his perpetual golden tan. He wore a tartan skirt over the school-issued gray tights, which he had neatly tucked into a pair of Doc Martens.

"I thought we could interview some of her friends, share their stories. I know Candela has some wild ones to tell—the two of them were as thick as thieves."

I sat down and pulled my laptop from my bag.

"You know her boyfriend, Rad, don't you?" he continued.

"Yeah," I said, instantly feeling guarded. "But we're not in touch anymore."

"Really?" said Angie, his perfectly shaped eyebrows shooting up in surprise. "Since when?"

"It's been a couple weeks or so," I said with a shrug.

"Oh," Angie shut the lid of his laptop and rested his chin in his hands. "I know it's none of my business, Audrey, but I heard through the grapevine that the two of you had something going on."

"What? From whom?"

"Just a few of my sources—you know."

I rolled my eyes. "Aren't there more interesting things to talk about?"

"It happens to be the trending topic at the moment."

"Well, it must be a slow news week."

"Is it true that Rad looks like River Phoenix?"

I thought about it for a moment. "Kind of, yeah."

"Is he more like Mike Waters in *My Own Private Idaho* or Eddie Birdlace in *Dogfight*? Both are equally hot by the way."

"Mike Waters."

"I am so jealous right now."

"Don't be. There's nothing to be jealous about."

"So nothing happened between you?" Angie's voice dropped to a conspiratorial whisper. "Not even a pash?"

"Of course not," I insisted. "I have a boyfriend—remember?"

Angie sighed. "I love Duck. Everyone loves Duck. He's a great guy, but he's wrong for you, honey."

"No, he's not."

"Yes, he is. You sit with a different clique. You two don't have anything in common. Don't get me wrong: Duck is great husband material, and he's cute as hell. But the two of you—" he drew his hand across his neck in a cutthroat motion "—are doomed. Sorry to be the bearer of bad news."

MY MOTHER WAS at Duck's place when I arrived there late that afternoon, sitting at the kitchen table with Zoe, a glass of wine in her hand.

"You look exhausted, Audrey. Have you been burning the midnight oil?" Zoe asked as I walked through the archway that separated her kitchen from the lounge room.

I nodded, putting my bag down by my mother's chair.

"Poor kid. Duck has been the same." She gave me a sympathetic smile. "The pressure they put on you is ridiculous, isn't it? I still wake up in the middle of the night sometimes thinking I'm back at school and forgot to do my homework."

"Seriously?"

"I'm afraid so."

"Did you hear the latest news, Zoe?" said my mother. "Candela's dropped out of school. You know, Amita's girl?"

"Really? Right in the final term? What a shame."

Mum shook her head. "I always knew that girl was bad news."

"Don't be nasty, Mum," I said. "You don't know the full story."

"I've been hearing all sorts of things through the grapevine about the type of people she's hanging out with now. Poor Amita—after the whole fiasco with Jeff walking out, it's the last thing she needs."

"Well, Lucy and I are going to meet up with her tomorrow," I said.

"You're not going to her house, I hope?"

"No," I lied, "we're going out for a coffee."

Duck surfaced from his room a few moments later.

"Hi," he said to me and turned to Zoe. "What's for dinner?"

"Your dad is picking up some pizza on his way home. Should be here any minute."

My mother glanced at her watch. "I didn't realize how late it is. I'd best get home. Audrey, are you going to stay here for dinner?"

"Yeah, Duck is going to talk me through calculus later on."

"Okay then. I'll see you tonight."

"I BUMPED INTO Lucy and Freddy today while I was in town," said Duck. "They said Rad got you a birthday gift. How come you never mentioned it to me?"

It was shortly after dinner, and we were sitting in his dad's study, our textbooks sprawled between us across the large desk. Duck's dad ran a law firm in the city. His study at home was like an extension of his office, all mahogany and leather with rows and rows of intimidating legal books.

I put my pen down and looked up. "I don't have to tell you every single detail of my life. Anyway, why would they mention that? Were you interrogating them?"

"No, we were just chatting about your birthday night, and Lucy asked if I saw the gift Rad got you because, in her words, it was *so sweet.*"

I cringed inwardly. I didn't want Duck to get the wrong idea. I hadn't even spoken to Rad since that night. Though there were times when I wished I could call him—and I would have too, if I hadn't deleted his number from my phone.

"So, he got you a snow globe."

"Yeah."

"Why is that sweet? What's so damn special about a snow globe?"

"Because I mentioned something about liking snowcapped mountains . . ."

"Oh, great, so now he knows more about you than I do."

"Don't be ridiculous."

"I thought you said you didn't invite him."

"I didn't! I didn't invite anyone—it was a spur-of-the-moment thing."

"Then how did he know to get you a gift?"

"How am I supposed to know?"

"Well, he's your friend. Apparently you seem to know a lot about each other."

"You're acting crazy again, Duck! It's been weeks since I last spoke to him."

"Why *did* you stop speaking to him? Did something happen between you?"

"No, of course not. The truth is we didn't know each other that well, anyway, so it's not a big deal."

"If it's not a big deal, then why don't you keep hanging out with him?"

I didn't have an answer.

"Everyone is talking about how the two of you have something going on. And you seemed pretty friendly with him at your birthday party."

"I was friendly with everyone at my party. That's how you behave toward your friends."

"I saw the way you were looking at each other. I'm not a fucking idiot."

"Stop it, Duck. Seriously. I'm *your* girlfriend, okay? Everyone knows that. I'm not going to talk to Rad anymore, especially if it upsets you this much. It's not worth us fighting over."

"Don't talk as if you're doing me a huge favor, Audrey."

I felt tired all of a sudden. I couldn't seem to do anything right. I stopped seeing Rad, and a large part of that was because of Duck, but it still wasn't enough for him. What did he want from me? Not to talk to another boy for as long as I lived?

"Look, I think I should just go." I grabbed my books and shoved them roughly into my bag. "I get enough shit from my mother." My voice quivered and tears sprung to my eyes. "I don't need it from you too."

"Audrey, come on, don't cry," he said, his tone softening.

"What do you want, Duck? Tell me! Rad and I were just friends, and now we're not even that. What do you want me to say?"

He stood up and came around my side of the table.

"I'm sick of fighting about this," I continued. "I didn't do anything wrong, so stop crucifying me."

He sighed. "You can't blame me for being worried, not when my girlfriend starts hanging around some guy. But I'm sick of fighting too. Let's just drop it."

He took my bag gently from my hands and pulled my books out again, spreading them across the table. I felt a wave of tenderness as I watched him. I knew how much he cared about me, and I was grateful to have him in my life. I just wished I could return his feelings in equal measure. Everything would be a lot simpler that way.

"Besides," he said with a grin, "our exams are next week, and given how terrible your math is, I'm your only hope."

THE NEXT DAY Lucy and I caught a bus out to Alexandria to visit Candela. It was hard to believe I hadn't seen her since the housewarming party—the last month had gone by in a flash.

The first thing I noticed when Candela opened the door was her disheveled appearance. Her hair was matted, and her skin looked like it was covered in a slick, oily film. The circles under her eyes were so dark they looked almost like bruises. She was dressed in an old tie-dyed T-shirt with a large red wine stain and ripped denim shorts. Candela had always been slim, but now she looked emaciated, like she hadn't eaten in days. "It's past four already?" she said peering out at us, as though the sunlight was hurting her eyes. Then she grinned widely. "So good to see you both." She drew me into a weak embrace. "It's been way too long."

"What's with all the trash?" I asked. The porch, which had been spotless on our last visit, was now in complete disarray. Bags of rubbish, pizza boxes piled up by the door. Flies buzzed around the debris, and a sour, rancid smell hung in the warm, still air.

"Oh yeah," said Candela, looking around the porch. "Ally had some kind of mental breakdown, so she's moved back in with her parents, and Ramona and I—well," she gave us a hopeless smile, "we've been pretty shitty at keeping the place in order." She opened the door to let us through, and we followed her into the hallway. When we got to the lounge room, Lucy and I exchanged a look. It was a complete mess. Dirty plates, cigarette butts, and empty beer bottles were strewn all across the coffee table. Used tissues, food wrappers, and half-eaten bits of fruit littered the three-seater sofa. Even the bright blue beanbag next to it was covered with crumbs and a sad-looking Rubik's Cube with half its colored stickers peeled off.

"Sorry about the mess," she said nonchalantly. "I've been too busy to tidy up." She made a half-hearted attempt to clear the table but gave up midway. Instead, she pushed the rubbish from the sofa onto the floor and plonked herself down, inviting us to do the same. "So how are you both?" she asked, as we sat on either side of her. "How's school?"

"It's okay," said Lucy. "A bit of a drag—you know."

"Not the same without you," I told her honestly.

"Yeah," said Lucy. "All the teachers ever talk about now are the exams. They're really laying on the pressure."

"They are," I said. "They keep saying that if we screw this up, that's it. It's all over—" I stopped and looked at Candela. She had a glazed look on her face, and I couldn't tell if she was even listening.

"Do you guys want a drink?" she asked, distracted.

"Sure," I said. Candela got up and made her way to the kitchen.

"Do you think she's okay?" I whispered to Lucy. She turned to look at me, a worried expression on her face. "I don't know," she mouthed, with a shrug.

We heard the fridge door slam shut as Candela made her way back to us, with a couple of Diet Cokes. She passed them over to us, before sitting back down again.

"So what's new with you, Candela?" asked Lucy, as she flicked back the tab.

"Well," said Candela, "I've started seeing this guy."

"You have?" I asked.

"Yeah, his name is Dirk. I think you met him at the housewarming."

"The biker guy with tats all around his neck? Seriously, Candela?"

"Why, what's the problem?"

"Isn't he, like, forty or something?"

"Thirty-five."

"So he's basically twice your age?"

"And your point is?" She shot me a defiant look.

"He kind of gave me the creeps, Candela," I said quietly.

She glared at me. "Well, maybe you're just too sensitive."

"What's that supposed to mean?" I snapped.

"Hey, we should go out for dinner next week," Lucy cut in quickly. It was clear she was trying to change the subject before it escalated into an argument. "Just the three of us. We haven't done that in ages."

"Okay," I said.

"Sure," said Candela, with a noncommittal shrug of her shoulders.

Something in her tone made my anger flare up again. "Don't come out with us if you don't want to, Candela. There isn't a bloody gun to your head."

"Jeez, Audrey, calm the hell down. What's your problem?"

"You've been so distant since you moved out. I don't hear a thing from you. You don't answer my calls or text back."

She stood up, glaring down at me. "It's always about you, isn't it, Audrey? Why don't you just get over yourself for a second and see that people have lives of their own. The world doesn't revolve around you."

"Oh, shut up. I'm the one having to pander to you. I'm sick of being the one doing all the chasing. I'm not asking you to make me a priority—I know you've got a lot going on. But at least meet me halfway."

She opened her mouth to speak but stopped. Her expression told me something I said had sunken in. "Look," she sighed, sitting back down. "I know I've been distant. I'm just messed up about Ana—even if I don't always show it . . . I've been trying to get away from anything that reminds me of her." She clasped my hand in hers and then reached for Lucy's. "The two of you—you're like sisters to me. I love you both; that will never change. But I need to forget for a while—to be away from Three Oaks, from Barrett, and that god-awful bottle-green uniform." Her eyes flickered over my school dress. "I just need everything from that part of my life to disappear for a bit."

Her words brought on a heavy feeling in my chest. Until now, I was unable to grasp the depth of Candela's suffering. I wanted desperately to be there for my friend, but not if my presence was causing her further pain.

"If you need your space, Candela, we'll respect that," said Lucy quietly. "But at least come to graduation. Please? It would be so weird not having you there."

I winced at the desperation in Lucy's tone, but I felt the same. Everything was dull without Candela. Nothing felt as special.

"Of course I'll be there," she said with a tight smile. There was a troubled look in her eyes. "I wouldn't miss it for the world."

Eight

It was the day of our exams, and I could barely stomach anything as I sat down at breakfast.

"Nervous?" asked Dad, sliding a pancake onto his plate with a fork.

"Yeah."

"So what's first on the agenda?"

"English in the morning, and then we have history after lunch."

"Well, at least you're starting out with the two subjects you're good at," said Mum.

"I suppose." I frowned as a fresh wave of anxiety gripped my stomach.

"So there is really nothing to be nervous about, is there?"

I stiffened. There was something in her tone that was irking me. I think Dad must have noticed because he shot her a warning look.

"Edwina," he said, "I'm sure Audrey will knock it out of the park, especially with English. But you know as well as I do that examinations are scary as hell, even at the best of times."

"Thanks, Dad." I gave him an appreciative smile.

"Aren't you going to eat anything?" Mum asked.

A car horn sounded outside.

"Duck's here. I've got to go." I grabbed my school bag and slung it over my shoulder.

"Good luck, Audrey," my dad called after me.

THE ATMOSPHERE WAS unusually subdued as the teachers lined us up and led us into the hall. I walked past the desks and chairs that stood in neat, evenly spaced rows, my heart pounding in my chest. I took my seat and glanced over at Lucy, who was sitting near the front. She smiled and waved at me, then mouthed, "Good luck." To my right, Duck, with a pen in his hand, was staring intently at the clock that hung on the far end of the hall.

Mr. Sadowski stood up and took us through the rules as my history teacher, Mrs. Douglas, placed a sheet of paper facedown on my desk. As I stared at the blank white sheet, I felt a wave of panic. Desperately, I flicked the rubber band around my wrist, but it was akin to throwing buckets of water at a raging inferno. The walls around me began to shimmer and shrink. I was hyperventilating, hunched over my desk. Duck was at my side in a flash, and I felt his hands grip my shoulders. His voice was faint and recessive, like a signal dropping in and out. "Audrey . . . Audrey, what's wrong?"

I stood up blindly, my chair scraping loudly against the parquetry floor. I could sense a hundred pairs of eyes on me, and I couldn't stand to be looked at—not for another second.

Somehow I made it outside and stood with my hands gripping the metal railing, desperately sucking at the air. Someone had their palm pressed against my back and a voice—I think it belonged to Mrs. Douglas—was saying over and over, "It's okay, darling; it's okay; it's okay."

MY MOTHER CAME to collect me from the school office an hour later. She had a quiet talk with the principal in the hallway while I sat in a room with the school nurse, straining to catch bits of their conversation. I'd been in such a panic earlier I didn't realize I was digging my fingernails into my wrists. That was something I resorted to when the rubber band wasn't working, but this time I had actually drawn blood. When Mum came into the room a few minutes later, her eyes went straight to the white bandage that wound its way around my left wrist.

WE DIDN'T SAY much to each other on the short drive home. I was still shaky when she led me up the stairs to my bedroom and tucked me into bed fully clothed. She left the room and came back with a cup of chamomile tea. I took it from her gratefully and sipped the warm liquid, letting it flow through my body, allowing it to bring me back down to earth. That was the funny thing about anxiety; you weren't entirely sure if you were real or if anything around you was, either.

Mum sat on the bed and stroked my head gently. "Audrey," she seemed to be choosing her words carefully, "I think it might be a good idea for you to take some time off."

I blinked at her, confused. "Time off?" I echoed dumbly. "Yes."

"You mean because I'm an embarrassment to you," I said, tears welling up in my eyes. "I'm right at the finish line, Mum. I can't just quit now."

"Audrey," her voice was strained, "I know things between us haven't been that great lately. But you're still my little girl, and I'm sorry—I didn't realize it was this bad."

"What am I supposed to do?" I said, suddenly angry. "You keep telling me all the ways I am going to screw up, so I hope you're happy now."

"Please, Audrey," she said in a small voice, "I'm really trying here."

DAD CAME HOME a few hours later, and I heard him talking quietly to Mum downstairs. Their voices were barely audible as I struggled to make out their words. After a while, I heard footsteps on the stairs and then a knock. "Audrey," my dad called, "can I come in?"

"Sure," I answered weakly.

Dad walked into the room as I sat up in bed. He sat down next to me and smiled. It was such a sad smile that it brought me to the verge of tears again. "For once your mother and I agree on something," he said. I could tell he was trying to keep his tone light.

"You don't think I should finish my exams either?" I asked.

He took a deep breath and let it out slowly. "How do you feel about it, sweetie?"

"I'm scared, Dad. It was so hard today. I could feel every-one staring at me. I feel like I'm a freak show, and everyone is laughing at me and—" I broke down.

"Audrey," he put his arms around me, and I sobbed quietly against his shoulder.

"It's okay, sweetie. You don't have to do anything. You can take your exams again when you're feeling up to it."

"I feel like a failure."

"Hey, you're not a failure. This is just a minor setback; that's all. It's not the end of the world."

"It sure feels that way."

"I know, baby. But I don't want you to worry about it right now."

"I'll never hear the end of it from Mum."

"Your mother only wants what's best for you, Audrey. Even if she has a funny way of showing it sometimes."

"I don't know what to do next," I said. "I just don't." I started to cry again.

"You don't have to do anything. Your mother and I will take care of you. You don't have to worry about a thing. Okay?"

"Okay."

"Everything will be okay, Audrey. Life has a way of working itself out. You'll see."

Nine

"I THOUGHT I was getting better," I said. I was sitting back in Ida's chair as she sat at her desk, by the open window. She took a long drag of her cigarette, before turning her head to blow the smoke outside.

"Anxiety is a tricky thing, honey. It's kind of like the weather, you know? You can have a whole lot of blue skies, then all of a sudden, it goes El fucking Niño on you." She stubbed her cigarette out and picked up her pen, clicking and unclicking it again. She looked up at me. "How are you coping, sweetheart?" Since my panic attack in the school hall last week, it had become a standard question. Not just with her but everyone else as well.

"Fine, I guess." I gave her my standard reply.

"How do you feel about taking time off school?"

I shrugged. "I don't know. Like a screwup."

She flashed me an encouraging smile. "Well, I've got good news for you. You're not a screwup. It's about running your own race, honey. Remember that."

"Okay," I said numbly. My fingers traced the outline of my rubber band. I looked up at Ida. "Do you think I need to be on medication? My friend Candela—her mother has anxiety. She's on Xanax. Apparently, it helps."

Ida let out a breath. "I can't prescribe medication, Audrey, but I can write a note for you to take to your doctor." She frowned. "But I don't think it's the right thing for you at this stage."

"I feel like I need something extra when the rubber band isn't working. You know, when it becomes too much and I start to spin out."

She pulled open her drawer and drew out a notepad. With a click of her pen, she wrote something down, before tearing the paper and handing it to me. "Take this to your doctor; he'll know what to do."

"Thanks," I said, tucking the note into the pocket of my jeans.

"Personally, I think you can manage without the medication. I would try to hold off if I were you. But some people find it's helpful to have that safety net."

I nodded. "I'll keep that in mind."

AFTER I LEFT Ida's office, I walked to the park at the end of the street. I sat at a bench, by the duck pond, and spaced out for a while. Then, taking my phone from my purse, I called Candela. For months I had been carrying this awful secret about Ana, and I could feel it ticking away inside of me like a time bomb. I had to tell someone. I knew Candela would probably never speak to me again, but that was something I would have to live with. My heart began pounding as I held the phone to my ear. It went straight to her voicemail. Getting up, I walked over to the nearest bus stop and caught the first bus to Alexandria.

As I WALKED up the steps leading to Candela's porch, I was hit with the nauseating smell of rubbish. The pile that was there on my last visit was now twice as high. Doing my best to side-step it, I rang the bell. There was no answer, so I rang it again. On my third try, the door opened a crack, and Ramona's face peered out from behind it. Her eyes lit up when she saw it was me. "Audrey!" she exclaimed, throwing the door open and grabbing my hand. "Come in! Candela's inside."

I wasn't prepared for the scene that greeted me when we got to the end of the hallway. At the kitchen table sat Candela, her back against a cane wicker chair and her legs wrapped around Dirk. He was holding a small silver spoon in one hand and a lighter in the other as he leaned over the table, frowning with concentration. They both looked up as we came into the room. Candela stood up suddenly, knocking Dirk so he lurched for-ward, sending a sprinkle of brown sugary powder across the table.

"What the *fuck*, Candela," he said, infuriated.

I opened my mouth to speak but couldn't think of a single thing to say. I turned to leave and heard her calling me from down the hall.

"Audrey, wait."

I was near the front door when I heard Ramona say, "Jesus, what the hell is her problem?"

I grabbed at the doorknob roughly and felt a sharp stab of pain against my palm. When I was outside, I saw a trickle of blood and realized I must have cut my hand on the sharp edge of the lock. Candela followed behind me, grabbing the back of my wrist. I spun around to face her. "I was going to tell you," she said.

"Tell me what? That you're shooting up now? What the hell are you doing?"

"Why are you so angry?" She looked genuinely surprised. "It's my fucking life. I'm just having some fun."

"Fun?" I said incredulously. I grabbed her by the shoulders and shook her. "Candela, wake up! This isn't about you popping pills or putting shit up your nose. Do you know what this kind of *fun* leads to?"

"Audrey, chill out for a second." She stepped away from me.

"No! I'm not going to watch someone I love throw their life away."

"Oh God, you sound like my mum." She looked away from me. "I can stop anytime I want."

"Does your mother know about this?"

"Quit being so judgmental. This is something I would expect from Lucy, not you."

"Does your mother know about this?" I repeated. "Does Eve? Candela, look at me!" She wouldn't meet my gaze. "Well, do they?"

She didn't answer.

"Is this about Ana?" I continued. "Is this how you're *dealing* with it?"

Her expression darkened at the mention of Ana's name. "I wouldn't go there if I were you," she warned.

"You know, there was a picture of you in her locket."

"And?" She put her hands on her hips, daring me to go on.

"What was going on with the two of you?" I demanded.

"Well, you seem to know more than me, Audrey. You're the one who saw Ana with her dad; you're the one who got all cozy with her boyfriend—so why are you asking me?"

I was taken aback by the hostility in her voice. I opened my mouth to respond, but she cut me off.

"Maybe you're the one with the schoolgirl crush."

"Candela, I—"

"I know what you're implying about me and Ana, and do you know what? It's none of your fucking business," she said, her bright green eyes piercing mine. "Do you hear me, Audrey?" Her voice rose in anger. "So get off my back and worry about your own screwed-up life." She turned suddenly on her heel and stormed back into the house, slamming the door shut behind her.

Ten

GRADUATION CAME AND went with little fanfare. Laughter and relief rang through the air. People signed T-shirts with Sharpies and scrawled meaningful quotations in each others' yearbooks. Out on the sports field, my classmates were burning their schoolbooks in large metal bins—a tradition that continued every year in spite of the oppressive heat.

Candela didn't show up—not that I expected her to. We hadn't spoken since our argument, even though I tried calling several times. When I told Lucy what I saw at Candela's house, she suggested we stage an intervention, but I knew it would be pointless. Candela had always done things on her own terms.

I was making my way over to the English block to meet up with Lucy when Angie came and found me.

"Hey, Audrey, I've been looking everywhere for you."

"What's up, Angie?"

"What are your plans for next year?"

"I don't know. I didn't finish my exams, so I suppose I'll have to take them again or something."

"Well, my aunt Sam is the editor for *See! Sydney*, and they're looking for an intern. I was meant to take the position, but my ultra-glam cousin Cecelia who lives in New York is getting married." He mouthed the words "shotgun wedding" as if it was the most scandalous thing in the world, and I laughed. "So," he continued, "Mum and I are going to her wedding, and I think I might stay on in New York for a while and do my own thing. You know, check out the fashion, do some gallery hopping."

"Sounds neat!"

"I know!" he exclaimed, doing a short, impromptu dance. "I can't wait!"

"Take me with you!"

He sighed. "I wish I could, sweetie, but I have a feeling I'm going to need the extra baggage space."

I laughed.

"Anyway, I told Sam about you, and she wants to know if you want to take the intern position at *See! Sydney* in my place."

"Wow, really?"

He nodded. "I told her you were my right-hand man with the school mag."

"Thanks, Angie, I would love that!"

"Cool! I'll pass on your number, so expect a call from her soon."

"Do I have to do an interview or anything? I know internships are really hard to come by."

"Yeah, but just between you and me, you've already got the position."

I hugged him warmly. "Angie, you're the best!"

I FOUND LUCY by the English block accosting Mr. Sadowski with a Sharpie in one hand and her yearbook in the other.

"Write something that will make sense to me in ten years," she instructed. Mr. Sadowski took the Sharpie from Lucy with a sigh and scribbled in her yearbook: *Youth is wasted on the young.*

LATER, WE MET Freddy at the school gate, and the three of us stood waiting for Duck. After a few minutes, I spotted him walking in a throng of students who, I realized with a sense of relief, I would never have to see again.

"Duck!" Lucy called. "We're over here."

He looked up and waved at us. When he reached the gate, he took my hand, threading his fingers through mine.

"What should we do now?" said Lucy as we made our way up the street.

I shrugged. "Don't know."

"Did you drive this morning?" Lucy asked Duck.

"No, we took the bus."

"Okay, good, we can all go in Freddy's car then . . ."

"It's a gorgeous day; why don't we head down to the beach for a swim?" I suggested.

"Yes!" said Lucy. "What a great way to celebrate."

"Sounds just like another typical day for me," said Freddy with a grin.

"Well, your extended holiday is coming to an end soon, buddy," said Lucy.

"Really? Have you finally decided on something, Freddy?" I asked.

"Business." He put his arm around Lucy's shoulder. "We're going to enroll in the same course next year."

"Aw," I said. "That's cute."

"We're going to be tycoons," said Lucy happily.

"I don't doubt it," said Duck.

When we got to the end of the street, Lucy stopped suddenly and licked at the air.

"Mmmm . . ." she said. "Freedom."

"Weirdo," said Freddy.

"Where did you park, anyway, babe?"

"About two streets down, over by the corner store."

Lucy pouted. "But that's miles away!"

"Do you want a piggyback?"

"Uh-huh."

He hoisted her onto his back, and she wrapped her arms around his neck.

"So Candela didn't turn up today," said Duck.

"Nope," said Lucy, a trace of annoyance in her voice. "So much for sticking to her word."

"I didn't think she'd come," I said.

"Honestly, I've washed my hands of her," said Lucy. "I'm sick of working so damn hard for crumbs."

"Don't say that, Lucy," I said quietly. "It's been the three of us forever. She's just going through stuff at the moment."

I knew Candela didn't mean to alienate us. She was just sad about losing Ana, and even though she would never say it out loud, she blamed me for what happened. Maybe she sensed it was my fault, that I was responsible for Ana's death. And the awful thing was she was right. I took a deep breath and pulled my hand free from Duck's, reaching quickly for my rubber band.

"That doesn't give her the right to treat us like shit," said Lucy. "And I don't like the crowd she's hanging out with." She swung her head back to face me. "I don't mean to sound like your mum, Audrey, but I think it's best you keep your distance."

Eleven

AFTER SCHOOL BROKE, each day seemed to blur into the next. I had no structure or purpose, no reason to get up in the morning. I was going to bed late every night, and I spent the hours reading penny dreadfuls, surfing the web, or watching reruns of *Doctor Who*. My mind kept ricocheting between Ana, Rad, and Candela. Like an unofficial tally of the lives I had inadvertently wrecked when I told that lie.

One morning, my phone buzzed loudly, waking me from a restless sleep. I reached for it blindly, knocking it from the nightstand. It fell to the floor with a clatter.

"Shit," I swore, hanging over the edge of my bed and grabbing it at lightning speed.

"Hello?"

"Is this Audrey?" spoke a woman's voice that I didn't recognize.

"Yes."

"Hi, it's Sam, Angie's aunt. I'm the editor at *See! Sydney*."

"Hi," I said, suddenly feeling wide awake. "I've been expecting your call."

"Great! Angie mentioned that you were interested in taking the intern position here. Are you free to come at ten tomorrow morning for an interview?"

"Absolutely! I'll see you then."

I ARRIVED AT a gray nondescript building half an hour before my meeting time. I sat downstairs at a coffee shop and grabbed a copy of the latest paper. I was absorbed in a story about taxi drivers claiming to have picked up ghost passengers when my phone began buzzing. I peered at the screen. It was Lucy.

"Hey, Lucy. What's up?"

"Guess what?"

"What?"

"Guess!" Lucy always got a perverse joy from holding back exciting news and making you work for it.

I sighed. "Lucy, I have, like, fifteen minutes before my meeting starts, so let's not do the guessing game today."

"Fine then, you killjoy. You know my uncle Harry? The one who works in advertising?"

"Mr. Fancy Pants?" I said, with a smile. Lucy's uncle Harry was a flamboyant man who had a ruddy nose and perpetually flushed cheeks. He had no children of his own and had always doted on Lucy. I remember him at their family gatherings when we were kids—often performing magic tricks and taking great delight in our astonished faces.

"Yes, Mr. Fancy Pants. He just got a job offer to work in Paris for a couple of years. Anyway, he asked me to housesit for him while he's away. Which is fantastic because Freddy and I are starting our course at Sydney U next year, and his house is nice and close. He says you can move in too, if you want. As long as we take good care of the place."

I let my mind play catch-up with her words. *Move out.* My brain seemed to single out the phrase from the jumble of sentences.

"Us, move out?" I asked dumbly.

"Yes! If you get the internship with *See! Sydney*, we can room together in his house."

"But what about rent and stuff? I'm not getting paid for my internship."

"We don't have to pay rent. We just have to take care of the place."

"Seriously?" I said.

"Yeah, isn't it great?"

"Oh my God!" I was suddenly jubilant. "I can get away from my mother!"

"Exactly," said Lucy happily.

"Like, I don't have to see her every single day." The thought was almost too wonderful to process.

"And our boyfriends can stay over too! Duck's starting his course next year, so it's perfect. Audrey, we're going to have a blast!"

"We'll have to get part-time jobs, for groceries and stuff," I said happily.

"We can figure all that out. I think we can get some government grants or whatever, and I get access to my trust once I start university. We can do this, Audrey!"

"We totally can!" I answered, feeling exuberant.

"Are you doing anything after your meeting?" she asked.

"No, I'll text you when I'm done."

"Okay, I'll pick you up afterward; we can go and check out the house together."

AN IMMACULATELY DRESSED woman in her midthirties was standing in the elevator when I walked through its heavy doors. I gave her a half-smile.

"Which floor?" she asked.

"Uh, seven," I said, as she reached for the set of buttons to the side.

"You wouldn't happen to be Audrey, would you?"

I turned to look at her. "Sam?"

She nodded, sticking out her hand. "Nice to meet you," she said with a warm smile.

I smiled back as we shook hands. I liked her immediately.

"Angie has told me so much about you," she said.

"He has?"

She nodded. "He gave me the latest copy of your school magazine. Outstanding work."

"Thank you. It was his baby."

There was a *ding* sound and the elevator doors slid open.

"Yours too, apparently," she said, as we stepped out of the lift. "Your articles were great to read. A little dark perhaps—but I do like your style."

She led me down the narrow hallway and through a frosted glass door with the words *See! Sydney* imprinted in bold black lettering.

"Hi, April," Sam said to a twenty-something girl sitting behind a simple white desk.

"Hi, Sam," said April. "Is this your ten o'clock?" She motioned to me.

Sam nodded.

"You must be Audrey, then," she said with a smile. "Welcome to our little office."

Behind her was a small open-plan office with an exposed brick wall at the back and large block windows throughout the length of the airy, bright room. There were steel pipes and wood beams across the ceiling from which terrariums hung on thin metal wires. A handful of desks, most of them empty, were scattered in a random formation with only a couple of journalists milling about, and there was a waiting area with a lounge and coffee bar. Overstuffed beanbags sat in the corners atop gray rustic floorboards. A track by Pink Floyd was playing softly.

"We have a very lax work ethic here," said Sam. "Most of our writers don't get in until after eleven. They can come and go as they please, as long as they hand in their articles on time."

"It's a good system," said April. "Everyone's happy, and the work is better as a result."

I had spent a great deal of time researching this publication. It was established five years ago and had already won a slew of awards.

"Although when we have a deadline, this place can be a madhouse," said Sam.

"Oh yeah," said April. "It can get pretty crazy." She gestured behind her. "But, usually, this is the kind of vibe you'll get here."

I FOLLOWED SAM to her desk, and we sat facing each other. A picture of Angie in a silver frame caught my eye. It looked like a recent one, taken with him standing in a canoe, wearing a large sombrero hat and red heart-shaped sunglasses and brandishing a paddle like a sword. "That picture always makes me laugh," she said, following my gaze.

"Angie is probably the most photogenic person in the world."

"Isn't he?" Her voice was full of affection. "He is the light of my life, you know. I still remember the first time I held him. He looked like a bean sprout. I tell him that all the time."

I laughed.

"So, Audrey," Sam put her palms flat on the table, "tell me about yourself. What are your ambitions?"

I considered her question for a few moments. "I love writing; I always have. I suppose my ultimate goal is to write a book one day."

She nodded thoughtfully. "I suppose this position will be a good start. You'll get to cut your teeth on an award-winning publication and mix with like-minded professionals." She smiled at me. "Are you thinking of taking any courses next year?"

"I don't know," I said. "I didn't finish my exams, so I might have to at some stage."

"Interesting. I know most publications only hire kids with degrees. But I'm a bit of a maverick, and it's worked well for me so far. When I'm hiring, I always look for something very particular. It's hard to explain. I suppose, in a way, it's instinctive. I seem to have a knack for knowing whether a writer is capable or not."

I nodded and waited for her to continue.

"And I definitely see potential in you. I think with a little guidance you'll brush up great in no time. I'm not sure what Angie has told you about the intern position, but I'll go through it with you now. Have you had any prior work experience?"

"I did a short internship at my dad's office about a year ago. He works in finance."

"Basic office duties?"

"Yeah, answering the phone, getting coffees, lots of filing."

She smiled. "Well, you'll have a similar role here. You'll be doing research and accompanying our senior journalists on interviews. And you'll have the opportunity to pitch story ideas at our meetings. Our brainstorming sessions are always great fun."

"Sounds perfect!"

"Good. The length of the internship is three months. I am looking to add a new writer to our team, so if it all goes well, there could be a paid position made available in mid-March."

I felt a jolt of excitement. "Really?" I could hardly believe my luck.

She smiled and nodded. "Yes, really."

"That would be wonderful! Truly."

"Well, then I guess you start Monday." She stood up and stuck out her hand at me from across the desk.

I got up from my chair and shook her hand, a grin plastered across my face.

"Thank you so much."

"No problem at all. Welcome to the team, Audrey. I think you're going to love it here."

Lucy came to pick me up after my meeting.

"How did it go?" she asked, as I slid into the passenger seat of Octopus One.

"Fantastic!" I said, beaming at her.

"So tell me all about it."

"The internship is three months, and then I might get a paid job after that."

"No way!" said Lucy. "Even lit graduates are having a super hard time getting a position."

"I know. It's actually surreal."

"Well, I guess we have another thing to celebrate!"

A few minutes later, Lucy pulled up in front of a quaint terrace house on a leafy, tree-lined street.

"Wow, you weren't kidding when you said it was close. I could walk to work."

"I told you it was perfect," said Lucy.

We got out of the car and walked through the gate and up the short flight of steps.

"It's so cute," I said. The door was painted a steampunk black and had an ornate brass knocker. The number *42* was painted on the door in large gold lettering.

"Wait until you get inside," she said, fishing the key out of her pocket and sticking it in the lock.

"Oh, wow," I breathed when we stepped across the threshold and into the house. I stood with my mouth agape as I took in the polished cherrywood floors and the retro-style furniture that gave the place a fun, playful vibe. There was a full-sized jukebox in the main hallway, accompanied by a vintage flip ball machine and fortune-telling wheel. Lucy's uncle was an art collector, and there were numerous paintings and limited-edition prints in ornate frames along the walls. We began walking through the house, marveling at the high ceilings that were a perfect complement to the open-plan layout that led us from the hallway to the lounge area and through the kitchen. There was a small room in the back, piled up high with an assortment of DVDs, books, cardboard boxes, and other paraphernalia. The back door opened to a charming English-style courtyard. A small outdoor table and chair set made of decorative wrought iron stood in the center of the yard, surrounded by lilies, white roses, and potted gardenias. "My uncle says my life won't be worth living if we let his plants die," said Lucy. Upstairs, there were two sun-drenched rooms, each with an en suite bathroom.

"Candela would have loved it here," I said, feeling suddenly wistful.

"I know," said Lucy. "We always said we'd move in together after school—the three of us. It kind of feels weird doing it without her."

"It does. Hey, what day is it today?"

Lucy checked her phone. "The fourteenth."

We looked at each other as the significance of the date dawned on us. It was Candela's birthday. I couldn't believe we almost forgot.

"We should call her," said Lucy.

I raised an eyebrow. "We can try."

My mind shot back to that day at Alexandria, outside Candela's house. Even though we hadn't spoken since then, I thought about her constantly. I had long since given up trying to make amends, but I couldn't ignore her birthday.

"Well, what have we got to lose?" said Lucy, tapping her number.

"Fingers crossed she'll pick up," I said.

"Hey, Lucy." To our surprise, Candela answered almost right away.

"Hi, stranger," said Lucy. "I'm here with Audrey."

"Hey, Candela," I said cautiously.

"Hey," she replied brightly. There wasn't a trace of hostility in her voice, and it made me feel hopeful.

"Happy birthday!" Lucy and I chimed in unison.

She laughed. "Aw, thanks guys."

"We miss you," said Lucy.

"I miss you both too," she said. There was a hint of sadness in her voice. It was her first birthday without us. "So what are you guys up to?"

Lucy told Candela about her uncle's house and how we would be house-sitting in the near future. "You know, you can crash here whenever you want."

"Thank you," said Candela. She sounded touched. "Maybe I can come and visit you both when you're settled in."

"You're welcome anytime," said Lucy.

"I have to get back to work now," said Candela. "Thanks for the call."

"You're working on your birthday?" I asked.

"Yeah, double shift," she said, with a sigh. "I'm just on my lunch break."

"Okay, we'll let you go, then," said Lucy. "It's good to hear your voice, Candela."

LATER THAT EVENING, I brought my parents up to speed about the exciting events of my day. As a tactical move, I told them about the internship and possible job offer first.

"That's wonderful, honey," said Dad, beaming at me.

"Congratulations, Audrey," said Mum. She looked genuinely happy for me. "Maybe a good time to go for your driver's license?" This was something I had been putting off, despite Mum's constant nagging. The idea of being in control of a dangerous hunk of metal while in the throes of a panic attack was a scenario that I did not want to find myself in.

"Actually, Lucy's uncle just accepted a job offer in Paris, and she'll be house-sitting for him while he's away. It's a big house, and it's really close to the *See! Sydney* office, about a ten-minute walk," I said in a rush, watching my mother's face transition from its calm, placid state to something that did not bode well for me. "Lucy says I can move in with her and—"

"No," Mum said. She put her fork down. "You're too young to be living out of home, Audrey."

"I'm eighteen!" I stood up, my chair loudly scraping the floor. "Most of my friends are leaving home."

"And look how it's turned out for Candela."

"Don't bring her into this. I'm not Candela, Mum."

"How do you think you'll support yourself? On an internship? How about rent and bills?"

"Lucy says we don't have to pay rent. And I can apply for a grant while I'm on my internship or get a part-time job."

"Audrey, you can barely take care of yourself. Maybe in a few years."

"A few years?" I cried, stunned. "Mum, I am not an invalid! Besides, I don't even need your permission, anyway."

"I beg your pardon?"

"Dad?" I looked over at him, my eyes pleading. "It's only house-sitting; I'm not going to be there forever."

He sighed and looked at Mum. "Audrey's right, Edwina. The girls are just house-sitting." I felt a tiny flicker of hope flare up in my chest. "Maybe it might be good for Audrey to get out there and learn a thing or two about responsibility."

She glared at him.

"And it's not too far away." He kept his tone light and jovial. "I'm sure she'll be back with her laundry every other day."

My mother looked from my dad to me. Then she stood up abruptly and pushed her chair back. "You're too soft on her; you always have been," she said to my dad. She picked up her plate—with half her meal still on it—and took it into the kitchen. I could hear the sharp clatter of the plate hitting the kitchen sink, then the sound of cupboard doors and drawers opening and slamming shut. My dad and I exchanged a look.

"No wild parties," he said, as a huge grin broke across my face. "You're living in someone else's house, so you have to treat it with respect."

"Dad!" I said, rushing to his side of the table and throwing my arms around his neck.

"Also," he continued, "I want you to visit your mother at least once a week—I'm serious, Audrey," he said when I let out a groan. "And you have to find a way to support yourself financially. No handouts from us."

"Okay," I said happily. I couldn't wait to call Lucy and tell her the good news.

Mum came out of the kitchen and looked at the two of us crossly. She had a handful of assorted kitchen utensils in her hands. "I suppose you'll be needing these," she said, laying them out on the table. "I don't want you girls living off pizza and burgers."

I leapt up and threw my arms around her. "Thanks, Mum," I said, kissing her on the cheek. My dad smiled at her and shrugged.

"Looks like our little girl is growing up."

Twelve

"I NOTICED YOU'RE not wearing your rubber band today," said Ida. It had been almost three months since I last saw her. I had been doing so well lately we were able to scale back our sessions.

I glanced down at my left wrist. "I must have forgotten it today," I said with a shrug. I sat down in the chair and dropped my brown leather satchel by my feet. It was a gift from my parents when I began my internship at *See! Sydney.*

"That's a great sign, Audrey."

"Yeah?"

She nodded and smiled. "How have you been? The last time we spoke, you had just started an internship at a magazine."

"I've been great," I said. "I was offered a full-time position last week." I reached into my bag, pulled out a business card, and passed it across the table. "Sam, my editor, got these cards printed up for me."

"Audrey Field, Journalist," said Ida with a smile. "Good for you, sweetheart. What an amazing achievement for someone your age."

"Thanks. I got lucky."

"And you're living out of home now, aren't you?"

I nodded. "I'm house-sitting with my friend Lucy."

"How has that been?"

"Wonderful. I don't have to put up with my mother on a daily basis anymore."

"How does that make you feel?"

"Like a huge weight has been lifted," I said, with a happy sigh. "I feel like I can relax and be myself. The other day I sat in my room and ate a whole pack of mint cookies just because I could."

Ida laughed. "Sounds like quite a revelation you had there."

"One of many."

"And do you still see your mother?"

"I go home for dinner every Thursday night. I also visit on some weekends. She's almost bearable in small doses. I think she's almost disappointed that I haven't screwed up yet. She has this irrational fear that I'll wind up like Candela."

"Speaking of Candela, have you heard from her?"

My smile waned. I shook my head. "No. Lucy and I called her up on her birthday, but we haven't heard from her since. That was months ago. I sent her a text with our address, but she's never bothered to show up."

"How does that make you feel?"

"Sad. I miss her a lot. We've been friends as far back as I can remember—we wouldn't go a day without talking. I love Lucy to death, but I've always had this special connection with Candela. It's hard to describe. I feel like I can talk to her without a filter, that she would never think less of me, no matter what I said. And she was the only one who understood how I felt about Rad—" I stopped.

"You're still thinking about Rad?"

"Yeah," I admitted. I had tried my best to put Rad out of my mind, but it was easier said than done. I kept thinking about the last time I saw him, at Blues Point when we had erased one another from our phones on the count of three. Sometimes, I wish I could go back to that night and stop that from happening. "I feel bad about it. I mean, Duck literally has no idea that Rad is still on my mind. We used to fight about it all the time, but it's almost like he's forgotten the whole thing ever happened." I looked down at my hands. "I wish I could forget."

"How is Duck doing?"

"Duck's great. He's just started his law degree, and he loves it. Since we left school, his ambitious streak has gone into overdrive."

"How so?"

"Well, he's gotten into self-help books in a big way. And there's always some business seminar in town that he's enrolled in."

"How do you feel about that?"

"Fine, I guess. As long as he is happy. We don't get to spend as much time together as we used to, though."

"Does that bother you?"

I shook my head. "Not really. There's lots to keep me busy."

"I'm glad to hear it." She scribbled something down in her notebook. "I know I wrote you a note for the doctor, some time ago. Did you ever fill the prescription?"

"No. After my fight with Candela, I was thinking about how she used to sneak a pill here and there from her mother's supply. And I didn't want to go down that road. I mean, I was coping okay with the rubber band."

"Have you had any more panic attacks since I last saw you?"

I shook my head and smiled. "Not a single one."

Thirteen

THE NEXT MORNING Sam came up to my desk and placed a book on top of a stack of papers.

"Novellas are making a comeback," she said, her tone matter of fact.

"They are? I thought publishers never touched them."

"Well, this one is making waves at the moment," she said tapping the cover lightly with one perfectly manicured finger.

"Pretty." There was an image of a snow-covered field with the title *A Snowflake in a Snowfield* and the author's name printed underneath. "Colorado Clark?" I said. "Is that a pen name?"

"I don't know, but you can ask him yourself. He's your first feature."

"Really?" I said, perking up. After weeks of pleading, Sam was finally tasking me with my first feature article. I was ecstatic. I jumped up and hugged her.

"Yes, really," she grinned. "April has set up a time and place for you to interview him on Monday. She'll e-mail the details to you. Make sure you read the book this weekend."

"I will," I promised, clutching the book to my chest and grinning at her. After sitting on the sideline for all these months, I was raring to go. I couldn't wait to see my name in print.

"The book has already made the Elliott Tate short list, by the way," she said as she was walking away.

"Seriously? A novella?"

She stopped and turned around. "It's not the first time a novella has been short-listed."

"I know, but it's rare."

A paper airplane landed squarely in front of me. I looked up. Trinh, a senior journalist, grinned at me from her desk. She got up and walked over.

"Congrats," she said.

"You knew?"

She nodded. "Uh-huh. Sam asked me if I thought you were ready, and I said 'hell yeah.'"

"Aw, thanks, Trinny," I said, flashing her a grateful smile.

Since I started at *See! Sydney,* senior journalist Trinh had taken me under her wing. She was in her midtwenties and already had an Ayres Award under her belt—the Australian equivalent of a Pulitzer. She had a passion for politics and wanted to write for the *Washington Post* one day. Like Sam, Trinh took pride in her appearance and always looked like she'd just walked off a fashion shoot. I envied women like that, the ones who could throw together an outfit and make it work—who could coordinate their shoes, makeup, and jewelry and make it all seem effortless.

"So are you excited?" she asked, her gold hoop earrings shimmering against her jet-black hair.

"Yes. You know how badly I've wanted this."

"I've read the book. It's powerful stuff—hard to believe someone so young wrote it. Word on the street is that he's gorgeous too."

"Is Colorado Clark his real name?"

"Apparently. It's an interesting name, isn't it? Sounds like a superhero."

"Yeah," I laughed. It certainly was an intriguing name.

"Anyway, I'd better get back to work. Good luck with the interview on Monday. Can't wait to hear all about it!"

"YOUR MOTHER HAS been calling me nonstop," said Lucy as I walked through the front door. "She says you're not answering your phone again." She was sitting upright on our royal-blue loveseat painting her toenails red.

I put my keys down on the kitchen bench and kicked off my shoes.

"God," I moaned. "There's a reason why I left home. When will she realize I plan on avoiding her for the rest of my life?"

"Audrey, I know she can be tough on you, but she's still your mother."

"You have no idea," I said with a sigh. "Your parents are perfect."

"Anyway," said Lucy, her face fixed in intense concentration as she dipped the tiny brush into the bottle of red polish, "can you just call her? I'm tired of playing gatekeeper."

"Fine." I grabbed a mug from the kitchen cupboard. "I'll do it after I have my cup of tea. Do you want one?"

"Sure." She put the bottle of polish on the coffee table and looked up at me. "Hey, want to go out tonight?"

"I probably shouldn't," I said, as I put the kettle on. "I've just been given my first feature."

"No way! Audrey, that's fantastic. Congrats! You've been wanting this for ages."

"I know," I said, beaming at her.

"Who's the feature?"

"Some hot new writer. I have to read his book over the weekend. It's a novella, which is kind of neat. I can't remember the last time I read one."

"A novella? You should be able to finish it in no time. C'mon, Audrey! Freddy and Duck are both free tonight. The four of us haven't gone out together in ages. Plus, now we have a reason to celebrate!"

"Okay. I suppose I can start the book tomorrow."

LATER THAT NIGHT, we met up with Freddy and Duck at Spag Bowl. It was someone's (probably drunken) idea to attach a small Italian joint to a bowling alley. The food was awful, but it had a great atmosphere and the Bolognese was passable as long as you drowned it with Parmesan.

Lucy and I were sitting at one of the tables draped in red-and-white gingham and decorated with a small vase of fake red roses. The place was buzzing with people talking over the offbeat notes of a piano sonata, occasionally interrupted by the smack of bowling balls into pins. "Should we get a snack before joining the boys?" I asked.

"I'm starving! Let's have dinner. Besides, Freddy gets so competitive when he plays against me. He's such a bad loser." She rolled her eyes.

I smiled. When it came to bowling, Lucy was formidable.

"Hi, gorgeous," said Freddy, sneaking up behind Lucy and planting a kiss on her cheek.

"Gross, you're all sweaty," she said pushing his face away.

"Hey," said Duck.

"Hi," Lucy and I said in unison.

"Are you two going to join us?" asked Freddy, picking up

Lucy's beer and taking a swig.

"Maybe later," said Lucy. "We're going to have dinner."

"Okay. I'm kicking Duck's butt. Three strikes in a row." He made a bowling motion for emphasis.

"You're amazing, babe," said Lucy dryly. He grinned at her proudly, pounding his chest, Tarzan style. He took another swig of Lucy's beer before turning to Duck.

"Ready for round two?"

"GOD, HE'S SO embarrassing," groaned Lucy. "I can't take him anywhere."

"He's got a sweet side to him, though," I said. "Like the other day when you stepped in dog poo and he spent the afternoon scrubbing your sneaker in the courtyard."

"That was really nice of him," she agreed.

"Anyway, the two of you are disgustingly cute."

"I know. We even make ourselves sick sometimes."

I laughed.

"I'll have the puttanesca." Lucy shut her menu and put it down on the table.

"Pepperoni pizza for me."

"Are you going to have some wine?"

I shook my head. "No, I want to stay off the alcohol tonight."

"You're such a nerd."

"Says the girl in the T-shirt with a math pun on it."

Lucy grinned.

We heard a shout of glee and turned our heads to see that Freddy had just scored another strike. He gave us the thumbs-up sign as Duck grinned at us and shrugged his shoulders.

"Duck looks happy," said Lucy.

"He is. Things have been really great between us." Duck's mood had improved dramatically once Rad was out of the picture. For him, it was a case of out of sight, out of mind. It wasn't that simple for me, but that was something I kept to myself.

"Well, he deserves it; he's a great guy."

"I know. I'm lucky to have him."

LATER, THE BOYS joined us at our table, and Freddy helped himself to some of my pizza.

"Did Audrey tell you? She got her first feature story."

"No kidding?" Duck said. He put his arm around my shoulder and kissed me on the cheek. "Way to go!"

"Congrats, Audrey," said Freddy. "We should celebrate!" He flagged the waiter down for a new round of drinks.

"I'm not drinking tonight."

"Why not?" Freddy asked.

"She wants to stay sharp," said Lucy, her eyes brimming with laughter.

"So who's the feature on?" asked Duck.

"Some up-and-coming writer. I have to interview him about his new book on Monday."

"Well, you have the entire weekend ahead of you," said Freddy. "A drink's not going to kill you."

"I suppose not," I said, caving in. "Maybe just one, then."

LATER THAT NIGHT, I found myself lying wide awake in bed. Duck was fast asleep. I always envied how he could do that. Sleep was like clockwork for him.

I crept out of bed and went in search of my brown leather satchel. I found it lying on the kitchen table, reached into the front pocket, and pulled out the copy of *A Snowflake in a Snowfield*. I made a cup of tea and settled myself on the loveseat with the book on my lap.

It was a chilly night, and I drew my favorite woolen throw up to my chin and curled my legs under my body. I breathed a sigh of contentment and reached for my tea. After taking a sip, I flicked open the book and turned to the first page.

An unnerving feeling settled over me as I began reading. It grew in intensity as I progressed further. The book was set in 1920s Wisconsin, a story about a woodcutter's daughter that read almost like a fairy tale. There was a dark undercurrent of abuse and neglect I found deeply disturbing. In the closing scene, Emily, the protagonist, trudges across the snow toward her favorite iron-wood tree, a length of rope clutched tightly in her hands. In the last few moments of her life, Emily's thoughts play out on the final page in a series of flashbacks that felt strangely familiar to me.

I snapped the book shut and realized my hands were shaking. I got up to get myself a glass of water. I barely made it to the kitchen sink when my legs gave out under me and I collapsed onto the floor, gasping for breath. For the first time in a while, I reached for my rubber band, but I didn't have it on. I pinched as hard as I could at the skin above my thighs. The pain was excruciating and I bit down on my lip to stop myself from crying out. Tears flooded my eyes and spilled down my cheeks.

After a few agonizing moments, the tension in my body began to ease and I clutched my knees tightly to my chest, rocking back and forth.

I had no idea why the book had been so triggering. Somehow, it was written in a way that mirrored many of the feelings I had kept buried since Ana's death—the sorrow, the regret, the overwhelming guilt. It was as though this writer had understood me in the most intimate way.

Taking a deep breath, I picked myself up and walked to the kitchen table. I withdrew my laptop from my satchel and flipped up the screen. With trembling fingers, I typed "Colorado Clark" in the search box. It was such an unusual name that I had no trouble finding a photo of the author. My heart pounded wildly in my chest as image after image flooded the screen. Colorado was the boy I had met the night of Ana's funeral who was still on my mind all these months later. "Rad," I whispered.

Fourteen

I ARRIVED AT the café where April had arranged for me to meet Rad. I found a corner booth and sat down, staring out the rain-splattered window where intricate letters spelled out the words "Callisto" in reverse. Every so often, drops would burst onto the glass like newly formed stars on a flat, translucent galaxy.

I checked the time on my phone. He was ten minutes late. I drummed my fingers nervously on the table. It felt like a lifetime since we last spoke. A teenage girl with frizzy brown hair walked by with a handful of dirty plates. "I'll be with you in a minute," she said before disappearing behind the counter. She came back a few minutes later with a menu. "Give me a holler when you're ready."

"Sure, I'm just waiting for someone." Just as the words left my mouth, I saw Rad outside the window, pulling up his coat collar against the rain. Moments later, he was through the door. His eyes scanned the café as I stood up.

"Hi, Rad," I said, as he strode toward me.

"Audrey?" he said with a jolt of recognition. "What are you doing here?"

"I'm with *See! Sydney.* I'm here to interview you," I explained.

He broke into a grin and shook his head in amazement. "You're kidding me, aren't you?"

I shook my head. "Nope."

"But you're barely out of school. How did you become a journalist so quickly?"

I shrugged. "You know, slept my way up."

He laughed. "God, what a strange coincidence."

"Isn't it?" I said. "Congratulations on your book, by the way. I had no idea your name was Colorado."

He grimaced. "Mum is the only person who calls me Colorado. To everyone else, I'm just Rad."

"You know, I had this poster of Colorado stuck on my wall when I was a kid. Come to think of it, that's probably what started my fixation with snowcapped mountains in the first place."

"Really?"

"Yeah. Isn't that weird? It's like something out of a novel."

"Well, that supports my theory—you know the one about us being characters in a book."

"I can't argue with you there."

The waitress walked by our booth and threw us a look. "Do you want a menu?"

"Yes, thanks," Rad said.

Rad slid into the booth opposite me, and the waitress came back with a menu. "Let me know when you're ready."

Rad took off his dark blue coat and put it on the bench beside him. His hair was wet from the rain, and he reached up and ruffled it with his fingers.

"Nice day, huh?"

"Not so much," I said, a small smile crossing my lips.

"Parking was a nightmare! How did you manage?"

"I caught the bus."

"Really? In this weather?"

"I've been meaning to go for my driver's license, but things have been so hectic over the last few months."

He nodded. "I can imagine."

"So, I have to ask. How did you wind up with a name like Colorado? There must be a story there."

"Well, my mum was obsessed with the book *On the Road*—do you know it?"

"Yeah, by Kerouac."

"That's the one. She was saving up for a big road trip across America, but then she met Dad. Soon after, she was pregnant with me."

"So she never went?"

"No, though she still talks about it sometimes. She had this affinity with Colorado. It used to be a running joke with Dad—the closest she ever got to Colorado was me."

I smirked. "Very funny."

"My dad used to think so, but he was probably the only one."

"So are you still living at home?"

"No, I moved out a few months back. I just needed a change of scenery. I couldn't walk down the street incognito. Everyone I bumped into would give me that look. You know, that 'There's the guy with the dead girlfriend' look."

I nodded.

"So I got a job stacking shelves at the supermarket and signed a lease for a shoebox apartment in Paddington."

"Oh, that's not too far from me."

"You moved out too?"

"Kind of. I'm house-sitting with Lucy at her uncle's place. We're in Surry Hills."

"Really? Hey, that's great! How's Lucy?"

"Really good. She's studying business at Sydney U. Freddy's there with her—they're enrolled in the same course."

"I have to give Freddy a call. I owe him a beer," said Rad. "I've literally been a hermit while writing this book. It's time to come out of hibernation, I suppose."

"What was that like? Hibernation, I mean. A lot of writers talk about this creative vacuum when they're busy working on a project, and I've always been curious about it."

"You kind of lose perspective after a while. At least, it was that way with me. You become insular. I barely left my apartment the whole time I was writing *Snowflake*. I kept odd hours. I was stacking shelves at night, so I would sleep in during the day. There's a café downstairs, which was handy. Sometimes, if I felt up to it, I would walk up to Centennial Park, feed the ducks."

"It sounds perfect, actually."

"Oddly enough, I did enjoy it, but only because I was working on something I cared about. I think I'd go crazy if I was just doing time."

"I can't believe you talked about doing something and actually accomplished it. I mean, not only did you write a book but you also got the Elliott Tate nomination."

"It was a nice surprise," he said, with a shrug. "But the biggest thrill was getting the publishing deal."

"How did it happen? Take me through it."

"I didn't have an end goal in mind when I was writing *Snowflake*. It was something I was compelled to do—I felt like I would go mad if I didn't. Writing was cathartic for me. Before I knew it, I'd finished the book, and I parked it to one side for a few weeks. Then, one night I was surfing the web, and I came across a competition that Geidt & Ekstrom was running. Do you know who they are?"

"I've heard about them. They've only been around a few years, but they've published a string of hits."

"Yeah, they've had a good run."

"I wasn't aware of the competition, though."

"I don't think it got any media attention, probably because it was the first year they ran it."

"That makes sense. So how did it work?"

"They were on the lookout for a novella. The prize was a publishing deal and a decent sum of money. Kind of like an advance."

"My editor, Sam, was telling me that novellas are coming back in vogue."

"Yeah, there is definitely a trend, which is great. Some of the best classics are novellas."

"I know. *Animal Farm* is one of my favorite books."

"Same."

"And I'm guessing you won the competition?"

"I did."

"Amazing," I said, sitting back in my seat and shaking my head. "So what happened next?"

"I quit my job as soon as the prize money came in. It's kind of neat that I can focus all my attention on writing now. At least for the next year or so. What about you? How did you get this gig? I know some graduates who are still struggling to get their foot in the door."

I told him all about Angie and Sam, my internship, and then my full-time position.

"Wow, lucky break."

"I know. Things are going so well for me at the moment."

"I'm glad to hear it. You deserve it."

"Thanks. I'm crossing my fingers for the Elliott Tate Award. I think *Snowflake* definitely has a good chance of winning."

"So I'm guessing you've read it?"

I nodded. "It's part of my job description. I loved it by the way."

"You know, some of our conversations went into *Snowflake*."

"Well, I had no idea you were the author, so you can imagine how freaked out I was when I was reading it."

"Sorry." He looked sheepish. "I actually didn't think it would ever see the light of day."

I waved my hand at him. "Don't worry about it."

"You're not going to sue me?"

"The thought did cross my mind."

THE RAIN OUTSIDE was slowing down to a patter. We ordered coffee and a basket of fries. The café was now almost empty on account of the bad weather. It was also an odd time of day—too late for lunch and too early for dinner. The dull light from the gray sky lending a quiet ambience to the room, a slow, lazy tempo punctuated by the faraway clatter of plates and cutlery.

"So I suppose we should start the official interview."

"Sure."

"Do you mind if I record this?"

"Not at all."

I pulled my phone from my bag and placed it on the table between us. Then I tapped the Voice Memos app and sat back in my seat.

"Why don't you tell me more about the book? Why did you choose Wisconsin as the setting? Have you ever been there?"

"No, I haven't been there. I always imagined a stark backdrop, and I suppose Wisconsin automatically puts you into that landscape. I liked the idea of setting it in winter, the bleakness of it."

"I really love the ending. It was poetic. That sense of isolation Emily felt walking into the snowstorm. She thought that everything she had done would be covered over by the snow and her footprints would disappear from the world along with everything that had ever validated her existence. Then—and you wrote this beautifully—we follow the single snowflake as it makes its slow, hypnotic descent down to land on Emily's cheek and melt into a single teardrop. It felt like at that moment, every snowflake in that field was a teardrop and the whole world was crying for her."

"I knew you'd get it. When I finished the book, I wanted to call you. I would have if I hadn't deleted your number from my phone."

"I would have liked that."

"I'm glad we're here now. It feels important somehow."

We were quiet for a few moments.

"Are you still with Duck?" he asked.

"Yeah."

"Oh."

I flushed at the obvious disappointment in his voice. There was an awkward pause, so I hurried back to the interview. "You have many powerful scenes in *Snowflake*. Aside from the ending, I love the scene where Emily finally stands up to her father. I mean, it was heart-wrenching, but at the same time—triumphant."

Rad sat back, a small sigh escaping his lips. "When Ana died, it was like a rupture. You know those scenes in the movies where something tears through an airplane and everything gets sucked through the void? Well, that's what it felt like, only I was the plane, trying to keep my insides from spilling out. I know it sounds weird."

My hand, resting under the table, reached for my rubber band. I knew Ana would come up in our conversation. It was inevitable since there was so much of her in the book. I had been steeling myself for this moment, and I gave myself a couple of sharp tweaks.

"Not at all." He had just described exactly how it felt for me, the perfect analogy. But, of course, I couldn't tell him that. Not without revealing my lie. It was something I had pushed so far down that I couldn't bring myself to tell anyone. Not even Ida.

"Grief is such a potent thing," he continued. "That's what I've learned. It's like a hot iron; you can barely stand to hold it. But you don't have a choice. The only way you can set it down, even if it's temporary, is to refocus the energy elsewhere. I've only been able to do that through writing."

"It's amazing what people create using their pain. Work that is touched by melancholy has its own unique beauty. Even the word 'melancholy' is pretty, the way it rolls on your tongue. I think sadness adds something to literature that is unique. It's an ingredient like . . ." I thought for a moment. "Like salt. Salt has that power to completely transform a dish. I think sadness has that same transformative effect in literature."

"That reminds me of a story. A fairy tale, actually. It's about this king who has three daughters. He was trying to work out whom he should leave his kingdom to, so he rounded them up and asked them to describe their love for him. The first daughter said she loved him like the way she loved her most precious jewels. The second described how much she loved him by referencing her most beautiful dresses. The third likened her love to salt, which pissed off the king because in comparison to fancy dresses and diamonds, salt is kind of underwhelming. So he sent her away. I don't really remember what happens next, but I think somehow she begins working for a neighboring kingdom, catches the eye of the prince, and, then, as luck would have it, ends up marrying him. One day, she hosts a royal banquet, and her father is the guest of honor. She instructs the cooks not to use any salt in their cooking. So the king is sitting at the dinner table. He doesn't recognize his own daughter because, well, it's a fairy tale."

I laughed.

"He takes a bite of his meal and spits it out," Rad continued. "Then he says he would rather die than eat another bite of food that isn't seasoned with salt. Of course, the princess reveals her true identity, and the king realizes the point she was trying to make before he threw her to the wolves."

"I like that story," I said.

"I knew you would."

"I suppose salt has a negative rap, like sadness. We're always told to watch our sodium intake or smile."

He grinned. "I like that."

"Actually, I kind of had this epiphany the other day."

He raised his eyebrows. "You did?"

"Yeah," I shook my head. "Forget it; it's stupid."

"Now you've got me curious. Come on," he added when I shook my head again. He gave me an encouraging smile. "I'll buy you a muffin," he offered.

I laughed. "Okay, then." I held up both hands in a gesture of surrender. "It happened after I read your book." I stopped and chewed my bottom lip, trying to find the appropriate words to describe my revelation while Rad sat there with an expectant look on his face. "I've sat in on several interviews with writers, and not all of them strike me as tortured souls. So it got me thinking, because a lot of literature is about struggle. But I don't think all writers are sad. I think it's the other way around—all sad people write. It's a form of catharsis, a way of working through things that feel unresolved, like undoing a knot. People who are prone to sadness are more likely to pick up a pen."

Rad nodded thoughtfully. "And because they do, some will inevitably end up as writers," he said.

"Exactly."

"So we've had it backward this whole time."

"Well, it was just a thought," I said with a shrug.

"I like it." He smiled at me, and I found myself smiling back.

SEVERAL CUPS OF coffee later, the rain was coming down thick and fast. Only a few cold, soggy fries remained in the basket. The sky was growing darker. "I should head off," I said, glancing at my phone. "I'm going to miss my bus."

"I can give you a lift home," he offered.

"Are you sure?"

"I don't know," he said playfully. "I think I am starting to have second thoughts now."

WE LEFT THE café and made our way to Rad's car, doing our best to dodge the rain.

"You still drive the same car."

"It hasn't been that long since we last saw each other," he said, getting in the driver's side.

"But it feels like a lifetime ago, doesn't it?" I slid into the passenger seat, and it was like entering a time capsule. "I suppose it's because so much has happened since."

We looked at each other for a moment, our expressions quizzical. Drops of water slid from our hair and fell onto the gray fabric upholstery. I felt along the seat, and that same tear was still there. Rad reached into a duffle bag in the back seat and pulled out a large beach towel, passing it to me. I dried myself as best as I could before handing it back. As Rad toweled his hair, a flicker of something passed through me. I wasn't quite sure what it was, but for a split second, it felt almost intimate. "So," he said, tossing the towel carelessly into the back seat, "where to?" I gave him my address as he pulled out of the parking lot.

"Do you know what's ironic about writers?" Rad said, as we sat in heavy traffic. The sky outside was almost pitch black, and the rain was pounding steadily on the windshield.

"What?"

"Writers take things that are deeply personal, things said to them in confidence, often during moments of great intimacy, and strip them down into words. Then they take those words, naked and vulnerable, and give them to the world. Yet in spite of this, writers struggle more than most when it comes to sentimental attachment. They only write about things they've felt deeply. That's the thing about writers—on one hand everything is sacred to them, but, on the other, nothing really is."

"Is that off the record?" I smiled.

"Is anything?" he replied with a grin.

"I think you're right, though." My face grew serious. "Some of my colleagues have admitted to sacrificing their integrity for a really good story. I suppose the act of writing is in itself a form of betrayal."

Rad nodded. "I agree. Writing is a conduit. It opens up a passageway into the past. Not just for the writer, but for the reader too. Both readers and writers are linked by the commonality of human experience."

"Yeah," I said. I looked at the figures walking on the street outside, their silhouettes warped by drops of rain sliding down glass. "But it's always a little skewed. You can never relive a moment through writing. You can only retell it."

"Yet things always seem less artificial when you're looking back. Time lends it an authenticity that nothing else can."

"I think it's because we romanticize the past. We give it more than it deserves."

The traffic began to clear, and we were quiet the rest of the way to my house.

I felt a twinge of disappointment when Rad turned the corner onto my street. I was enjoying our conversation and wished we could keep talking. "It's just ahead. You can drop me here." He slowed down to a stop just outside my house.

"Hey," he said, turning to face me. "Want to keep driving?"

"Okay."

Fifteen

I SURREPTITIOUSLY CHECKED my phone in the pocket of my brown satchel. No text. I slid it back down into the bag with a sigh. I looked out the car window and smiled at Duck, who was getting gas for the car. I didn't have to go into the office that day, and Duck's morning lecture got canceled, so we decided to go for lunch. He came around and tapped on my window. I wound it down.

"Want anything?" he asked.

"Can you get me a Diet Coke?"

"Okay," he said, kissing me as his thumb and forefinger gently snatched my chin.

As he walked away, I felt a stab of guilt, thinking about the night before. After we left the café, Rad and I drove aimlessly for hours, lost in conversation. By then, it had stopped raining, and the night air was warm and still. We had no idea where we were. None of the street names were familiar, but we didn't care. It felt almost dreamlike, as though we had slipped into a new reality.

It was well past midnight when we realized how hungry we were. Thankfully, we found a twenty-four-hour McDonald's with a drive-through. We ordered burgers and thick shakes that we ate in the deserted parking lot. Outside, the rain-drenched asphalt was an incandescent blur: hues of white, red, and yellow refracting the light from the nearby streetlamps and the golden arches overhead. Maybe it was the free-flowing conversation or the thrill of being somewhere unfamiliar, but it was hands down the best burger I'd ever had.

This morning, I was ready to tell Lucy about Rad, but she had to rush off to class. Now I wondered whether I should hold back from telling her. If I kept it a secret from Lucy, then perhaps I could justify keeping it from Duck.

The sound of the door clicking open snapped me back to the present. Duck got into the car and handed me my drink. Then he looked at me and smiled for the longest time. "What?" I smiled back.

"I really love you, Audrey." He leaned over and kissed me softly on the cheek. "You make me so happy."

"AUDREY," TRINH CALLED, when I walked into the office Wednesday morning. She was sitting on the couch in the common area and motioned for me to come over. I sat down next to her.

"So how was your interview?"

I took a deep breath. "You wouldn't believe this, but I know the author."

Her eyes widened. "Colorado Clark?"

"Well, I knew him by the name Rad—no one calls him Colorado," I explained.

"Oh. How do you know him?"

I gave her a quick recap of the history I shared with Rad.

"Wow," she said. "That's really cool—especially about the snow globe. And then you deleted each other's numbers?" Her eyes were unusually dreamy. "I mean, I'm not a romantic, but God, that's like fate, destiny—whatever you want to call it. Don't you think?"

"I suppose." I didn't know what Rad's sudden appearance in my life meant. But it was wreaking havoc with my emotions. All the feelings of guilt that were tied to Ana had come rushing back. At the same time, the connection I felt to Rad was growing more intense by the day.

"I mean, what are the chances?" Trinh continued. "It's almost like you were meant to meet up again."

THE FOLLOWING SATURDAY, Duck was away at a seminar, and Lucy had locked herself away in her room to cram for her first exam. The night before, she'd given me strict instructions not to disturb her unless it was an absolute emergency.

It was a beautiful, crisp morning, and I was out in the courtyard with the paper and a fresh cup of coffee. I was flicking through the Lifestyle section, wondering whether I should go and see a film, when my phone rang.

"Hey." It was Rad.

"Hi."

"What are you up to?"

"Just reading the paper."

"Anything interesting?"

"There's a documentary called *Killer Clouds* coming out soon. Apparently they are the most dangerous things in the sky."

"Those fluffy, marshmallowy things?"

"You mean those angry, lightning-inducing, tornado-facilitating monsters."

"Wow, I will never look at a cloud in the same way again."

"They are the original wolf in sheep's clothing."

"Long before there were wolves."

"Or clothing."

Rad laughed. "Hey, are you doing anything today?"

"Nope. How about you?"

"Nothing. I'm kind of bored. Want to hang out?"

I thought about Duck and felt immediately guilty. I knew he wouldn't like the idea of me seeing Rad again, but I couldn't help myself.

"Okay."

RAD CAME TO pick me up about an hour later.

"So what should we do?" I said, when we were pulling away from the curb. "Want to see a movie? There's one about the US economy that everyone at work is raving about."

"That sounds like a good option," said Rad. "It's such a beautiful day, though; do you really want to spend it inside a cinema?"

"I suppose not."

"What about a hike?"

"A hike? Are you kidding me?"

"Why, what's wrong with hiking?"

"Nothing, other than the fact that it involves walking."

We were silent as we thought of things to do.

"You know, it's been, like, a million years since I've gone down to the trails. The weather is so great today I wouldn't mind going for a ride."

"On a bike?"

"I was thinking more along the lines of a horse," said Rad.

"Oh."

"Have you ridden before?"

"Sure." I had no idea why I said that, since I had never ridden a horse in my life.

"Excellent! I used to ride a lot when I was a kid. I miss it."

"Uh-huh," I said, thinking back to Lucy's tenth birthday when her parents had hired a pony and we took turns riding him while a lady led us slowly up and down the yard.

"My mum is mad about horses," Rad continued. "We drove out west every weekend to the stables. I used to ride a horse named Periscope. He was a scraggly brown thing, but I absolutely adored him. He got sent away when I was about thirteen, and I was beside myself."

"That's strange. I knew this guy who went through the exact same thing."

"Really?"

"Yeah, his name was Sodapop," I teased.

"This is what I get for baring my soul to you."

ABOUT AN HOUR later, Rad pulled into a dirt driveway off the Central Coast with an overarching sign that read "Eureka Equestrian."

Rad parked the car, and we got out, making our way over to the log building up ahead. A teenage girl in riding gear sat behind a glass booth.

"Hi," she said. The tag pinned to her shirt read "Sally."

"Hi," said Rad. "We'd like to book two horses for an hour."

"Sure. That will be seventy-five each."

SALLY LED US to the stables, where a burly man in a plaid red shirt was running a hard wire brush over a handsome black horse. He looked up as we approached.

"Two for an hour ride on the Bereewan Trail," said Sally, motioning to us. She grabbed a couple of helmets that were hanging on the side of the stable and passed them over to me.

"That's a good track, especially for a day like this," he said in a low, gruff voice. "I'm Bill, by the way."

"I'm Rad; this is Audrey."

"Hi," I said, strapping on my helmet.

"And this is Midnight." He patted the side of the horse affectionately.

"He's beautiful," said Rad.

"He sure is. You two ridden before?"

"Yeah," said Rad. "I used to ride almost every weekend."

"Great," Bill replied.

"I'm a little rusty," I said.

Bill nodded. "Okay, then, Rad you take Midnight." He handed the reins to Rad. "And for you, Audrey, I'll go and get Molly. She's a little old and slow."

"Sounds good."

Bill disappeared into the stable and came out a moment later with a white mare. She had large gray patches across her body and big, doleful eyes.

"So how long since your last ride?" asked Bill, as he threw a saddle across Molly's back.

"Um, a couple years," I lied.

"How often were you riding?"

"Not too often."

"Do you remember the basics?"

"Uh, I might need a quick reminder."

Bill buckled up the saddle and placed the bridle over Molly's head. Then he pulled up a stepladder and placed it on the left side of her body.

"This is a mounting block," he explained. "Just step up onto it, put your left leg in the stirrup, and swing yourself up over the horse."

"Okay," I said and followed his instructions.

"That's the way," Bill confirmed.

"Holy shit," I said, when I was sitting in the saddle. The sudden height was giving me vertigo.

"Are you okay?" said Rad. He had already mounted without any assistance and was now sitting back in his saddle like it was the most natural thing in the world.

"I'd forgotten how tall horses are."

Bill handed me the reins, and I took them with nervous hands. "Okay, so when you want Molly to start walking, sit straight up in your saddle, put your heels down, and squeeze gently."

I did as he directed, and Molly moved into a slow walk. I let out a yelp, and Rad gave me a strange look.

"You sure you've ridden a horse before, Audrey?"

"Of course I have."

"You're doing good," said Bill. "Now, if you want Molly to go right, pull on the right rein and hold. Same thing if you want to go left. Got it?"

"Uh-huh."

"If you want to go into a slow trot, give the old girl another squeeze and lift your butt off the saddle. If you want her to stop, sit down in the saddle and pull gently on both reins. She will also respond to 'whoa.'"

"Okay."

Bill let me walk Molly around the paddock until he was satisfied I knew what I was doing.

"Now, come to a stop," he said.

I sat down into the saddle, pulled back gently on the reins, and said, "Whoa." Molly came to a halt.

"Good," Bill smiled. "All right, then, you're all set to go."

ABOUT TEN MINUTES into our ride, I was actually enjoying myself. I had gotten used to the height and the motion as we bounced along in a slow trot. The scenery around us was stunning. A dense forest edged the trail and paved it with dappled light. Birds chirped in the eaves above us, and in the distance, we heard the faint roar of crashing waves.

"This was a good idea," said Rad, as though reading my thoughts.

My horse, Molly, let out a snort. "She agrees."

Rad smiled at me. "So how come you've got the weekend free? What's your boyfriend up to?"

"He's away at a seminar. W-Y-S-A." I spelled it out. "It stands for World Youth Success Academy."

"Sounds kind of like *Star Trek*."

"You're not that far off, actually. It preaches a holistic, new age kind of ideology. There's, like, a career element to it, but most of it has to do with how you run your life—from your mind-set, spiritual values, even down to your diet—it almost borders on theology."

"You seem pretty clued in."

"I looked them up when Duck was trying to convince me to join."

"Sounds kind of cultish, doesn't it?"

"A little," I admitted. "Hence the research. I was actually thinking of doing a story on it. I pitched it at one of our meetings, but my editor, Sam, says it's been done to death."

"Doesn't it bother you that your boyfriend is involved with them?"

"No. Duck's mainly there for the career side of things."

"And he's doing all this on top of his law degree?"

"Uh-huh."

"Wow, busy guy. I've only got a book to write, and I'm

having trouble with that."

"You're working on another book already?"

"I kind of have to if I want to keep paying rent."

"But I thought *Snowflake* was selling by the truckload. I mean, I saw a copy sitting in the window of Ariel."

"The book industry is a lot smaller than everyone thinks," said Rad. "I'm barely covering my living expenses."

"Oh. I thought you were set for life."

He laughed. "Not even close. The Elliott Tate nomination has helped, but I have a long way to go."

"So what's the new book about?"

"To be honest, I don't know. I saw a documentary a couple months back about bees and how they've been dying out in masses."

"I read an article about that the other day."

"It's really sad. They're like a barometer of our ecosystem. It's just one of the major signs that we're screwing it up."

"Do you know why they're dying?"

"Probably a combination of things like pesticides, predators like wasps, global warming. Bees pollinate a lot of our crops, so we're pretty screwed if they die out completely."

"Yeah." I glanced over at Rad, who was staring straight ahead, his expression serene. He had on the same shirt he wore that night at Blues Point. I remembered his arms around me, the way his warm skin felt against my cheek. I'd thought about that night a lot, and now he was here and I longed to be that close to him again.

He caught me looking at him and smiled. I turned away quickly.

"So how is work going for you?"

"It's going great. Your article is coming along well, so Sam is giving me lots of new assignments. She's happy with my progress and says I could be up for a promotion soon."

We came to a turn where the trail was only wide enough for one horse to pass through. Rad held back and let me go in front of him. I tugged the rein gently with my right hand when, all of a sudden, a small gray blur shot out in front of us.

"What the hell—" I began. Then Molly let out a whinny and reared. I screamed, pulling frantically on the reins. "Whoa!" I cried as she broke into a gallop. "Rad! What do I do?"

"Audrey," I saw a flash of him in my peripheral, reaching out toward me. "Hang on!"

My heart was going a million miles per hour. "Oh my God!" I shrieked when Molly bounded forward at lightning speed, turning everything around me into a blur. The forest cleared, and, before I knew it, we were on sand, racing toward the waves. My saddle was coming loose, and I could hear Rad's horse, Midnight, galloping behind me.

"Audrey! Let go of the reins," he called.

"Are you kidding me?" I screamed back.

"Get your feet out of the stirrups and let go of the reins. Do it! Now!"

"Shit!" I cried. I kicked my legs free and let go of the reins, my stomach lurching as I was thrown off the back of my horse. I tumbled onto the sand and came to an abrupt standstill. As I strained to sit up, I saw Molly bolting off back the way we came.

Rad came to a stop and looked down at me from his horse. "Audrey, are you okay?" he asked, breathing hard.

"I think so. God, my butt is killing me."

Rad dismounted and came over to me. I saw a hint of laughter in his eyes when they met mine.

"Glad you think this is funny," I said, wincing.

"I'm sorry," he said, holding his hand out to me. "But you look so cute with your helmet dangling from your head like that."

I took his hand, and he pulled me up. "Never again. From now on I'm sticking to merry-go-rounds."

He looked at me, a strange expression on his face.

"What?"

"Nothing," he shook his head and smiled.

"No, seriously, why are you looking at me like that?"

"Just what you said about merry-go-rounds. You're the only person I know who would say something like that." He grinned at me and shrugged. "I just like how your mind works; that's all."

I was taken aback by the compliment and wasn't sure how to respond. I looked at my feet and smiled.

"So have you fallen off a horse before?" I asked.

"Sure, lots of times."

I stared at him. "Are you serious?"

"Yeah," he gave me a look. "You've never ridden a horse before, have you?"

"No," I admitted.

"Audrey, why would you lie about that?"

I shrugged. "I don't know. I figured I could pick it up as I went along."

"You are ridiculous. You could have been seriously hurt. Luckily, you had a soft landing."

"What the hell happened, anyway?"

"I think a rabbit ran out onto the trail. It must have startled your horse."

I sighed. "We're miles away from anywhere. What the hell are we going to do now?"

"Do you have your phone on you?"

"No, I put it in the saddlebag."

"Oh. You're not supposed to put anything important in the saddlebag."

"What about your phone?"

"It's dead."

"Great. What are we going to do?"

Rad chewed on his lip for a few moments. "I know," he said, walking back toward Midnight. "Why don't you get on with me?"

"No. Forget it."

"Audrey, you know what they say when you fall off a horse . . ."

"Don't you dare."

He grinned. "You get back on."

"I hate you."

"Come on; you'll be fine." He held out his hand. "I'll boost you up."

"There's no room for me on the saddle."

"There is if you sit up front. I saw it in a movie once."

"It sounds awfully dangerous."

"We'll go slow; I promise."

Reluctantly, I took his hand, and he helped me up onto the saddle.

"Holy shit, this horse is even taller than Molly." Rad's horse gave a soft whinny, practically giving me a heart attack.

"It's okay," Rad said reassuringly. "You'll be fine."

He got up behind me with almost no effort and put his arms around my waist. "Okay, now just hold onto the reins gently, and he'll take us back to base."

I took a deep breath. "Okay. Okay, I can do this."

"See; this isn't so bad," said Rad as Midnight began moving into a slow trot. "It's actually kind of nice."

All of a sudden I was hugely aware of Rad's arms around me and that I was practically sitting in his lap—not to mention that the bouncing motion of the horse had put us in a kind of compromising position. I felt a wave of guilt, thinking about how Duck would feel if he caught a glimpse of this. But then the guilt was replaced by something else, something far more insistent. It was chemical, the way my body reacted to his. A raw, undulating lust was making me ache all over. I felt the heat rise to my cheeks, and I was glad Rad couldn't see my face.

"You better not be taking advantage of this situation," I muttered, under my breath.

"The thought barely crossed my mind."

WE MADE IT back in one piece, and I was both glad and disappointed to get off the horse.

"We were a bit worried about you when Molly showed up," said Bill, taking the reins from Rad. "I was ready to send the boys out in the pickup truck."

"I'm glad Molly made it back safe—she had a bit of a freakout." I took off my helmet. "And I think I left my phone in her saddle."

"You sure did—Sally found it. You can pick it up from her on your way out."

"Great, thanks."

"Molly's usually pretty good. What happened out there?"

"I think she was startled by a rabbit," said Rad.

"Ah, I see," said Bill. "We'll have to check on our fencing, then."

A family of four were ambling over toward us, and Bill gave them a quick nod of acknowledgment. Then he turned to us and tipped his hat. "Thanks for your patronage. You two lovebirds have a nice day."

Sixteen

"THERE'S SOMETHING I have to tell you, Lucy," I said one morning as she and I were catching up on housework.

"What is it?" She closed the door of the dishwasher and stood up.

"I'm hanging out with Rad again."

She frowned. "Rad? Freddy hasn't seen him in ages. He kind of just dropped off the radar."

"He was busy, working on his book. You know my first feature? The author I had to interview?"

"Yeah. You were pretty vague about it when I asked you how it went."

"I know. That's because the author was Rad."

"What? I thought you said his name was Colorado."

"Rad *is* Colorado—that's his actual name."

It took Lucy a few moments to grasp that.

"Oh, I see," said Lucy slowly. "God, what a spinout!"

"His book is in the running for the Elliott Tate Award."

"Jesus Christ, that's huge! Audrey, this is big news. Why haven't you told me?"

"Well, I'm telling you now."

"Does Duck know?"

I shook my head. "I don't think he'll be that happy about it. He always had this thing against Rad."

"But you and Rad are just friends, right?"

"Of course we are." I looked down at my hands.

"Audrey?" She had a worried look on her face. "Is there more to this than what you're telling me?"

"No. Well, I don't know."

"What do you mean?"

I looked at her. "I have feelings for him, Lucy. I just—" I let out an exasperated sigh. "We've always had this connection, or whatever the hell it is. I don't know." I gave her a helpless look.

"Oh, Audrey," she said, giving my arm a quick squeeze. "I think if Rad is in your life again, he's there for a reason."

I nodded. "You know, it's like Duck and I have hardly anything to talk about. We need constant background noise—like a movie, or an activity, or friends, or something. Otherwise, we bore each other to death. Does that make sense?"

"It does."

"But when I'm with Rad, we have so much fun. We could be doing nothing at all—it doesn't matter. We laugh all the time, and he just gets me. Like how you get me, but this is a boy, and because of that, there's this whole other dimension."

"I know," said Lucy softly. "I love Freddy like that."

The word "love" hung in the air between us, like an ax.

"But how can I break it off with Duck?" I said, sadly. "We've been together since we were kids."

"Audrey, do you remember my lucky Chuck Taylors?"

"The bright orange ones?"

Lucy nodded.

"Oh God, yes. You wore them until they fell to pieces. Even then you refused to part with them."

"Everyone kept telling me I should throw them out."

"Your mother did throw them out at one point."

"She did. And I went through the trash bin and fished them out again."

I laughed. "You were obsessed with them."

"I was. If Candela hadn't tossed them into the river that day, I might still be wearing them now."

"I don't doubt it."

"Well, I think the point I'm trying to make is sometimes we get attached to things, just for the sake of it. Long after we've outgrown them. Do you know what I mean?" I knew she was referring to my relationship with Duck.

"Yeah," I said quietly.

"I know you love him, and he sure as hell loves you. But if you have feelings for Rad, you can't keep pushing them to one side. Even back when you first met, we all knew there was something between you two. I think Duck sensed it too."

"I know. I just don't want to hurt him."

"You can't go through your life without hurting people. That's unrealistic."

"Yeah, but this is me and Duck. We have so much history."

"I know, sweetie. It's part of my history too."

I looked at her. "He saved my life, Lucy. If it weren't for him, I wouldn't even be here."

She sighed. "He did a wonderful, noble thing, and do you know what you owe him for that?"

I shook my head. "What?"

"Your gratitude—that's all."

I felt like crying. "What if I'm making a huge mistake?"

"Then make it. You can't go on living a lie."

A FEW NIGHTS later, Rad sent me a text just past midnight.

You up?

Yes

Want to go for a drive?

Ok

I knew it was a bad idea. I was playing with fire. The right thing to do was to tell Duck I was seeing Rad again. It was wrong to sneak around behind his back, especially now that Lucy knew. It felt like my life had split into two paths and I was living both simultaneously, knowing that, eventually, they would have to collide.

I put on my jeans, grabbed my Audrey jacket and my house keys, and walked outside. "Hey," Rad said as I got into the car.

"Hi," I replied.

We were unusually quiet as we cruised the streets of Sydney. It wasn't until we were heading north over the Harbor Bridge that he broke the silence. "It's kind of weird, isn't it? How we are hanging out so often?" It was an innocent enough question, but I knew he was heading into dangerous territory, and I was frightened. My attachment to this strange new world was steadily growing. There was something addictive about it—that free, exhilarating exchange we shared.

"Yeah," I said quietly, hoping he would drop the subject. I wasn't prepared for what came next, though.

"Audrey." His voice was a little strained. "I've met someone." A wave of nausea hit me. I swallowed hard.

"That's great, Rad," I said, trying to steady the quiver in my voice. "I'm happy for you."

"Are you?" He glanced over at me. I felt a surge of anger, but I knew I had no right to feel the way I did. It was irrational. I had a boyfriend. Rad and I were just friends.

"Of course I am," I said tightly. "So who is she?"

"That's not important," he said.

"Then why haven't you mentioned her?" I tried to keep the bitterness from creeping into my voice. "If it's not important, why wouldn't she come up in conversation? Seems like a weird thing to leave out, since we've been talking every day—sometimes for hours." I knew I was making a fool of myself, but I couldn't stop. "What's her name? Where did you meet her?"

"Her name's Claire. I met her at a party. We've only been on a few dates, Audrey; it's not serious."

"It sounds pretty serious to me." I tried to picture Claire but saw Ana instead. I snapped my rubber band, then glanced at Rad, whose eyes were fixed on the road. I wanted to backtrack ten minutes and stay frozen in that pocket of time forever. It felt like I was waking from a dream, dragged against my will, back to reality.

"Well, you're free to see whomever you want," I said.

"Audrey, I like you. A lot. But you have a boyfriend, and we've been hanging out for weeks now. As far as I know, you haven't told him you've been spending time with me. I don't really get that." I felt tears well up behind my eyes. I turned my head away from him. The last thing I wanted was for him to see me cry. "What the fuck am I supposed to do?" he continued. "I don't know what I am to you."

"I don't, either," I blurted out. "I don't know what we are to each other. But whatever it is, I know I don't want to lose it."

"I don't, either," he said after a while. "I don't know what this is, but I like it."

"Me too."

Seventeen

It was a lazy Sunday morning, and Duck and I both had the day free. That was rare nowadays, with Duck's studies and newfound preoccupation with WYSA taking so much time. The weather was light and breezy as we strolled hand in hand down the main street of Paddington.

"What should we do today?" I asked.

"I don't know. They have those gondolas at Centennial Park; maybe we can catch one—get some ice cream as well."

"They are so cheesy," I said, with a laugh.

"Ice cream?" he teased.

"No, gondolas."

"They remind me of Venice." Duck's parents took him on a tour around Europe when he was nine.

"Venice," I sighed, my heart swelling up with the vision of an exotic, faraway place.

"I'll take you there for our honeymoon."

My stomach tightened. "Yeah," I said absently.

We were walking past a jewelry shop when he stopped suddenly, pulled my hand, and led me to the window.

"I need to get a new watch," he said, scanning the display. "What do you think of the blue Coach one?"

"It's nice, but the Rolex is more *you*."

"Like I can afford one."

"Well, you're going to be a hotshot lawyer one day. You'll have plenty of cash then."

"If I spend my money on anything, it will be on one of those." He pointed at a display of diamond rings farther up along.

I laughed. "Well, that's a long way off, isn't it?"

"Is it really?" He looked at me, his expression serious.

"Of course it is, Duck. We're way too young."

"You used to say how you couldn't wait to turn eighteen because then we could get married."

I sighed. "I was a kid, Duck. Seriously."

"Why are you acting like this?" He looked hurt.

"What do you mean? Like what?"

"Just—I don't know. You seem distant lately, and I can't work out why."

I drew in a deep breath. I didn't realize he had noticed anything was different about me. But now that he had brought it up, I knew I could no longer keep Rad a secret. This was the moment to tell him the truth. My heart was drumming loudly in my chest. I swallowed.

"Duck—" I began.

"Look—" he said at the same time. "Sorry, what were you going to say?"

"It's fine; you go first."

He sighed. "I know we haven't been spending a lot of time together lately, and that's mostly been my fault. I suppose I've been caught up with my studies and getting ahead. I'm just working toward the future, our future."

"I've been working hard too."

"Well, your work is different from mine."

"Why is it any different?"

He looked away, and I realized what he was implying.

"God. You think my career is less important than yours, don't you?"

"That's not what I meant."

"What did you mean?"

"Forget it," he said, with a sigh. "I just have this whole plan in my head, you know. And you're part of it. You always have been."

"Having babies and scrubbing the floor—is that your vision for me?"

"You make it sound so awful. You love kids; you've always wanted them. What the hell has changed?"

"I think this is a conversation we should be having ten years from now."

"Fine. Whatever."

"Look, this is the first weekend you've had free for ages. I don't want to spend it fighting with you."

"Don't do that, Audrey,"

"Do what?"

"What you're doing. It's emotional blackmail."

"Emotional blackmail? Are you kidding me?"

He was quiet, and he seemed to be thinking things over. His expression softened.

"I was looking forward to spending the weekend with you," he said after a while. "I'm sorry; I don't want to fight either."

"It's okay. You've been busy. I'm not going to hold that against you."

He smiled. "I just—well, I really miss you. Lately, you're almost like a stranger." He took my hand and pulled me to him.

"I'm still the same person."

"I know, and I'm proud of you. Okay? Don't ever doubt that."

I nodded. "Okay."

"No more arguments today." He smiled. "Deal?"

I put my head down on his shoulder. There was a dull ache in my chest. "Deal," I said.

Eighteen

I SENT RAD an e-mail with my article about him attached before it was due to go to print. A few moments later, my phone rang. "Shit," I swore, digging through piles of paper and other office junk to find it. "Hi?"

"Hello!" It was Rad. "Nice article. Especially the reference to my boyish good looks."

"That was Sam's idea. I think she has a crush on you."

"Who can blame her?"

I laughed. "Did you read the bit where I mention how modest you are?"

"I haven't got to that part yet." He was quiet for a moment. "Hey, did I really say that?"

"Say what?"

"'An author's first novel is always, at least in part, an autobiography.'" He was quoting a line from my article, word for word.

"You did say that. I have a recording of it."

"Wow, that's profound." He sounded pleased with himself, and I couldn't help but smile.

"That's the reason why it got the extra attention."

"Yes, the red type really jumps out against all that other stuff I said."

"Not to mention the bump up in font size."

"And the generous application of semi-bold."

We laughed.

"Hey, are you doing anything right now?" he asked suddenly.

"I just got into work."

"Can you take the day off?"

"Uh," I said chewing the end of my pen and surveying the office. It was abuzz with activity, but since it was Friday, I knew it would slow down toward the afternoon. "I have to finish up an article, but I can probably slip out just after lunch. Why?"

"I have a surprise for you."

"You know I hate surprises."

"I think you might like this one."

I STOOD ON the sidewalk outside the office scanning for Rad's car when a pastel-pink Cadillac—top down—pulled up beside me.

"Hi," said Rad, looking up at me from the driver's seat.

"Hi." I looked down the length of the car. "Something seems different about you today, Rad."

He laughed and pushed open the passenger door. I slid into the seat beside him. It was a beautiful day. The air felt electric, like anything could happen.

"So what's with the car?"

"Just doing a favor for my dad's friend. He asked if I could drive his new Cadillac up to his house in the Northern Beaches. Want to tag along?"

"Sure—why not?" I put my seat belt on. "We'll be back in time for dinner, right?" Duck was coming over for dinner that night, and I had planned to tell him I was hanging out with Rad again, before my article went to print. I wasn't looking forward to his reaction, but I was sure he'd come around eventually. After all, Rad and I were just friends.

"Yeah, we can be back by dinner," said Rad.

"How are we getting back, by the way?"

"There's a rental car waiting for us at the other end."

"Perfect."

I ENJOYED OUR conversation as we sped away from the city and through the streets of suburbia. I had never felt more alive, with the wind rushing through my hair and Duran Duran blaring on the stereo. "What's this radio channel?" I called over the music.

"It's a cassette. This car comes with a tape deck. There are stacks of them in the glove compartment."

I pulled the latch, and, sure enough, there was a small collection of cassette tapes scattered inside.

"They're '80s tracks," I said, delighted.

"I thought you'd like them. They were thrown in with the car. Dad's friend is crazy about the music of that era."

"I don't blame him."

"Neither do I."

"It's been ages since I've seen one of these." I held the cassette tape in my hand like it was a holy relic. "Look at this compilation: the Bangles, Tears for Fears, Talking Heads."

"Great mix!" Rad agreed.

I ruffled through the collection and picked out another tape.

"Oh my God. *Dazzle Ships*! I loved this when I was a kid."

"By OMD?"

"Uh-huh. Can I put it on?"

"Sure."

I fiddled around with the buttons on the dash and got the deck to spit out Duran Duran. I put it back carefully in its casing and popped in *Dazzle Ships*.

The sounds of orchestral trumpets rang through the cackling speakers in what sounded like the lead-up to a radio broadcast. Then a man said something in Czech before the track broke into an upbeat melody. I began bopping to the music, and Rad joined me as best as he could.

"Do you know this album basically killed them? OMD, I mean," I said.

"I read something about that. It was the follow-up to *Architecture & Morality*, which was a huge commercial hit. Then they released *Dazzle Ships*, and it bombed. It's such a shame. I've always thought it was underrated."

"I suppose it was just ahead of its time. Now the album is getting the acclaim that it didn't back then. It's like when *Blade Runner* first came out: half the critics didn't like it, but now it's a classic. Isn't that weird? You can create something that is pure genius, but you have to get your timing right. I always thought that was so unfair," I said.

"Especially if you don't live to see the applause. Like van Gogh."

"That would be tragic. He died a failure, and look how revered his work is now, over a hundred years later."

Rad shook his head. "Crazy, huh?"

WE HAD ALMOST reached our destination when Rad suggested we take a short detour.

"Isn't your dad's friend expecting you?" I asked.

"It's cool. I'll just send him a text."

Moments later, Rad pulled over outside a quaint-looking general store with a wraparound porch and a grandfather clock by the entrance.

"So this is what you wanted to show me?" I teased.

"No, Audrey," he said wryly. "I just thought we should pick up a few supplies."

We got out of the Cadillac and walked up the steps and through the entrance. A blonde woman with her hair in a bun and wearing a blue sweater over khaki slacks was sitting at the counter, engrossed in a crossword puzzle. She looked up at us with a nod of acknowledgment and went back to her puzzle.

We walked along the aisles past imported biscuits, raspberry licorice in old-fashioned packaging, and tiny jars of artisan honey. As we browsed the shelves, I wondered what Rad had planned. I felt a flicker of excitement, and I let my imagination run wild. Then I immediately felt guilty because a majority of the scenarios I imagined were X-rated. I bit my lip and tried to get my mind out of the gutter.

We walked by a section of fresh fruit and picked up some grapes and mandarins. We added a couple of bags of Kettle chips and Diet Cokes and put them on the counter. The lady looked up at us and smiled.

"Will that be all?" she asked, as she tallied up our purchase.

Rad nodded. "That's all, thanks."

WE ARRIVED IN the small seaside town of Newport and drove for a short time through the hilly streets, the ocean slipping in and out of view.

Rad slowed and turned into the drive of a charming cottage painted a muted turquoise with gray-and-white striped awnings over the windows.

"What an adorable house," I said.

"It's my dad's place. We used to come here all the time before he and Mum split up."

The inside was quaint and cozy, decorated with conch shells and antique oil lamps, wall hangings of old maps, and nautical paraphernalia. In the center of the room was an overstuffed couch with candy-striped pink-and-red cushions that faced an old stone fireplace. Toward the back, there was a tiny kitchenette and an alcove with a small bedroom. Rad threw open the bifold doors to reveal a large wooden deck and a jetty, with the sea stretching out into the horizon.

"It's beautiful," I said, looking out at the view. Suddenly, I got an overwhelming sense that everything was going to be okay. Tonight I would tell Duck about Rad, and he would be fine with it. Then I would be able to see Rad anytime I wanted without feeling guilty.

"Dad and I used to fish off that jetty. We caught a bluefin once. It was huge." He smiled at the memory.

"So does this place just sit empty now?"

"It's mostly rented out as a holiday house, but it's pretty quiet this time of year. Dad comes up with my stepmother whenever they can."

"I don't blame them—I would live here if I could."

We were putting our supplies away in the fridge when Rad pulled out an unopened bottle of rosé.

"Do you want a glass?"

"Are you having any?"

"I shouldn't," he said, shaking his head. "But no reason why you can't."

"Sure."

He rummaged through the cabinets and found a wineglass.

"Are you hungry?"

"A little," I said.

He opened up the freezer. "There are some frozen pizzas in here. I can put one in the oven."

"Sounds good."

"Pepperoni was your favorite, right?"

I smiled, touched that he remembered. "Yeah."

THE DAY SEEMED to slip away as we nibbled on our makeshift banquet set up on the small wooden table that overlooked the sea. The sky was a perfect blue as we watched the seagulls glide through the cool breeze while the sun dived in and out of the thin, translucent clouds.

"I bet the sunsets here are amazing," I said with a sigh.

"They are. It's a shame we have to leave soon. Looks like it will be a stunning one."

"I can imagine." I smiled and took another sip of my rosé.

"This is also the perfect spot for stargazing. You can almost see the outline of the Milky Way."

"I bet it would be magical."

Rad turned to me. "Well, why don't we stay? I can always drop the car off tomorrow morning."

"Your dad's friend won't mind?"

"Not at all."

I thought about it. I did have dinner plans with Duck, and I wanted to tell him about Rad, but there was no reason why I couldn't do it on Saturday night instead. I could always text him with an excuse. The truth was I would rather hang out here with Rad.

"Yeah, what the hell," I shrugged. "Why don't we stay?"

"Great. Well, in that case, I'm going to pour myself a glass of wine."

THE BOTTLE OF rosé was almost empty when the sun began its slow descent.

"Do you want the rest?" Rad asked, his hand on the bottle.

"Are you trying to get me drunk?" I teased.

"I thought you already were. I know I am."

He poured the rest into my glass, then he got up and positioned his chair so it was next to mine. We were quiet as we watched the sky transition from pink to gold to orange in a stunning interplay of color and light.

"You weren't kidding about the sunsets, were you?" I said, downing the last of the rosé.

"No."

"God, it's so beautiful."

"I'm glad I brought you here. This place has always been special to me. It reminds me of a time in my life when things were less complicated."

"How old were you when your parents split up?"

"I was fourteen. Mum moved away, so I chose to live with Dad. A few years later, he met Sophia, my stepmother. She's great."

"So the two of you get on?"

"Yeah. She's a belly dancer."

"No kidding!" I had never known anyone with that job title before. I imagined it would be a great topic of conversation at a dinner party.

"She performs with a band. They do the odd birthday or office party. She's really good."

"That's so cool."

"It is. I'm just glad Dad's happy."

"Mum cheated on Dad when I was a kid."

"She did?"

"Yeah," I said, thinking back to that dark period. "She always wanted to be an actor, and I get the feeling I came along and took her off that trajectory. When I was about eleven, she ran off with some hotshot producer who promised her the world. Dad and I never saw it coming. One day she was there, acting her normal self, then the next she was gone."

"God, how awful."

"She called us up the day after she disappeared and said she wasn't coming back. Just like that. She sounded so cold on the phone—like a stranger. Then a few months later, she turned up crying on our doorstep, and my dad took her back. But it was never the same. It was like something vital was missing. It didn't feel like we were a family anymore—we were just going through the motions."

"That must have been so hard."

"Yeah."

"I knew my parents were having problems, but it was still a shock when they split up."

"Was there someone else in the picture?" I asked.

"No, I don't think so. I suppose they just grew apart. My mum was probably in a similar situation to yours—she wanted more."

"Did she ever get to do that road trip?"

Rad shook his head. "Strangely enough, no. It's not like there was anything to stop her. She had the freedom and the means to do it. But she moved back to the small town in New Zealand where she grew up. Now she lives with her partner, Miriam, and their brood of horses."

"Do you visit her often?"

"I used to spend my school holidays there, but it's been awhile now. We talk on the phone regularly, though."

"That's nice."

"I think I resented her for leaving, but in hindsight, it was the right thing for her to do. I mean, the alternative would have been worse. I think if my parents had stayed together purely for my sake, the bitterness would have eaten away at them."

"I think that's where my parents are. They're together, but I don't think they're happy. I know Mum definitely isn't."

"Relationships are weird like that. Most people I know are together out of habit more than anything else. I don't know many couples who are truly happy."

"Other than Lucy and Freddy, of course."

"Lucy and Freddy are an anomaly." He smiled.

The light was fading fast now, and soon the sky was a different kind of beautiful.

"It's not even completely dark yet, and you can already see the stars," I said.

A small gust of wind came from nowhere, and I shivered a little.

"Are you cold?" Rad asked. "Do you want to go back inside?"

"No, let's stay out here awhile longer. It's so pretty."

He put his arm around my shoulder and pulled me into him. I tucked my head into his neck. His skin was warm and inviting. He brushed my hair away from my face, tucking a lock of it behind my ear before placing a tentative kiss on my cheek. I turned toward him, so our faces were only inches apart. "Oh, what the hell," he said under his breath. And then he kissed me full on the mouth, long and hard. I had read about kisses like this in books. On many nights I had seen them flicker across the TV screen as I watched with detached fascination. But it had never felt this way with Duck. I didn't know it could be like this.

I let out a sigh when our lips finally parted.

"Holy shit," Rad breathed. "I can't believe I just did that."

I couldn't believe it either. It was better than anything I could have imagined.

"Do it again," I said.

AGAINST MY BETTER judgment, we stumbled inside, making our way through the alcove and falling onto the bed. Rad wrapped his arms around me and pressed his body into mine. When he kissed me again, I felt like all the bones in my body had liquefied.

"God, Audrey—" He sank his teeth gently into my shoulder, and I felt a violent jolt somewhere below my abdomen.

"Rad," I murmured, pulling him closer to me.

He tugged at my sweater, pulling it up over my head and kissing his way slowly down my neck. I reached behind my back and fumbled with the clasp of my bra, pulling it free.

"Wow," said Rad, his eyes pinned to my chest.

"Thanks," I laughed.

As his hands traveled down my body, I was suddenly aware of every cell and synapse, every electrical current that sparked between them. Every touch, every caress, sent a shiver down my spine. Soon, his hands had found their way to the top button of my jeans when Duck flashed into my mind without warning.

"Rad . . ." I said softly. "Hey, I think we should stop."

There was a pause.

"Okay," he said, letting out a deep breath. He pulled away from me gently, lying down flat on his back. I propped myself up on my elbow and kissed him softly on the mouth. "It's not that I don't want to, because I really, *really* do."

"I know. But your boyfriend—"

"Yeah, and I don't think either of us is thinking straight at the moment. I don't want to regret this tomorrow."

"It's okay—this isn't the way I want us to start either."

I loved the way he said "us." How strange that, all of a sudden, one little word could make me so certain of my true place in the world.

"What about Claire, the girl you were seeing?" I searched his face. He hadn't mentioned her since that night, and I never asked.

He shook his head. "It didn't work out."

"No?" I tried not to look too pleased. "Why?"

Rad reached up and stroked my hair. "She wasn't you."

We kissed again, and my body gravitated toward his like one of those rides at the fun fair where you're spinning so fast that the motion pins you to the wall.

After a while, I pulled away from him reluctantly, and he let out another deep breath.

"Are you okay?" I asked him.

"Barely," he winced.

"Is it hurting you?" I teased, my hand resting at the top of his thigh.

"Shut up," he said, his hand reaching for mine. "I can't stop thinking about all the things I want to do to you. So just give me a minute."

"I can always give you a Lexy Robbins." I put my head down on the pillow and laced his fingers through mine.

"A what?" he laughed.

"Lexy Robbins is a girl I went to school with. She was always preaching to us about her virginity. But apparently, she wasn't so precious when it came to dealing out hand jobs."

He laughed again, pressing his face into my hair. "You're such an idiot."

We were quiet for a few minutes.

"I'm going to end it with Duck. I want to be with you."

"Don't say his name. It drives me insane when you do."

"I'm sorry."

My hand was still in his. "I just want you all to myself. I can't help that."

I squeezed his hand. "Me too."

We lay there for a few moments, and he turned to face me.

"Hey," he said. "I have a confession to make."

"What is it?"

"Do you know that day we went to the trails and you fell off the horse?"

I grimaced. "Don't remind me."

He smiled. "When you were sitting on the sand looking up at me, that's when I felt it."

"What?"

"This," he said, his hand running down the side of my waist. "I had this insane urge to kiss you."

He pulled me into him, his mouth closing over mine. "I also wanted other things," he murmured.

"Like?"

His hand rested on my hips, and his eyes looked into mine. "I wanted to go down on you."

I drew in a deep breath. "Oh—"

"But I also wanted to hold you, tell you stupid jokes, and make you cups of tea. I just got this flash of a life with you, of the two of us together."

"I want the same things with you. That night at Blues Point, when we agreed to stop seeing each other—that was really hard for me."

"It feels so long ago," said Rad, his expression wistful.

"I thought about you a lot during that time. I didn't know if I'd ever see you again, but you were always on my mind."

"I thought about you too. I would see something funny or cool and think, 'Audrey would love this.'"

"It's weird how we met up again, don't you think? Especially the way it happened."

"It almost feels predetermined." He reached over and took my hand again. "There's so much I want to do with you."

"We'll do everything you want."

"Promise me?"

I nodded. "Cross my heart."

I WOKE UP the next morning with a head full of screeching bats. My tongue felt like a desert, and my legs were two pillars of wet cement. I struggled to open my eyes as the events of the night before came back to me in flashes.

I sat up slowly in bed, wincing from the effort, and looked around the room. It was empty. "Rad?" I called tentatively, but there was no answer. Then I noticed a note on the side table.

Hey,
I was up early and didn't want to wake you. I've gone to
swap over the car. Be back soon.

I sank back into bed, the note clutched in my hand. A smile spread across my face as I thought of Rad and the things he said, the things we did. Then suddenly I remembered that I had forgotten to text Duck last night.

"Shit," I said, getting up and throwing off the sheets. I padded across the rustic wood floors in search of my satchel. I found it on the couch and ruffled through it, looking for my phone. I fished it out and looked at it with a sinking feeling. The battery was dead.

I heard a key in the door, and Rad appeared with a paper bag in his hand.

"Good morning," he smiled, then frowned when he caught my expression. "Everything okay?"

"I forgot to text Duck last night to cancel our dinner plans. Now my phone is dead."

"Oh—want to use mine?"

I shook my head. "I don't think that's a good idea."

All of a sudden, I was overcome with guilt. I put the phone back in my satchel and sat down on the couch.

"God, my head's killing me," I said, wincing.

Rad put the paper bag on the kitchen counter and ruffled through the drawers.

"There are some aspirins here; want one?"

I nodded as he went to fill up a glass of water.

"I got some bagels while I was out. Are you hungry?"

"I'm sorry, Rad," I said, looking up at him. "I think I should get back home."

"Okay, we can leave right now."

THERE WAS A gray rental car in the driveway where the pink Cadillac was parked the previous day. This stark change brought me firmly back down to reality.

Rad and I barely said a word to each other until we got to the main freeway.

"Look, Audrey, about last night—"

"It's fine," I said, my hand nervously tracing my rubber band.

"We had too much to drink, and we got carried away. I shouldn't have let it happen. I'm sorry."

"It's not your fault; I was part of it too. The truth is I don't regret what happened between us. I wanted it to happen, but at the same time, I just feel like an asshole about it."

"You're not an asshole," Rad said. "And besides," he looked at me, "we didn't . . . you know."

I smirked. "You turned down my Lexy Robbins offer."

"I'll take a rain check on that."

We were quiet as "Karma Police" played on the radio.

"I'm not going to pressure you, Audrey. This is something you have to figure out in your own time. But I don't think we should see each other anymore until you do."

"I know. It's getting too complicated."

He nodded. "I don't want to be the guy who is messing around with someone else's girlfriend. And, to be honest, I don't think I can keep holding back when I'm around you—not anymore."

"Me too." The thought of not seeing him made my stomach drop. Yet I knew it was the right thing to do. I had to end things with Duck before I could even consider a future with Rad.

RAD DROPPED ME off at a cul-de-sac just minutes away from my house.

"So I guess this is goodbye, then."

"For now."

He looked over at me. "God, I really want to kiss you."

"Me too."

"Will you call me when you're a free agent?"

I nodded. "Yeah, it might be a while, though."

"Take as much time as you need, Audrey. I'm not going anywhere."

As I TURNED the corner onto my street, my heart began pounding wildly. I wondered why I was so anxious as I made my way, key in hand, toward the house. When I got to the gate, I saw Duck, sitting on the steps leading up to the door. He looked up at me, eyes red and bloodshot, his hair disheveled. "Where the fuck have you been?" he said, standing up. I could feel the blood pounding in my ears. My mouth went dry.

"I was with a friend."

"A friend?" He looked incredulous. "And you didn't call me? For the whole night? Do you have any idea how worried I was? Even Lucy didn't know where the hell you were."

"I'm sorry; it was a spur-of-the-moment thing, and my phone died," I said in a rush.

"Who is this friend you were with?"

I looked down.

"Audrey? What is going on?"

"We should talk inside, Duck," I said quietly, pushing past him and sticking my key into the door. He followed me into the house.

"Okay, we're inside now," he said impatiently. "Can you tell me what the hell is going on? You're acting weird, and it's freaking me out."

I turned to face him.

"God, Audrey," he said, as if seeing me for the first time. "You look awful."

"I'm just hungover," I said truthfully.

"Do you want a glass of water?"

"No, I'm okay." I felt like the worst person in the world.

"I'll get you one." He grabbed a glass from the kitchen cabinet and filled it at the tap. "Audrey, why aren't you telling me what happened? Where were you?"

I took a deep breath. I had to tell him the truth. I owed him that, especially after what happened last night.

"I was with Rad."

The color seemed to drain from his face.

"Rad? You were with *Rad*? But I thought you'd stopped speaking to him," Duck said slowly.

"I did, but about a month ago, I had to interview him for a book he wrote—"

"He wrote a book?"

"Yeah, he was my first feature."

"And you never bothered to tell me this?"

I remained quiet.

"So you've been seeing him since then? Behind my back?"

I nodded again.

"Where did you see him? How many times did this happen?" He was getting angry now.

I bit my lip and turned away.

"You're fucking him, aren't you?" he spat.

"No!" I said, my head snapping back to face him.

"So nothing has happened between you? Nothing at all?"

I looked down at my feet, then shook my head slowly. "No."

"I don't believe you."

"It doesn't matter, anyway."

His mouth opened in astonishment. "What do you mean it doesn't matter? What the hell is wrong with you? Audrey, look at me!" He was still holding the glass, and it shook in his hand, the water spilling over the rim onto the cherrywood floorboards below. I concentrated on that sad pool of water. I couldn't bring myself to look at him. Tears welled up in my eyes.

"How far did it go? Did you kiss him? Did he touch you?"

I began sobbing quietly, holding my face in my hands. I didn't answer him, but we both knew my silence was an admission of guilt.

"Fuck!" He ran his hand through his hair. "Fuck, fuck, fuck. I'm going to kill him."

"It's not his fault."

He looked at me, livid. "So he didn't know we were still together?"

"Well, yeah, he did—"

"Audrey!" Duck yelled. "How the fuck can you stand there and defend him?"

"I'm not defending him!"

"*Yes, you are!*" His face twisted into an expression of rage, and with one smooth motion, he hurled the glass of water at the wall behind us. It crashed and splintered, spraying glass across the room.

"What are you doing?" I screamed, backing away from him.

His eyes were wild, and he was breathing hard. We stood facing each other, unsure of where to go next. We had never been here before.

After what seemed like an eternity, his expression changed from fury to despair.

"I don't know who the hell you are anymore."

I felt all the adrenalin leave my body in a rush. "Maybe you never did in the first place."

"Don't say that, Audrey."

After a few moments, he went back to the kitchen and pulled out a dustpan and broom from the cupboard. Without saying a word, he began sweeping up the broken glass.

I walked over to him, my vision blurred with tears. "Duck, don't," I sobbed, putting my hand on his shoulder. "Leave it."

He turned to face me. There were tears in his eyes now too. "This is it, isn't it? We're breaking up."

I nodded.

"But—you and me, we're meant to be rock solid, right? I always thought if nothing else worked out in my life, I'd still have you."

"I'm so sorry," I whispered.

"Oh God," he said, his voice choked up with tears. "Oh God."

He let go of the broom and pulled me into his arms. "I love you," he whispered, into my ear. "I can't remember a time when I didn't." He pulled away from me gently and took my hand in his, running his thumb over my ring finger. "You know, I've always wondered about your ring size."

I completely broke down then, sobbing and clutching at his shirt. My heart was clenching like a fist in my chest. I had no idea it would hurt this much. My mind went back through the years like a person dying. I thought of Duck waving to me from his deck, summers at his parents' lake house, jumping into the water from the pier, our laughter ringing through the air. Sitting for hours on the lawn, the sun on our faces. Chasing the ice cream truck down our street. The first time we made love, when I was so certain this was the person I would spend my whole life with. I looked back on all of that with new tenderness as it was disintegrating before me.

"I can't do this," Duck said, pulling away from me suddenly. "I've got to get out of here."

"Where are you going?"

"I don't know."

"Are you going to be okay?"

"How can you ask me that?" I could see the anger flash into his eyes again.

"I'm sorry."

He shook his head. "I wish I could hate you right now; I really do."

"Duck—" I said, reaching out for him.

"Don't." He brushed my hand away roughly and pushed past me. Moments later, the house shook with the sound of the door slamming.

LUCY CAME HOME later to find me balled up on the couch.

"Audrey," she said, approaching me tentatively, "are you okay?"

I looked up at her, my eyes aching from the effort.

"Duck and I broke up."

"Oh, sweetie," she said, sitting down beside me. She pulled me into her arms, and I cried softly against her shoulder.

"Is Duck okay?"

"No."

"Poor Duck."

I put my head into her lap and lay there, feeling almost catatonic. "I didn't know it could hurt this much. Honestly, I didn't."

Lucy stroked my hair. "Do you want me to do anything? I can get Freddy to check on Duck."

"Okay, thanks, Lucy."

My phone had been charging on the coffee table, and now it rang suddenly. I reached for it quickly, hoping it was Duck. My heart dropped when my mother's name came up on the screen.

"Shit, this is the last thing I need."

I let the phone ring out, but later it started up again. I sighed and picked it up.

"Hi, Mum."

"What the hell is happening, Audrey? I just got off the phone with Zoe. She said you and Duck just broke up. Is that true?"

I winced at the shrillness of her voice.

"And what's this about Rad coming back on the scene? How can you do this to Duck, Audrey?" I could tell she was gritting her teeth. "I did *not* raise my daughter to sleep around."

"I haven't slept with Rad," I said, angrily.

"Well, something must have happened between the two of you! What's the matter with you, Audrey? I knew it was a bad idea—you moving out."

It was unbearable. My nerves were already shot, and this was way too much. I felt ready to take it to DEFCON 1. "Mum,"

I said, "what makes you think you can judge me like this? At least I wasn't *married* to Duck. You know, like how you were *married* to Dad."

She fell silent, and I knew my accusation was like a slap in the face.

"How could you—"

I hung up the phone and switched it off, slamming it down onto the coffee table. "Hypocrite," I spat.

"Audrey, your mother cheated on your dad years ago. You can't keep punishing her for it."

I knew Lucy was right, and it made me feel even worse.

"You know what they say about the apple not falling far from the tree," I said bitterly.

"You didn't sleep with Rad, though, did you?"

"No, we only fooled around. I know that still doesn't make it right."

"Oh, Audrey, you should have told Duck earlier about Rad, before it got to that point."

"I know; I'm a shitty person."

"No, you're not. You're just human; that's all. We all make mistakes."

I looked at Lucy, the eternal optimist. "At least I don't ever have to break up with you," I said, with a wry smile.

She reached over and took my hand in hers. "No, you're stuck with me for life."

THE NEXT MORNING, I got a text from Duck.

Can we talk?

We met at our favorite café. I was relieved to see that he looked much better than yesterday and told him so.

"Thanks. You hungry?" he said.

"Not really." My stomach had been in knots ever since our breakup. Hard to believe it was only yesterday.

We got a coffee each, and I busied myself with tearing the sugar sachet, pouring it into my cup, and swirling it around with my spoon. I wasn't sure if I could meet his gaze without crying again.

"I'm really sorry about yesterday," Duck said after a while. "I didn't mean to lose my temper like that."

"It's okay; you had every right to be upset."

"Audrey, look at me, please." He reached out and took my hand.

I looked up at him. He gave me a sad smile. "It's not okay. I was out of line. It was just a shock; that's all."

"You've got nothing to be sorry for."

"Yes, I do. I've had some time to process it all, and it's starting to make sense to me. We've been growing apart for a long time now; I just didn't want to face it."

I nodded.

"Look; if I could click my fingers and have things go back to the way they were, I would do it in an instant. But I know that's not realistic. We've been together for so long maybe we need some time apart to figure out who we really are."

"Maybe."

"The truth is I want the world for you, Audrey. I want you to do all the things you ever wanted to do, without me there to stop you."

It was a complete one-eighty turnaround from yesterday. I expected him to be angry, to call me names or throw more accusations at me. God knows I deserved it. But he was acting so *reasonable,* so selfless. I knew I should have been glad, but something about his attitude was irking me.

"Is this you talking, Duck? Because it sounds like one of

your self-help books." I didn't mean for my words to come out so harshly, and for a moment he looked stung.

"This is me talking, Audrey. I mean everything that I've said."

"Okay, fine."

"What's the matter? I thought this is what you wanted."

"It is."

He smiled at me. "We can still be friends, can't we?"

"Of course we can, Duck."

Nineteen

"DID I EVER tell you that Rad has heterochromia?" I was bringing Ida up to speed about the last few weeks since my breakup with Duck as we sat facing each other across her desk.

"No, I don't think you've mentioned it."

"His eyes are so beautiful. One is a stormy gray, the other a summer blue. That's how tornadoes are formed, you know. When dark, brooding thunderclouds come into contact with sun-drenched skies."

Ida nodded. "Yes, that's exactly right."

"I feel like ever since he's come back into my life, everything has gone haywire. I'm wearing my rubber band again."

"I noticed." Her eyes glanced at my left wrist with the thin band of rubber peeking out from under the sleeve of my sweater.

"I feel anxious all the time, like everything is spinning out of control. But I can't seem to stay away."

"Are you still seeing him?"

"Not since that night we went up to Newport. But I think about him all the time, and that isn't right, is it? I've just broken up with Duck, whom I've been with since I was a kid. He has been nothing but wonderful to me, and all I can think about is Rad. I feel really shitty about that, but I can't help it."

Ida leaned back in her chair and sighed. "Our emotions pull us in different directions. The stronger the emotion, the greater the pull. Feelings are not always practical, nor do they make any logical sense. That's just the way it goes."

"I've been worried about Duck. He deleted his Facebook yesterday, and I haven't been able to get in touch with him since."

"Does he have someone to talk to?"

"His family is great, especially his mum. She's fantastic, and Freddy has been keeping him company over the last few days. But I think I should see him. I've been avoiding it because then I'd be obligated to see my mother too."

"I take it that she isn't happy with the breakup?"

"No. She was hysterical when she called me. I haven't spoken to her since either. Do you think I should go and see her?"

Ida nodded. "I think that might be a good idea."

AFTER I LEFT Ida's office, I caught the bus to Duck's place. I walked the familiar pathway up through the garden, a lump rising in my throat. Memories came to life around me like a ghostly matinee. Duck and I had spent so much time here, and I couldn't take a step without bumping into some fragment of our history.

"Oh, Audrey," said Zoe, when she came to the door. She opened her arms, and I fell into them. Suddenly, I was a little girl again with a scraped knee, craving the kind of comfort my mother did not know how to give. Tears fought their way through my shut eyelids and trickled down my cheeks.

"Come in, sweetie," she said. I walked into the hallway and noticed at once the empty space on the wall where that dreadful picture of Duck and I had hung.

"You took the picture down."

"I'm sorry," said Zoe, her hand rubbing gently at my back. "Duck took it down just yesterday."

"Can I have it?"

"Of course you can."

"Thank you." My voice was barely a whisper.

She led me down the hallway and into the neat, sunny lounge room. We sat down on her brown leather sofa.

"How is he?" I asked as she handed me a box of tissues. I took one and blew my nose.

"He's doing really well, actually, which is surprising. He's philosophical about it all." She reached over and took my hand, peering at me with a worried look on her face. "How are you, darling?"

I shrugged. "I'm okay, I guess. I'm more worried about Duck. I tried to call him today, but his phone is disconnected."

Zoe frowned. "It is?"

I nodded. "And he deleted his Facebook page too."

She sighed. "I'll have a talk with him. I'm sure he just needs some time to process everything. It must have been a shock."

"I know." I looked down at my hands. "Do you know where he is now?"

She shook her head. "He left early this morning, and he hasn't been back since."

"Oh."

She must have read the expression on my face because she put her hand on my arm and said, "He'll be okay, Audrey. He just needs time. You both do."

"I just wish—" I shook my head, and tears welled up in my eyes again.

"I know. But these things are bound to happen. You know, I was madly in love with someone once, and I was heartbroken when we broke up. But I'm glad it happened, because then I never would have met Duck's dad. Things have a way of working themselves out in the end."

"I guess you're right."

"Of course I am." She reached over and gave me a brief hug. She smoothed my hair away from my face and said, "You should go and see your mother. She's worried about you."

When I left Duck's place, I walked up the street to my mother's house. She was in the front yard, dressed in her gardening gear, tending to her roses.

"Hey, Mum," I said.

She looked up. "Audrey, what are you doing here?"

"I just went to see Zoe."

"I see." She went back to her roses.

"Mum," I said.

She stopped.

"I'm sorry I hung up on you and for what I said. It happened a long time ago, and I know it's wrong for me to keep bringing it up."

She stood up to face me, pruning shears in her hand. It looked like she had been crying. "I've never been good at playing the housewife, Audrey. Some of us aren't made that way. I love your dad. Not a day goes by where I'm not thankful for his patience and his forgiveness. But I'm a stranger in my own life. Do you understand?"

"I do."

"I'm scared for you, Audrey, now that you've chosen Rad over Duck. Every time I've followed my heart, it's turned out badly for me. When I met your dad, he swept me off my feet." A soft look came over her face. "I wanted to be a star. I was heading in that direction. But I fell madly in love with a boy, and I lost my head. I was seeing someone else at the time, someone I cared about, but I was still *myself*, Audrey. He didn't affect me the way your dad did. At the time, I couldn't see that the crazy, passionate love I had for your father would lead me here to this life—this slow death." She motioned around her. "Before I knew it, I was pregnant—at twenty-two!" She shook her head. "That's too young—not much older than you are now. This isn't easy for me to say. It's not that I didn't want you; I just wish it happened ten years later. I just wanted those ten years for myself, to find out how far I could have gone." She closed her eyes, as though it pained her to say these words to me. "I don't want you to lose that time—that precious, precious time. If you have to be with someone at all, then be with someone who makes you feel like you are still in control. Someone like Duck. Because sooner or later, all kinds of love—crazy love, wild love—fade into the same thing. The love becomes old and predictable—safe. So why not start there if that's where you'll end up?"

"Mum, I'm not you. I'm never going to be you. You don't have to worry."

She sighed, peeling off her gloves and tossing them on the ground. "Come with me, Audrey. There's something I want to show you."

I followed her into the house, up the stairs, and into the spare room where we kept our odds and ends. She walked over to the bureau in the far corner and pulled open the bottom drawer, crammed full of junk. Lifting out a black-and-white striped hat box, she put it on top of my old writing desk and took out the contents. There were pictures of young couples, radiant and glowing, basking in the sun. My mother picked up one of the photos and handed it to me. A boy in a leather jacket with a cigarette dangling from his mouth stared at me with dark, brooding eyes.

"Who's that, Mum?" I asked, thinking it must have been an old friend or ex-boyfriend.

"That's your dad, Audrey."

My mouth fell open. "That's Dad?"

She nodded. "He was going to be a writer. Did you know that?"

"No," I said, shaking my head slowly. As far as I knew, my dad worked in an office. I never thought he had aspirations to do anything else. I guess that was ignorant of me.

"You should have seen him back then," she said, looking down at the photo. Her eyes were dreamy again. I wondered when she had stopped looking at him like that. "I would have done anything for him. Hell, I would have followed him right off a cliff. That's what boys can do, Audrey; that's the power they can wield over you. It's like being under a spell."

If she was right, it was already too late. I felt that for Rad, that mysterious pull. I had from the moment my eyes fell into his. I couldn't stop it any more than she could all those years ago.

"But you can break the spell, Audrey, before it takes you over completely," she said, as if reading my mind. "I am standing here now, where you will be some day, and I don't want you to have the same regrets that I do. I don't want you throwing your potential away on some boy. I made that mistake—I squandered my youth and my talent—but you don't have to. It's not too late for you." Her eyes were so sad, so desperate. I wanted to tell her not to worry, that Rad was different and everything would work out fine.

"I won't let it happen to me, Mum. I'll be careful; I promise."

"Oh, Audrey, it's already happened. I saw it that night at Ana's funeral. The way you looked at Rad. I saw myself all over again. I'm not stupid. I know what I'm up against trying to convince you. But I'm on your side, even if it seems that I'm the enemy." Her voice broke. "I'm your mother, Audrey, and I'm on your side."

LATER THAT NIGHT, Lucy and I were awakened by the sound of screeching tires, followed by a blaring horn. I raced to the front window with Lucy following closely behind. We peeked out from behind the curtains. "Oh shit," said Lucy. "It's Duck." He was standing in the street outside, with a half-empty bottle of Jack Daniels in his hand.

"Audrey!" he screamed as he began ranting away in a torrent of verbal abuse while shouting my name repeatedly, at the top of his lungs. I could see lights down our street coming on as neighbors woke up to the commotion.

"I have to go out and speak to him," I said, stepping away from the window.

"No. No way, Audrey, stay in here. I'm calling the police."

"But Lucy," I said dumbly, "it's Duck."

She grabbed my shoulders and looked me in the eye. "Audrey, I'm not letting you go outside. Stay here." She disappeared into her bedroom and came back moments later with her phone in her hand. She was about to dial when I stopped her.

"Lucy, someone has already called the cops," I said, as a police vehicle came down our street, lights flashing. They parked near Duck's car, and two officers got out. He turned to face them, his stance aggressive. One officer tried to reason quietly with him, but it only made him more hysterical. The other one reacted swiftly, grabbing the bottle from Duck's hand and pinning his arms behind his back. After a short struggle, he managed to break away and ran toward our window, where

Lucy and I stood watching the nightmare unfold. He stood there, eyes wild and animal-like, looking straight into mine. "Oh God, what is he doing?" said Lucy as he lifted up his shirt. To our horror, we saw deep red cuts all across his bare chest.

"This is what you did to me, Audrey! Do you hear me, Audrey? I should have left you at the bottom of that lake, you fucking bitch!" he screamed, his voice coarse and broken. At that moment, the two officers pounced on Duck, and he was wrestled to the ground and handcuffed.

Once he was bundled into the back of the police car, one of the officers knocked on the front door. I opened it. "Do you know that man?" he asked.

"He was my boyfriend. We just broke up."

"Has he hurt you in any way?"

I shook my head. "No, never."

NEXT MORNING, LUCY and I were sitting at our kitchen table after being up all night. "I don't think I'm going to any of my classes today," she said, glancing at the clock.

"I'm going to skip work too," I said miserably, taking a sip of my tea.

Lucy's eyes were red from crying, and she had dark rings of fatigue under her eyes. "I still can't believe that was Duck out there last night." She shook her head. "How could he do that to you?"

"It's not his fault—it's mine."

She gave me an incredulous look. "Audrey, do you have any idea how crazy that sounds? People get dumped all the time, and it sucks, but you know what you do? You cry; you smash a few plates; you go to a karaoke bar and make a fool of yourself. However you choose to deal with it, it's *your* shit to handle. It's *your* burden to carry. You don't drag other people down with you. You don't turn up on the doorstep in the middle of the night acting like a raving lunatic."

I began crying again, holding my head in my hands. "I shouldn't have disappeared like that last week."

"It was a shitty thing for you to do; I won't deny it. I would have been livid if Freddy had done the same to me. But it still doesn't justify Duck's behavior last night. He had every right to be angry, but not like that."

"What if he comes back again?"

"I don't know."

There was a knock at the door. Lucy and I looked at each other, and we cautiously went to the front door. "It's Duck's mum," said Lucy, peeking through the front curtain. We opened the door.

"Hi, Zoe," I said.

"Audrey, Lucy, can I come in?"

I nodded and closed the door as we headed to the kitchen.

"Want a coffee?" asked Lucy.

"No, thanks, it looks like you girls have been up all night. Why don't you have a seat? I'll make you both coffee." She busied herself in the kitchen, and Lucy and I sat back down. Zoe set our coffee on the kitchen table, then sat down across from me. She reached out and took my hand. "I'm sorry about last night, Audrey," she said with a frown. Tears began welling up in my eyes again. She gave my hand a squeeze. "Now, I don't want you blaming yourself in any way, you hear. Duck knows full well he was in the wrong."

"Zoe's right, Audrey." Lucy handed me a box of tissues. "It's not your fault."

I nodded, tears streaming down my cheeks.

"I should have been paying more attention," said Zoe. "I thought he was fine, but I guess I was way off the mark."

"He knows how much I still care about him, doesn't he?"

"Of course he does, Audrey. The two of you go way back. That's something that never goes away."

My lips trembled, and fresh tears spilled down. "No," I whispered. "Never."

She smiled at me. "I'm sure you'll be the best of friends again—in time."

"I hope so," I said as Lucy put her arm around my shoulder.

"Now, I had a trip planned to see Duck's grandma in Europe," said Zoe. "I'm going to take Duck with me too. The change in scenery will do him good."

"When are you leaving?"

"Next week and we'll be away for a while, so it will give you both some breathing space."

"Okay," I said softly. "Please take care of him."

"You know I will." She reached over and squeezed my arm. "Now—I have a million things to do before the trip, so I'd better get going." She got up, slinging her handbag over her shoulder. "You girls take care."

Twenty

ALTHOUGH A GOOD amount of time had passed since Duck and I broke up, Rad and I had agreed to take things one day at a time. So this was my first visit to Rad's apartment, and I was browsing through the books on his shelf. His place was tiny but cozy. It looked exactly how I had pictured it—messy in a way that was inviting—and I could see myself padding around in my pajamas with a cereal bowl in hand. Best of all, it was three floors above a French-style café, and the delicious smell of freshly baked croissants occasionally wafted in from the open window.

"Hey, I remember these," I said, spying a *Choose Your Own Adventure* book among a sea of science fiction titles and tattered paperbacks. I picked it up, running my fingers across the cover. "*Inside UFO 54-40*. Is this one any good?"

"Well, it's a strange book," said Rad. "Like, the goal is to get to Ultima—it's meant to be some kind of paradise, a nirvana or whatever. When I read it as a kid, I couldn't get to Ultima no matter what choices I made throughout the book. But it was right there, in front of me." He took the book from me and flipped through until he found the page he was looking for. "That's Ultima." There was an illustration of a futuristic cityscape surrounded by mountain greenery and piercing rays of sunlight.

"Why couldn't you get there?" I asked.

"That's what I was trying to work out as a kid. I got so obsessed that my mother had to take the book away from me at one point. Years later, I came across a thread about it on a forum. As it turns out, I wasn't the only one who couldn't get to Ultima. I followed a link someone posted to a wiki and learned there is actually no legitimate way to get to there. The author was a sadist."

"What a cruel thing to do to children."

"Tell me about it." Rad closed the book and passed it to me. "You can give it a try if you want."

"No, thanks, I'm not really into sadomasochism."

"You're not? Well, that's definitely a deal-breaker for me."

I laughed, tracing the spine of his books with my fingers. They felt vibrant and alive, like they carried parts of his DNA. My hand hit something cold on the middle shelf, and I craned my neck to get a closer look. A thin metal box was wedged between a copy of *Slaughterhouse-Five* and *The Dogs of Winter.* Curious, I took it out. "Office-Home, Deed Box" was printed in the top left corner in faded, dull gold. In the center was a silver lock. "What's this?" I asked.

"It's nothing important," said Rad, taking it from my hands. "Just my old Garbage Pail Kids collection. I lost the key years ago." He put the box down on the shelf and ran a hand through my hair. "I can't believe you're actually standing here, in my apartment. You have no idea how many times when we were out somewhere and you'd be laughing or biting your lip and

I'd wish I could take you home." He kissed me, softly at first, then his kisses grew more urgent. His hand traveled up along my thigh, past the hem of my skirt, brushing the elastic of my underwear and sending a shot of adrenaline through my body.

His eyes met mine and I silently willed him to go further. But he stopped and gently drew his hand away. "We're meant to be taking it slow . . . remember?"

"It's a lot harder than I thought it would be," I sighed.

"You're telling me," he laughed.

We broke away from each other reluctantly.

"Come on," I said. "Let's go out."

WE MET LUCY and Freddy at Luna Park in Lavender Bay. It was a beautiful, clear night. Summer was edging its way closer, and I felt a sense of magic permeate the warm cotton candy air. Rad and I walked hand in hand, absorbing the carnival atmosphere and the pretty lights that dotted the promenade.

"We were here for your tenth birthday party, Audrey. Remember?" asked Lucy.

"Yeah. Candela was throwing popcorn from the Ferris wheel."

"Didn't she get into trouble?" Rad asked.

"We all did, which was totally unfair. We were the ones trying to stop her!" said Lucy.

"She got us kicked out," I added.

"Your mum was furious," said Lucy. "She took us straight home after that."

"I was livid," I laughed. "I kicked her in the shins for ruining my birthday."

"When was the last time the three of you got together?" asked Freddy.

"I don't even remember," I said, sadly.

"She doesn't answer her phone anymore," Lucy said.

Shrieks of terror came from the roller coaster that wound its way above us. A small boy swung a giant hammer at the high striker, giggling with delight when the lights shot halfway up the tower.

"Hey, let's go on the ghost train," said Lucy, and the four of us went to join the line.

"Spoooooky!" said Freddy as we stepped into our carriages. The train jolted into life and began to move through a dark tunnel, decorated with hanging spiderwebs and silhouettes of ominous figures. I wasn't a stranger to ghost trains, but for some reason, this one made me feel edgy. I felt for my rubber band in the dark but realized with a jolt of panic that I'd left it at home. I moved in closer to Rad, and he squeezed my hand reassuringly. He almost had a sixth sense when it came to how I was feeling.

"You okay?" he whispered in my ear.

"Fine," I smiled brightly at him as a waxen Bride of Frankenstein suddenly dropped from the cavernous ceiling to confront us. There were several loud cries and shrieks, then I felt a tap on my shoulder and my head swung around sharply. My heart leaped into my throat. It was Ana. I opened my mouth to scream, but no sound came out.

"Audrey! Audrey!" Rad shook my shoulders gently as I sat frozen with fear. One of the operators came over looking concerned.

"I saw a girl in there," I told him, dazed.

"Wearing a white dress?" asked the operator.

I nodded.

"She must be one of our plants," he explained. "We have a few in there."

"Plants?" I was confused.

"Actors. Sorry if she gave you a fright."

"I had some dude with a gorilla head tap me on the shoulder," said Freddy. "Scared the living daylights out of me."

My heart rate began to steady. "Jesus, I had no idea they did that."

"Adds to the drama," said Freddy, raising his hands in the air like claws and rippling his fingers.

"Audrey!" Lucy's face was etched with worry. "You're as white as a sheet."

"You sure you're okay?" asked Rad as he led me off the platform.

"Yeah, I just thought I saw a ghost."

Twenty-one

BEFORE LONG, CITY streets and department stores were glittering with Christmas displays. Rad and I were coming out of a movie theater one afternoon when I got a call from Lucy. There was an urgency in her voice. "Audrey, it's Candela."

WE MET LUCY at the Royal North Shore Hospital about twenty minutes later. "How is she?" I asked.

"Not great." Lucy led us through the corridors. She stopped outside a ward, and we could see Candela through the doorway, lying eyes shut in a hospital bed. Her mother and sister, Eve, were sitting on either side of her. They both turned to us when we walked into the room.

"Audrey," said Candela's mother. Then she looked over at Rad and shot me a strange look. "Rad? Aren't you the boy who was with Ana?"

An icy cold feeling enveloped my body.

"Yeah." Rad looked a little uncomfortable. Eve's eyes widened as though her mind had just joined the dots. At sixteen, she was the spitting image of Candela on the night I told that terrible lie.

"Any change?" asked Lucy.

Candela's mother shook her head. "No, but we're all praying."

CANDELA WAS ADMITTED to the hospital earlier that day. The details were sketchy, but Eve told us the ambulance was called to her house in Alexandria in the early morning. Though her housemates were tight-lipped, blood tests had revealed a deadly cocktail of drugs coursing through her body. Shortly after her arrival at the hospital, she slipped into a coma and had been in that state ever since. Eve relayed this to the three of us as we stood in the hallway, drinking coffee from Styrofoam cups. "When will she wake up?" I asked.

"They don't know." Eve's voice was strained with worry. "The doctors said it was hard to tell with coma patients. We just have to wait and see."

THE NEXT FEW days were a blur as Lucy and I took turns keeping vigil at Candela's bedside. I brought a copy of Rad's book and read it out loud to her. Sometimes Rad came along, and other times Freddy would be there. Not once did Dirk or Ramona bother to show up.

Late one morning, I was having lunch with Eve in the hospital cafeteria. "I haven't seen Candela for months," she admitted, picking miserably at her salad. We were quiet for a little while. "If only I had kept my mouth shut that night," she continued, in a quiet, cautious tone.

I shook my head. "I was the one who should have kept my mouth shut."

"It's a strange twist of fate, isn't it? How you're with Rad now."

"Yeah."

"Does he know you were the one who saw Ana with her dad?"

"No," I said quickly. Every time the thought popped up in my mind, I pushed it back down again, like a jack-in-the-box.

"My mother blames herself," said Eve, putting her fork down. "When Candela found out Mum had told her friend about Ana, they had a huge fight. Then when we heard Ana had killed herself . . ." Eve trailed off.

"I know." I was anxious to get off the subject. I knew exactly what Eve was alluding to. If none of this had happened, then Candela might never have moved out. If things had been different, she might not be lying in a hospital bed now, fighting for her life.

LATER THAT NIGHT, Rad came over, and we decided to go for a drive. We were cruising up a long stretch of dirt road when he pulled over. I could tell something was on his mind. After a long silence, he said, "You're the first person I've been able to open up to, since Ana." As always, the mention of her name sent a chill through my body.

"You never talk about her."

"I know," he replied. "Being around the hospital these past few days has brought back some old memories. Ana wasn't a stranger to hospitals—you've heard about that time she rigged up the garage while her parents were away?"

I nodded, a lump forming in my throat. Everyone knew about the day Ana's parents had come back early from a trip to find her half-conscious in their garage, surrounded by a thick cloud of toxic fumes.

"It was lucky they came back when they did." He shuddered, as if trying to shake off the memory. "That wasn't her first attempt, you know. As horrible as it sounds, I think everyone assumed it would only be a matter of time with her."

"Yeah." It was common knowledge that Ana was reckless with her life, the kind of girl who would play Russian roulette with a loaded gun. It made her seem almost immortal, the casual way she flirted with death.

Rad took my hand and held it in his, tracing my knuckles with his thumb.

"After what happened with Ana, I vowed never to let myself care about anything again. It was just too damn hard." He reached out and gently pulled my chin around to face him. "But then I met you. I didn't want to care about you, but I couldn't help myself." He smiled, his hand cupping the side of my face. I reached up and put my hand over his. "Sometimes it scares me, though, when I look at you. I see that same expression on your face that I used to see on Ana's." He ran his thumb softly across my lips. "I don't want to fall in love with another sad girl."

CANDELA WOKE UP the following Sunday. Lucy and I went straight to the hospital when we heard.

She was sitting up in bed, pushing morosely at a tub of red Jell-O. "Hey," I said, sitting down on the side of the bed. She looked up at me.

"It's been awhile," she said and broke into a grin. A flood of tears blurred my eyes as I threw my arms around her.

"I REMEMBER BITS and pieces," said Candela, when we asked her if she was aware of anything during her coma. Her mother and Eve had just left, and Lucy and I were now keeping her company. "Audrey, you were reading some book to me, I think. And Lucy was talking about Freddy—something to do with *The War of the Worlds.*"

Lucy's cheeks turned pink. "You heard that?"

"Yeah, what's that about?"

"Freddy plays the Jeff Wayne album whenever he's annoyed with her," I explained.

Candela snorted. "Seriously?"

Lucy nodded. "He puts it on full blast."

Candela's expression suddenly turned serious as she locked Lucy's gaze in hers. "Ullaaaa," she uttered in a low dramatic voice.

"Ullaaaa," I echoed.

Lucy glared at us for a moment, but she must have seen the funny side because we all broke into laughter. It felt like old times again.

"God, I would sell my soul for a cigarette," Candela said with a sigh.

"So what happens next?" asked Lucy.

Candela suddenly turned serious. "I think this was a wake-up call. I mean, you can't get more of a slap in the face than a near-death experience." She gave us a meaningful look. "I've talked to Mum, and we've decided on rehab. I'm checking in tomorrow."

"I'm so proud of you," I said kissing her on the forehead. "We've missed you."

"I've missed you both too," she admitted. "I wanted to call, but, you know, I was so messed up. I didn't want you to see me the way I was."

"You can always call us," said Lucy. "We're your family."

Candela turned her head away, and I could see she was trying to blink back tears. "I've done things, you know," her voice wavered. "Things I'm not proud of."

"Candela," I said, putting my hand on her arm, "who hasn't?"

She wiped her eyes with the corner of her bedsheet, then turned to face us, smiling brightly. "Lucy, most probably."

Twenty-two

I spent Christmas Eve at my parent's place and woke up the next day to the sound of carols drifting through my window from our neighbors' house. They played the same Michael Bublé soundtrack every single year. I glanced at my phone and realized with a shock that it was almost noon.

I slipped into my favorite sundress, brushed my teeth, and ran a comb through my hair. When I got downstairs, I could see my parents were already setting up Christmas lunch. It was a tradition we had for as long as I could remember. "Why didn't you wake me?" I asked.

Dad was clutching a stack of placemats, and he looked up from the table and beamed at me. "Good morning, beautiful. Merry Christmas!"

"Merry Christmas, Dad." He drew me into a bear hug and kissed me lightly on the forehead.

I wandered into the kitchen where Mum was checking on the turkey. "Merry Christmas, Mum," I gave her a quick peck on the cheek. "Do you need me to help out with anything?"

"I think I have it under control," she said with a smile. She turned and looked at me, her gaze traveling down the length of my dress. "Do you want to put something else on?"

"What do you mean? What's wrong with what I'm wearing?"

She sighed. "It's a little plain for Christmas lunch, don't you think? How about that nice dress I got you, the dark green one with the buttons down the front?"

"I'm happy with the dress I'm wearing," I said, a little tightly. I had sworn to myself that I wouldn't let my mother get to me today. Besides, it was only lunch, and then I was free to meet up with Rad later in the day. I was looking forward to spending our first Christmas together.

"We have guests coming," she said, pulling on her oven mitts.

"We do?"

The doorbell rang.

"Can you get the door, Audrey? I have to deal with this turkey."

"Sure." I made my way to the front door and opened it, a ready smile painted on my face.

"Hi, darling." It was Zoe and Duck.

My smile froze. "Zoe," my voice strangled. "Duck."

"Hey, Audrey," said Duck. "It's good to see you." He looked like he had lost a lot of weight, and there were dark circles under his eyes. I felt a stab of guilt when I thought of how quickly I had moved on with Rad.

Zoe pulled me into a quick embrace. Duck stuck out his hand as I leaned in for a hug, my nose bumping awkwardly against his ear. It was on the tip of my tongue to ask what they were doing here, when the realization struck me. This was my mother's doing. She had invited them here. A sick feeling gripped my stomach.

"I didn't know you were back from your trip."

"We just got back a few days ago. Didn't your mother tell you?" Zoe gave me a curious look.

I opened my mouth to respond when I heard Mum come up behind me. "Zoe, Duck!" she beamed, kissing Zoe on the cheek and cupping her hands affectionately around Duck's face. "Look how tanned you are! You're such a handsome boy." She linked her arm through his. "Come inside; lunch is almost ready."

Dad was coming down the stairs, just as we got to the dining room. "Perfect timing! What would you like to drink? Beer? Champagne? I just opened a bottle."

"Champagne sounds wonderful," said Zoe.

Dad disappeared into the kitchen and came back a few moments later with champagne glasses and a bottle of Moët.

"Mum, can I talk to you for a minute?" I asked.

"Sure," she replied.

I headed to the kitchen, with Mum in tow.

"What the hell, Mum?" I hissed, when I pulled the kitchen door shut behind us.

She looked nonplussed. "What's the problem, Audrey?"

I wanted to scream. "What's the problem?" I said incredulously. "Mum, why is Duck here at Christmas lunch? Have you gone insane?"

"They just got back from their trip to Europe, so I thought it would be nice to catch up," she said.

"And you didn't consider how I would feel about this?"

"I didn't think you'd mind. It's just lunch, Audrey. You know Zoe and Duck are like family to us."

"This isn't *just* lunch," I tried to keep my voice level. "It's a fucking ambush."

She blinked. "I would have told you they were coming, but I didn't get a chance this morning."

"Don't give me that bullshit, Mum. You did it on purpose. Why would you do this? Why?" I could feel hot tears pushing their way out from behind my eyes. "Why, why, why?"

She sighed. "Audrey, I'm not trying to push you back into Duck's arms; honestly, I'm not. You and Duck have so much history. He was here long before Rad came into the picture. There's no reason why you can't be friends. That's all I'm saying."

"Mum—you can't do this. I'm with Rad now. You can't invite my ex to lunch without checking with me first. A normal person doesn't do that; don't you see? It's a nasty thing to do. Not just to me but to Duck as well."

"I think you're being overly dramatic."

I took a deep breath. I felt like I was ready to explode.

"Listen to me, Mum." She opened her mouth to interrupt me. "*Listen to me!*" I screamed, my fists banging at the sides of my head in frustration.

"Audrey, calm down—they can hear you out there."

"Don't you *dare* tell me to calm down!" I was breathing hard now. I knew Zoe and Duck could probably hear every word I was saying, but I was beyond caring.

"I'm your mother, Audrey. I know what's best for you even if you can't see it yourself."

A cold rage filled my body. I grabbed the nearest plate from the kitchen counter and hurled it at the floor. It smashed into pieces.

My mother looked stunned. "Audrey, what are you doing?"

I picked up another plate and threw it at her feet. She jumped, startled. The door swung open, and Dad came in. "What's going on?" He looked from me to my mother to the broken plates on the floor. My breath was ragged. I had the crook of my forefinger coiled around my rubber band.

"Come on, Audrey." Dad took my arm and walked me toward the back door. He turned and glared at my mother, shaking his head.

When we got outside, he peered at me with an expression of concern on his face. "What happened?"

"It's Mum," I said. My breathing was a little less patchy, but I was sobbing. I gulped, wiping the tears that were now streaming down my face. "I didn't know she invited Duck and Zoe."

"You didn't?" My dad looked genuinely surprised. "Your mother said it was your idea."

"Well, she's a liar," I spat. I couldn't contain my bitterness.

A look of realization dawned on his face. He sighed. "Audrey, I'll speak to her tonight about this. I don't agree with what she did, but I think she meant well."

"How can you say that? Seriously, Dad."

"I know she has a funny way of showing it, but your mother does love you, Audrey. You have to believe that."

I shook my head. "I don't want anything to do with her anymore. She drives me insane."

"I know things have always been rocky between the two of you, but it's Christmas Day. Can you at least stay for lunch? Please?" He gave me a pleading look. "Later you're free to do anything you want."

I looked at his tired, lined face and felt a pang of sadness—he had spent far too many years caught in the crossfire between Mum and me.

I felt fresh new tears well up in my eyes. "Okay, Dad, I'll stay for lunch."

RAD CAME BY to pick me up later that afternoon. I breathed a sigh of relief when I slipped into the passenger seat of his car. "Everything okay?" he asked.

"Yeah, it's just my mum being a complete asshole as usual."

"What happened?"

"Just the regular stuff. Let's not talk about it, okay?"

He started the engine. "Okay."

I didn't want to tell him about the setup Mum had orchestrated. It seemed unnecessary and would only hurt his feelings. He already sensed that Mum was less than thrilled about our relationship.

"So where to?" I asked as we pulled away from the curb. I was starting to feel a lot better.

He smiled at me. "I have a surprise for you."

"I hate surprises."

"You always like mine, though."

RAD WOULDN'T TELL me where we were going, but I figured it out by the time we were a few streets away from his place. When we got to his apartment, he put one hand over my eyes. "Don't peek," he warned. I heard the key turn in the lock, and he guided me in with a hand on my waist. After a few steps, he said, "Okay, you can open your eyes now."

"Wow!" We were standing in his apartment with the shades pulled down. Strung up around the room were multicolored fairy lights and tinsel. There was a mini Christmas tree draped in candy canes on his writing desk in the far corner of the room. Above his bed hung a foil banner that read, "BY GOLLY, BE JOLLY."

"What do you think?" Rad asked.

"Very festive!" I replied.

My eyes adjusted to the dark, and I caught sight of a small gift-wrapped box under the Christmas tree. "I thought we weren't doing gifts."

"We're not. It's for me too."

"You wrapped up a gift for yourself?" I teased.

"Just open it, Audrey," he said dryly, handing it to me. I took the box and tore through the wrapping. Inside were a box of chocolates and two DVDs—*Cat People* and its sequel, *The Curse of the Cat People.*

"I thought we could spend Christmas in bed watching them instead of the Christmas shit they have on TV."

"I thought the bed was off limits for us."

He took a step toward me and put his hands on either side of my waist. "Well, during World War I they had a truce on Christmas Day. The Germans climbed out of their trenches and came over to say hello to the Allies. They even played a friendly game of soccer."

"What on earth are you talking about, Rad?"

"Clearly, if they can manage a truce on Christmas Day, then I think we can too."

He tilted my chin with the crook of his finger and kissed me. All of a sudden, I was struggling to catch my breath. My hands tugged at his shirt, and he reached down, pulling it up over his shoulders. I nuzzled his neck as he unzipped the back of my dress until it fell to the floor with a soft rustle. He got onto his knees and kissed my bare stomach. "Jesus, Audrey," he said, letting out a deep breath. "You're a goddess."

"WHERE DID YOU get that banner?" I asked later. We were stretched out on the bed, my leg flung carelessly over his.

"That old thing has been in the family for seven generations."

I laughed. "You're such a moron."

He kissed the top of my head. "Do you want it?"

"Yes, but I don't know if you should be giving me family heirlooms just yet."

"You're right. Great-grandma Clark would be rolling over in her grave right now."

We were quiet for a few moments.

"I should get back on the pill," I said absentmindedly.

"Don't. Get pregnant."

"Shut up." I broke into laughter.

"I'm serious," he said playfully. "Have my baby." He reached out and put his palm flat on my tummy.

"Stop it." I brushed his hand away.

He reached over again and began tickling me.

"Rad, seriously! No! Rad—" I shrieked between fits of laughter, trying to fight him off. "Stop it! Rad! Stop it right now! I will kill you—I swear."

Somehow, I managed to get on top of him, pinning his arms back. "Nipple cripple!" I declared, reaching for his chest.

"Don't you dare!" he cried, grabbing my wrist. We were laughing so hard at this point I could barely catch my breath. We wrestled around for a moment, and before I knew it, he had me in a vice-like grip.

"Truce?" he said, breathing hard.

"Okay, okay, truce."

He released me from his iron grip, and we lay there quiet, staring up at the ceiling. He reached over and took my hand. "Seriously, though, don't you ever think about it?"

"About what?"

"You know, kids."

"Sure, but there's so much I want to do first. I mean, my mother had me in her early twenties, and I think part of her feels as though she missed out on so much because of that. When she talks about her life before I was in the picture, she gets this look in her eyes, like she's yearning to go back. I'll bet if given the chance, she would do it in a flash."

"I think my mum was the same in that she wanted something more from her life. Something neither Dad nor I could give her—a kind of fulfillment, I suppose. Not that she didn't do a great job with me, under the circumstances. But I think she must have felt like she walked into something she couldn't get out of. I always sensed that she felt trapped in a life she never would have chosen had she known any different."

"That's what I mean. It takes time to find out who you really are. I think it's important to get that part right before anything else."

"Absolutely. I know it's one of those things people roll their eyes at, but I do believe you have to figure out who you are before you take on that kind of responsibility. I always wonder what my mum's life would have been like if she didn't have me. Maybe she would have gone on that road trip, and somewhere along the way, she might have realized that she didn't want the white picket fence or that she preferred women over men. Even though she got there in the end, she had to go through hell for it."

"That's something I am going to do my best to avoid."

"Me too, though it's not hard to imagine how it can happen, especially the way I feel about you. I like the idea of the two of us in a little house by the sea with a brood of our own—maybe a dachshund or two. But I know there's no rush."

I laughed. "You know I'm a cat person."

"Okay, how about a Shiba Inu? They're very catlike dogs, apparently."

"How about a cat?

"You can have as many cats as you want."

"Can I have that in writing?"

He laughed. "I'll get my lawyer to draw up the papers."

I put my head down on his chest. "Why are you so good to me?"

"Because you're the only girl in this world who can make me happy. Other than Lexy Robbins, of course."

"Idiot."

Rad combed his fingers gently through my hair. "Do I make you happy?"

"Yeah."

"Good, that's all I want to do."

I tipped my chin up to kiss him. I could never get tired of kissing him. "Well, you're doing exceptionally well so far," I yawned.

"Tired?" Rad asked. I loved the weight of his body next to mine.

"Uh-huh. I think I'm falling asleep."

"Audrey." His voice was like a lullaby, and I could feel my eyelids growing heavy.

"Mmmm," I murmured.

"Merry Christmas."

Twenty-three

AUTUMN CREPT UP slowly, as the tree-lined streets of Surry Hills made their slow transition from green to yellow. I got a text one morning from Eve to let me know Candela had just come out of rehab.

Lucy and I went to her mother's house later that day. Candela was in the garden hosing the lawn when we arrived. She wore a pair of jeans and a Velvet Underground T-shirt. "You look amazing," I said and meant it. The last few months had been good to her. She had put some weight back on, and her skin had cleared up dramatically. She was looking like her old self again.

"They had us eating lots of fruits and veggies. All the boring shit. We weren't allowed to smoke, so I was climbing the walls. But it was worth it. I haven't felt this great in ages."

We went into her bedroom, and she put a record in her old vinyl machine. The crackling melody of "At Seventeen" filled the room. "Your bedroom is exactly the same as when you left it," said Lucy.

"Yeah, it's a fucking museum. Still, it's kind of nice being back here again. But I'll give it a week before Mum starts driving me crazy."

Lucy threw a glance at me. "Well, you know that spare room we have? It's a little small, but there's a bed under all that junk. It's yours if you want it."

"Yeah!" I agreed. "Why don't you move in with us?"

Candela looked from me to Lucy, a smile slowly spreading across her face. "Really? You don't mind?"

"We'd love to have you," said Lucy. "Truly."

"Mum has set me up with a job, so I'll be able to chip in for groceries and stuff." Her face was glowing.

"Then it's settled, roomie!" I said.

A FEW WEEKS later, we had a small gathering at our house to welcome Candela.

"Candela looks great," said Rad, as we sat in the courtyard with Freddy and Lucy.

"Doesn't she?" said Lucy. "Audrey and Candela are genetically blessed. I kind of lucked out there, but at least I've got a great smile."

"Babe, you're gorgeous." Freddy kissed her on the cheek with a loud smack.

"Aw, thanks, babe."

Candela walked over, cigarette in hand. "Look at your little garden." She picked one of our gardenias and stuck it behind her ear. "Who knew you and Lucy were such homemakers?"

"Wish they were just as good in the kitchen," joked Freddy as Lucy slapped at his hand.

Candela laughed. "Well, that's probably where I'll come in."

THE NEXT FEW weeks drifted by in a blissful haze. For once, everything was going right in my life, and I was the happiest I had ever been. Candela brought a new spark and energy to our house. She had a knack for cooking, a skill that Lucy and I lacked, and our neglected kitchen was now humming and singing with the sound of banging pot lids and the delicious aroma of freshly cooked meals.

Sam promoted me to senior journalist, which involved interviewing famous authors and a bigger pay check. There was nothing I loved more than sharing a cup of coffee with a writer who had years of wisdom to impart. I got along with my coworkers, especially Trinh, who was always singing my praises to Sam. I had a feeling she played a part in my promotion.

Things with Rad were better than I could have imagined. There was a magical sense of discovery between us, like an archaeological dig. I loved the unraveling and the undoing, as though we were peeling back through layers of skin and muscle and tissue to peer into the very heart of our most authentic selves. The bond we shared was so intrinsic, so deeply rooted, that I imagined it was always there waiting for us to make the connection.

The only dark cloud to blot my perfect sky was the idea that at some point, I had to tell Rad about Ana and my lie that ultimately drove her to end her own life. Whenever this dawned on me, I sank into a state of despondency that sometimes took days to shake off. During one of my sessions with Ida, I almost revealed the lie. The truth, desperate to see the light, had made its way up from the pit of my stomach to sit at the tip of my tongue, only to be swallowed back down again.

ONE NIGHT, LUCY and I were in the kitchen when Candela came out of her room with a flat, rectangular box in her hand. "Look what I found under my bed."

"What is it?" I asked.

Candela slid the box open to reveal a wooden carved Ouija board. "Oh shit," said Lucy, recoiling in horror. "I hate those things."

"Oh, come on, Lucy," Candela smiled. "I've joined in on a few séances before. It's fun."

"Does it actually work?" I asked.

"Well," said Candela, "one time when we asked if the spirits had a message for anyone in the room, the pointer skittled across on its own and stopped at the letter P. This girl Patricia just stared at it, white as a sheet." Candela paused for dramatic effect. "Then she fainted."

Suddenly, there was a loud knock on the door, and we all screamed in unison. "Lucy, open up! I forgot my key again!" Freddy called out.

"Jeez." Lucy let out a deep breath. "I forgot he was coming over tonight."

FREDDY INSPECTED THE Ouija board with great interest, running his hands over the lines and grooves. "We've got to give this a go."

I glanced over at Lucy, who was very much dead set against it. "Not sure if that's a good idea, guys. Audrey?" She looked at me for support. I had to admit—I was a little curious.

"Why not? What's the worst that can happen?"

It took a few more minutes of cajoling to convince Lucy. Then we all scrambled around the house, searching for candles. "Where should we do it?" asked Freddy.

"Coffee table." I cleared away some magazines and a tea-stained mug. Candela put the board on the table, and we set the candles on ceramic plates, placing them on the floor around the room.

When the candles were lit, we raced around the house switching off the lights, then we assembled back in the lounge room. The atmosphere was a little unnerving as the shadows cast by the flickering candlelight fell across the Ouija board like a scene straight out of a horror movie. "Is anyone else having second thoughts?" queried Lucy.

"Oh, come on, Lucy," Candela said cheerfully. "We've gone to this much effort already."

We arranged ourselves around the coffee table and each put a finger on the pointer.

"Is there anyone there?" Candela's tone was somber. We held our breath for a few seconds, and then it began to move. I looked up sharply. "Is anyone moving it?"

"No," they all echoed in unison. I watched mesmerized as the pointer spelled out the word "yes" in response to Candela's question.

"Who is it?" Candela's voice was a little shaky.

"Hey, I think we should stop, guys," said Lucy nervously.

"Shhhh." Freddy looked transfixed.

The pointer moved again and landed on the letter *A*. My body stiffened, and a new fear gripped me as it made its way with slow deliberation to the letter *N*. Then it completed its journey on *A*. *Ana*. The word exploded in my mind like a hand grenade and sent me reeling into a state of panic. I withdrew my finger immediately as if I had just been scalded. Then Freddy collapsed into fits of laughter.

"You asshole!" cried Lucy, getting up and flicking the lights on. I stood up quickly, knocking my knee hard against the underside of the table, and ran straight upstairs to my bedroom, slamming the door shut behind me. I fell onto my knees, gasping for air. *I'm dying,* I thought. My lungs were screaming for oxygen, and in my panicked stupor, I couldn't find a way to oblige them. Candela came bursting in and hurried over.

"Audrey! Oh my God." She put one hand on my arm and tossed her head back and screamed, "Lucy, grab the bag of mushrooms in the fridge."

"What?"

"Just grab the bag of mushrooms." Almost in a heartbeat, Lucy was there with the paper bag. Candela dumped the mushrooms on the floor and put the bag over my mouth. "Audrey! Breathe . . . breathe . . . breathe."

"Is she okay? I've never seen her this bad. Do we need to call anyone?"

"She'll be okay." Candela ran her hand soothingly up and down my back. Soon, my pulse steadied, and my breathing grew less ragged. When it was over, I sat there dazed and looked up to catch Freddy standing by the door, looking down at me with his mouth agape.

Twenty-four

IT WAS LUCY's birthday, and we were celebrating at Spag Bowl. Rad and I joined Lucy and Freddy sitting at their favorite table.

"Hey, birthday girl!" I leaned down to kiss her cheek. "Did you manage to get in touch with Candela?"

She shook her head. "No, I've been calling her all day. She didn't come in last night, and she hasn't been answering my texts. I hope she hasn't forgotten."

I pulled my phone out of my purse and tapped Candela's number. After a few seconds, it went to voicemail. "Candela, where are you? We're all at Spag Bowl for Lucy's birthday dinner. Call me back."

"What should we do?" said Lucy checking her watch. "It's quarter to eight."

"We should probably start without her."

WHEN LUCY AND I got home, Candela was sitting on the steps outside the house holding the string of a red helium balloon. She grinned sheepishly when she saw us. "I'm such a shitty friend." She stood up and gave Lucy a hug. "Happy birthday, sweetie. I'm sorry I missed it."

"Where were you?" I asked.

"I was with a friend, and we lost track of time."

"Who?" I could see Candela tense up in response to Lucy's innocent question.

"What are you, my mother now?" I think the words came out harsher than she intended.

Lucy flinched. "Candela, I didn't mean anything by it."

"Sorry," Candela sighed. "Look, I'm just tired. I haven't slept all night."

She handed Lucy the red balloon, and in the fumbled exchange, it slipped out of their grasp. The three of us stood watching its slow ascent into the dark, starless sky.

Twenty-five

OVER THE NEXT few weeks, Candela's disappearing acts grew more and more frequent. Our kitchen once again stood neglected; cutlery and dirty dishes piled up in the sink. Lucy was complaining about the mess in Candela's room and the fact that she hadn't paid her share of the bills for over a month. One morning, a strange number popped up on the screen of my phone.

"Hello?"

"Hi, is this Audrey?" It was a female voice I didn't recognize.

"Yes, speaking. Who is this?"

"Sorry to bother you. I'm Candela's boss. She hasn't been to work for the past few days, and I'm trying to contact her. Do you know where she is?"

"No. Sorry."

I heard Lucy coming up the stairs as I ended the call. "Audrey, have you seen my mother's pearls?" she asked.

"No. When did you have them last?"

She cocked her head to one side in the way she always did when sorting through her memory archives—which I pictured to be in neat, orderly compartments, with color-coded labels. "The last time I wore them was the night of my birthday dinner, at Spag Bowl. Anyway, Mum wants them back, and I can't find them anywhere." She chewed on her bottom lip.

"That's weird." It was hard to believe she could misplace something as important as her mother's pearls.

"You don't suppose . . ." she trailed off and looked immediately guilty.

"Candela? No way."

"She's been so behind on her share of the bills," said Lucy, winding a lock of hair around her finger. "And she hasn't come home in days."

"I just got a call from her boss. It was weird. She said Candela hasn't been in, and she was trying to get ahold of her."

"God, I wonder what the hell is up with her."

"Maybe she met someone?"

"I don't know," said Lucy with a shrug. "You know what Candela's like. She hates having to answer to anyone, so I don't want to push her."

"Me neither."

As if on cue, we heard a key turn in the door and the thudding sound of Candela's boots in the hallway. Lucy and I went out to meet her, and she stopped when she saw us, a little startled.

"Hi, guys. What's happening?"

"Where have you been?" I asked. "You haven't been home in days."

She rolled her eyes. "So you're going to give me the third degree now?" She walked past us into the kitchen and grabbed a Diet Coke from the fridge.

"Candela," I said cautiously. "We're not trying to cramp your style. We're just worried; that's all."

"Worried? Audrey, you're the one having panic attacks." She must have seen how much her words had stung because she gave me an apologetic look. "I'm sorry; that was mean."

She looked from me to Lucy. "Guys, I'm fine. I've been busy at work."

"Really? Your boss just called looking for you. She wants to know why you haven't been showing up."

Candela looked at me, her eyebrows shooting up in surprise. Then she looked away, an expression of annoyance crossing her face.

"Well, I was planning on quitting anyway." There was an awkward moment as we stood there, not knowing what to say. Then Candela threw up her hands. "Okay, you've got me. I've met someone, and we're just having fun hanging out, okay? I don't make a thing of it when you're off with your boyfriends, so give a girl a break." She took a long swig of her Diet Coke and in her typical fashion walked off into her room, pulling the door firmly shut behind her.

LUCY AND I hoped Candela was just going through a phase and it would blow over. After all, when Rad and I began seeing each other, I disappeared for days on end. But to our dismay, Candela's behavior got more and more erratic as we edged into spring. Aside from the pearl necklace, we noticed other missing items. A five-dollar bill here, a twenty there. Then there was Lucy's Burberry purse and my iPod. Things that you don't realize are missing until you look for them. One day, it all came to a head when Candela turned up after being absent for over a week.

"I'm just here to pick up a few things," she said dismissively, walking past Lucy and me sitting on the love seat playing Mario Kart.

I got up, following her. "Candela, wait."

Lucy came up, and in a few minutes we were all standing in her bedroom.

"I'm kind of in a hurry," she said, shoving some of her clothes into a small duffle bag.

"We need to talk to you," Lucy insisted.

"What is it?" Candela looked from Lucy to me. She sighed and put her bag on the bed, spreading out her arms in a gesture of surrender. "I'm all ears."

"We've noticed things have gone missing around the house," I said.

"And?"

I gave an exasperated sigh. "Look, Candela. If you're short on cash, we're happy to help—"

"You think I'm stealing from you?" She cut me off, put her hands on her hips, and glared at me.

"Are you?" asked Lucy.

"Come on, guys. It's me."

"Are you using again?"

"No!" said Candela, raising her voice. "What the hell, Audrey?"

I reached out and grabbed her arm.

"What the fuck are you doing?" she yelled, pulling away. I grabbed her arm again, pushing her sleeves up.

"Let me see your arms," I demanded.

She shoved me backward, tugging her sleeve back down. "Audrey," her eyes flashed dangerously, "I'm warning you!" She threw a few more things into her bag and stormed out, with Lucy and I trailing closely behind.

When we got outside, we saw a heavyset man on a motorcycle, with obscenities tattooed around his bulging neck. My heart sank.

"Jesus Christ," I swore under my breath, "she's back with Dirk again."

"Candy Cane!" he called gruffly. "Move your ass, baby."

Lucy reached out and grabbed Candela's arm. "You're not going anywhere with him."

Candela looked at her, eyes wide with disbelief. "Excuse me?"

"Lucy's right," I said, grabbing her other arm. "Come back inside, Candela."

"What's going on, Candy Cane?" Dirk called out again. To our dismay, he got off his bike and sauntered over. "Hey, let her go," he said, towering over us.

"Fuck off," I said.

"What did you just say?" he said, taking a menacing step toward me.

I glared at him. "I told you to fuck off. Get lost."

"You're lucky you're a girl." He crossed his arms and glared down at me. "I don't hit girls."

"Well, Candela," my tone dripped with sarcasm, "looks like you've got yourself a real gentleman here."

"Don't talk to her like that!" Dirk barked at me.

I turned to him. "Oh yeah? Where the fuck were you when she was in hospital, fighting for her life? *Where were you then?*" I screamed.

He shifted from one foot to the other. "Candela knows why I wasn't there," he retorted. "I don't have to answer to you."

"You're going to screw up her life again." Tears of anger welled up in my eyes.

"Oh shut up, Audrey," said Candela. "Seriously, I am so sick of your shit. Why can't you both just leave me alone?" She hurled the duffle bag on the ground at our feet. "I don't need a single damn thing from either one of you, okay? Come on, Dirk. Let's just get the hell out of here."

Twenty-six

Days after Candela's departure, I found myself sitting at Rad's kitchen table staring at a black metal box—the one I'd come across on my first visit to his apartment. He was out, and I wanted to tidy up before I left for an interview with author Elsa Reed.

I came across the box tucked away in the back corner of his bedroom closet when I was putting away some laundry. It beckoned to me, like Pandora's box. So now I was sitting here, staring at it with a mix of curiosity and dread. The sunlight streaming in between the slats of the window highlighted a paper clip, already complicit in my pending crime. Its silvery glint drew my gaze the same way a raven is mesmerized by a discarded bottle cap.

For some reason, my mind dragged up a memory of Candela from a long time ago. It was one of those warm summer days that shone like a beacon flickering somewhere in the dark chambers of my mind like a photograph taken with a pinhole camera. We must have been no more than thirteen. We were sitting on plastic seats suspended in the air by metal chains, kicking the tips of our matching white-and-blue Converse sneakers against the asphalt, in a local park where we used to play.

I still recall that day like a scene from a movie or a tattered picture book with edges blunted and pages marred by crayon scribbles. Candela's long dark hair swung back and forth like a silken sheet; her beautiful green eyes were framed in thick, curly lashes. She was more like a boy than a girl, with perpetually scraped knees and a steely determination.

Her head was turned sideways, and her gaze was fixed on the seesaw in front of us where on one bright yellow seat someone had left behind a scrunchie made from a pearly white fabric with red polka dots. "Let's play confession," she said.

"What's confession?"

She went into a detailed description of the process, right down to the lattice screen that hid the priest and the smell of stale varnish in the confessional. She asked me if I had anything to confess. I thought long and hard, but I couldn't think of anything impressive. When it was Candela's turn, she rattled off a long list of things. Money snuck from her mother's purse, cigarettes in the girl's shower block at summer camp, and going to third base with the boy who lived next door. "What does it feel like?" I asked about the boy, my voice dropping to a whisper. She shrugged, her eyes still pinned tightly to the red-and-white scrunchie.

"It doesn't feel like anything." Then she began to cry as I watched, feeling strangely removed.

"Candela, don't cry."

She turned to look at me, her tiny hands wiping furiously at her tears as if she was trying to punish them for betraying her. "Audrey," she said, her glassy eyes staring straight into mine, "I'm going to hell."

Shaking off the memory, I picked up the paper clip; with a little encouragement, the silver lock clicked open. I sat there for a few more minutes, drumming my fingers on the glass table-top, my heart fluttering like a panic-stricken bird inside my chest. I was hoping to find a stack of Garbage Pail cards, like Rad had said, but the feeling of dread in my stomach told me otherwise. After drawing a deep breath, I flipped the lid open and carefully withdrew the contents, placing them on the table before me. I knew right away the box was a time capsule of his relationship with Ana. There were concert tickets, pressed flowers, and other keepsakes, each with their own mysterious significance. Photographs of Ana and letters to Rad written in her impossibly tiny handwriting. Pictures of the two of them, smiling, his palm flat against her back, their heads turned to greet the camera.

I wondered whether he still looked through this box. Did he sift through its contents on those whiskey-fueled nights he spent here alone? I wondered whether she came to life again for him in these photographs.

I picked up a piece of wrinkled paper—a receipt from a stationery store—and turned it over. On the back was a poem in Rad's messy scrawl.

Her name was Aphrodite
she, my sage, my aversion
to the razor blade
She was life itself hung
on a hook and from me
took, the shock of day
where breath expelled
from earthly gaze
and heavenward

in hands she held
I will see her when
the harps command,
a tune, a dance,
a book, her arms.

I read it several times, finding meaning that wasn't there or no longer was. Cutting this same wound open, over and over again.

I put it back down on the table and shook my head. What the hell was I doing? Tears blurring my vision, I began putting away the contents of the box. As I held the edge of a creamy envelope between the tip of my thumb and forefinger, a Polaroid photo dropped out and landed, flat on the table. It was Ana, topless and sitting cross-legged on a bare mattress, her eyes looking fixedly into the camera. I turned the Polaroid over, and once again, I was confronted by the rude shock of Rad's scratchy writing.

I love you, I'm sorry

I went to put the photo back into the envelope when I noticed there was a piece of notepaper inside. It was folded up many times over, like a letter meant to be inserted into a bottle. With trembling hands, I withdrew it and pulled it open slowly, my heart thumping in my chest. I recognized Ana's tiny writing at once, and as I read, I realized it must be a page torn from her diary.

I'm going to do it this time. My parents will be
away this weekend, and I am going to seal up the
garage with Dad's beloved red Thunderbird running

inside. Then I'm going to fall asleep to the sweet
perfume of carbon monoxide and "Sugar Baby Love"
blasting on the stereo. Seventeen seems like a good age
to leave this shitball of a world . . .

I heard footsteps in the hall outside, and my heart leapt to my throat. I quickly folded up the diary entry and stuck it into the pocket of my Audrey jacket. Then I scooped the remaining items into the box and shut the lid. I got up, my chair scraping loudly against the kitchen floor, and raced over to Rad's closet to put the box back where I found it. The key turned in the lock, and a few seconds later, he was through the door.

"Hey," he said, dropping his keys on the kitchen table and looking around the apartment. "You tidied up."

"Hey," I said, a little out of breath.

"You okay?"

I nodded. "I'm fine."

"Audrey?" His eyes scanned my face. "Have you been crying?"

I shook my head. "No, it was just a little dusty in here; that's all." I tried to muster up a smile. "Allergies."

"Okay." He looked unconvinced.

"I should get going. I have an interview this afternoon." I grabbed my satchel and draped it across my shoulder.

"Hey." He reached out and touched my arm as I walked past him toward the door. "Audrey, this is nuts. You're obviously *not* okay. Can you please tell me what's wrong?"

I stopped. Tears filled my eyes. I wish I had never looked into the box. I so wish I could pretend it didn't exist.

Rad put both hands on my shoulders and peered down at me. "Audrey, I hate seeing you like this. Please tell me what's wrong. Was it something I did?"

"No, it's not you."

"What is it, then?"

"I just—" My voice caught in my throat. I looked down at my feet. "I just need to know that you want me," I said finally.

He looked at me stunned for a few moments, before his expression softened. "I want you—of course I want you." He drew me into his arms. "More than anything." I felt his lips against my ear. "*So much.*"

THAT AFTERNOON I met up with author Elsa Reed at the Tuscan-style villa near Bondi Beach, where she lived. The entire time, I couldn't stop thinking about the contents of the black metal box. Not even the gorgeous sea view from Elsa's deck or the fact that I was actually speaking to one of my idols could keep my mind from trailing back to that morning. The photograph, the poem, and the page from Ana's diary kept popping up in my head, one after another, like pieces of luggage on a carousel. Luckily, Elsa didn't seem to notice how distracted I was as we discussed her writing process.

"I get up around five every morning," she said. "I don't know why. No matter how late I go to bed the night before, the next day at 5 a.m. sharp," she clicked her fingers, "I'm up and ready for work."

"But how do you manage to cope with all the day-to-day stuff?"

"Well, I think it helps that I've never been married and I don't have any children. It means I can nap during the day if I want."

"So you've never wanted children? I'm sorry if that's too personal a question."

She smiled at me, her eyes creasing gently in the corners. It was a warm smile. "I don't think I went out of my way *not* to have children," she said thoughtfully. "I suppose I never made it a priority. Other things seemed more important to me during my thirties and forties. Then before I knew it, I was in my fifties, and by then, I knew it was a little late." She laughed. "Not that I feel as if I've missed out. I've spent much of my life traveling, and as you know, I've written several books during that time. I can't say that I would have preferred to settle down like most responsible adults, because you only get one life, and I don't have that comparison to make. What I do know is that I like my life—very much so—and I am possessive about the way I live. I can't imagine having it any other way."

"I grew up devouring your books," I said. "I hope this doesn't sound selfish, but I'm glad you had all that time to write. I feel your books are a gift to the world. And, what's more, you've found the holy grail in that your books have enjoyed critical acclaim as well as commercial success."

"Yes, I have been very fortunate in that regard."

We were quiet for a few moments, as we sipped the green tea she had prepared earlier.

"There's something I have always wanted to ask you."

"Go ahead."

"There is a recurring character in your stories. The man with the bumblebee pin. You write about him with so much tenderness—I can't help but wonder if he's based on someone you know."

Her eyes lit up. "Ah, the man with the bumblebee pin. Yes, he is based on someone I know or rather, someone I *knew*—a very long time ago. I suppose you can say he is my muse."

"Am I allowed to ask what happened?"

"Do you know about Saturn return?"

"No."

"It's an astrological transit that happens about every twenty-eight years when Saturn returns to the same place in the sky it stood on the day you were born."

"And what's the significance of that?"

"Do you know the opening line of *A Tale of Two Cities?*"

"'It was the best of times, it was the worst of times . . .'"

She nodded. "Around the time you turn twenty-seven, Saturn begins to close in on its first cycle. Many people believe this will herald a tremendous change in your life. It's supposed to be the period where you cross the threshold into adulthood. And it's meant to be a time that is as magical as it is unsettling. Your life is thrown into chaos and disarray. Think of it as your own tiny revolution."

"Was it that way for you?"

She nodded. "That was the year I met the man with the bumblebee pin."

"And what happened?" I asked, fascinated.

A mysterious smile played on her lips. "Well, I won't go into any detail—I let my books speak for me in that regard—but I will tell you that when I turned twenty-seven, I learned a very important lesson."

"What was it?" I asked, leaning in.

"I learned that writing is the consolation prize you are given when you don't get the thing you want the most."

I LEFT ELSA's house, my head spinning. I decided to go for a walk along Bondi Beach to process everything that had happened that day. *Writing is the consolation prize you are given when you don't get the thing you want the most.* I couldn't help but attach those words to Rad and the book he wrote after Ana's death. Seeing that box and its contents, I finally understood the depth of his feelings for Ana, and it was as if the rug had been pulled out from under my feet.

I was walking down the busy footway, the ocean before me shimmering like a jewel, when suddenly, I stopped. I remembered the page from Ana's diary. I slipped my hand into the pocket of my Audrey jacket, but nothing was there. I frowned. I was dead sure I had put it in there. I checked the other pocket, but it too was empty. Frantically, I dug into all the pockets of my jeans—there was nothing. My head began to spin. My throat felt like it was closing in on me. I reached down and tweaked my rubber band, blindly stumbling to a nearby bench. A teenage boy on his skateboard stopped by me. "Hey, are you okay?"

I nodded. "Asthma," I said, hoping he would leave me alone.

"Do you need me to call the ambulance or anything?"

"No," I managed to gasp, "I'll be okay."

I collapsed on the bench, my chest rising and falling rapidly. I snapped my rubber band again and gripped the side of the bench, forcing myself to concentrate on my hand, to acknowledge that it was connected to something solid. I clutched the bench like a life raft.

It felt like an eternity before I managed to get my breathing under control. Then it was like a fog clearing, and, gradually, I felt as if I was back in the real world again, and I became aware of the odd looks I was getting from passersby.

I reached into my satchel, my hands still shaking, and took out every last thing in there, hoping I would now find the page from Ana's diary. Maybe I could put it back in the box before Rad noticed it was missing. But I looked and looked, and it was nowhere to be found.

I grabbed my phone and called Lucy.

"Hey, Audrey."

"Hey."

"Are you okay?" she asked, even though she must have known from my voice that I wasn't.

"I don't know. I'm at Bondi Beach. Can you come and pick me up?"

"Sure, sweetie. Just hang on—I'll be there in twenty minutes."

Lucy took me home and settled me onto our blue couch. She wrapped our large throw around me and squeezed my shoulders.

"What happened today?"

I told her about my morning, how I found the time capsule Rad kept in his apartment.

"Oh, Audrey," she said with a sigh. "You shouldn't have looked in there. I mean, most people keep old love letters, and it hasn't been that long since Ana died. I don't think it would in any way diminish what he feels for you."

"I know. I guess I just thought what we had was the most amazing and rare thing. I suppose I always imagined his relationship with Ana was similar to the one I shared with Duck. But now, seeing the poem and the photo . . ." I didn't mention the diary entry.

"I know. It must have been a shock for you."

I nodded. "I hardly ever think about Duck anymore. I still care about him but not anything romantic—that faded so quickly. But I think it's different for Rad. Even though he never talks about Ana, his pen tells me she's still there in his heart. She's in every damn line he writes."

"Audrey, if you had the choice, would you rather be his muse or be in his arms?"

"I want to be both. I know it's the exception rather than the rule, but I can't help what I want."

"Of course not, sweetie," she said, giving me a sympathetic smile.

"Do you know about Schrödinger's cat?"

Lucy nodded. "Yeah. It's the theory about the cat in the box with the flask of poison. The idea being that the cat in the box is both simultaneously alive and dead—it's only when you open the box that it is one or the other."

"Exactly. If I had never looked into that box, it would still be a pile of old trading cards—at least to me. But I've opened up a new reality, and I want to go back to the old one."

"Audrey," Lucy let out a deep breath, "this kind of thinking isn't healthy. All these what-ifs. You can go on and on forever."

"I know. I just can't believe he would lie about what was in the box. I think that bothers me more than anything. That he could look in my eyes and tell me something that is completely contrary to the truth."

"I don't think he did it out of malice, Audrey. You just caught him off guard. I mean, we've all been guilty of that at some point."

"I suppose you're right."

"Haven't you ever told a lie that you regretted?"

Out of nowhere, an icy cold finger traced a line down my back. I shivered and pulled the throw tighter around me.

"I mean, everyone does," Lucy continued, oblivious to the effect her words had on me. "Freddy still believes I'm a natural blonde."

"Seriously?"

She nodded. "He has no idea."

"He hasn't noticed that the carpet doesn't match the drapes?"

She looked at me and shrugged. "Now you know why I'm so OCD about my waxing appointments."

I gave her a wry smile. "Well, your secret's safe with me."

LATER THAT NIGHT, I got a text from Rad.

Want to go for a drive?

Sure

It had been a long day, and I wished I could just close my eyes and fall asleep. But my mind was racing, and I was on the verge of a panic attack. I didn't know if seeing Rad would soothe my anxiety or make it worse.

HE WAS OUTSIDE my house about twenty minutes later.

"We haven't done this in ages," I said, as we turned the corner.

"No." Rad turned and smiled at me.

"It feels nostalgic."

We drove for a while with no destination. The moon swam through the sky, pale and ghostly, dipping in and out of clouds like a retro arcade game. I looked over at Rad, and as usual, a feeling of tenderness swept through me. Sitting there beside him in the car—it was all I wanted for the rest of my life. "I know you looked inside that box," he said suddenly. My entire body prickled with fear. I kept silent. "It's okay," he continued. "I think in a way I wanted you to."

He must have noticed that the page from Ana's diary was missing.

He switched gears and slowed down, then turned into the empty parking lot of a supermarket. He parked the car and looked at me, his face partly covered in shadow.

"Did you read anything?"

"Only a poem," I said truthfully. "And there was a diary entry, but I only read the first few lines."

"I noticed it was missing from the box. Do you still have it?"

I shook my head. "I'm not sure why, but I stuck it in the pocket of my jacket, and now I can't seem to find it. It must have fallen out somewhere. I'm sorry."

"Oh. Hopefully it will turn up."

"Why did you have a page from Ana's diary?"

"I took it on the night of her wake. I knew she kept her diary under a loose floorboard in her bedroom. I'm not sure why I went through it." He shook his head. "Grief makes you do weird things."

"You don't have to explain. I probably would have done the same thing myself."

"I'm not sure why I chose to tear out that page in particular. I suppose I wanted to punish myself in some way for what happened to Ana. I wanted something that would hurt me each time I read it."

"But that's crazy, Rad. Why would you do that to yourself? It's bad enough you lost her."

He looked at me, and a strange expression crossed his face. "Audrey, I've never told this to anyone before. What happened to Ana was my fault. I'm the reason why she did it."

"Why on earth would you think that, Rad? How could it be your fault?"

His eyes, pained and haunted, looked straight into mine. "You know that rumor that was going around, the one about Ana screwing her dad?"

I swallowed hard. "Yeah."

"I was at her house right before they found her in the bathtub. I went there to confront her about the rumor." He closed his eyes, as though it hurt him to remember. "She told me it was a lie, that someone had made it all up. But I got the feeling she was hiding something from me. I told her I thought she was lying, and we got into a fight—the worst fight we'd ever had."

I reached over and took his hand. It was cold and clammy.

"I should have been there for her," he continued. "Regardless of whether the gossip was true or not. She had the whole town against her. She just needed someone on her side. But I chose not to be that person. A few hours later, her father called and told me she was dead." He shook his head and buried his face in his hands.

"Rad," I put my hand on his shoulder. "What happened to Ana wasn't your fault."

He turned to face me. "What do you mean? I just told you—"

I drew in a deep breath. "Rad, Ana was telling you the truth," I said softly. "The rumor—it was a lie."

He looked at me blankly. "A lie? But how do you know for sure?"

I opened my mouth to speak and then closed it again. My heart was beating so fast I felt like it was going to burst out of my chest. I swallowed hard and looked him straight in the eye. "Because I was the one who made it up."

Rad stared at me as if I was an apparition. Like I had just materialized from thin air to occupy the passenger seat across from him. "You made it up?" he said dumbly.

I nodded. "I told the story to Lucy and Candela one night, and Eve overheard us. She passed it on to her mother, and that's how the rumor got started."

"Audrey, what are you saying?" He grew more and more distressed. "Why are you saying this shit?" He looked around the car wildly.

"Because it's true," I said, my voice breaking with emotion. "And I live with my guilt every single day."

"You're fucking with me, aren't you?"

I shook my head and bit down hard on my lip. "I wish I was, but I'm telling you it's true. It was a lie. I made it up."

"Why the fuck would you make up something like that?" he said, grabbing my shoulders and shaking me. "Why the fuck would you do that?"

"I don't know," I said, tears welling up in my eyes.

"*What were you thinking?*" He was shouting now, his eyes flashing with anger.

"I don't know," I said again, my voice small and unsteady. "Kids say stupid things. I had no idea it was going to end the way it did, or I never would have said anything."

"What the hell did Ana ever do to you?"

"Nothing! She did nothing at all."

"What the *fuck*, Audrey! Do you know what you've done? Do you have *any* idea?" His hands were clutching the steering wheel so hard that his knuckles were white.

"Yes, I do," I said helplessly. "That's what landed me in therapy. That's why I couldn't get through my exams. Don't you think I would take it back if I could? I know what I did, Rad! Believe me—I do."

"You don't know," he hissed. "You've got no fucking idea." He was breathing hard.

I tugged at the door handle, and it opened with a click. "Audrey, what the hell are you doing?" he said, grabbing my arm. "It's the middle of the night."

"I have to get out of here." I tried to pull my arm free.

"C'mon, Audrey." He didn't sound so angry anymore. "It's not safe out there, for fuck's sake. I don't want another dead girl on my conscience."

"But what happened to Ana wasn't your fault. You know the truth now—it was mine."

He turned away from me so I couldn't read his expression. "Just shut the door, Audrey. I'll take you home," he said quietly.

Twenty-seven

SEVERAL WEEKS HAD gone by without a word from Rad. My whole life had come crashing to a halt. I couldn't even bring myself to tell Lucy what had happened. She skittled around me cautiously during those dark days, worried about doing or saying the wrong thing.

I hardly got out of bed, ignoring my deadlines with *See! Sydney* and the frantic calls from Sam and Trinh. Lucy must have told them what had happened because after a while, the calls stopped. I knew I was jeopardizing my career, but all I could think about was Rad. Now that he was gone, nothing seemed to matter. I kept going over that night in the car when I confessed to him about Ana, and I wished I could take it all back.

The minutes, hours, and days crawled slowly by, as a sickening feeling grew in the pit of my stomach. I could still perform the basic human functions, but I felt soulless. Every time I came across something that reminded me of Rad, the dull, throbbing ache would rise to a sharp, painful crescendo, and the shock of it was almost too much to bear.

One day, Lucy, tired of tiptoeing around me, finally had enough. She marched into my room that morning and threw the curtains back. "Audrey, you're a mess. Have a shower; have something to eat. If you don't, I'm calling your mother."

The sunlight hurt my eyes, and the thought of food made my stomach turn. But the threat of my mother's involvement was much worse, so I got up and stumbled blindly like an automaton into the shower. The water felt good on my skin, and when I emerged twenty minutes later, I actually was a little hungry.

Lucy made some cheese toasties and set them outside on the courtyard table with two cups of coffee. I sat down, taking small bites at first, then wolfing the rest down.

"I don't really know what's going on with you and Rad," she said, taking a sip of her coffee, "but I know how much you miss him." She looked at me, putting her mug down with a sharp clatter. "Look, I know he must be thinking about you too. I see how you are with each other. He lights you up. I've never seen you so happy."

I thought I was all cried out, but the tears rolled from my eyes like they had been lying in wait, ready to ambush me.

"Audrey, why don't you call him?"

"He doesn't want anything to do with me."

"Why? What did you do that was so bad?"

I shook my head and looked at her, bitter despair coursing through my body. "It's over, Lucy. I don't want to talk about it anymore."

I DROPPED BY the office later that afternoon. It had taken all my strength and willpower to leave the house. As I walked into Sam's office, her expression was a conflicted mix of reproach and concern. "How are you?" The concern seemed to win out, as her eyes scanned my face.

"I'm sorry I've been such a shit. Just going through some stuff."

"That's okay," she said, motioning to the chair across her desk. I sat down, my palms flat on my knees. "Trinh has been covering for you these past few weeks, and we have a new girl in too. She doesn't have your flair, but, hey, that's why we have editors."

"I'm really sorry to leave you and Trinh in the lurch."

Sam sighed. "Is this about Rad?"

"Yeah, we broke up."

"Sorry to hear that, sweetie—he was a real darling too." She shook her head regretfully. "What a shame."

"Sam, I have to get away."

"Away?" A look of alarm crossed her eyes. "What do you mean?"

"I don't know," I said, not quite sure where I was going with the conversation. It was something I hadn't realized until that moment. "I need to get away from here."

"Are you telling me you want to quit? Audrey, think about this carefully. You've got a great thing going here."

"I know; I've been so happy here—"

"And I've been very happy with you," she cut in quickly. "Everyone in the office adores you."

"You've all been so good to me, and I appreciate it—I truly do. But I need to get away, even if it's just for a while."

"How long?"

"I don't know."

"You've come such a long way since you've been here, and you're now one of my best writers. But you know I can't keep your job on hold."

"I understand that," I said, numbly. "I'm so sorry, Sam. I've got to go someplace and clear my head. I can't stay here any longer."

She looked at me for the longest time. "Where are you planning on going?" she asked finally.

"I have to go to Colorado." The words came as a surprise, but as soon as they were out of my mouth, I sensed it was the right thing. At once, my mind conjured a vision of a new life in a small town where no one knew who I was. "I have some savings leftover. I'm just going to take some time out. Maybe write a book."

Sam sat back in her chair and sighed. "You'll send me a postcard, won't you? When you get there?"

"I will," I promised.

I stood up, and she walked me through the office and out the door.

"I'll miss seeing your pretty face around here," she said, giving me a hug. "Trinh will be disappointed. She had a soft spot for you."

"Is she in today?"

Sam shook her head. "She's coming in tomorrow. I'll pass on the news to her then."

"Thanks, Sam." I gave her a grateful smile.

She nodded. "You take care, now."

LUCY BEGAN FUSSING over me like a mother hen when I told her my plans. "Colorado? Why Colorado?"

"I don't really know," I said, folding another T-shirt and placing it neatly into my suitcase.

"Has Colorado got anything to do with Rad?"

"No, this is what I need to do—for myself."

"But Colorado—that's Rad's name. I thought you were trying to get over him. I mean, why not . . . I don't know . . ." she threw up her arms, "Denmark? Why Colorado?"

"Because—" I began, then sighed. "Look; I can't explain it. I know it sounds crazy, but I just have this feeling that I need to be there."

"Okay," she said, looking bewildered. "And do you have to go right away? What's the rush?"

I took my Audrey jacket from its hanger and put it on my bed.

"I'm going to leave you with some money for the bills and stuff."

"Don't worry about it. Mum and Dad have my back."

I smiled at her gratefully. "Thanks, that would be a great help."

"Have you told your parents?"

"Yeah, they're cool with it."

"Even your mother?"

"Even my mother."

My relationship with Mum had sunken to an all-time low after the stunt she pulled at Christmas lunch, so she had been on her very best behavior ever since. She even loaned me a generous sum for my trip.

"Audrey," Lucy was suddenly tearful, "what am I going to do without you?"

WHEN I TOLD Ida, she raised her eyebrows and stubbed out her cigarette on the red heart-shaped ashtray that was a permanent fixture on her desk. She leaned forward and looked as though she was about to say something, but I quickly cut her off.

"I know what you're going to say. The Colorado thing is some kind of coping mechanism that my anxiety-addled brain has conjured. That somehow going there will bring me closer to Rad. Even if it makes no logical sense."

"I wasn't going to say that at all. Sometimes we look too deeply into these things."

"Maybe the name is just a coincidence."

She smiled at me. "Or serendipity."

"Sometimes it feels like I'm following bread crumbs."

"Like in *Hansel and Gretel*?"

I nodded. "Are you a fan of *Doctor Who*?"

"I wouldn't say a fan exactly . . ."

"Do you know the general gist of it?"

"Yes, he's a time lord who pilots a ship called the TARDIS. Usually, an earthling joins him on his adventures."

"Pretty much. There was an episode titled 'Bad Wolf' where Dr. Who's companion, Rose, hooks into the heart of the TARDIS and becomes this entity with the power to influence time and space. Armed with this power, she scatters the words 'bad wolf' throughout oceans of time and in several different worlds. The words were like a code that the past versions of herself could recognize and follow in order to save the world—well, the universe. I suppose that every time she saw the words 'bad wolf,' whether it was a piece of graffiti or the name of an evil corporation, it was like a bread crumb leading her to a predetermined conclusion. That's what it feels like for me. Like I'm being guided somewhere, and there's a reason for it, only I won't know what it is until I get there."

"So that's what you mean about following bread crumbs." She sparked up another cigarette. "Sounds very insightful."

"It's just a thought," I said with a shrug.

She was quiet as she seemed to be thinking something over.

"I know it seems like you're in this infinite loop: one step forward, two steps back. But I do think you're making strides, even if you're not aware of it yourself. That's very important for you to know—you have come a long way."

"Really?"

She took another drag. "Yes. The fact that you're going on this trip is quite a remarkable progression."

"I still find it daunting." My hand traced the line of my rubber band. "I'm putting on a brave face, but I *am* terrified. At the moment it doesn't feel real. But there are times when it sinks in that I am going, that I am really doing this and . . ." I gave her a wry smile. "Well, you know."

"It's absolutely normal to feel that way, Audrey. I do believe this will be good for you, and if you ever need me, you can find me on Skype. But I kind of have a feeling I won't be hearing from you again."

I took a deep breath. "It's kind of crazy, isn't it?"

"We all need to follow our intuition, even if it takes us down the wrong path. Otherwise, you'll always be second-guessing yourself."

"I know. This was always my dream—to live in a quiet mountain town and write a book. It's been my dream for as long as I can remember."

"Then how lucky you are that circumstances have allowed you to follow it."

"Yeah, I just wish—" I shook my head. "No, forget it."

"That Rad could go with you?"

I nodded, tears once again welling up in my eyes. "I can't believe how hard it is. The pain is *indescribable*. It's like I've been turned into sandstone and my insides are being slowly hollowed out by a chisel and mallet."

"First love," said Ida with a sigh. "That's the one that kills you."

"But Rad wasn't my first love—Duck was."

"Well, that's the thing," she said. "Your first love isn't the first person you give your heart to—it's the first one who breaks it."

On the day before my flight, there was a knock at the door. Lucy was out, so I went to the front window to see who it was. My heart pounded wildly when I saw it was Rad. "Hey," he said when I opened the door. "Can I come in?"

"Sure." The last few days had been good for me. I felt in control again, like I was making progress. But now, seeing his face, being close to him—I was ready to fall to pieces. "Want a coffee?" I asked as he followed me inside and down the hall. I willed my voice not to betray me.

"Are you going somewhere?" said Rad, spotting the suitcase, next to the door.

I turned around to face him. "What are you doing here, Rad?"

He sighed. "Can we sit?"

"Okay."

We sat on the blue couch facing each other. "It's been a shitty few weeks," he said. "I'm sure for you as well."

I nodded, swallowing hard.

"I'm sorry I lost it that night; it's just a really hard thing to get your head around, you know?"

"Yeah," I said quietly.

"But I'm glad you told me. I mean, I always felt there was something you were holding back." He raked his fingers through his hair and looked around the room as if he was trying to search for the words he wanted to say next. Then he turned back to face me. "The thing is, I know you're not a bad person, Audrey. You just did a stupid thing, and I know you'd take it back if you could. I know how sorry you are—it all makes sense to me now. I was angry when you told me, and I have tried to hold on to that anger because it seemed like the right thing to do for Ana. But I couldn't stay mad at you, even though I wanted to." He reached over, taking my hand in his. "Then I found myself just thinking about you and not about what you said that night. Just you. And I couldn't bear the thought of never seeing you again."

Tears flooded my eyes and ran in watery streaks down my face. Rad reached up, gently wiping at them with his thumb. I looked away, trying to steady myself. "I'm in love with you, Audrey. I love you so much that I can't see straight, and the truth is, I don't even want to."

"Rad," I said, my voice all choked up. "No, we can't do this."

"Yes, we can. We can start all over again from the beginning. Clean slate." He peered at me hopefully. "Please?"

I shook my head, pulling my hand away from his. "No, it doesn't feel like a clean slate, not to me. Not yet."

"Audrey, you can't be serious." His face fell.

"I'm just trying to be realistic," I said, looking down at my hands.

"Fuck being realistic. Too many great things in this world get lost to reason."

I bit my lip and shook my head, trying to gather as much resolve as I could muster. I thought of what Mum had said the day she showed me that old picture of my father. *That's what boys can do, Audrey; that's the power they can wield over you. It's like being under a spell.* Somewhere during my heartache, my insufferable pain, there was something else stirring within me, and it was growing stronger and more insistent with each day. I had the sense that I was coming back to myself—that I was the one in charge again. Anxiety took that away from me, and in a way, so did love. And now I wanted to reclaim it in the only way I knew how. As much as it hurt, I knew this was my last chance to be free, to learn to stand on my own.

"Please," said Rad.

"I can't."

"Why?"

"Because I don't know who I am, and I need to find out. I have to do it on my own."

"Whatever you're going through, we can work through it together, help each other." He reached over and held my face gently between his hands. "Please, Audrey," he pleaded. "We can't just throw this into the fire; it's too important."

I looked at him, his eyes glassy and wet with tears, and I knew—I knew I was just a hairline away from cracking, from taking him in my arms and telling him he could have anything he wanted.

"I'm so sorry, Rad," I whispered. "I love you, but I can't."

ON THE MORNING I was due to fly out, Lucy came into my room with a breakfast tray of scrambled eggs on toast and bits of burnt bacon.

"Ta-da!" she announced proudly.

"Thanks, Lucy," I said, taking the tray from her.

"So you're all set?"

"All set."

A FEW HOURS later, I was putting my phone and passport into my leather satchel.

"All packed?" asked Lucy.

"Yes, I've been all packed for the last week."

"You sure you don't want me to drive you to the airport?"

"No, I want to do it alone."

Her eyes filled up, and I held my arms out and hugged her. "Love you, sweetie," she said. "I'm going to miss you."

"Me too." I squeezed her tightly. "I'll call you first thing when I land."

There was a honk outside, and I pulled away from Lucy, holding both her hands.

"My cab is here. You'll be okay, won't you?"

"Of course. You know Freddy practically lives here anyway. Maybe I'll convince him to move in officially."

"Good luck dragging him away from his momma," I said, with a smile. Freddy was a kid at heart, and I couldn't imagine him flying the coop just yet.

She rolled her eyes. "That woman drives me mad!"

"She loves you, though. His whole family adores you."

"Can you blame them?" She grinned, then her expression saddened. "I can't believe you're really going."

I gave her another quick hug. "I'll be back before you know it."

As THE CAR pulled out of my street, I nervously fingered the rubber band around my left wrist. I gazed out the window anxiously, as the city streets flashed by. Every sight, every sound, felt so much like Rad. I thought of that beautiful spring day when he turned up at my office in the pink Cadillac. That night when we kissed for the first time, under the stars. My phone rang all of a sudden, jolting me out of my daydream. I picked it up, my heart drumming loudly in my chest.

"Audrey." It was Sam.

"Hey."

"Have you left yet?"

"I'm just on my way to the airport."

"Do you a have a minute to stop by? There's a package that just came for you."

I checked the time. I was running early. "Yeah, I can make a quick stop."

SAM WAS WAITING for me downstairs with a brown envelope in her hand. "A courier brought this in for you just after lunch," she said as I got out of the cab. I took it from her outstretched hand and looked at it curiously. My heart skipped a beat when I recognized Rad's writing on the front.

For Audrey

I tucked it into my satchel and pulled the zip across. "Thanks, Sam."

She gave me a warm smile. "Take care." She gave me a quick hug and glanced quickly at her watch. "I should get going; I'm running late for my eleven o'clock. Don't be a stranger now, okay?"

Sam hurried off, blowing me a kiss. I stood there for a few moments, taking in the buildings that I knew like the back of my hand. I realized how happy I'd been here, and with a small pang of regret, I wondered whether I was making the right decision. In the distance I could hear the familiar sound of rock music coming from the Stairway to Heaven Church a few buildings down. The music came to a stop, and a small crowd of people filed out of the large, heavy doors and made their way down the street.

"Audrey?"

To my surprise, I turned around and saw Duck standing there.

"Hi!" he said, with a smile.

"Duck, you look great!" I thought back to how he was at the Christmas lunch, quiet and withdrawn. Now he looked like his regular old self again.

"I feel great," he said, his head motioning toward the church. "I think I've found what I've been looking for."

A pretty brunette wandered up to us and linked her arm through Duck's. "Audrey, this is my girlfriend, Angela."

She smiled brightly at me. "Hi, Audrey. Lovely to meet you."

"Lovely to meet you too," I said.

Duck beamed at me. "I told you, didn't I? Everything happens for a reason."

DUCK'S WORDS RANG in my ears as I sat in the cab heading toward the airport. I felt like a bird, feathers shed and poised to take flight.

Everything happens for a reason.

I dug into my handbag and took out the brown envelope, running my fingers across the ink where Rad had dragged his pen in the shape of my name. Whatever happened next, I knew it would never compare to what was. I would have to live my whole life knowing I would never find someone else like him, but I already knew I wouldn't. Taking a deep breath, I ripped open the envelope and reached inside, my stomach wound tightly in knots. It was a copy of *Inside UFO 54-40*. I flipped through the pages until I saw Rad's writing, scribbled on the page where Ultima shone like a beautiful mirage, an impossible dream.

We never made it, did we?

PART TWO

Whirlpools

I thought of you and how you love this beauty,
And walking up the long beach all alone
I heard the waves breaking in measured thunder
As you and I once heard their monotone.

Around me were the echoing dunes, beyond me
The cold and sparkling silver of the sea—
We two will pass through death and ages lengthen
Before you hear that sound again with me.

—Sara Teasdale, *Sea Sand*

One

Rosie's Diner was at the end of a small trek down a hilly road and up the main street of Delta. For the past few weeks, it had been my ritual to trudge along the same path, rain or shine or (as I've grown accustomed to) snow. I'd make my way on many cold, dismal days, like a moth to flame, into the warmth of those four walls.

I arrived in Colorado at the start of winter without a plan or destination in mind. After a short and uneventful stint in Denver, I flew to Montrose before boarding the first bus that struck my fancy. It took me to Delta, where I spent the last few weeks in a dingy motel with a dodgy radiator, pouring through the local classifieds for a place to stay. I walked a lot during those first days—all over the main part of town past quaint shops with brightly colored awnings and festive murals painted on the sides of buildings. I hiked across parklands and rushing rivers with no direction in mind. I returned at the end of each day and slipped back into my room like a ghost, wondering what the hell I was doing out here all on my own. During those cold, sleepless nights, I felt desolate and unsure, discouraged and homesick.

The turning point came when by chance I wandered into Rosie's Diner, which was staffed by Rosie herself, a cheerful middle-aged woman with strands of silver hair threaded through her dark, wiry locks. On my first visit, I tried a slice of her gooseberry pie, and it warmed me in a way that nothing else had in a long time. After that, I kept going back day after day, and we struck up a friendship.

"Morning, sweetheart," said Rosie as I pushed through the heavy glass door.

"Morning, Rosie," I answered, sliding into my regular booth. She came over with a slice of lemon tart and a pot of coffee.

"You're still looking for a place to stay, aren't you?"

"Yeah, I'm not having much luck. I can't seem to find anything in my price range, and I'm burning through my savings quicker than I thought."

"Well, I've got some great news for you."

"Really?" I unzipped my brown satchel and pulled out my laptop.

"Some friends of mine, Graham and Dale, are going away for the winter. They're looking for a house sitter, and I told them you'd be perfect. They live right on the edge of town, so it will be easy for you to get around."

"That sounds promising," I said, a spark of hope flaring up in my chest.

"There's not much to do in the garden this time of year, but they have a little Yorkie who needs taking care of."

"Oh, I love Yorkies. They are adorable."

"What are you doing later today, around three?"

"Nothing."

"Great! Why don't you meet me back here, and I'll drive you over to the house."

"Okay, thanks, Rosie."

"Still working away on your book?" she asked. She set the tart down on the table and poured coffee into my mug. I wrapped my gloved hands around it, watching the steam rise up in wispy white coils.

"Yeah, I think it's going to be a collection of short stories."

"Well, I'll leave you to it, then." She flashed me a warm smile. "Oh, by the way. I read that book you gave me, *A Snowflake in a Snowfield*."

My breath caught in my throat. "What did you think?"

"It was beautiful. Read the whole thing in one sitting. That kid sure is talented."

"I thought you might like it." I couldn't help feeling a flush of pride.

She shot me a cautious look. "Have you spoken to him at all?"

"No."

"You still miss him, though." I nodded, and she gave me a sympathetic smile. "You know, missing someone can sometimes be the best thing for a writer."

LATER THAT AFTERNOON, I met Rosie outside the diner, and we walked around back to her old pickup truck. A short drive later, we arrived at the house, and Rosie pulled into the driveway. It was a charming chalet made entirely from timber, and it reminded me of a gingerbread house, especially with its quaint sloping roof that was heavily caked with snow.

"It's pretty," I said.

"The lake is about a five-minute walk from here. It will be frozen over in a month or two. The locals even skate on the outer edges."

"Skating's not really for me, but I bet the view will be stunning."

We walked up the drive and knocked on the wood-paneled door.

A few moments later, it swung open, and we were greeted by a burly man with a heavy beard wearing a red-and-white checkered shirt.

"Rosie!" he roared, pulling her into a bear hug. He swung his head back. "Dale, they're here!"

"This is the girl I was telling you about," said Rosie when he let her go.

I heard footsteps coming down the hallway, and another man appeared at the door. He had closely cropped hair, and his clean-shaven face was framed by a pair of rimless glasses.

"Audrey, this is Graham, and this—" she motioned to the man in glasses, "is his partner, Dale."

"Hi," I said.

"She's gorgeous," said Dale, planting a kiss on my cheek.

"Thank you," I laughed.

A little Yorkie poked her head from behind his ankles. He scooped her up. "And this little thing here is Apple."

"Hi, Apple." I reached down and stroked her head. She tipped her head back and licked my fingers.

"Come in, come in," said Graham, and we followed him inside.

"Oh, it's beautiful," I said, as my eyes took in the wooden beams and their quaint triangular formation. Expansive windows opened to a stunning view of snowcapped mountains and fir trees dusted with white. The place was immaculate and beautifully decorated with antiques, Persian rugs, and charming lampshades; it was full of warm hues of red, pink, and earthy browns. A large cream-colored couch wrapped around a roaring fire in the center of the room. My heart gave a small flutter of hope. No more cold, damp nights at the motel if this worked out for me.

Graham walked over to the bar and came back with two drinks in his hand.

"These are our famous Pink Flamingos," he said, handing one to me and the other to Rosie.

"Oh, these are legendary," she said, taking a sip from her neon-green straw.

I took a sip of mine. It tasted like a mix of cotton candy, grapefruit, and Cointreau.

"Yum," I exclaimed as Dale winked at me.

We settled ourselves on the couch, and Apple bounded up into my lap.

"She likes you," said Graham. "That's always a good sign."

I smiled. "I like her too."

"So, Audrey, I suppose Rosie has told you we're looking for a house sitter while we're away for the winter."

"Yes, she has."

"Our regular girl pulled out last minute. Met some guy and took off with him to Spain—all quite sudden. These whirlwind romances." He rolled his eyes. "So we were in a bit of a fix until you showed up."

"It was meant to be," said Rosie.

"It seems that way, doesn't it?" He smiled. "Now, Audrey, I'm sure you're a model citizen, but we'll need two references from you. It's just a standard thing we do."

"That's fine. I was house-sitting in Sydney for my best friend's uncle. I can get a reference from him. And I'm sure my editor, Sam, would be happy to provide one as well."

"Perfect!" said Dale, clapping his hands together. "Let's talk about payment."

"Oh, no, I'm happy to do it free of charge, honestly. I mean, you're the ones who are doing me the favor. It's been really hard finding a place, and I'll be glad to get out of that motel."

"No, no, we insist."

"No, really—"

"Oh, darling," said Dale, his hand on my arm. "We don't mind at all—honestly."

Graham chimed in. "Well, if it would make you feel better, why don't you do a little work for us on the side as well?"

"Work?"

"Of course!" said Dale, his eyes lighting up. "The antiques."

Graham turned to me. "Dale and I import antiques, and we have a whole shed full of them that need some TLC. So if you'd like, you can work on them while we're away. That would be perfect, actually. What do you think?"

"I've never worked with antiques before. Is it hard?"

"Not at all." Graham waved his hand. "Easy as pie. We just need to have them cleaned up and oiled. Dale and I will take you through it."

"Sounds great! I'd love to make myself useful while I'm here."

There was a *ding* sound.

"Aha! The Bombe Alaska's ready," said Dale, jumping to his feet. "Can you give me a hand, Gray?"

"Sure." Graham followed Dale into the kitchen.

"They're smitten with you," Rosie announced when they were out of earshot.

"I feel terrible about taking their money. Look at this place; I feel like I should be paying them."

"Oh, don't worry about it, Audrey," she said, patting me on the knee. "They're just thrilled to have found someone on such short notice. Besides," she winked, "they won't miss the money, if you know what I mean."

I looked around at the lavishly decorated room and nodded. "I suppose you're right. Well, hopefully I can make it up to them with the antiques."

"That's sweet of you, honey. They would really appreciate that."

The two men came back with four slices of the Bombe Alaska served on bone china plates. Dale handed one to me along with a spoon.

"Dig in."

"You're in for a treat, Audrey," said Rosie. "Dale makes the best Bombe Alaska."

"I'd have to agree with you there," said Graham.

I took a bite. It was phenomenal. The sponge was soft and sweet; the dark chocolate ice cream was a perfect companion to the orange-flavored meringue.

"Wow, this is amazing, Dale."

"I don't know why you won't give me the recipe," said Rosie, after taking a bite of hers.

"Sorry, darling, you know I promised my mother on her deathbed to keep it secret. Anything else you are welcome to."

"I got my gooseberry pie recipe from Dale," she explained.

"Really? I'm impressed!"

"Oh stop it," Dale said, but he looked immensely pleased.

A FEW WEEKS later, Graham and Dale left on their trip, and I settled into the house. I was grateful to be out of the motel, and Apple was great company. When the weather was good, I took her for walks around the lake where we fed the ducks leftover bread and chatted with the locals. I often came across a lady with a German shepherd who recommended a good coffee shop just minutes away.

Spending time with the antiques turned out to be an unexpected joy. There was an assortment of furniture in the shed—tables, chairs, side cabinets, and writing desks that were old and tired, covered in dirt and dust. Dale and Graham had shown me how to bring them to life again using stiff brushes, old rags, and oil. The transformation was astonishing, and every new piece of furniture I worked on gave me a sense of pride and satisfaction.

Some days I stayed in working on my book of short stories, stopping every so often to admire the view. On the mantelpiece above the fire, I had put the snow globe Rad gave me that night at Blues Point Park. I often wished I could call him up and tell him I had made it to my little mountain town, that outside my window I could see mountains capped in snow, and that I was writing the book I had always wanted to write.

The isolation made me miss home, but I kept in regular contact with Lucy, who was anxious to know every detail about my new life. I never asked her about Rad, even though I wanted to, and she was careful to avoid the topic.

One morning, I logged onto my e-mail and saw Angie's name in my inbox. Since graduation, we had written to each other every now and then, but it had been ages since I last heard from him. I clicked it open.

Hello old friend!

It's been a while. New York is fab, as you know. I'm in my element here.

Couple months back I officially became a junior agent at Annie Otto. Turns out my cousin Cecelia married a publishing magnate and he recommended me when a position opened up in their NY office. So here I am!

Anyway, I was chatting to one of my colleagues, and you know, novellas are coming back into fashion. So

*are short stories, and would you believe it (gasp) poetry.
Apparently the kids today are into speed reading. I
blame Twitter.*

*I thought of you right away, and an idea came to
me. Sam tells me you're in Colorado working on a
book. Would you consider having me rep you? I'd love
to peddle a book of your short stories. The one about the
bookcase still haunts my dreams at night. I think you
would be a real hit.*

Thoughts?

Lots of love, Angie. xx

I grinned. I was thrilled for Angie. Annie Otto was one of the best literary agents in the world. I wrote back and accepted his offer.

The next day I got to work. I sat down with my pen and notepad and spent the morning brainstorming ideas. After lunch, I began tapping away on my laptop. Hours later, I looked up at the clock and was surprised to see it was well past dinner. It had been a dreary day, so I barely noticed how dark it had gotten. I stretched my arms and got up, my legs numb from sitting for so long, then went to fix myself a quick dinner. I was pleased with the work I had done, and I fell asleep that night with a feeling of satisfaction. I wondered if it was like this for Rad when he was writing his book. I found myself wishing I could share my experience with him.

I jumped out of bed the next morning, eager to get back to my writing. I made myself a cup of coffee before going over all the work I'd done the previous day. It was awful. The writing was all over the place. The ideas were good, but I couldn't seem to bring them to life. I let out a groan of disappointment. What the hell was wrong with me? Why couldn't I get the stories down when I could see them so vividly in my head? But I couldn't give up now, not when I had a real shot at getting my work published. With a sigh, I shut the lid of my laptop and went back to the drawing board.

DAYS LATER, I was at Rosie's with a mug of coffee and a caramel slice. I had my laptop open in front of me, and I was staring sullenly at the screen.

"Everything okay, sweetheart?" Rosie asked, stopping by my booth.

I looked up at her and sighed. "I don't know, Rosie. Ever since Angie wrote to me, I can't seem to get myself together. I think the possibility of getting published has spooked me. Whenever I write anything, I think it's amazing—brilliant. Then the next day when I go over my work, I hate it. With a passion."

"The one you wrote about the bookshelf is pure genius."

"I know, but this is Annie Otto, after all. Every story I write has to be as good as that one, if not better. Angie says I'll need seven to eight pieces. So far, I've written only a couple I'm happy with."

She smiled at me. "Just give it some time, Audrey. I'm sure you'll work it out."

ONE DAY, THE weather was exceptionally good. The sky was a dreamy blue, and I didn't feel like staying in. I called Rosie, who had the day off, and she agreed to meet at the Creamery Arts Center, where the locals held a market every third Sunday.

I arrived there a little earlier than planned, so I strolled through the busy park where a number of stalls were set up in white tents. A cold wind hit me from nowhere, and I shivered, zipping up my anorak and pulling my wine-colored beanie snugly over my ears. I was kicking myself for not putting on my gloves before I left that morning. My hands were freezing, and I stuck them in my pockets.

I stopped to admire the bronze statue of dancing elephants when I heard Rosie call out my name.

"Hi, you!" I said, giving her a quick hug.

"Hey! I'm early."

"So am I!"

We laughed.

"How about these elephants, huh?" I said.

"Aren't they beautiful?" Rosie remarked.

I nodded. "They look almost alive. Who's the artist?"

"Jim Agius. His sculptures are just wonderful."

We began our leisurely stroll around the markets, stopping every now and then to admire the wares put out by the locals. Several of the stalls sold handmade jewelry and assorted metal-work. From candelabras to photo frames to pickaxes—it was a mixed bag. There were also cakes, pies, and other baked goods. The aroma that drifted from those stalls made me feel suddenly hungry, and I decided I would take something back with me on the way home.

Up ahead, I spotted an old-fashioned cart selling chestnuts.

"Hey, it's been ages since I've had chestnuts," I said to Rosie. "I love them."

"Oh, looks like Gabe's manning the stall today. You see that tall, gorgeous black dude standing behind the cart?"

I followed her gaze to where a man in his early twenties was handing an elderly couple a bag of chestnuts.

"Why don't you grab us a bag?" she suggested. "I'll pick us up some coffees, and we'll have ourselves a little picnic."

"Sure. I'll meet you by the dancing elephants?"

"Perfect. Make sure you tell Gabe I said hi."

As I approached the cart, Gabe looked up, his eyes locking on to mine.

"Hi," he said with a warm smile. His eyes were iridescent—like the changing of seasons, a myriad of brown hues married with golden flecks of light. He had angular cheekbones, a shadow of a beard, and a dark blue beanie pulled over his closely cropped hair.

"Hi," I replied.

"Would you like some chestnuts? It's five dollars a bag."

"Sure."

Using a pair of tongs, he filled a brown paper bag with chestnuts and passed it to me.

"You should have them while they're warm. They taste the best that way."

I took one out of the bag and attempted to remove the skin.

"Here," he said, reaching over. "Let me show you a neat trick."

He put his hand over mine; it was warm from the chestnuts.

"See, you have to squeeze it like this." He pressed down gently on my thumb and forefinger. Sure enough, the shell loosened and broke away cleanly, leaving a perfect chestnut behind.

"Hey, that's really amazing. Thank you!"

I dipped into my pocket and handed him a five-dollar bill.

"You're welcome. It's one of those tricks, you know, that will serve you well in life."

I laughed. "Is that so?" I popped the chestnut into my mouth. I had forgotten just how good they were.

"Uh-huh." He smiled again. "You're not from around here, are you?"

"No."

"Are you just visiting, then?"

I shrugged. "To be honest, I don't really know. I'll be staying here for the winter at least, and I'll just take it from there."

"I have a feeling you're from somewhere a long way away."

"I am."

"Australia?"

"The accent is a dead giveaway, isn't it?"

He smiled in response. "So you're on an adventure, then."

"I suppose you can say that."

"I think that's really great. I have plans to travel too."

"You do?"

"Yeah. At the moment, I'm just saving like crazy. I work at my uncle's garage five days a week, and on weekends, I pick up odd jobs."

"Where are you planning to go?"

"I have it all figured out. Once I get enough cash together, I'm going to Alaska to work on the oil rigs. I hear it can be tough, but on the upside, you earn really good money. So I'll do that for a few years until I have enough cash for a boat. Then I'm going to sail around the world."

"That's quite a detailed plan."

"I believe in having a goal and working hard for it. I mean, you won't believe it, but I couldn't even swim a year ago. I knew that had to be fixed if my plans involved being around water. So I set myself a deadline, signed up for lessons, and now I'm a pro."

"Hey, that's really great."

"So what about you? Is there something you wish you could do?"

I thought about the walk this morning, trudging through the snow. Some of it had snuck into my boots and my feet were damp and cold. I was already looking forward to getting home, peeling off my socks, and warming my feet by the fire.

"I wish I could drive," I said. Since being here, there had been many situations when driving would have been ideal. Shopping for groceries, for example, would be a heck of a lot easier. What's more, Graham and Dale left me the keys to their car, so it sure would have been helpful if I had a driver's license.

"You can't drive?"

"No, I never got my driver's license when I was back home, and I'm sure it would be tricky to get one while I'm here."

"Well, my uncle's friend is a cop. Why don't I give him a call and check with him—see what the rules are for visitors?"

"Oh, no, I don't want to be a bother."

"It's no problem at all."

"Really? That would be great, then, thanks."

"I suppose I should get your number, then, so I can let you know what he says."

"Yeah, good idea."

He pulled his phone from the back pocket of his jeans. "So where are you staying?"

"I'm house-sitting for a couple just at the edge of town. Graham and Dale."

"Oh, I know who they are. Graham drives a Saab. Totally impractical." He shook his head. "They are great guys, though; my uncle went to school with Dale."

"Small world."

He shrugged. "Tell me about it. So . . . your number?" He passed me his phone, and I keyed in my name and number before passing it back.

"Your name is Audrey?"

I nodded.

"I've never met an Audrey before. It's a real pretty name."

"Thank you. Oh, Rosie says hi by the way."

"You know Rosie?"

"Yeah, she's kind of taken me under her wing since I've been here."

He smiled. "Rosie has a heart of gold—so you're in good hands."

A FEW DAYS later, Gabe called.

"Hi, Audrey. I talked to my uncle's friend about getting a driver's license here, and he says it's doable."

"Really?"

"Yeah. Have you got a pen and paper handy?"

"I'll grab one." I stood up, almost stepping on Apple. "Sorry, baby," I whispered under my breath. She looked up at me with her sweet, doe-like eyes, oblivious to her near-death experience.

I found a pen in a kitchen drawer and a paper towel on the counter. "Okay, I'm ready."

"So, first thing you have to do is get together your passport and your birth certificate."

"Sure, I have my passport here, and I can get my parents to fax me my birth certificate."

Gabe gave me the phone number and address of the registry, and I wrote it down on the paper towel. It was in the basement of the Delta County Courthouse, which happened to be just a short walk away.

"Now, you'll have to take a test, but it's pretty easy. You can pick up the study booklet at the office ahead of time."

"Okay, I'll do that."

"Once you get your leaner's permit, you can start taking driving lessons."

"Oh," I said, feeling a little disheartened. "I don't think I can afford driving lessons at the moment." I couldn't believe that hadn't even occurred to me.

"Well, I know someone who can help you there."

"You do?" I asked. "Who?"

"Me, of course."

"Oh, no, Gabe. I can't ask you to do that."

"I'd be happy to. I taught my nephew last summer. He passed with flying colors."

"That's very kind of you," I said, feeling reluctant, "but I don't want to put you out."

"Don't worry about it, Audrey." His voice was kind and reassuring. "It will be no trouble at all."

"I'VE DECIDED TO try for my driver's license, and Gabe's offered to give me lessons." I was at the diner, sitting on a stool at the counter. Rosie was brushing some crumbs into the sink with a rag. She stopped and looked up, setting the rag down.

"Gabe? Since when did the two of you start talking?"

"I gave him my number—you know, the day we were at the markets."

"You gave him your number? You didn't mention anything about this to me, young lady."

I shrugged. "It was for a practical reason, and I didn't really expect him to call."

"Well," she said, hands on her hips, "this is interesting."

"Rosie, don't read too much into it. It is definitely too soon for me to be thinking about *that*."

"I wasn't implying anything," she said, even though it was obvious she was. "But I will say he's a sweet kid. *And*," she smirked, "quite easy on the eyes too."

"Really? I didn't notice," I lied.

She rolled her eyes. "Of course you didn't."

"So how do you know him, anyway?"

"I know his uncle Daryl. He runs the local auto repair shop."

"Gabe mentioned he works there. He was also telling me about his plans—he wants to sail around the world one day. It's a pipe dream for most people, isn't it? But Gabe has figured out how to get there, step by step. I mean, it's impressive."

"I'm telling you now: that kid is going places. Don't let those good looks fool you. He scored off the charts on his SATs, and they offered him a scholarship to Stanford."

"Wow. Why didn't he take it?"

"I'll leave it up to him to tell you."

"Do you think I should take the lessons? I don't want to be a bother. I mean, he seems like a pretty busy guy."

"If he's offering, then yes—why not? I'm sure the two of you would get along like nobody's business. Plus, imagine how great it would be if you got your license. No more trudging through the snow."

I brightened at the thought. "Yeah, I spoke to Graham about it, and he says his insurance will cover me. So I'm free to use his car if I do get my license."

"That's great, honey. I definitely think you should go for it, then. It would make your life a heck of a lot easier."

ON MY FIRST driving lesson, Gabe picked me up in his battered station wagon, and we practiced around the back streets.

At first, it was terrifying. It felt as if the car was going way too fast and the tires were made of glass and couldn't possibly keep us pinned to the road.

"Easy on the brake—you're doing okay," said Gabe, after I jammed my foot down sharply on the brake for the hundredth time.

"Shit—okay." I took a deep breath.

"It's a bit freaky the first time you get behind the wheel, so don't worry. You'll get the hang of it soon."

He was right. After a while, I managed to avoid doing the stop-start thing and drove down the entire length of the street.

"Oh my God! I can't believe I'm actually driving!"

"See? Nothing to it—just takes a bit of getting used to; that's all," said Gabe. His face broke into his trademark good-natured grin. "Now signal for the turn up ahead."

I continued to drive at a crawl, pulling over each time a car came up behind me. I got used to signaling and making turns. It was actually not that different from playing a video game.

"So how come you've never gone for your license, back home?" Gabe asked.

"I'm not sure," I frowned. "I suppose I didn't have a big enough incentive. I moved out of home after I left school, and my work was in walking distance." I didn't want to tell him it was mainly because of my anxiety issue.

"And I'm sure it doesn't snow where you were."

"No, the weather in Australia is pretty tame compared to here."

"How was the test?"

"It was easy. I mean, a memory game more than anything, and a lot of it was common sense." I had gone for the written test a few days ago and left the office proudly with my learner's permit in hand. It felt oddly liberating. I wanted to call Rad and share the good news, but something told me to stay strong. I had come this far on my own. I had to see how much further I could go.

I signaled for a turn up ahead. "You know what the weird thing is? If I hadn't stopped at your cart that day, I probably wouldn't have done this. And I'm so glad I did."

"Me too. You know that movie *The Matrix*—the scene where Morpheus shows Neo how he can download all these different skills?"

"Uh-huh."

"I think life is kind of like that. You are a toolbox, and you have to add stuff to it and build on it. I think the more tools you have, the better life gets."

"I like that idea."

"That's my mission in life. To keep adding to the toolbox."

"You know what? I think I'm going to do the same."

A few days later, Gabe called to tell me he had something special planned for us the following day.

"You'll have to get up before dawn, though. Do you think you can manage that?"

I groaned inwardly. I was not a morning person.

"Sure, I can do that. I might need a wake-up call, though."

He laughed. "Okay, noted."

Next morning, true to his word, my phone went off at five, interrupting a deep and peaceful sleep. Against my better judgment, I had stayed up late the night before working on an idea for a new story. I was so engrossed in it that I lost track of the time. Reluctantly, I reached toward the nightstand and fumbled in the dark for my phone.

"Hey," I said, groggily.

"Good morning." Gabe's baritone cut through the chilly air.

"I'm going back to sleep. It's too cold to go out."

"No, you're not. Put on some warm clothes and a good pair of hiking boots. I'll be at your house in twenty minutes."

ABOUT AN HOUR later, I was riding shotgun in Gabe's car as we headed out farther and farther away from civilization.

"It's not dangerous all the way out here, is it?" I asked.

"Not really."

"What about bears?"

"It's winter." He grinned at me broadly. "They're all asleep, Audrey."

The road got more and more gritty, with stones jumping up and biting the underside of the car. We were driving by a rocky mountain face when Gabe slowed down and parked by the side of the road.

"We're here," he announced cheerfully.

We got out, and he popped the trunk, grabbed a backpack, and slung it over his shoulders. He pulled out a pair of flashlights and handed one to me.

"So we're going for a hike, I guess?"

"You guessed it." He motioned to the top of the cliff face that loomed over us at an impossible height. "We're heading up there."

My face fell. "Seriously? In the dark? What if we get lost?"

"We won't; I've done this a thousand times. I'll admit it's a tough track, but it will be worth it when we get up there."

"Okay," I said, still a little reluctant. "Lead the way."

BY THE TIME we made it near the top, I was struggling to catch my breath, and my legs felt ready to give way. Gabe had just pushed off the last foothold to step onto the summit, and he turned and stretched his hand out to me. "Almost there."

I grabbed his hand and, dipping into the last reserves of my energy, lunged upward and over onto the rocky surface. "Wow!" I stammered, as my eyes drank in the view before me.

We were caught in that brief moment when the sun is just on the cusp of the horizon; golden streams of light burst from its pale, soft glow. Below us, the wilderness stretched on and on right out to the horizon, and it was like we were the only two people in the world. "This is Ultima," I said under my breath and wished Rad was here to see this.

"What was that?" asked Gabe.

I shook my head. "I was just thinking out loud—the view here is spectacular."

"It's really something, isn't it?"

He peeled off his backpack and sat down on a large, flat rock. I went to join him. Reaching into his bag, he pulled out a bright red thermos.

"Coffee?"

"Oh yes!" I said.

I watched as he carefully poured the coffee into plastic cups before passing one to me. I took the cup from him and sipped the coffee slowly, feeling mildly euphoric. Being in Gabe's company made me feel at ease. It was hard to believe we'd only met recently. I felt as though I had known him all my life.

"How often do you come out here?" I asked.

"Every chance I get. It's been really busy at the garage lately, so I've been helping my uncle out with extra shifts. But he made me take the day off today."

"The two of you are close, aren't you?"

Gabe grinned. "Yeah, we are. He's a good guy. He's always had my back."

"How about your parents? Are they here in Delta?"

"No, in Denver. Dad's a software engineer, and Mom teaches middle school. Dad is still furious that I turned down my scholarship to Stanford, so I haven't been back home for a while."

"Rosie told me about that. Why didn't you go for it?"

"I suppose I just wanted to see the world a little before I made that kind of commitment. Nothing more to it than that." He took a sip of his coffee, his eyes staring out at the horizon. "How about you?" He turned to look at me. "Did you ever go to college?"

I shook my head. "I didn't have the option because I kind of messed up my exams."

"Why? What happened?"

I took a deep breath and told him about my panic attack. "At the time, it was like the end of the world, you know? But then, life just carried on, and I landed this amazing position at *See! Sydney*—they're an award-winning publication. And I've learned so much since—more than anything a degree could have taught me. I'm a lot further ahead in my career than I would have been if I'd done it the regular way."

"I guess it was a blessing in disguise, then."

"It was."

"So what are you planning to do now?"

I told him about Angie and the opportunity to have my work published.

"Wow, Annie Otto, that's huge!"

"I can't believe something that big fell into my lap. But now I'm scared shitless, and I can't make the words do what I want."

"It's just performance anxiety. You'll get past it in no time."

"I hope so." As I gazed out at the picturesque scene, I felt suddenly upbeat. Gabe was right; it was just performance anxiety, nothing more than that. As soon as the nerves settled, I would write like I used to, and the stories would come rushing onto paper.

"In the meantime, just sit proud and think of how much you've accomplished."

I grinned. "You know, life isn't all that different from a snakes and ladders game, is it? A ladder appears out of nowhere, and all of a sudden you're that much closer to the finish line."

"But it works the other way too."

"It does," I said, thinking back to my breakup with Rad. "Everything was going so well for me, then it was like a slippery slope. My best friend, Candela, went AWOL, my relationship ended, and I just couldn't function. I left my job, which was a crazy thing to do. There are hundreds of grad students who would kill for my position, but I just couldn't do it anymore. I needed to be somewhere different, forget the real world for a while."

"I think you've been pretty brave, coming out here all by yourself."

"It was hard the first few weeks. I felt like I had made a terrible mistake. But I couldn't go back home, not after telling everyone this was my dream. I couldn't face it, so I stuck it out in that shitty motel. But now, as each day goes by, it becomes clearer to me that I *did* make the right choice. I don't have anything solid to go by; it's just a feeling."

"It's good to get out of your comfort zone. All my life, I was book smart—your stereotypical nerd."

"You, a nerd?" I laughed.

"Yes, a full-blown nerd. We're talking glasses, braces, Dungeons & Dragons—the works. I even went on this game show called *Battle of the Brainiacs*. I was the chubby, happy-go-lucky kid who aced all his exams and cleaned up at the chess tournament. All my life, I'd spent so much time inside my head. One day—it was only a few weeks after I sat for my SATs—it was almost like I snapped and my brain wanted a vacation."

"Snapped?"

"Yes, a panic attack. Similar to yours. One minute I was wolfing down enchiladas with some friends at our favorite hangout; the next I was on the floor, clutching my chest and thinking I was having a heart attack."

"But you're the most stable and level-headed person I've ever met."

"I wasn't always like this. It took a lot of work for me to get there."

"How did you do it?"

"My parents sent me to a see a guy. He recommended that I start running, so I did. Once I started, it became an addiction. I'd spent so much time developing my mind I had neglected my body. It was starved for attention. So the second I put a little focus there, my body lapped it up like nobody's business. That was when I realized how important it was to find a balance between the two. So now I run and hike as much as possible. Sometimes I go kayaking or mountain biking, and as you know, I recently learned to swim. I was never any good at sports—I didn't think I could do those things. But the more I got into it, the easier it became. Now it's as natural to me as breathing. And it all started one morning when I laced up my running shoes and went for a jog around the block."

"That's amazing," I said, feeling suddenly inspired. "At home, I barely did anything physical. I walked to work and back—that's about it. But when I got here, I walked a lot because there was nothing else to do. Even though I didn't realize it at the time, walking was making me stronger not just physically but mentally as well."

"That's what I mean about getting out of your comfort zone. That's where you learn the most about yourself."

We were quiet for a few moments, watching the sun creep upward, painting the sky a cotton candy pink.

"So you don't ever get panic attacks anymore?" I asked, breaking the silence.

"Well, you know what Hunter S. Thompson said about the 'edge.'"

I nodded. "Only the ones who have gone over know what it's really like."

"Exactly. Once you cross over, you can't go back. It never goes away completely. You just get better at dealing with it."

"My therapist gave me this." I pulled back the sleeve of my Sherpa jacket to show him the rubber band around my wrist. "Whenever I feel anxious, I just snap the rubber band against my skin."

"Does it work?"

"It does, most of the time. It definitely helps to have it there."

"Do you know what I do?"

I shook my head and let him continue.

"I picture a ship tied to a mooring. I imagine the rope between the two is made of this indestructible material. It's impossible to break. Not even an atomic bomb could sever it. And as I picture this infallible piece of rope, I imagine the ship is my mind and the mooring is my body."

"I like that. I might have to borrow it sometime."

He grinned his good-natured grin. "Are you hungry?"

"Starving."

He reached into his backpack. "Do you like peanut butter and jelly?"

"Absolutely," I smiled.

A FEW WEEKS later, I spoke to Lucy via FaceTime and brought up Gabe for the first time.

"I've made a new friend. His name is Gabe."

"What's he like?"

"He's really great, so much fun to be around. He's funny

and smart—so different from Rad—" I stopped. I hadn't said Rad's name out loud in such a long time that it felt like I was breaking some kind of taboo. "Not that I'm thinking about Gabe in a romantic way," I added.

"But you're still thinking about Rad?" said Lucy cautiously.

"Of course I am. I think about him all the damn time."

"Oh, sweetie. The two of you had something pretty special. I mean, anyone could see that."

"I know," I said quietly. "He was the only person who understood me in a way that was profound, in a way that mattered. How can you get past something like that? Something that meant that much—" I stopped, feeling the same old anxiety rear its ugly head. I closed my eyes and took a deep breath.

"Anyway. Let's not talk about Rad anymore."

"Okay, then, why don't you tell me about your new friend?"

"Well, he's been teaching me to drive—"

"You're learning to drive? Audrey, that's amazing! When did this happen?"

"I got my learner's permit a few weeks back."

"Oh, why didn't you tell me?"

"I don't know," I shrugged. "I guess I wasn't sure if I'd go through with the lessons and how I'd do. But it's actually going well. Better than I ever thought! Gabe thinks it won't be much longer before I can go for my test. We're doing lessons practically every day."

"That's really nice of him."

"I know. I'm so thankful."

"So what else do the two of you get up to aside from driving lessons?"

I told her about our hiking trip. "We took some pictures. Do you want to see?"

"I'd love to! Send away!"

I texted her some pictures we took on the mountaintop that morning.

"Holy shit, Audrey. *That's* Gabe?"

"Uh-huh."

"Boy, you weren't kidding about the view. And I don't mean the mountain scenery. Is he like a model or something?"

"No, he works for his uncle at the local auto shop."

"Seriously, Audrey, and I don't say this lightly—he is *magnificent.* Like, probably the most beautiful person I have ever seen. Ever."

I laughed. "He's really smart and funny. And I'm learning a lot from him."

"You are?"

"I am. He has a way of taking something complex and making it dead simple. His mother is a teacher, so maybe that's where he gets it."

"He sounds like a heck of a guy," she paused. "So you're telling me there isn't an attraction there? Not even a bit?"

"I like him a lot, but as a friend. I can't think of him as more than that."

"Audrey, please," she said, unconvinced. "I'm already half in love with him, based on those pictures alone."

"Who are you in love with?" I heard Freddy's voice in the background.

Lucy clapped her hand over her mouth. "Oops," she said, her eyes brimming with laughter. She turned her head back. "I'm just chatting to Audrey."

Freddy's goofy face appeared next to hers on the screen a few moments later.

"Hey, Audrey," he said with a wave.

"Hey, Freddy. How's it going?"

"Great, can't complain. We went bowling yesterday. I beat Lucy for the first time." He beamed as Lucy rolled her eyes.

"My arm was sore. Your momma made me roll a mountain of dough the day before."

"No excuses, babe." He grinned.

She gave me a wry smile. "I'm never going to hear the end of this, for as long as I live."

He kissed her cheek and playfully ruffled her hair. "Nope, you definitely won't."

I laughed. "Congratulations, Freddy."

"Thanks, Audrey. How are you doing all the way over there?"

"Really good. I've made some new friends, and I've taken up hiking."

"You? Hiking?" He gave me a dubious look.

"I have pictures to prove it!"

"Here, babe, check these out." Lucy showed Freddy the pictures I sent.

He whistled softly under his breath. "So that's your new friend, huh?" He teased.

"Yes, Lucy's kind of in love with him." I laughed.

"I don't blame her. I think I might be a bit in love with him myself."

EVERY SATURDAY—RAIN or shine—Gabe and I went for a hike in the woods. It was something I looked forward to each week. Gabe was always great company. He was such a cheerful person that no matter what mood I was in, he could always wrangle a smile from me.

During our long hikes, I learned that Gabe was a movie buff. His taste was eclectic. He loved action flicks—anything by Tarantino—but he also loved quirky, introspective films like *Being John Malkovich*. His absolute favorite was a toss-up between *Scarface* and *Over the Top*, the latter being a B-grade movie about an arm-wrestling tournament, starring Sylvester Stallone. We saw it one night at his place, a one-bedroom flat above his uncle's workshop. It wasn't a movie I would have picked off the shelf at Blockbuster, but I did find myself enjoying it a lot.

One Saturday, we had just finished our routine hike and were heading back to Gabe's car when we were simultaneously struck with a wild craving for quesadillas.

"Want to go to Fiesta?" he asked. Fiesta was a Mexican place in town.

"Great idea."

"Do you want to drive?"

"Sure." He handed me the keys.

We arrived at Fiesta, and I was delighted to see there was a parking space on the street, right out front.

"It's way too tight, Audrey."

"I'm going to give it a try."

"Okay, but it *is* really narrow, and this is parallel parking we're talking about. I don't think I could get in it, and you know my parking skills are out of this world."

I laughed. "Bet you ten bucks I can park it."

"I'd feel bad, taking your money."

I signaled and began to reverse into the spot, biting my lip in concentration. A few moments later, to Gabe's surprise, I had perfectly parked his car. He got out, a look of astonishment on his face. I was next to him a few moments later, surveying my handiwork.

"What did I tell you?" I couldn't help but gloat.

"Looks like you're ready for that test."

LESS THAN A week later, Gabe dropped me off at the registry for my driver's test. I was a bundle of nerves, so he gave me a quick pep talk before wishing me luck and setting off on foot to his uncle's shop.

The test itself was a lot easier than I expected. My driving instructor, Bob—a wearied middle-aged man with a handlebar moustache—barely spoke as we drove around the main streets of Delta, along the test track that I had already done a thousand times with Gabe. Every once in a while, he wrote something down on his clipboard.

When Bob told me I had passed, I couldn't help but hug him, and he made a half-hearted attempt at reciprocating. When they took my photo, the lady behind the counter had to tell me to stop grinning like a maniac.

As soon as I left the registry, I drove straight to Rosie's, honking the horn loudly out front. She came through the doors as I stepped out of Gabe's car.

"Congratulations, honey!" Rosie cried, arms open. We hugged on the pavement.

"Thanks," I beamed at her.

"Have you told Gabe the good news yet?"

"I'm going to surprise him when he gets off work later. We're having dinner at my place tonight."

"Come inside. I made you some lemon tarts."

"Okay, I'll just park Gabe's car round the back."

THE DINER WAS empty when I made my way in. I sat at the counter while Rosie busied herself, plating the lemon tarts and pouring freshly brewed coffee into a mug. She set them down in front of me with a smile.

"Thanks, Rosie." I could hardly keep the grin off my face.

"If I had known, I would have baked you a cake."

I took a sip of my coffee. "You know you don't have to do that."

She smiled. "So you're having dinner with Gabe tonight?"

I nodded. "I've been watching those cooking shows that come on late at night, and a few days ago, I made my first dish."

"What was it?"

"Spaghetti with meatballs," I said, proudly.

"Sounds delish."

"It's not that difficult, if you get step-by-step instructions. It tasted pretty good."

"And that's what you're cooking up tonight?"

"Uh-huh. I'm going to pick up some handmade egg pasta from the deli and a tub of Ben & Jerry's, and I think I'll splurge on a really good bottle of Pinot."

"Sounds like you have a fun night planned."

"It's the least I can do for Gabe—he's been so great. I mean, if I had never met him, I don't think I would have done this. He's been such a good friend."

"Friend?" Rosie raised her eyebrows.

"Yes, Rosie," I said wryly. "We're just friends."

"You don't have any feelings for him?"

I frowned. "Not those kind of feelings. I'm not ready to dive into anything new. Not just yet."

"Well, I can say, hand on heart, Gabe has feelings for you. I've seen the two of you together. The kid can hardly take his eyes off you."

I knew Rosie wasn't making it up. I sensed that Gabe had feelings for me, and I didn't want to lead him on. Nor did I want to stop seeing him.

"I don't know about that, Rosie."

"You're such a bad liar, Audrey."

I PICKED GABE up from his uncle's later that afternoon. It was my first day as a mobile person, and I was loving every minute of it. I had no idea how restrictive my life had been prior to this independent, self-sufficient me.

Gabe was in blue overalls bent over the open hood of an electric-blue Chevy when I walked in. He looked up, caught my eye, and smiled. For the first time, I did feel something, a small flutter in my chest.

He gave me an expectant look. "So?"

"I got it!

He grinned. "Another one for the toolbox."

I smiled. "I guess so."

AFTER GABE FINISHED up, I drove us back to my place, and he helped me out in the kitchen with the spaghetti and meatballs. The sauce was bubbling away in the pan when we decided to start on the Pinot. He was telling me a funny story about a customer who came in that day and was trying to barter his way out of paying the bill. Soon he had me in stitches.

"Look at you," said Gabe.

"What about me?"

"When I first met you, you were like this fragile china doll. I just wanted to pick you up and put you in bubble wrap."

I laughed. "You did?"

He nodded. "You just seemed kind of lost, unsure about yourself. Now it's like you're a different person."

"How so?" I leaned my hip against the kitchen bench and took another sip of Pinot.

"You're just . . . so alive now. You seem so strong and capable, like you're ready to take on the world. You're like the living version of a *Karate Kid* montage."

I laughed.

"And your cheeks are glowing," he continued. "It must be the mountain air."

"I think it has a lot to do with you as well." The words slipped out before I could stop them. I bit my lip and looked away.

"Do you mean that, Audrey?" Slowly, I turned my head back to meet his gaze.

I nodded. "I do."

He took a step forward, his hand brushing my cheek. "I really like you," he said.

I looked up at him. "I like you too."

He leaned in and kissed me. His lips were soft and warm, and I suddenly realized how much I missed this kind of intimacy.

"I've wanted to do that for ages," he said, when he broke away.

"Why didn't you?"

"I wasn't sure how you felt."

We moved into each other and kissed again. I put my wine glass down and wrapped my arms around his neck, wanting desperately to lose myself in the moment. Then out of nowhere and without warning, I was hit by a wave of sadness.

I pulled away.

"Are you okay?" he asked, his eyes searching mine.

"No." My voice was barely a whisper. "I don't think so."

"What's wrong?"

"I don't know, exactly," I said, shaking my head again. The sadness that had begun in the pit of my stomach was spreading through my body and growing in intensity. "I just—" my voice caught on a sob, catching me completely off guard. Tears rolled down my cheeks one after another, like a sudden deluge of rain erupting from a perfectly blue sky.

"Audrey," he said and took a step back as I wiped at my face with my hands.

"I'm sorry. I don't know why I'm crying. It's not you . . . you've been nothing but wonderful." I gave him a helpless look.

He sighed. "Rosie mentioned there was someone back home—someone you were trying to forget. She said that was the reason you came all the way out here. Is that who you're crying about?"

I looked at him. "I don't know—maybe."

"Look, I'm not here to rush you into anything. I like you, but I'm just as happy to be your friend. Okay?"

"Okay," I whispered.

We were quiet for a few minutes. Then I reached over and took his hand. "Just because I'm not ready right now doesn't mean I won't ever be."

"I know," he said, giving my hand a squeeze. "This kind of stuff—you can't set a time or date to it."

"No, you can't."

"Especially when you lose someone who meant a lot to you."

I drew in a deep breath. "I think it was the first time I was truly in love, if you know what I mean."

"I do." A sad look crossed his face. "A girl broke my heart a few years back, and I still think about it sometimes."

"What happened?"

"Birdie's an artist. She got a job offer in New York with an ad agency. We tried to do the long-distance thing for a while, but she met someone else."

"I'm sorry."

"What happened with your guy? How did it come to an end?"

"To be honest, I don't know if things did end with Rad— that's his name. I feel like we're still unfinished business, like we're in limbo. I suppose that's why I can't seem to move on.

There's this connection between us that will probably always be there. Even if I never see him again."

"Like the rope between the ship and the mooring?"

"Exactly like that."

BEFORE I KNEW it, we were barreling our way toward spring, and I got an e-mail from Dale with the date of their return. I was sad to be leaving this beautiful house and especially to be parting ways with Apple, whom I adored. Still, I knew how lucky I was to have spent the winter here. After the first hike with Gabe that day, the anxiety about my writing had lifted, and I was churning out some decent work. I had sent a handful of short stories to Angie, and his response was encouraging. I didn't want to think too much about what I would do next—where I would live and how to pay my bills. I just hoped that my luck would hold out and something would turn up.

One day, Gabe came over, and I could tell there was something on his mind. We were lounging on the couch by the fire, with Apple bounding between us in excited bursts, when I decided to bring it up.

"Gabe? You've been so quiet today. Is everything okay?"

"Everything's fine, Audrey," he said. "I've just been thinking. You know Dale and Graham are coming home soon."

I nodded.

"What are you planning on doing when they're back?"

"I suppose I should start house hunting. I've been careful with the money they left me, so I should have enough to rent a place for the next few months. I was also thinking of getting a job in town. I saw a sign posted at the veterinarian—they're looking for a new receptionist. Anyway, I'm thinking of applying."

"So you want to stay here? In Delta, I mean."

"Yeah. This town has been good for me. I can drive now, and I'm learning to cook. I'm at least halfway through writing my first book. Plus," I smiled, "I can crack open a chestnut with one hand and pull the shell away clean. How many people do you know who can manage something like that?"

A soft smile played on his lips, and I knew he was thinking back to the day we met when he was selling chestnuts at the market.

"All in all," I continued, "my toolbox is looking pretty healthy these days."

"Is that so?" He raised his eyebrows, and I blushed, realizing the suggestive nature of that line.

"Anyway," I said quickly, "I know it sounds really cliché, but you know when people talk about finding themselves? Well, I'm starting to get where they're coming from. So in answer to your question, yes, I think I'll stay put—unless you have another suggestion?"

"I do," he said quietly.

"Yeah?" I looked at him, surprised.

He nodded. "Something I've been thinking about."

"Okay, let's hear it, then."

"Well, it's been ages since I've had any time off. I could do with a vacation, and I thought—" He looked a bit embarrassed. "Well, this is where it gets really cliché . . ."

"Go on. No stalling, Gabe."

"I thought we could go on a road trip. Maybe head out to the West Coast."

"A road trip," I said slowly. My mind shot back to that rainy day when I interviewed Rad at Callisto. I remembered how he told me his mother had planned a road trip across the States—one she never took. I shrugged it off as another strange coincidence.

"We could take turns driving," Gabe continued. "I have a bit of money saved up, and Alaska can wait a few months. We can get a tent, pitch it where we want. Or stay in cheap motels—twin beds of course." He was talking quickly now.

"Gabe, it's okay. You don't have to convince me. I like the idea."

A slow grin spread across his face. "Yeah? Really?"

"Yeah, I think it will be fun."

He leaped to his feet. "We could visit Reno, swim in Lake Tahoe—Yosemite has some great hiking trails. I mean, there's so much to see and do!"

He looked almost like a kid, and I loved seeing him so animated. His excitement was contagious, and soon I was on my feet and we were doing a ridiculous impromptu dance around the room and laughing like children. I felt wild and free, like a stringless kite. My heart was soaring, and in that moment, it was like I had finally broken free from the shackles of my past. Rad, Ana, the lie—I had stepped out of the shadow and into the light.

We stopped dancing and collapsed back onto the couch, a little out of breath. Gabe kissed me, and this time, I didn't pull away.

WE SPENT THE remainder of the days leading up to Graham and Dale's return meticulously planning our road trip. We kept finding new things we wanted to see or do, adding detours to our already packed itinerary.

"We're never going to make it to L.A. at this rate."

"Does that matter?" asked Gabe.

"I suppose not."

"Though I really do want to go to the Margaret Herrick Library," he said.

"That's the nerd in you talking."

"They have the original screenplay for *The Godfather*," he grinned. "The *actual* first draft. And they have the original notes and sketches from *The Shining* by Stanley Kubrick himself."

There was a look of wonder in his eyes that went straight to my heart. On impulse, I grabbed at the sides of his face and kissed him firmly on the mouth.

"What was that for?"

"Do I need a reason?"

BEFORE LONG, IT was the night before Graham and Dale were due to arrive, and I spent it packing up my things. Gabe was out getting some last-minute supplies for our trip. We planned to stay at his place the following night before leaving on our big road trip first thing in the morning. I smiled, thinking about the big adventure ahead.

"I'll miss you," I said to Apple, who wagged her tail at me anxiously. I picked her up and gave her furry neck a kiss. "I'll come back and visit you lots."

I went to put her down when I heard my phone beep. It was a text from Lucy.

FaceTime?

Sure.

I realized it had been ages since I last spoke to her. I hadn't even told her about the road trip.

I found my laptop lying on the couch and pulled up the screen. A few moments later, Lucy was there, grinning at me from the other side of the world.

"Hey, stranger," she said.

"Hi! How have you been?"

"Great. How about you?"

"Really good!"

"How's Gabe?"

"He's doing great too."

I was just about to bring up the road trip when she blurted out, "Anyway, I have news! Big news!"

"Oh, what is it?"

"Well, guess who turned up on our doorstep today?"

"I have no idea, Lucy."

"Guess!"

I sighed. "Okay, I know you're dying to tell me, so just come out with already."

"Okay, *fine*," she said, in a singsong voice. She paused for dramatic effect. "It was Candela!"

"Candela? Really?"

I hadn't spoken to Candela since her dramatic departure with Dirk.

"Uh-huh. And do you know what else?"

"What?"

"She's getting married, Audrey!"

"Married? To whom?"

"To Dirk."

I groaned. "Seriously?"

"Actually, he's cleaned up now. They both have. Candela looks fantastic! Dirk took over his dad's garage a few months back, and he's been doing custom bikes. It's going really well for him. Apparently, some celebrity musician just ordered one."

"Really? Who?"

"She was pretty evasive about it, but I think it was Keith Urban."

"That's awesome!"

"Anyway, she still feels really shitty about what happened— you know, the day when she stormed off. But she really wants you at her wedding. And even though she can be a real shit sometimes, she's still Candela. She's practically family."

"I know," I said, biting my lip.

"Will you come back?"

"When is the wedding?" I asked cautiously.

"Uh, well, it's kind of late notice. You know what Candela's like . . ."

"How late?"

"Well, it's not *this* Sunday—"

"You are fucking kidding me."

"It's the Sunday after that," Lucy finished. "Can you make it?"

I DIDN'T GET much sleep that night. I kept tossing it over in my head. I could always come back here after the wedding, I thought. The road trip could wait a few weeks. But already I could feel a tightness in my chest, as though something was pulling me back into the past. Like when you've driven halfway to a dinner party and you have to double back home because you remembered you left the iron on.

THE NEXT DAY, Graham and Dale came back. Apple raced out to greet them, and I followed closely.

"Hi, honey!" Graham called out as he scooped Apple up into his arms. "Hi, baby, Daddy's home. Did you miss me?" In response, she licked his face with great enthusiasm. After putting her down, he wrapped me in one of his iron-grip hugs. Dale had come up behind him, and he planted a firm kiss on my cheek before grabbing my hand and twirling me around.

"Welcome back," I laughed.

I helped them with their luggage, and we made our way back into the house with Apple running around clumsily at our feet.

"The house looks wonderful!" Graham exclaimed when we got inside. "Exactly like how we left it."

"The antiques are all done as well. I hope you'll be happy with them."

"I'm sure you did a fantastic job, honey."

I put the kettle on, and soon we were settled on the couch, sipping cups of chamomile tea.

"So how was your flight?"

"Long and tedious," said Graham. "It's good to be home."

"Amen," said Dale.

Apple interjected with two sharp barks, and we laughed.

"So, Audrey," said Dale. His eyes had a mischievous glint to them. "Rosie says you've been spending a lot of time with Gabe."

"I have," I admitted. "Gabe's been wonderful." I thought about my dilemma and was hit with a sudden avalanche of emotion. It must have shown on my face because the two men exchanged a worried glance.

"Trouble in paradise?" asked Graham cautiously.

I sighed. "Well, there's something I'm wrestling with at the moment."

I brought them up to speed with my predicament: the road trip I had planned with Gabe and Candela's wedding.

"I see," said Dale with a frown. "What do you think you'll do?"

"I don't know. I honestly don't."

"Why can't you do the road trip with Gabe after the wedding?"

"I suppose I can," I said, chewing on my bottom lip.

Dale gave me a questioning look. "Audrey, I hope I'm not out of line here," he glanced at Graham, "but we get the feeling that you were running away from something back home, and that's the reason why you came out here." He held up both hands. "Just an outsider's perspective."

I smiled at him. "You're not an outsider."

Graham put his arm around my shoulder and gave it a squeeze.

"And you're right. I was running away, and I've been dreading the idea of going back home. But I think I've gotten past that. I think I'm ready to face my demons head-on."

"I thought there was something different about you," said Graham.

"What do you mean?"

"Well, it's like you were this—no offense—wisp of a girl when we left. Like you were a two-dimensional cardboard cutout. But you've blossomed into this beautiful young lady. It's quite a transformation."

"In other words, you look like you've really gotten your shit together," said Dale.

I laughed. "It's the mountain air."

"You're a regular Heidi," said Graham with a wink.

I grinned and sipped my tea.

"Or maybe it's because of Gabe?" Dale raised his eyebrows. "Nothing makes your cheeks glow like young love."

"I wouldn't say 'love,'" I said quickly, feeling a jolt of panic at the word. "I mean, I adore Gabe and all . . ." It was true. I thought the world of Gabe. Finding him was an incredible stroke of luck, but it still didn't come close to what I felt for Rad, not by a long shot. At that moment, I realized I still felt it. I didn't know where Rad was or what he was doing. I didn't know whether he had moved on or not, but all of a sudden, I knew it was something I had to find out.

"There's someone back home, isn't there?" said Dale, reading my mind.

"Is it that obvious?"

"Honey, if you haven't fallen head over heels in love with Gabe by now, it's pretty clear you're still hung up on someone else."

LATE THAT AFTERNOON, I heard Gabe's car pull up, and with a sinking feeling, I went outside to greet him.

"Hey," he said, as he got out of the car. The backseat was already bulging with supplies for our trip.

He must have caught the look on my face. "Audrey, have you been crying? What's wrong?"

I told him about my talk with Lucy and Candela's wedding.

He drew in a deep breath after I finished.

"Boy, talk about bad timing."

"I know."

He shook his head. "I guess you're going, then?"

"She's like a sister to me. I can't miss her wedding."

He nodded. "No, you can't."

"I suppose our road trip can wait until I get back? What do you think?"

He looked so dejected that I felt tears spring to my eyes. "Audrey, I would be more than happy to wait if I thought for a second that you'd be coming back."

"Gabe—" I started to say.

"I suppose I was always meant to go on this trip alone."

"Don't say that." The tears spilled over. "Don't."

He stared at me for a few moments before reaching out to me. I collapsed against his chest, and he wrapped his arms around me. He held me tightly for a while, his lips pressed against my ear. "You've got to do what your heart tells you, okay? There's no point in us going through with this if you're just going to keep looking back."

"I thought I'd let it go," I whispered. "I really did, Gabe."

"I thought so too," said Gabe. "But we know differently now."

"God, I'm going to miss you."

He pulled away and smiled. "Well, maybe we'll run into each other again. Stranger things have happened."

"We'll keep in touch, won't we?"

He shook his head. "I think it's best we just leave it here for now. I don't think I can do the friend thing. Not with you."

"But what if I need you?"

"You can always find me, if you really have to. It's the twenty-first century, after all."

"Okay."

"You take care of yourself, Audrey."

"So this is it? We're saying goodbye?" I felt a wave of panic and realized how much I had come to depend on him. It was hard to believe it was only yesterday we were planning our trip, blissfully unaware of what lay ahead.

He nodded. "This is goodbye."

I threw my arms around his neck and pressed my lips against his cheek. "You're my angel, you know," I whispered. I didn't want to let him go.

He gently pulled my arms free and stepped back. He looked down at me and grinned his good-natured grin. "You're going to be okay, Audrey. You don't need anybody anymore. Remember that."

Then just as swiftly as he appeared in my life, he was gone. I stood on the sidewalk and watched as the station wagon turned the corner at the end of the street and disappeared. I stood there for a long time in the dying light, a dull thudding in my chest and the feeling I was more alone than I had ever been.

Two

CANDELA'S NUPTIALS FELT more like a small house party than a wedding. It was held in the tiny garden of her duplex in Chippendale. Eve was her maid of honor, and Lucy and I were the bridesmaids. The whole ceremony had a casual, laid-back vibe to it.

Dirk and Candela looked very much the picture of young love. To see them each glowing with health and happiness gave me a wonderful sense of optimism.

Lucy and Candela had been waiting for me when I walked through the arrival gate in Sydney a week earlier. Candela held up her two fingers in a peace sign when she caught sight of me from a distance. I grinned broadly when I saw it. Since we were kids, we'd hold our fingers in the same way when we wanted to make a show of peace. I felt a wave of affection wash over me, despite the ugliness of our last parting. There are some friendships that weather the greatest storms, and I knew the one I shared with Lucy and Candela could make it through anything.

Now the three of us were sitting cross-legged on the soft lawn under a lemon tree. Candela was still in her wedding dress, a simple white satin garment with lace trim. Intricate patterns were inked in henna on her hands and wrists. Lucy and I were in matching blue linen dresses we'd picked up just the day before on a last-minute shopping stint.

Dirk was in the shed with the door rolled up, showing his latest work to his friends who stood around, beers in hand, nodding with appreciation.

"I know whom you're hoping to see," said Candela, as she caught me surveying the guests. She and Lucy exchanged a meaningful glance. "But he's not here."

They both knew Rad was a sore spot for me, and with all the last-minute wedding preparations, I didn't get a chance to bring him up. "How is he?" I asked, trying to sound impassive.

Lucy gave a long sigh. "I didn't want to worry you," she said, "but it's not good, Audrey. I ran into him one day." She tilted her head to one side and chewed thoughtfully on her bottom lip. "About five months after you left, maybe? He had no idea you had gone to Colorado. I think he had tried calling you, but, of course, you changed your number. Anyway, he was just heading home from some big meeting that didn't go down well. I'm not sure what happened after that, but he turned up at Freddy's a couple of weeks later and asked Freddy if he would look after his MacBook and a few other things. After a month or so, we got a postcard from someplace up north called Bell Rock Trailer Park, and no one has heard from him since."

"What did the postcard say?" This news about Rad was the last thing I expected to hear. Why would he be at a trailer park? Why did he leave his MacBook with Freddy? His whole life was on that thing.

"The postcard just said, 'Having a great time, wish you were here.'"

I smiled inwardly. It sounded so like Rad—the wry, sarcastic humor I adored. I pictured him with pen poised over the postcard, writing that tired cliché with a smirk, and my heart gave an involuntary flutter.

"So no one has heard from him since?"

"Nope."

"Well, how do you know he's still there?"

"We don't."

"He didn't leave a number?"

Lucy shook her head. "We still have the postcard, though. His address is on it. Maybe you can write to him there."

Three

I PULLED INTO Bell Rock Trailer Park and found a space under a large tree. I turned off the engine and sat there chewing thoughtfully on the tip of my thumb. When I told Lucy I was going to set out on this wild goose chase, she said, "Take Octopus One!" She offered to come with me, but I wanted to do it on my own.

I had no idea whether Rad was still here—there wasn't a number listed for the trailer park, and they didn't even have a website. I figured if he had left, someone there might know where he went.

After a few more minutes of staring into space, I snapped into action. Opening the car door, I stepped out into the warm summer day. I was hit with a dose of cool, salty air, and it felt good in my lungs. I caught a glimpse of the sea just beyond the group of trailers parked haphazardly across the rolling lawn. There was barely a week of summer left, and the weather was starting to turn. I walked up a bumpy asphalt path littered with dry white sand toward a small wood building. It was red and white, with the paint chipping away along the slats and window frames.

I pushed through the door and walked into the air-conditioned cool inside. Two wildly excited black and tan Chihuahuas greeted me—their little tails wagging furiously between sharp, intermittent yelps. "Gin! Tonic! Stop harassing the nice lady," said a throaty voice. My eyes adjusted to the dim light, and I saw an old woman with wiry gray hair sitting behind a counter. She stood up, revealing a purple gypsy dress decorated with mystic symbols. "Hello, dear," she purred, looking me over. "I'm Maud, the owner. Are you after a trailer?"

"Uh, no," I said, a little bemused.

The room looked more like a fortune-teller's den than the office of a trailer park. There were sumptuous velvet throws draped over a small round coffee table and a shapeless couch complete with matching cushions. Old movie posters in thin black frames were hung on the wood paneled walls. Displayed on a bench that stretched wall to wall behind the counter were gaudy trinkets and a pack of illustrated tarot cards next to a large crystal ball. She looked me over again, her expression pensive. "Then how can I help you?"

"I'm looking for someone. You may know him," I said nervously. "His name is Rad." I wasn't sure what else to say, so I added, "He sent a postcard from here a few months ago."

She regarded me carefully. "You're looking for Rad," she said, with a mysterious smile. "Then you must be Audrey."

MAUD LED ME down a narrow, winding path to a white trailer with muddy-orange trim parked in an area partly hidden by trees and shrubbery. A makeshift washing line was strung from the trailer to a nearby tree, and my heart skipped a beat when I recognized one of Rad's T-shirts fluttering in the gentle breeze.

"This is him," said Maud.

"Thank you."

She pressed her gnarled hands into mine. "Good luck, dear." She turned and ambled back down the path.

Taking a deep breath, I walked toward the door and knocked.

A moment later, the door swung open, and Rad stood there, framed by the doorway, wearing a pair of board shorts and clutching a towel in his hand. He looked at me with an expression I couldn't quite interpret. After a few tense seconds, he finally said, "Audrey."

"Hi, Rad." He looked different. There was something about his face and body that looked harder and more defined. A thin layer of stubble had grown on his usually clean-shaven face, and his fingernails were chewed and brittle.

"What are you doing here?" he asked, unsmiling.

"I don't know," I said truthfully. "I just wanted to talk to you."

He looked nonplussed. "Well, I was just about to go for a swim." His tone wasn't rude exactly, but it was dismissive. He pushed past me, heading toward the beach.

"Rad," I walked after him. "What the hell? I came all the way here. Can you at least talk to me?"

He stopped and turned around. "Talk to you?" he gave me an incredulous look. "You disappeared, Audrey. You changed your fucking number. It's a little bit too late for talking, isn't it?"

I was taken aback. This person in front of me looked and sounded like Rad, but he seemed like a stranger. It was like knowing your favorite song by heart and then hearing a live karaoke performance sung with an odd staccato and off-key.

"I had to get away," I said, hating the pleading tone in my voice. "I didn't know what else to do."

He shrugged and continued walking.

"Rad," I called after him.

"Just leave me alone, Audrey," he said quietly, his back still toward me. I ran up past him, jogging backward, and peered up into his face.

"Hey, I just want to talk—please."

He stopped walking. "How the hell did you get here, anyway?"

"I drove."

"Since when did you learn to drive?"

"When I was in Delta. Gabe taught me." As soon as the words were out of my mouth, I wanted to take them back.

"Gabe?" he said, his eyes narrowing.

"Just someone I was kind of seeing." I avoided his gaze.

"Well," he said wryly, "that didn't take long."

He walked past me again, crossing the threshold from lawn to sand.

"Rad," I said helplessly. "I don't know what to say."

My eyes were fixed on his back as he walked farther and farther away toward the shoreline.

"Just go back home, Audrey." His voice was barely audible over the crashing waves. "There's nothing for you here."

"How did it go, dear?" asked Maud as she caught me walking back to my car. I wiped at the tears spilling from my eyes and shook my head. "Not good." She reached out and took my hand. "Come with me, dear. Let me make you a cup of tea."

I soon found myself sitting beside Maud on her couch. Our empty teacups and chipped saucers were perched near the edge of the coffee table. "I still remember the day he came through here. I took one look at him and thought to myself, 'This kid looks down on his luck.' He rented one of the trailers for a month or so, then when the general manager left, he took on the role."

"Rad? But he's a writer."

"Not anymore," she said, with a small shake of her head. "He told me he wanted a job that didn't require too much thinking. Said he was tired of thinking."

"What happened to him?"

"I'll leave that up to him to tell you."

"He won't talk to me."

"Maybe not," she said, "but I can tell you this. You're the only thing he ever talks about."

I CHECKED MYSELF into a motel a few streets away from Bell Rock. The room was a lot nicer than I expected, with a view of the sea through double glass doors that led onto a small balcony. I even found a chocolate mint on my pillow when I climbed into bed, exhausted.

I picked up my phone from the side table and dialed Lucy's number. She answered right away.

"Hey!" she said cheerfully.

"Hey, I just arrived at Bell Rock."

"You okay? You sound tired."

"Yeah, I'm fine. It was a long drive, and it took me awhile to get used to driving on the other side of the road."

"Oh, I should have come with you."

"No, I think it's better I came alone."

There was a short pause.

"I found Rad—he's still here."

"Oh, good. How is he?"

I sighed. "He didn't want to talk to me."

"You serious? Why?"

"I don't know. He's still angry, I suppose."

"Well, maybe it was a shock for him, seeing you after all this time."

"Maybe." I put my head back on the pillow and stared up at the ceiling. "It's just that he seems so different."

"In what way?"

"He took a job managing the park."

"Really? What sort of work is that?"

"General maintenance stuff, I guess. I'm not really sure."

"So he's not writing anymore?"

"I met Maud, the owner. She says he's given up on writing."

"He's so talented, though," Lucy protested. "Why would he give that up?"

"I don't know." I chewed on my thumbnail. "He looks different, too. It's his eyes, I think. They seem—" I struggled to find the right word. "Empty," I said finally.

"Oh no. God, I wish Freddy and I had checked up on him a little more."

"It's not your fault. I shouldn't have disappeared all of a sudden."

"Don't blame yourself, Audrey. People are allowed to leave if they want."

"Yeah. It's just that . . . well, I think he might be going through a really hard time at the moment."

Lucy sighed. "What are you going to do?"

"I'm not sure. I think I might hang around here for a few days. See if I can get through to him. I'll text you the details of where I'm staying."

"All right. Get some rest and call me if anything changes."

"Okay, sweetie, I will. Good night."

I DROVE UP to Bell Rock again the next day, and after wandering around the park for twenty minutes, I saw Rad walking out of a trailer with a box of tools in hand. It was so uncharacteristic of him, this handyman role. I tried picturing him changing a lightbulb, and the image just didn't fit. He caught sight of me, but his expression didn't change. "I thought you were leaving," he said.

"Actually, I'm thinking of staying awhile."

He sighed and gave me a resigned look. "Want a beer?"

WE SAT ON lawn chairs outside his trailer with cold beers clutched in our hands. Rad looked out toward the ocean, a dull expression on his face.

"What happened, Rad? Why did you come here?"

He was quiet, then shrugged. "Just a series of bad luck that snowballed into everything turning to shit." He took a swig of his beer. He turned to me. "Your little confession that night was probably the start of it all."

I winced.

"Then you left." He waved his hands in the air like a magician. "Poof! Audrey vanishes, and I had no idea where you were. But you know," he smirked, "you left me with all this free time to work on my novel." He tipped his beer in my direction. "So, thanks for that."

I remained silent, not knowing what to say.

"And then," he continued, "I finished the novel, and you know what? I was actually proud of it. It was pretty damn good. I was excited. I sent a few chapters to my publisher, and she was excited. In fact, so excited that an exec from their New York branch flew out to meet me. They had *big*"—Rad emphasized the word—"plans for me. I was going to be, in their words, 'the next Vonnegut.'"

"That's huge, Rad."

He threw me a cynical look and continued in a bored, monotone voice. "I was like an eager schoolboy on the day of the meeting. I printed out the manuscript and took it down to the copy shop to have it bound." He swallowed the last of his beer and put it down by his feet. "I even wore a tie." He stopped talking for a little while, the heel of his foot tapping against the metal frame of the chair. "So we met up at Galileo. Me, my Australian publisher, and the exec. It was a gorgeous day, and I was feeling pretty good about everything. I thought, 'Hey, here it is, my big break.' Then about fifteen minutes into the meeting, I realized what a dick the exec was. He flicked through my manuscript and said all this inane crap. Basically, he wanted to butcher it, change the title, the names of the characters. Hell, he even suggested I write under a new pen name. Apparently Colorado Clark sounded too contrived."

"What did you do?" I asked, feeling apprehensive.

"I lost it. I told him he could get back on the fucking plane because there was no way he was touching my book. Then I stormed out." He shook his head as he relived the moment. "It was a stupid thing to do; I know. I should have just sat through it like a trained monkey and not made an ass of myself. I mean, this guy was a real heavyweight, you know. Not the person you want to piss off. That night I got really drunk, like stupidly drunk. I burned the hard copy of the manuscript and then deleted all the digital files. It was one of those apocalyptic 'fuck you' to the universe kind of moments."

"Oh shit, Rad. You didn't."

"Of course, when I woke up the next morning," he shot me a wry look, "it wasn't pretty. I searched everywhere for a backup, but I had been really thorough. The whole thing was gone."

"Jesus."

"So I thought, 'That's my writing career—over. Done and dusted.' Since I was unemployed with no prospects, I wasn't going to keep making rent, so I figured it was better to leave than to spiral down the path into eventual eviction. I went to Freddy's house and dropped off some of my stuff, then I just got into my car and drove." He finished his story with a sigh, staring sullenly at the horizon. "So that's me. Now you're all up to date." He turned to look at me, his expression unreadable. I turned away, looking out toward the ocean.

"Let's go for a walk on the beach," I said.

OVER THE NEXT few weeks, we walked a lot. Up and down the length of the beach, slogging up sand dunes and climbing rock pools. After my insensitive slip of the tongue about Gabe that first day, I was careful to avoid the topic. Rad told me about a brief fling he had with a Swedish tourist. Even though it didn't come to anything, the mere mention of it drove me mad. I imagined her blonde and gorgeous in a tiny bikini, Rad kissing her smooth, tanned shoulder. I wondered if he found her fascinating, if he ever talked about me when he was with her. I wondered a thousand things, but all I said was, "Oh, she sounds nice."

Being around Rad felt like I had never left, as if my time in Delta was a dream that had happened to someone else. Even after all the time away, the love was still there, bright as the sun. At least on my end—I wasn't sure how he felt about me, and I was afraid to ask.

The thick of winter arrived, and, one after another, the summer holiday campers packed up and left, giving the park a melancholy vibe.

I finally saw the inside of Rad's trailer one day. He invited me in after a long trek on the coastal path. It was small but had a nice and cozy atmosphere, kind of like a fort. There was a small table stuck to the wall with a bench on either side. Piled on top were Sudoku puzzle books and old newspapers.

One night we built a bonfire. It took much longer than expected to get the fire going, but, eventually, it created a warm, intimate atmosphere. We found marshmallows in one of the cupboards and speared them onto sticks, pointing them at the swirling flames.

It was a beautiful, clear night, and we sat on his green-and-white striped lawn chairs and tipped our heads up to the sky. He reached toward me, wrapping the crook of his finger around my rubber band like he used to.

"You're still wearing this."

I remember the first time he brought it up. It was that magical night in Newport when we kissed for the first time. "Interesting piece of jewelry," he had said. Over the course of our relationship, he would play with it absentmindedly during our conversations in bed, his fingers gently flicking the elastic against my skin.

Now, the touch of his finger against my wrist brought the warm memories back in a flood, sending an unexpected thrill through my body. He looked as though he wanted to kiss me, and I was readying myself. But then he looked away, and the spell was broken. We sat in quiet contemplation for a time, listening to the ocean crashing in the distance. When he turned to face me again, his eyes were unbearably sad. "I used to think people were like lighthouses. That they were there to protect you. But they're not. People are like whirlpools. They pull you in; they drag you under. You have to work so hard just to keep your head above water."

DURING THE WEEKS that I spent at Bell Rock, I got to know Maud pretty well. Back in the '50s, her late husband ran a small theater that screened art house films. When he passed away,

Maud sold it (just wasn't the same without him, she explained) and bought Bell Rock, fulfilling her lifelong dream of living by the sea.

Most of her clientele were vacationers, but she also had a few permanent residents. One was an elderly man who kept mostly to himself. We saw him some mornings, sitting outside his trailer on a foldout chair, reading the paper. "Hey, pretty girl," he'd call out to me whenever I walked by. There was also a young hippie couple with a baby boy and a mysterious woman who always wore dark sunglasses and never smiled. Aside from renting out trailers, Maud also told fortunes for the locals. When she was young, she traveled around the United States with a small circus troupe. She told wonderful stories of her adventures, including the time she did a tarot reading for a famous movie star during the year she spent at Coney Island. I saw her life captured in pictures pressed into old leather-bound albums, their plastic sleeves sticky and yellow with age. It was hard to believe the young spirited gypsy girl draped in velvet and lace was Maud. "Wasn't I gorgeous?" she'd say. It was a rhetorical question.

ONE NIGHT, RAD and I were walking barefoot along the beach when the subject of Maud came up in the conversation.

"She wants to read my fortune, but I don't know if that's such a good idea—knowing what's ahead."

"Well, you should take everything she says with a grain of salt. I know what she's like when she's had a few too many."

"Has she ever read yours?"

"Yeah, she says one day I'll have people lining up for my autograph."

"Well, I'd better get mine now."

"Sure, do you have a pen on you?"

I laughed. It was the first time since I came here that Rad seemed almost like his old self again. We walked in silence a little longer.

"Tell me about your book. The one you wrote when I was away."

"It was called *Honeybee*. I don't really want to talk about it."

"I wish I could have read it."

"Do you know the Chinese have a tradition of burning fake money because they believe it goes to their dead relatives in the spirit world?"

"It's a nice idea."

"Well, that was going through my mind when the manuscript was burning. Maybe in some other alternate universe, there are people reading my book. Who knows?"

"Maybe."

"I think writing is over for me," said Rad. "I've sat for ages with a pen in my hand, and nothing comes out. So I end up doing Sudoku puzzles."

"It's probably just writer's block."

"Or some karmic force that is punishing me for destroying my own book."

I reached out and put my hand on his arm. "I don't think it works like that."

He stopped and turned to face me. "It's weird, isn't it? The coincidences, I mean. It's almost like everything is decided for you, like it's already been written."

"Yeah, you know me. I have an existential crisis every five minutes."

He smiled at me. "I love that I can talk to you about all this stuff. Most people wouldn't get it."

"You can talk to me about anything."

"I know."

I followed his gaze upward, and we thought our individual thoughts, sending them out into the universe like parallel lines. At that moment, I felt a sense of something that was bigger than us, an inexplicable force that willfully drew Rad and me to this convergence, to this particular alignment with the stars. We were always meant for each other. This was something I knew right down to the depths of my soul. "You know," said Rad, his face turning toward me, "Maud was right about something."

"What was that?"

"She said you would find me again."

THE NEXT DAY, I was awakened by a sharp knock on my door. I got up and pulled on my robe. "Who is it?" I called.

"It's me!" announced Lucy.

"Lucy!" I opened the door and grinned widely at her. "What are you doing here?"

"Surprise!" she said, throwing her arms around me as I squeezed her tightly.

"Why didn't you call to let me know you were coming?" I was suddenly aware of how messy my room was, and I began picking up bits and pieces from the floor.

"Relax, Audrey." She came inside and shut the door behind her. "I used to live with you, remember?"

"I know," I said, tossing a pile of clothes into the bathroom. "How did you get here?"

"Borrowed Mum's car," she said, walking over to the window. "Wow, you've got a great view."

"It's really pretty here."

She turned to face me. "You look great. How's everything? Is Rad doing okay?"

"He's doing a lot better. He's even writing again."

"Oh, if I'd known, I would have brought up his laptop."

"Never mind. He tends to stick to pen and paper, so we get by sharing mine for now."

She sighed. "I'm glad he's getting back on his feet again."

"Do you want a coffee?" The motel room had a small Nespresso machine, and I popped in a capsule.

"Sure." Lucy sat down on my bed. I made us both a coffee and sat down next to her. "Do you think you'll get back together with him?"

I shrugged. "I don't know. It's up to him."

"So you don't think you're going back to Delta?"

I shook my head. "Rosie said Gabe has left, so there's no real point in going back. It wouldn't be the same without him."

"Are you guys still in touch?"

"No. He said he didn't want to do the friend thing."

There was a short pause.

"He was pretty special to you, wasn't he?" she asked, even though she already knew the answer.

"More than he'll ever know."

LUCY AND I had lunch together later that day. There was a little fish and chips place by the local wharf, and we sat at one of the tables watching ships sway in the docks and throwing bits of our chips at the seagulls. "Look how crazy they are," said Lucy, as the squawking birds clawed and pecked each other for the scraps of food.

"This reminds me of that lolly scramble you had at your tenth birthday. Remember? Your mum was throwing bags of lollies onto the lawn, and the kids went nuts, pushing and shoving each other to get at the loot."

"Someone grabbed my hair and wrestled me to the ground—all for a Sherbie," said Lucy.

We laughed.

"Time is going by so quickly, isn't it?" she said, gazing out at the ocean.

"Yeah. The last year has gone by in a flash."

"Now Candela's married, and you're off doing amazing things. Sometimes I feel like I'm the only one who is standing still." She twisted a lock of hair around her forefinger.

"Lucy." I put my arm around her shoulders. "There's plenty of time left to do anything you want to do."

"I suppose."

"Plus, you have Freddy. He's a real sweetheart."

"Yeah," she said with a smile. "But he was my first real boyfriend. I don't have anyone else to compare him with. What if he isn't the love of my life and I'm just sticking with him because I've never known anything else?"

"You love him, don't you?"

"Of course I do. More than anything else in the whole world."

"It's a beautiful thing, Lucy, to love someone and have them love you back. Everything pales in comparison."

She smiled at me. "Audrey, why don't you tell Rad how you feel? What have you got to lose?"

"What if he doesn't feel the same way about me anymore?"

"You love him, don't you?"

"Yes," I said, without hesitation. "I do."

"Well," she said, tossing another handful of scraps at the overzealous seagulls, "don't you think he has a right to know?"

LATER THAT NIGHT, I tossed and turned in bed, going over my conversation with Lucy. With a sigh, I got up and pulled on my jeans. Minutes later I was knocking on Rad's door. He opened it almost right away, and his alert face told me he couldn't sleep either. "Hey," he said, opening the door wider, to let me in.

We sat side by side, our legs hanging off the side of his bed. There was a copy of *Snow Crash* sitting open, by his pillow. "How long are you planning on staying?" asked Rad.

"I don't know. I'm not sure if I will go back."

"What about Gabe? Is he still in the picture?" he asked, his tone casual.

"No, that ended before I came here."

He looked thoughtful for a while. "I'm really glad you're here," he said finally. He looked down at his hands. "To be honest, I didn't think I'd see you again."

"It was hard to come back home to Sydney. At least in Delta I could pretend I wasn't the girl who told that lie."

"Do I remind you of that?"

"Yeah." I gave him a reassuring smile. "But not in a bad way. Not anymore."

He bit his bottom lip, and his expression grew distant, as though he was thinking hard about something. After a while, he turned to face me again. "Do you ever think about us, Audrey?"

"Of course I do."

He looked relieved, as though a weight had been lifted from his shoulders.

"Do you?"

"Yeah," he said, his voice heavy with emotion. "All the time." He reached over, cupping my face in his hands and gazing softly at me. Then he kissed me. It was a deep, yearning kiss, like his mouth was searching mine for all the words that belonged to him but had been kept from him in his self-imposed exile.

A deep realization reverberated through my body, like the ringing of a church bell. All at once, I understood why the pain of separation, that carving out of the insides, had to happen. I used to have this sense that I felt too much for Rad, that the feelings inside me would start spilling over and I wouldn't be able to contain them. Now I knew why I had been hollowed out, why my insides were chipped away with a chisel and mallet. It was to make room for this new feeling, this love that was so vast, so expansive it could not have fit into the vessel I once was.

He undressed me with a rough urgency that felt fresh yet familiar, his fingers pulling and tearing at my clothes, until I was naked and breathless. I felt a new strength in his arms as he pulled me down with him onto the tiny bed. "I've missed this," he murmured, his face buried into my neck.

Afterward, we lay silent, lulled by the hypnotic sound of waves beating against the rocks. Gradually, I could tell from his breathing that he had drifted into a peaceful sleep. I turned to face him, my fingers curling gently around his dark brown hair. A feeling of tenderness swept through me like an ache; it almost felt maternal. "I'm going to take care of you," I whispered.

THE NEXT MORNING we were shy with each other when we made our cups of coffee with unnecessary clumsiness in the cramped space. "So," said Rad, letting out a deep breath, "last night." I grinned at him, without meaning to. It was as though my mouth had a mind of its own.

"Last night," I echoed.

We stood there, half-empty coffee cups in our hands, grinning at each other with a comical awkwardness that made me want to burst into laughter. Or perhaps it was because I was so damn happy. He put his cup down and held his hand out to me.

I took it, and he pulled me to him. I crashed into his chest with a soft thud, and my coffee tipped over the edges of the mug and spilled onto the linoleum floor in splotches like inkblots.

"What now?" he asked, searching my face.

I kissed him warmly. "If you're still up for it, I want us to start again. Clean slate."

"Yes," he said, letting out a breath. "I'd like that."

IT WAS DIFFERENT this time around. There was a realness to our relationship, a grounding that had never been there before. I'd never felt so sure about anything in my life. I knew I didn't want to be away from Rad ever again.

I moved into the trailer, and we spent one blissful day after another, our hearts filled with love and our heads full of dreams. The happiness we had found at the start of our relationship was always tinged with a shade of uncertainty, but now that had lifted, and I felt like I could surrender myself completely.

"Do you know what I thought, the first day you came here?" asked Rad.

We were cocooned in his tiny bed, where we had spent most of the morning. Outside, the sky was a moody gray. I looked up at him as the first drops of rain drummed softly on the tin roof.

"No, what was going through your mind?"

He smiled at me. "When I opened my door to find you standing there, I couldn't help thinking, 'I've been here all summer long, but for the first time, the sun's come out.'"

LATER THAT DAY, I was on my way to the shower block when I ran into Maud. She was just about to take Gin and Tonic for a walk on the beach.

"Audrey," she said.

"Hey, Maud." I bent down to pat Gin and Tonic, who were both vying for my attention by climbing over each other.

"I was actually just about to stop by your place. You know the winter solstice is next week."

I shook my head. "I didn't realize. I'm losing track of the days."

She smiled at me. "The bohemian life."

I grinned at her. "So what's the significance of the solstice?"

"We're having a party."

"We are?"

"Yes, we do one every year, over on the shore. We build a huge bonfire and have a band come out to play. The locals bring a dish each—kind of like a potluck. We do some fun stuff for the kids as well. Like bobbing for apples, you know."

"Sounds fun!"

"There will be fireworks too."

"Really? I love fireworks!"

"So you and Rad will be there?"

"Of course," I said. "Wouldn't miss it for the world."

"Wonderful," she beamed. "I'm picking up some leaflets from the printer tomorrow. I'll make sure to drop one by."

"Great. Looking forward to it!"

THE FOLLOWING WEEK, Rad and I stood by a raging bonfire on the beach, toasting marshmallows and chatting to Linda, who taught at the local elementary school. The band was a trio of women who played folk music with an assortment of instruments—banjo, flute, and tambourine. Throngs of children were laughing and running around with glow sticks and sparklers.

"I can't wait for the school holidays," said Linda. "Just four more weeks and I'm off to Fiji. I love my kids, but it's nice to have a break every now and then." She took a sip of her beer. "How about the two of you? What are your plans?"

"Audrey's almost finished her first book," said Rad.

"Really?" Linda turned to me. "What's your book about?"

"It's just a collection of short stories."

"Oh, I'd love to read it when it's done."

"You'd love it," said Rad, putting his arm around my shoulder. "She's a regular Mary Shelley."

"Well, I wouldn't say that," I protested.

"Sounds like my cup of tea," said Linda, with a sigh. "Look at you two, a couple of budding young authors. Living the dream."

Rad shrugged and grinned. "I'll admit it's good to be writing again after a long hiatus."

"My friend read *A Snowflake in a Snowfield* a few weeks back. She loved it. Nearly fell over when I told her I knew the author. We're all keen on a second book." She paused. "Will there be a second book?"

"Yeah. I sent the outline to my agent a few days back. Just waiting to hear from her."

"I'm sure she'll be over the moon."

"Any clues about the story?" Linda asked.

"I'd better not talk about it; I don't want to jinx it," said Rad.

"I totally understand." Linda pulled a freshly toasted marshmallow off the stick in her hand and popped it into her mouth.

"I think I'm going to grab another slice of pizza. Do you guys want anything?"

Linda groaned, "I couldn't eat another bite."

"I wouldn't mind another beer," said Rad.

"Sure, I'll grab one for you."

I left them talking and made a beeline for the trestle table ladened with an assortment of food. I bumped into Maud. With her skirt partly hitched, she was dancing merrily by the band.

"You made it!" She stretched her arm out toward me. "Have a dance with me?"

I laughed. "Okay." I took her other hand and tried my best to keep up with her.

"You look happy, sweetheart," she said, a little out of breath.

"I am happy." I meant it.

"You deserve it. I think you and Rad have something truly magical." A touch of sadness fell on her face. "It reminds me of what I had once. Something you get once in your life and only if you're very lucky. Speaking of Rad, where is he? I don't think I've seen him at all tonight."

"I just left him over by the bonfire, talking to Linda."

I glanced over my shoulder, but Linda was standing there with her husband, and Rad was nowhere to be seen. I frowned. "He was there just a second ago." My eyes scanned the crowd, but I couldn't see him anywhere.

"You'd better go and find him, dear; the fireworks are going off soon."

"I'll see if I can track him down. I know he wouldn't want to miss it."

I walked back over to the bonfire and asked Linda if she knew where Rad had gone.

"He got a phone call but had trouble hearing over the music, so he went over that way." She pointed in the direction of the sand dunes farther toward the shoreline.

"Thanks, Linda." I headed down that way.

I finally spotted him in the distance, walking back toward the party, phone clutched in hand. He caught my eye and waved. When he got closer, I could see there was a shell-shocked expression on his face.

"Everything okay?" I asked cautiously.

"Yeah. I just got off the phone with my agent. You know the outline I sent her for my next book? She was calling me about that."

"Did she like it?"

"She did."

"That's wonderful!" I said, beaming at him. "I told you she would."

"But something really weird happened. My agent is friends with a major producer in Hollywood, and she sent my outline through to him. The producer fell head over heels for the story and wants to develop it into a film."

"You are kidding me!"

He shook his head slowly and let out a breath. "I'm not. They want me to go to L.A. to work with another writer."

"Are you serious?" My heart began thumping in exhilaration. "Rad, do you have any idea how amazing this is?"

We looked at each other, not quite knowing what to say.

"When do they want you out there?"

"As soon as possible."

"Oh my God," I said, as the realization sank in. "You're going to L.A.!"

"I guess so. Will you come with me?"

"Yes!" I said, without any hesitation. "Of course."

In one smooth motion, he picked me up and swung me around. A loud bang tore through the night air, and we looked up to see a burst of magenta sparks erupt across the night sky. There were animated cheers in the distance.

"Fireworks! How appropriate."

He laughed and then kissed me hard as the sky was suddenly

filled with bursts of multicolored light. We looked up, arms wrapped tightly around each other, our faces aglow.

"Everything is going to be okay from now on, Audrey. I just know it!"

LUCY WAS THRILLED when I told her.

"Actually, I have some news too. My uncle's contract has been renewed, so he'll be in Paris for the next few years. He's asked me if I could stay on, and of course I said yes. You know Freddy practically lives here anyway, but we wanted to make it official. You know, move in together for real."

"So you've managed to convince him—finally."

"Uh-huh," she said happily. "I'm really excited about it."

"How are his parents taking it?"

Lucy sighed. "He hasn't told them yet."

"No?"

"I'm giving him until the end of this month. I said if he doesn't, the offer is going to my barista, Samuel, who's house hunting at the moment. He may be gay, but he's dreamy as hell, and I wouldn't mind waking up to great coffee and eye candy every morning."

I laughed. "I'm sure Freddy will let them down gently."

I could almost picture Lucy rolling her eyes. "It's going to break his momma's poor, old heart. In her eyes, Freddy will always be twelve years old."

"It will probably destroy her," I agreed. Freddy came from an extremely close-knit family.

"Look at us! Soon we'll be married old ladies like Candela. Have you told her the news, by the way?"

"I tried her earlier, but she didn't answer."

"Typical," Lucy scoffed. "I'll bet she'll be over the moon

when she hears. I mean, L.A.! How glam. We'll definitely come over for a visit."

"That would be awesome! The three of us together, like old times."

"When do you guys leave?"

"In a couple of weeks."

"Wow, that soon?"

"They're really keen to get started."

"I'll bet! It must be so surreal for you both."

"It is. We're coming down to Sydney in a few days. I have to pack up my stuff, anyway."

"Great, we'll throw a party."

"Definitely," I agreed.

"Tell Rad congrats for me. No one deserves it more than he does."

"I will."

THE NEXT MORNING, I woke to my phone buzzing against my hip. Still half asleep, I picked it up and glanced at the screen. It was Candela. "Finally," I muttered, getting out of bed, careful not to disturb Rad, who was still fast asleep.

I threw on a robe and slipped out the door before answering the phone.

"Candela! Sweetie, I've been trying to get ahold of you. I've got some great news—"

"Audrey." She was sobbing. "I'm so sorry."

"It's okay." For some reason, I thought she was apologizing for missing my call the day before.

"I—I'm sorry," she sobbed again, and it began to dawn on me that something was terribly wrong.

"Candela, what's going on? Why are you crying?"

"It's Freddy. He was in a car accident."

"Oh no." I felt my legs buckle, my back hitting the trailer. "Is he okay?"

There was a brief silence followed by another sob. I felt a heaviness in my heart, and, somehow, I sensed what she was going to say next.

"I'm so sorry, Audrey. He—" she faltered, "he's dead."

Four

WE ARRIVED AT Lucy's house around midday. Rad and I barely spoke a word the whole way there. It felt like we were in a bad dream. How could things have changed so suddenly, so brutally? *Freddy is dead. No, no, it can't be.* Comprehension and denial swung in my mind like a pendulum: back and forth, back and forth. *Lucy. Oh God, Lucy.*

Rad woke up that morning to find me doubled over on the floor outside, my body wracked with sobs. He got down on his knees, pulling me into his arms and rocking me gently. It was a long while before I was able to steady myself enough to speak. His face grew ashen when I told him about Freddy.

Lucy's mother answered the door before we had a chance to knock. Like mine, her eyes were red from crying.

"Audrey," she said, pulling me into her arms. "I'm so glad you're here."

She nodded, "Hi, Rad," and motioned for us to come inside.

Candela was in the sitting room. She got up, and we held each other for a long time.

"How is she?"

Candela shook her head. "Not good. She's in shock, I think. She's almost catatonic. The scariest thing is she hasn't shed a single tear."

"What happened?" asked Rad.

"Freddy was on his way over to see Lucy in the middle of the night. We're not sure why. He was hit by a truck driver who was off his head on speed." She shook her head sadly. "They said he died on impact."

I let out a deep breath. "Oh my God."

"I told Lucy you were on your way," her mother said. "I think she would like to see you."

I nodded and made my way over to Lucy's old bedroom. My head felt heavy, like I was walking underwater. I stopped outside her door and took a deep breath. As gently as I could, I turned the doorknob and stepped inside.

Lucy looked smaller somehow. Like she had visibly shrunken since I last saw her, as though a vital part of her was now missing. Her lips trembled a little when our eyes met, but otherwise, she barely moved.

I sat down on her bed and took her hand, which was sitting limp on top of her bedspread. "I'm so sorry, sweetie."

She nodded, a faraway look in her eyes.

"He's gone, Audrey," she said in a low, monotone voice. "Freddy's gone. My Freddy."

I nodded, tears springing to my eyes.

"He's not coming back, is he?" She stared blankly ahead.

I reached out and smoothed her hair away from her face. Tears spilled down my cheeks. "No, sweetie, he's not."

Five

It was the day of Freddy's funeral. I had gone home to my mother's place the day before to pick up the same black dress I wore for Ana. My mother was uncharacteristically subdued, and Dad, as usual, said and did all the right things.

A heavy mood permeated the air as we made our way up the steps of Holy Trinity church, Candela and I on either side of Lucy, a hand each tightly clasped in hers. The last time we were here, it was for Ana, and I couldn't shake the feeling of déjà vu.

Freddy's mother walked ahead of us, her body weak with grief. In her hands, she clutched an old teddy bear with a missing button eye, a memento from Freddy's childhood. Freddy's dad had his arm around her, and the two shuffled wearily up the aisle.

At the burial, Lucy stood at the foot of the freshly dug grave watching with a glazed look as Freddy's coffin was gradually lowered into the ground. Something seemed to crack inside her then. She made a small whimpering noise, and the tears finally came. "Freddy," she sobbed. "Freddy . . . Freddy . . ." She clutched at her stomach, as though she was about to be sick. "Freddy . . . Freddy . . ." She called his name over and over again until her voice was hoarse and ragged.

THE WAKE WAS at Freddy's house, a modest bungalow with a large, sprawling lawn. The guests were Freddy's extended family and friends. He had always been the life of the party, and his gregarious nature made his absence so much more apparent.

Sometime toward the end of the night, I lost Lucy and went in search for her. I finally found her sitting on Freddy's bed in his old room, holding a jar of olives in her hand. I walked in, shutting the door behind me.

"Hey, you," I said, sitting down beside her.

She looked up at me. "He always kept a jar of green olives under his bed."

"He did?"

She nodded. "I always thought it was the stupidest thing. I mean, who the hell does that?"

"It sounds like something Freddy would do." I smiled at her.

Tears welled up in her eyes again. "He just had all these weird quirks, you know? They used to drive me crazy. I was always trying to change him. But he was perfect, wasn't he?"

"He was."

"But now he'll never know that. I can't tell him how wonderful he was." Her hands tensed around the jar. "I miss him, Audrey. So damn much."

She dropped the jar on the bed and put her head down on my shoulder. I stroked her hair.

"I know you do, sweetie. I miss him too."

There was a knock at the door.

"Come in," I called.

Rad walked into the room, and Lucy seemed to stiffen.

"Hey, Lucy," said Rad. His hand reached for her shoulder, and she flinched. She stood up suddenly and walked out of the room without a word.

Rad looked taken aback.

"Don't worry; she's not herself."

"I don't blame her. I've been there before."

I felt my stomach clench. Ana had been on my mind all day.

"It doesn't feel real, does it?"

Rad shook his head. "No, it's like we've woken up in a nightmare."

I nodded.

"Freddy's cousin is having car troubles," said Rad. "I'm going to give him a lift home."

"Now?"

"Yeah," said Rad. "It's been a long day for him. Are you okay to get home? I can double back and pick you up."

"That's okay; I'll just catch a ride with Candela."

"I'll see you later at the house, then."

I nodded. "Okay."

AFTER RAD LEFT, I went to look for Lucy again and ran into Candela, who was in the kitchen helping with the dishes.

"Have you seen Lucy?"

"I think she just went outside."

I made my way out the back door and found her sitting down cross-legged on the lawn.

"Hey, want to come back inside?"

Lucy looked up at me, her damp cheeks streaked with fresh tears.

"Audrey," she said. Her eyes were wide and tremulous. "There's something I need to tell you about Rad."

Six

I STOOD AT the door of my house, the key trembling in my hand. I felt like I was floating high above my body looking down from a terrible distance.

Rad came down the stairs just as I walked through the door.

"Hey, how are you?" His arms were open, inviting.

I took a step back.

He frowned. "Audrey? What's wrong?"

"Lucy said Freddy found something on your laptop."

"What? What do you mean?"

"Freddy was working on an assignment when his computer crashed. So he went to use your laptop, the one you left with him before you went to Bell Rock. He accidentally deleted a file and went into the trash to retrieve it. There was a document in there, a letter you wrote to me. It was called 'suicide note.'"

The color drained from Rad's face. "Oh no," he said. His hand shot up to his forehead, and he grimaced.

"What was in that document, Rad?"

He looked up. "Freddy didn't say?"

"He never got the chance."

"It was nothing, Audrey," Rad said quickly. "I just had a bad moment—that's all. It was a time in my life where everything had gone to shit. So yeah, for that split second I thought about ending it all. But I came to my senses, and that's why I deleted the file. I didn't expect Freddy or anyone else to ever find it."

He reached out for me again, and I shrunk back.

"Audrey, haven't you ever done anything stupid in the heat of the moment and then regretted it afterward? I made a mistake, but I'm okay now. It was a cry for help; that's all. It won't happen again."

"What was in the document, Rad?" I repeated.

"Nothing!" There was an edge to his voice. "Just the usual, about how sorry I was and how much I love you. All that kind of stuff you write when you're in that frame of mind."

"I don't believe you."

"I swear to you that's all it was."

"Then why did Freddy call Lucy up in the middle of the night? Why did he say, 'We have to warn Audrey about Rad'? Why did Freddy get in the *fucking car* and race over to see her because there was something you wrote in that document that scared the *shit* out of him?"

Rad's mouth opened, then closed again.

"Do you know they found your laptop?" I continued. "It was lying by the side of the road, completely smashed to pieces. Freddy had it with him. Why would he take *your* laptop to Lucy's place in the middle of the night? Why? What was so important that it couldn't wait until the morning?" I demanded.

He shook his head. "Audrey—"

"I need to know the truth, Rad. Right now."

He stood there for a few moments, staring at me. It seemed an eternity before he spoke again. "I wanted to tell you," he said, his face crumbling. He sat down on the step and sunk his head into his hands.

"Then tell me."

He looked up at me. His eyes had a terrible bleakness to them. All of a sudden, I was terrified.

"The letter—was there something in there about Ana?"

He nodded.

"It's bad, isn't it?"

He nodded again. "It was more of a confession than a suicide letter."

A shiver went through my body.

"Tell me what happened."

He took a deep breath. "I went to Ana's house that day to confront her about the rumor," he began slowly. "That part of it was true. It was exactly like I told you. She kept denying it, saying someone made it up. We got into a huge fight, and she slapped me. I was furious—I called her a lying whore. She reached out to hit me again, but I grabbed her arm and pushed her back. She tripped on a rug and fell, hitting the back of her head on the edge of the coffee table. I rushed over to her right away, but she wasn't moving. I tried to revive her, but she didn't wake up. I checked her pulse. She didn't have one. That's when I panicked. I was in shock. I mean, there wasn't even any blood. But she . . . she just wouldn't wake up."

I stared at Rad with horror, and a wave of revulsion washed over me.

"So I sat in the corner of the room for a while. I didn't know what to do. Then this weird sensation came over me, and what happened next was a blur."

"Rad," I stared at him, my eyes wide with disbelief. He turned away, looking straight ahead.

"When I was about nine, my mother took me to England for my uncle's wedding. We went to Stonehenge, but it's weird;

I don't remember ever going there. Even when I look at the photographs now, it doesn't feel real. Like it happened to someone else." He turned to face me again. "That's what it was like that day with Ana," he said, his tone almost mechanical. "I picked her up and put her in the bath with her dress still on. I ran the water. Then I found a razor in one of the cabinets. I got behind her so I would get the angle right when I cut into her wrists. I wasn't sure if she would still bleed since her heart had stopped by then, but she did. God, there was so much blood." He shivered. "Then, I dropped the razor into the bath and left."

I closed my eyes. Cold, spidery fingers crawled up and down my spine. "You . . . you cut into her wrists?" I whispered. An image of Rad, razor in hand, shot to the forefront of my mind, and I thought I was going to be sick.

"Audrey." He stood up.

I took a step back. "*No!*" I screamed, with a ferocity that took me by surprise.

Rad flinched and took a step back. "Audrey, I—"

"*You cut into her wrists!*" I shrieked. "You *cut* into *her* wrists!" The bile rose in my throat. I felt hysterical, out of control. My mind was spinning so fast I couldn't seem to hold on to the thoughts that flitted in and out. Was Ana already dead when he put her into the bath? If she had been alive, wouldn't that make him a murderer? And the lie I told—what part did that play in this tragedy? Nothing? Everything?

"How did you know Ana was already dead?" I demanded. "Are you a doctor?"

His raked his hand through his hair. "She didn't have a pulse; I swear! She wasn't breathing—there was nothing I could do. They wouldn't understand that it was an accident. I just panicked." He was scrambling now, eyes wild, ready to grab at anything.

"You panicked?" I said, incredulously. "People call the ambulance when they panic, Rad. They don't stage a fucking *suicide*."

His eyes widened, and his hand shot out to grip the banister, as if he'd been thrown off balance.

He stammered, "But you believe me, don't you, Audrey? You know I had no other choice."

"You did have a choice. You could have told me the truth. You were a coward," I spat.

"You're right—you're absolutely right. I was a coward. If I could go back in time, I would do things differently. I would have called the ambulance. Fuck, I would have told you—I should have told you. Wouldn't you do the same? If you could go back, would you have told that lie?"

"That's not fair, Rad. You can't—" I started.

"I know that now," he cut in quickly. "In the end, that was the thing that unraveled me. That I left you thinking you were in the wrong when I had done such a terrible thing. I wanted to tell you so many times, Audrey." His eyes were pleading when they looked into mine. "I love you so damn much. You came and found me when I was in that shitty place, and you brought me back to life. I tried to push you away, and you wouldn't let me. Then when we grew close, I wanted to tell you, but I couldn't handle the thought of losing you again."

I shook my head. "No, don't you dare!" I said, gritting my teeth. My fingers tugged fretfully at my rubber band, and it snapped in two, falling silently from my wrist to the ground.

"Audrey." His eyes locked on to mine. Those strange, beautiful eyes: one a stormy gray, the other summer blue.

Like a jagged rock pitched from a slingshot, my mind traveled back to the night I told that lie. I thought of Rad, his strong, gentle hands stained red with Ana's blood. Candela lying in the hospital bed, fighting for her life. Duck shoved into the back of a police van. Now Freddy—poor Freddy. Another one for the body count. And I had to add Lucy as well because you couldn't separate the two.

"Audrey," Rad repeated. There was a desperation to his voice. "I'm so sorry. I don't know what to do." He grabbed my arms. "Tell me what to do. I'll do anything you want."

I broke free from his grasp and stumbled back. "I don't want anything to do with you," I said weakly, my eyes watering and my voice trembling.

"I've put my life in your hands," he pleaded. "Don't you see? We have a fresh start ahead of us in L.A. We can leave all this behind."

All of a sudden, I felt an eerie calm settle over me. It was as though I was standing in the eye of the storm, and everything had stopped. In that moment of clarity, I knew I was just as culpable as Rad. I knew there was blood on my hands too. We had become caricatures of ourselves, trapped in this nightmare; the entry ticket for this grotesque carnival, my lie. I had cursed us from the moment the evil spilled from my lips. Yet beyond the madness, the utter horror of Rad's confession, I couldn't ignore the love that was there, pulsating with a life of its own, pulling us closer and closer, blurring the lines. We could start all over again in L.A., where no one knew us. I was stronger than I had ever been. I was strong enough for the both of us. Then the clarity dissolved, and I was pitched back into blinding chaos.

I sobbed violently, my shoulders heaving from the effort. I cried in a way I never had before. I felt everything I lost compound into this cruel, unforgiving moment. Rad put his arms around me, and I pushed back as hard as I could, thrashing wildly at his hands, his face, tearing at his hair. With all my strength, I pounded his chest with my fists, but still, he wouldn't let go. After a while, my arms grew limp, and I let him hold me.

Epilogue

THE EARLY MORNING sun streamed through the curtains of our one-bedroom flat in Santa Monica. I was on my second cup of coffee, and Rad was just waking up.

He opened his eyes and gave me a sleepy smile. "Morning," he said.

"Morning." I put my coffee mug down on the side table, then leaned over and kissed him gently. He ran his hands through my hair and buried his face in my neck. "You smell good," he murmured, pulling me down onto the bed with him. He wrapped his arms around me, and we stayed like that for a while.

"What time is it?" he asked.

"Almost ten, I think."

"You're already dressed."

"I was up early this morning and thought I'd go for a walk on the pier—pick up some bagels on my way back."

"Sounds good."

I gently untangled myself and got up.

"Blueberry for you?"

"Yeah."

I put my Audrey jacket on.

"Is it cold out there today?" he asked.

I nodded. "I was out on the balcony this morning, and it was a little chilly."

He sat up and stretched out his arms with a yawn, turning his head to the window. "Looks like it's going to be a beautiful day."

I smiled. "I think so too."

THE SUN HAD climbed high above the horizon. A seagull was hitching a ride on the wind. I watched as the tide swirled around the wooden legs of the Santa Monica Pier. People milled about taking photographs and talking animatedly on cell phones. The sea was a perfect backdrop to the spinning Ferris wheel and the colored umbrellas that dotted the promenade. In the distance, there were shrieks of delight coming from the bright yellow rollercoaster.

I leaned against the powder-blue railing and closed my eyes, letting the sun warm my face. It had been unusually cool these past few days, and I felt the cold a lot more than I used to. I took in a deep lungful of the salty sea air and let it out again with a sigh.

So here I was, several months after the night of Freddy's funeral. I had settled into my new life with Rad. I didn't want to think about the dark days that followed the night when Rad revealed the truth about Ana to me. We had agreed to leave all that behind. I left Lucy and Candela bewildered and begging for answers—answers I couldn't give without implicating Rad. I knew I could never tell them the truth because they wouldn't understand. How could I explain it to another person if I couldn't even justify it to myself? All I knew was that my decision to stay with Rad was not so much a choice as a necessity.

I thought about my time in Delta. About Gabe, that day we said goodbye. How he told me I didn't need anyone anymore. But he was wrong. I needed Rad—we needed each other now more than ever. Then I thought about the rope that kept the ship attached to the mooring—the one that should never fray, never break. Like the rubber band that used to occupy my left wrist, the rope had snapped, and I was free-falling, but I wasn't afraid anymore. I thought of Rad and the terrible secret we shared—the lie we chose to bury for good. It would always be there—we knew that—but we would no longer give it any power over us. It nearly drove us apart, but, instead, it had bound us to each other like a blood pact. And now here we were, in a whole new life. It was a blank canvas—the chance to start all over again.

I walked by a busker in a felt hat, a white feather stuck in its brim. He was strumming a muted rendition of "Strawberry Fields Forever." I stopped and put my hand in the pocket of my jacket for some loose coins. I could hear the jangle, but I couldn't seem to find the coins. I frowned, my fingers pushing deeper against the red satin lining. I felt a tear that I had never noticed before. As I fished the coins out, I heard the unmistakable rustle of paper. I dropped the coins into the busker's open guitar case and continued walking, my hand pushing through the tear until my fingers found a piece of folded up paper. It was the page from Ana's diary that had gone missing the day I opened up the metal box. It must have been caught inside the lining of my jacket this entire time. My heart skipped a beat, and I felt the old familiar panic rising up again. Then, almost as soon as it began, it was over. I took a deep breath and looked at Ana's tiny writing. As I read, her words seemed to travel from a time so long ago they felt closer to the future than the past. I sensed somehow that those words were always meant to find me here.

I'm going to do it this time. My parents will be away this weekend, and I am going to seal up the garage with Dad's beloved red Thunderbird running inside. Then I'm going to fall asleep to the sweet perfume of carbon monoxide and "Sugar Baby Love" blasting on the stereo. Seventeen seems like a good age to leave this shitball of a world.

I wonder who will be the first to find me. Maybe the lady next door, the one who keeps giving me the evil eye. I once heard her yelling at her husband about the way he looks at me. I can imagine her at the scene, that initial look of horror. Then her fat, rubbery lips will curve into a smile, secretly pleased with the discovery. Or maybe Rad will get to me before she does. I can just see those sweet, puppy dog eyes, wide with incredulity and brimming with tears. He can be so sentimental sometimes; it makes me want to gag. He still thinks I was a virgin when we fucked for the first time. Can you believe it? I know he thinks he's in love, but he has no idea what love is. Not yet anyway.

The truth is, everyone wants to believe they're in love but no one really is. So to all the girls out there who are stuck between two minds about some stupid crush, I have news for you. If you have to wonder, if you have to question what you feel, then deep down you actually don't give a shit. As for the rest of you who do get it, welcome to the club. If you know what it's like to want someone so much you would kill for them. If you know what it's like to feel someone so deep under your skin you would sacrifice everything to protect them—even if it screws up your own moral compass so you can't see right from wrong. If you're like me, then let me leave you with this: That's what love is. Don't let them tell you any different. Don't tell yourself otherwise.

Acknowledgments

Special thanks to Al Zuckerman. It has been a privilege and an honor to work with you on this book. Your wisdom and guidance have been invaluable, and you have taught me so much. I'm truly grateful for all the advice you have given me, and I can't wait to work with you again on the next novel.

Thank you to Kirsty Melville, Patty Rice, and the team at Andrews McMeel for your amazing support. I really appreciate how tirelessly you have worked behind the scenes to bring *Sad Girls* to life and make it available in bookstores all over the world.

Samantha Wekstein from Writers House, your wonderful feedback and notes have been such a big help to me. Thank you.

To my editor Chris Schillig, thank you for your advice and valuable input. You did an amazing job.

Mum, Dad, Niv, Jerric, Karen, Sherry, Sivvy, and Aleks: thank you for being the metaphoric rubber band around my wrist.

Dr. Gwendoline Smith, thank you for your valuable time and expertise on the subject of anxiety. I thoroughly enjoyed our little late-night chats and your incredible insights.

To Ollie Faudet, who has been an avid supporter of *Sad Girls* since day one. Your unique worldview has been a source of inspiration, and it wouldn't be the same book without you.

Thank you to Michael Faudet, who lived and breathed the world of *Sad Girls* alongside me. For years, we spoke extensively about the characters, settings, and plotlines. If this is my baby, it is in equal parts his as well. Our collaboration, both in life and work, has been the greatest gift of all.

Lastly, to my readers from all corners of the world, a big thank-you. You have shown me that love is the very thing that unites us. If it wasn't for you, I would never have written a single book.

Also by Lang Leav:

Love & Misadventure
Lullabies
Memories
The Universe of Us

Andrews McMeel Publishing
a division of Andrews McMeel Universal
1130 Walnut Street, Kansas City, Missouri 64106

www.andrewsmcmeel.com

17 18 19 20 21 RR2 10 9 8 7 6 5 4 3 2 1

ISBN: 978-1-4494-8776-8

Library of Congress Control Number: 2017932229

Editor: Patty Rice
Designer/Art Director: Diane Marsh
Production Editor: Erika Kuster
Production Manager: Cliff Koehler

ATTENTION: SCHOOLS AND BUSINESSES
Andrews McMeel books are available at quantity discounts
with bulk purchase for educational, business, or sales
promotional use. For information, please e-mail the
Andrews McMeel Publishing Special Sales Department:
specialsales@amuniversal.com.